Books by Jody Hedlund

The Preacher's Bride
The Doctor's Lady
Unending Devotion
A Noble Groom
Rebellious Heart
Captured by Love

BEACONS OF HOPE

Out of the Storm: A Beacons of Hope Novella
Love Unexpected
Hearts Made Whole
Undaunted Hope

ORPHAN TRAIN

An Awakened Heart: An Orphan Train Novella
With You Always
Together Forever
Searching for You

THE BRIDE SHIPS

A Reluctant Bride
The Runaway Bride
A Bride of Convenience
Almost a Bride

COLORADO COWBOYS

A Cowboy for Keeps

come back to me

JODY HEDLUND

Revell

a division of Baker Publishing Group
Grand Rapids, Michigan

© 2021 by Jody Hedlund

Published by Revell
a division of Baker Publishing Group
PO Box 6287, Grand Rapids, MI 49516-6287
www.revellbooks.com

Printed in the United States of America

Library of Congress Cataloging-in-Publication Data
Names: Hedlund, Jody, author.
Title: Come back to me / Jody Hedlund.
Description: Grand Rapids, Michigan : Revell, a division of Baker Publishing
     Group, [2021] | Series: Waters of time
Identifiers: LCCN 2020047618 | ISBN 9780800738433 (paperback) | ISBN
     9780800740047 (casebound) | ISBN 9781493430444 (ebook)
Subjects: GSAFD: Science fiction. | Romantic suspense fiction.
Classification: LCC PS3608.E333 C66 2021 | DDC 813/.6—dc23
LC record available at https://lccn.loc.gov/2020047618

This book is a work of fiction. Names, characters, places, and incidents are the product of the author's imagination or are used fictitiously. Any resemblance to actual events, locales, or persons, living or dead, is coincidental.

21 22 23 24 25 26 27   7 6 5 4 3 2 1

In keeping with biblical principles of creation stewardship, Baker Publishing Group advocates the responsible use of our natural resources. As a member of the Green Press Initiative, our company uses recycled paper when possible. The text paper of this book is composed in part of post-consumer waste.

To my agent, Natasha Kern.
Thank you for believing in this book and believing in me.
You have been there for me in countless ways—cheering,
advocating, encouraging, advising, editing, and educating.
Thanks for even taking the time to discuss with me in detail
the physics of time and energy. You are the kind of agent
that makes me believe anything is possible.

~ 1 ~

"Your father is in a coma."

"What did you say?" Marian Creighton fumbled with her phone and almost dropped it. "I don't think I heard you correctly."

"I'm sorry, Marian." Harrison Burlington's English accent on the other end was as loud and clear as if he'd been sitting at Jasper's desk opposite from hers. "Unfortunately, you did hear me all too correctly. I'm afraid your father is in a coma."

"My dad's in a coma?" The words reverberated all the way to the cells in her bone marrow, sending chills over her skin.

"Yes. He's here at Kent and Canterbury Hospital."

Marian shoved away the research sprawled in front of her and shot out of her leather chair.

"The hospital staff phoned me about an hour ago, and I came straightaway."

"What happened? Was he in an accident?"

"The doctors think not. But they're still trying to sort it out."

"I don't understand." The blue lights on the digital clock on her desk read 10:48 p.m., which meant it was almost four o'clock in the morning in Canterbury, five hours ahead of Connecticut.

"Apparently, your father arrived at the hospital and passed out in the lobby." Harrison paused, and in the background the beeping of monitors was unmistakable. "They've been doing tests on Arthur, but they haven't been able to locate any trauma that may have caused the coma."

"That makes no sense." She stared through the glass walls of the inner laboratory to the dark deserted offices beyond. The red exit sign gave off an eerie, almost haunted light that spread over the pharmacokinetics department of Mercer Pharmaceuticals' research lab. "Dad called this afternoon, and he sounded fine. Said he was feeling great."

She didn't talk to her dad often. They were busy with their pharmacokinetics research. At least that's the excuse she made for them both. Plus, there was that big body of water called the Atlantic Ocean separating them, although truthfully at times the ocean seemed small and shallow compared to the deep gulf that stood between them.

"I saw your father in the office yesterday morning, and he didn't complain of anything being awry. He acted a bit distracted. But there's nothing dodgy about that." Harrison was being too kind. But she supposed his ability to overlook Arthur Creighton's glaring idiosyncrasies was why he happened to be Dad's one and only friend.

"So the doctors have no idea why he's fallen into a coma?"

"None. They're gobsmacked."

"There's no visible sign of an accident, fall, head trauma?"

"Not that they can find."

"What about a brain aneurysm or cerebral hypoxia?"

"No and no."

What other symptoms could lead to unresponsiveness? "Maybe he experienced some kind of poisoning, like carbon monoxide? Or perhaps cardiac arrest or—"

"Marian, I've already queried the personnel about every possible cause." Harrison was a brilliant medical scientist, a coworker of her dad's at Mercer's Canterbury research and development headquarters. Of course, he'd know all the right questions to ask the physicians regarding Dad's situation.

Exhaustion hit her, and she lowered herself back into her chair. She regularly put in twelve- to fifteen-hour days in the lab. It was her life. She succumbed to sleep only when she had to.

"I'm truly sorry, love. I know the news is dreadful." Harrison's voice radiated with sympathy.

She pictured her father's friend in his power wheelchair. A young man in his thirties, Harrison was stately and scholarly, his dark waves untouched yet by silver compared to her dad's full head of gray hair. Behind thick spectacles, Harrison's eyes contained kindness, and he cared about what she had to say, unlike Dad, who rarely tore his attention away from the one thing that mattered most: finding a cure for the genetic disease that had robbed him of his wife.

Marian's throat tightened. "Thanks for being there with him."

"I'll be here as long as it takes."

Marian rapidly calculated the amount of time needed to drive to the airport and catch the first flight to Heathrow. "I might be able to make it to the hospital by tomorrow afternoon."

"Go home and have a rest first. I don't want you becoming ill in the process of rushing to get here."

Her? Ill? She almost laughed. "I'll be fine, Harrison. I always am."

"I know you can look after yourself, but I couldn't bear it if something happened to you too."

Too. The tiny word was a glaring reminder of all that had gone wrong in her family.

"Marian?" His voice dropped a decibel. "Let's not talk about this to Ellen yet."

"Definitely not."

After ending the call, Marian tossed her phone onto the detailed spreadsheets and charts scattered across her desk. The soft whir of the laboratory equipment behind her was the lone sound in the office, and their fluorescent glow the only light—other than her desk lamp, which spotlighted the results of her recent failed experiment.

Harrison had no cause to worry about her getting sick. She'd won the lottery and inherited the good genes in the family.

Ahead, the screen saver on her laptop displayed a gorgeous blonde-haired, blue-eyed woman with a whitened, orthodontist smile—a picture of perfection. But pictures were deceptive. They never told the true story. They couldn't reveal that underneath the beautiful exterior, Ellen was on the fast track toward death, that tumors were growing somewhere in her body again. If she didn't die of inoperable cysts in the brain like their mom, she'd likely die from cysts elsewhere in her body.

At twenty-six, Ellen was two years younger than Marian but had already suffered more than most people did in a lifetime. It wasn't a matter of *if* Ellen would end up hospitalized again. It was merely a matter of *when*.

"It's not fair, God." Marian whispered the same prayer she had a thousand times since the fateful day when the blood test revealed that Ellen had inherited the anomaly from their mom and Marian hadn't. "Ellen doesn't deserve it."

If either of them had to get stuck with VHL, Von Hippel-Lindau syndrome, Marian should have been the one with the mutated gene. Ellen had so much more to give the world— more love, compassion, kindness, laughter, and beauty. What did Marian have to offer, other than her frantic race to find a cure for VHL?

"Oh Ellen." Frustration clamored inside, looking helplessly for a release.

The scrolling laptop screen saver shifted to a different picture, this one of the two of them together from last month when Marian had flown to Haiti to visit Ellen, who was currently volunteering in an orphanage and using her pediatric nursing skills to make a difference there.

Even in the humidity and blazing heat, Ellen was as striking as a model. Yes, she was a tad thin. But with her long legs and ample curves, combined with her outgoing and sweet personality, she was irresistible. The orphans adored her. The local workers thought she was a goddess. And any man who came within a mile radius fell in love with her.

Marian snorted aloud at the differences in their appearances. Sure, their oval-shaped faces contained similarities—narrow chins and prominent cheekbones. And they both had long lashes framing upturned eyes.

But compared to Ellen's tanned face, Marian's complexion was pale, making her brown eyes too dark and brooding. Ellen had pulled her hair back into a messy bun, managing to look stylish and casual at the same time. Although Marian had used plenty of straightening products and her hot iron in an attempt to tame her long auburn waves, her messy bun looked just that—messy.

Marian picked her phone back up. She had to reserve a flight. One tonight, if possible.

The phone screen lit up with a recent text from Ellen still awaiting her response. Nothing serious, just Ellen being her usual sweet self and checking in to say hi. Marian's fingers hovered above the message, but then she swiped it away. She had to wait to reply. If she ended up having a conversation with her sister, she'd probably spill the news about Dad.

She'd never believed in her wildest dreams Ellen would outlive their dad. And she'd certainly never imagined she'd have to bear bad news to her sister about Dad. It was always the other way around—calling Dad to let him know of a new development with Ellen.

Last year Ellen had laser surgery to eliminate three tumors from the outer regions of her retina. The year before, she had one of her adrenal glands removed. Even now, her doctors were paying special attention to the tumors on her kidney, which would need to be taken out eventually.

Harrison was right. They couldn't say anything to Ellen. Not until they knew more. Otherwise her sister would jump on the first plane out of Port Au Prince to be by Dad's side. But the travel, the sleeplessness, the stress—it would take a toll on Ellen, weaken her immune system, cause high blood pressure, lead to more weight loss, and increase the rate and size of tumor growth.

The outer office door swung open, and the motion sensor lights came to life, revealing Jasper's brown hair and athletic frame. In his Under Armour shorts and University of Illinois at Chicago sweatshirt, he'd slung his gym bag over his shoulder after exercising in the company fitness center. Marian was never sure if he timed his nightly workouts to coincide with her late hours, but he was always there when she finished.

He smiled and lifted a hand in greeting.

She gave a half wave in return, too despondent to muster any enthusiasm at seeing him.

He wound through the hallway to the office they shared with several other researchers. "Hey," he said as he entered. "Almost done? I'll walk you out."

"My dad's in a coma." Saying the words aloud was like having the wind knocked out of her. She pressed a hand against her chest and tried to drag in a breath.

Brow furrowing with concern, Jasper shrugged his bag off his shoulder and eased it to the floor. His hair, damp from his shower, clung to his forehead, and his body emanated the citrus of his Axe body spray. "I'm sorry, Marian. Does anyone know what happened?"

"The doctors haven't found the cause yet."

Jasper crossed his arms and leaned against the doorframe. Mercer had hired Jasper Boyle at the Groton facility about the same time she'd started last year. They'd been partners on several chemical analysis projects and had quickly gotten to know each other.

Over time, she'd opened up to him about her frustrations with her dad, especially regarding his crazy research and theories. And Jasper had shared his disappointment with his dad's Lou Gehrig's disease.

Jasper had hinted recently at wanting more from their relationship, but Marian had been honest with him that she was married to her work. Besides, she hadn't wanted to ruin their friendship with romantic entanglements.

Of course, she'd never had many romantic entanglements to speak of. In high school, she'd been a geeky science nerd and had happily spent Friday nights dating her books rather than boys. That pattern had continued through college and graduate school. And she doubted it would ever end. Not until she found a way to save Ellen.

Now her plans had to widen to include saving her dad.

"You look tired." Jasper's gaze swept down the form-fitting black Dior top she'd paired with a slim charcoal skirt. The appreciative glint in his eyes assured her that while she might not have Ellen's jaw-dropping beauty, she had inherited the same long legs and womanly form.

"I'll be fine once I'm at the hospital with Dad."

"Have the doctors given him a prognosis?"

"Not that I'm aware of." She reached for the leather briefcase beneath her desk. "But as soon as I get there, I'll find out exactly what's going on and make sure they're doing all they can."

"I have no doubt you will." His tone was amused. He knew her well enough to realize she was capable of getting what she wanted. "When are you leaving?"

"I haven't booked a flight yet." She tucked her laptop into the briefcase along with the binder filled with meticulous records of all her experiments.

"You should take the company jet this time."

She shook her head. "You know how I feel about that."

He shrugged. "I thought you might like to get there faster."

Since her dad's family—her great-grandfather—had been one of the founders of Mercer Pharmaceuticals and her dad still owned a share of the business, she had access to the company jet whenever it suited her, but she didn't want to be known for using the family perks. The other employees already thought she'd landed her position because of her connections. Of course, no one said so to her face. But she had no doubt that's what they believed.

The truth was, she'd earned her research job at Mercer Pharmaceuticals the same way everyone else had. She'd spent long years in school, excelled in her studies, and pushed herself hard to get where she was.

She reached for the latest spreadsheet outlining the pharmacokinetic parameters, the columns of absorption rates and volume of distribution that were once again inconclusive. She was getting close. Intuitively, she knew that. But how could she convince everyone else without solid evidence?

With a frustrated sigh, she crumpled the sheet and tossed it toward the wastebasket in the corner. It bounced off the glass wall and landed on the floor near the other papers she'd already discarded.

Jasper straightened and combed his fingers through his damp hair. "Let me come with you."

Her gaze shot to him in surprise.

His eyes were warm and sympathetic. "You shouldn't be alone at a time like this."

For one brief instant, she was tempted to let herself need someone else. But just as quickly as the weakness surfaced, she stuffed it away like an item in her leather case. "Thank you, Jasper. But you have responsibilities here, and I don't know how long I'll be gone."

"I can take off some time—"

"What if he doesn't come out of his coma right away?" *Or ever?* She shuddered at the unbidden thought.

"I'll stay as long as I'm able." His expression was earnest.

"Jasper . . ." She didn't want to lecture him with the I-only-want-to-be-friends conversation again. She was too tired for it.

"Just as friends, Marian." He could read her well. "Friends are there for friends, aren't they?"

She snapped her briefcase closed.

He grinned one of his charming grins that could win over even the staunchest of hearts. He was attractive and amiable. And the impish quirk of his mouth told her he knew it.

Her lips gave an involuntary twitch of a smile, but she leveled him with what she hoped was her most serious look, one that said his charm didn't work on her—even though he was chipping away at her reserves. "I'll be fine. I promise."

He stuffed his hands into the front pocket of his sweatshirt. "If you're sure."

"I'll let you know if his condition worsens."

"Say the word, and I'll be on the first plane over."

She tidied the remaining items on her desk. "You're too nice to me."

"Friends are supposed to be nice."

She couldn't hold back her smile any longer. "You're a good friend, Jasper. Thank you."

He tugged the keys out of his pocket and jangled them. "Since you clearly don't intend to wait for a morning flight, I'll drive you to the airport." Sometimes it was scary how well Jasper knew her.

She made several quick phone calls, one to reserve her flight, a second to her boss to let him know of the family emergency, and another to her landlady. With no time to swing by her place and pack, Marian was glad her dad had insisted on her keeping a room and wardrobe at his Canterbury home. She'd always felt like he wanted the arrangement to make himself feel better. Maybe he truly had believed it would help draw them closer. But it hadn't.

Marian switched off several machines before giving the lab a final survey. Her gaze snagged on the silver-framed picture on her desk, the last photo taken of her family during a trip to Jennings Beach before Mom died. The happy faces stared back at her. With windblown hair and their arms draped around one another, they stood against the backdrop of the ocean stretching out behind them. Even her dad was smiling, his hair still red without any gray.

That day on the beach had been the last time not only for smiles, but for being together. Little had they known they'd existed in a sinking ship without a lifeboat. Cancer had been lurking beneath the surface, waiting to capture Mom in its sharp teeth and drag her away, leaving the rest of them lost at sea and floating further apart with every passing year.

Even if the abyss between Dad and her felt unbridgeable, she had to go to him anyway. She still loved him, had always been close to him growing up, closer than to her mom. She didn't want him to be alone during this medical crisis. Perhaps when he awoke from his coma, she could try harder to connect with him.

For a second, she considered snatching up the family photo and taking it with her, especially as a strange sensation came over her—one warning her she'd never see the picture again.

She shook her head to dislodge the silly feeling. Then she brushed past Jasper out the door and down the hallway without another glance at the lab or the silver-framed picture. She was coming back. She was on the verge of finding a cure for Ellen. No one and nothing could stop her from returning and saving her sister's life.

~2~

AT A TOUCH against her arm, Marian startled upright and blinked awake.

"Marian, love. Go home and have a rest." A gentle voice spoke beside her. "Take a hot shower and sleep in a bed."

She shifted in the hospital chair to find Harrison Burlington in his motorized wheelchair. Through his glasses, he regarded her anxiously. He'd changed his attire—another crisp suit with a bow tie and matching vest reminiscent of the 1850s. He even wore a pocket watch with a fob dangling out and looped to one of his buttons.

His dark hair was neatly combed away from his forehead. The scent of sandalwood aftershave lingered in the air about him but still couldn't overpower the ammonia and bleach that permeated the hospital room.

Her attention jumped to her dad, to his pale face, closed eyes, and the gentle rise and fall of his chest. His hand was still within hers where she'd placed it. She tightened her grip, but his remained loose and lifeless.

From what she could tell, he hadn't moved a muscle while she'd dozed. His body was in the same position, his arms at his sides, his head and chin facing the ceiling. Not a strand of his scraggly gray hair had shifted. Even the bedside monitors registered a steady pulse and normal breathing rhythm, unchanged from every other time she'd looked.

The heavy curtains across the window didn't let a sliver of light into the private room Harrison had arranged for her dad, and she had no idea whether it was the middle of the night or day.

"What time is it?" Her voice was raspy with sleep.

Harrison withdrew the elegant pocket watch and flipped open the lid. "Eleven o'clock in the morning."

She'd been at the hospital for almost twenty-four hours straight. After coming directly from the airport, she'd spent the majority of yesterday grilling the specialists and persuading them to order further tests.

She was sure by now that every physician at Kent and Canterbury was as anxious to see her leave as Harrison was—although Harrison's motives were out of kindness and not irritation.

She rubbed her eyes, the grittiness of her waterproof mascara assuring her that she was still wearing at least a little makeup. Even so, she guessed she looked a fright. Harrison was right. She needed a shower.

Harrison stuffed the watch back into his pocket. "Bojing is outside in the car park and will drive you to Chesterfield Park. I left instructions for the maids to make up a guest bed for you."

"Thank you, Harrison. But I have a rental car. And I don't want to impose on your home."

"With twenty bedrooms, you'll hardly impose."

Harrison's sprawling manor was located on the outskirts of Canterbury. Long ago, the estate had consisted of over a thousand acres of surrounding land. Although it wasn't as vast anymore, the remaining formal gardens and deer park gave the place a private, country-like feel. Set against such a magnificent backdrop, the ancient mansion house was stunning, always featured in travel magazines.

"I'd love to stay at Chesterfield Park. But I keep extra clothes at Dad's house. I'll be fine there."

"Right. But I don't want you to be alone at a time like this." He sounded like Jasper, fussing over her. In fact, Jasper had already called three times since her arrival.

"I'm a strong woman." She'd said the same thing to Jasper each time.

The crease between Harrison's eyes only deepened. He was a striking man, and she'd always wondered why he'd never married. Even though he'd lost the use of his legs as a result of a spinal cord injury during a car accident when he'd been a child, he was one of the most capable men she'd ever known. Surely, he could have his pick of women, especially with his prestige and wealth.

"Besides"—she fished for the car keys in her purse—"Dad's house is closer to the hospital."

Harrison opened his mouth as if he wanted to say more, but then he sat back in his wheelchair and pressed his lips closed.

She kissed her dad's cheek then stood and stretched. "I won't be gone long."

"Take your time. I'll stay with Arthur." His eyes still radiated worry, although he was evidently trying to rein it in.

She leaned down and placed a kiss on Harrison's forehead. "I don't know what I'd do without you."

As she made her way out of the hospital to the Lexus she'd rented, she listened to her voicemail, including a message from Ellen. She still hadn't told her sister about Dad's coma, and guilt nudged her. She couldn't put it off forever. But the longer she could spare Ellen the stress, the better.

Minutes later, Marian pulled onto St. Peter's Lane and parked in front of the tall terraced house her dad had purchased when he'd taken the position in Canterbury. As she exited her car, she released a breath containing the tension that had been building since Harrison called her with the news of the coma.

The street was always quiet even though it was situated within the original city walls and just a block away from shops, restaurants, and theaters.

She started up the steps to the front door, appreciating the Regency style of the house with its white brick exterior, multitude of large panes, and the half-moon window above the door. With four floors and seven bedrooms, the house certainly had space for two grown daughters who only came sporadically.

Even if the place was too big for Dad, Marian couldn't begrudge his choice. In her opinion, it was one of the most stunning properties within the old city walls as well as one of the richest in terms of history. It had lovely fireplaces in many of the rooms, shutters, lofty ceilings with ornate cornices and ceiling roses, a spacious welcoming hall, a Georgian-era staircase, and much more.

The home had come furnished, but her dad had hired an interior decorator to add the finishing touches, making it a unique but lovely blend of modern and Victorian.

Marian lifted the key to the lock but froze as the door inched open. Not only was the dead bolt not secured, but the door hadn't been closed tightly. Perhaps in the throes of distress and haste to reach the hospital, Dad had neglected to lock up.

A strange prickling formed at the back of her neck, an intuition that someone was watching her. She glanced both ways up and down the street, viewing more of the fashionable terraced homes and a few parked cars, but seeing nothing or no one out of the ordinary.

She shook off the unwelcome sensation and pushed the door fully open. The moment she stepped into the wide front hallway, she stopped abruptly at the destruction that met her. Upended tables, shattered glass, overthrown rugs. Every framed painting and porcelain plate that once so proudly graced the walls now littered the floor in broken pieces.

Marian pressed a hand to her mouth. What had happened? And was the intruder lurking in the shadows?

She held herself motionless for long seconds, listening, waiting. But only the eerie silence of a deserted home remained. Finally, she tiptoed through the debris into the front room, the lounge, only to find it had been ransacked like the hallway. The sectional couch cushions had been pulled out, the decorative pillows tossed aside, even the large Oriental rug at the center was tousled.

The adjoining dining room had suffered the same fate. Everything that could be emptied had been, every drawer in the mahogany sideboard and every chest. Antique coins, valuable knickknacks, and her mother's sterling silver place settings were kicked helter-skelter across the floor.

Marian made her way through the house, up the steep stairway to the next floor, her dismay and anxiety multiplying exponentially with each step she took. As far as she could tell, the break-in hadn't been done by thieves hoping to steal valuables. None of her father's expensive electronic devices had been taken. And none of the items of historic value had been stolen either.

She swung open the door to her father's study, her shoulders sinking at the disaster spreading out before her. Dad had never been tidy, but the room had been ripped apart from top to bottom until nothing remained in its original place—not a book, file, or spreadsheet. It was as if an F-5 tornado had been trapped in the room.

Had he been home when the intruder struck? Did that have something to do with his coma?

She shook her head. No, all the tests—the X-rays, MRIs, CTs, PET scans, and even a DXA—revealed no bodily trauma whatsoever.

If she had to guess, she'd say the break-in occurred after he'd gone to the hospital. Otherwise, he surely would have reported the vandalism.

What about the library? Her dad's collection of books was his life. When he wasn't working, he was reading. She backed out of the office and headed to the next room.

She flipped on the light switch to reveal the full destruction. The floor-to-ceiling shelves that covered three walls had been emptied of every single book, now strewn on the floor. All that remained on the glossy oak panels were dust bunnies.

Whoever had been there had left no nook or cranny unturned.

With trembling fingers, she reached for the closest hardback, which had fallen open to the first page. *The Architectural History of Canterbury Cathedral* by Robert Willis. She carefully smoothed the yellowed paper, noticing the tome had been written in 1845. Dad might be a scientist to the core of his being, but over the past ten years of living in Canterbury, he'd collected a sizeable number of history books as well.

She set the cathedral book upon the shelf, picked up several more, and then stopped herself. Before she moved anything or started cleaning up the place, she needed to alert the police. This was a crime scene, and if she had any hope of finding out what had happened and why, she needed help. She pulled out her phone and dialed the emergency number 999.

• • •

"The police constable claims the break-in was a random act of violence." Marian set the container of tikka masala from Kashmir Tandoori on the hospital tray table next to Harrison. The spicy cayenne wafted around her, making her stomach growl, especially with the realization that she hadn't eaten anything substantial since arriving in England.

After meeting with the police, she'd managed a quick shower and changed into one of her more casual outfits, a rose-colored blouse with gray twill trousers and a pair of ankle-strap heels. She'd pulled her hair up into a French twist and refreshed her makeup. Now she felt like a new person—even though she was still tired.

She retrieved two sets of plastic silverware from the takeout bag along with paper plates. "I told the police I want an investigator to come out to the house anyway."

"I could phone them and add my insistence to the matter."

"If they won't assign an investigator to our case, I'll hire a private detective." Marian began to divide the Indian food between the two plates.

Harrison touched her hand, pressed a finger against his lips, and tilted his head toward the door. Gravity drenched every move he made.

Without a word, she crossed the room and closed the door. On the way back, she paused beside her dad, squeezed his hand, and waited a fraction, hoping he'd squeeze back. But his fingers were as clammy and still as the last time she'd held his hand only five minutes ago. With a sigh, she released him and adjusted his sheet.

His skin had always been pale like hers, probably from spending so much time indoors. Plump, but clean shaven, his face reflected his gentle spirit. The grooves next to his eyes had been the result of constant study and reading.

Wake up, Dad, she silently pleaded before bending and pressing a kiss to his forehead. Whatever trouble he was in, she wanted him to know she'd do anything to help him.

As she lowered herself into the chair beside the bed, she picked up her plate. "So what's really going on, Harrison?"

"Your father's office at the lab was torn apart too." His tone was low and ominous.

Her blood turned cold. "It was? When?"

"I went over yesterday morning after I left here to let everyone know about Arthur, and I saw the upheaval then."

"Why would anyone wreck Dad's home *and* office? And who?"

"It has to be one of the other drug companies." Harrison

glanced at the door, his brow furrowing. "I had my suspicions about what happened at the office. But now that they've searched Arthur's house too, it's clear they're cracking on until they get what they're after."

Her dad had already perfected the formulas of two different drugs for Mercer, FDA-approved medications that had brought the company worldwide fame and fortune. Of course, during their creation, other pharmaceutical companies had attempted to steal Dad's research, and he'd faced ongoing threats. Had that happened again?

"So was Dad on the verge of developing another drug?"

Harrison leaned forward. "Not just any drug, Marian. *The* drug."

"The cure for VHL?" She hadn't known Dad was still working on it, had thought he'd given up when he passed along his research to her.

Harrison's eyes gleamed strangely behind his spectacles. "The ultimate cure for anything."

"Oh." Deflated, Marian slumped against the sterile chair. She didn't want to hear about her dad's obsession. She'd listened to enough of his theories throughout the years and had stopped paying attention to his rambling long ago.

Maybe if he hadn't spent so much time running down all those rabbit trails, he would have found the cure for VHL by now. Ellen would be safe. And Marian wouldn't have to spend every second of her life trying to succeed where he'd failed. Maybe they would have been together again instead of continually drifting farther apart, living separate lives in three different countries.

Whatever the case, she didn't want to talk about "the ultimate cure." Even though Harrison had always been willing to listen to her dad go on about his research, he knew how she felt about it.

She took a bite of the spicy chicken, savoring the blend of cumin and coriander and tomato. "This is delicious. We need to eat before it gets cold."

Harrison pushed his plate away, untouched. "None of the drug companies would stir up this kind of trouble for just any drug—they never have before. But they would do anything, no matter how vile, if they believed Arthur had completed his work on the ultimate cure."

She wanted to sigh in exasperation, but she finished her bite and responded evenly. "You and I both know his research for the ultimate cure was based on myths and historical gibberish."

"And you and I both know Arthur is a genius." Harrison glanced at her dad, studying him while she inhaled more of her dinner. "To be fair, what if his Tree of Life theory is valid?"

Marian released a short, bitter laugh. "Come on, Harrison. We're scientists, and we're trained to use empirical evidence. To test. To retest. To base results on solid observations not speculation. And most certainly not on tall tales."

"He was rather secretive of late. Maybe he finally discovered the location of the seeds from the Tree of Life."

Seeds? Tree of Life? Marian shook her head, her frustration escalating.

"We obviously don't know all the particulars." His voice was barely audible. "But Lionel Inc. pesters him unceasingly. I'd hazard a guess they're behind whatever happened to Arthur, especially if they fancy getting their hands on a discovery."

Whatever happened to Arthur . . .

During her last call with Dad, he'd been distracted and cryptic. One of his final instructions pushed to the front of her mind: *If anything happens to me, go to my safety deposit box at the bank, Marian. You're intelligent, and you'll figure out what to do next.*

At the time, she'd believed he was alluding to end-of-life decisions. But what if he'd known someone meant to do him harm? Or had he known he'd fall into a coma? If so, how?

Hunger fading, Marian placed her soggy plate onto the table.

Whatever was in the safety deposit box was likely what the intruders had been looking for when they'd broken into her dad's office and home. Perhaps it contained something important, something Dad hadn't wanted anyone else to know about, except her.

Why?

How would Mercer competitors know her dad had landed upon another medicinal discovery unless they had inside connections, perhaps someone close to her dad that they were paying to report to them? Perhaps someone working for Lionel Inc.? They had a branch in Sandwich, only thirteen miles from Canterbury.

Although the police suspected the trespasser into her dad's house had used an electronic lockpick or some other specialized tool that left no trace of tampering, what if the intruder was a trusted friend who already had a key to Dad's house, as well as a key to his office?

A trusted friend . . . like Harrison Burlington.

No, not Harrison. Kind, giving, gentle Harrison would never willingly bring Arthur Creighton any harm.

Even so, for now, it was best not to say anything about the safety deposit box. She picked up her plate of takeout and started to eat again, trying to don an air of indifference. But all the while she nibbled, she considered what kind of excuse she could give Harrison before she left again.

The bank closed in two hours. She had to see what was in the safety deposit box today. She wouldn't be able to rest until she did.

~ 3 ~

THE SAFETY DEPOSIT BOX sat on the tall table in front of Marian. Even though the bank attendant had closed the door and left her alone, she glanced around the tiny viewing room anyway— which was more of an empty closet, paneled in dark wood with a single light overhead.

A couple of years ago during a visit, Dad had gone through the process of having her and Ellen sign as joint renters on the box. When she'd arrived a short while ago, the bank hadn't given her any hassle as she'd signed the admission form.

Thankfully, she'd had no trouble finding the key to the box. The hospital staff had placed Dad's personal belongings into safekeeping. After she'd arrived, they'd given her the plastic bag containing his keys, wallet, several wadded tissues, a scattering of change— including old coins like those on his dining room floor—and the Rolex watch she and Ellen had given him last Christmas, the one with an engraving of their love on the back.

Marian hadn't found anything unusual in the assortment, nothing to give her any clues regarding what had happened to him in his last hours before he'd fallen into his coma.

She brushed a hand across the five-by-twenty-two-inch cold metal container. Now she could only pray she'd find some hint. She

27

wouldn't be able to rest until she unraveled the mystery of what her dad had been doing in his final days to attract so much danger.

Tree of Life. Seeds. Harrison's whisper came back to taunt her.

"No," she said. "That's nothing. Nothing but a stupid theory of a desperate man."

A man frantic to find a cure. A man who'd go to any lengths. A man who'd accept any hope no matter how ridiculous. All so he could save his wife from her rare genetic disease.

Marian had been a young girl when her mom had been diagnosed and when her dad had first started searching for the Tree of Life from the book of Genesis. At the time, Marian had loved her dad's story about how God had planted the original Tree of Life in the middle of the Garden of Eden—a tree God said would allow men to live forever.

Once the first humans sinned, God banned them from the Garden of Eden and placed an angel with a flaming sword in front of the garden to keep people out. Ever since then, the Garden of Eden had been lost to history. Or at least that's what most normal, sane people believed.

But not her dad. He wasn't normal or sane. He'd developed his own theories about what had happened to the mysterious Tree of Life, the tree that was supposed to help humans live forever.

According to Genesis, a river flowed through the Garden of Eden and separated into four headwaters, carrying water away from the garden. Dad speculated that the life-giving qualities of the Tree of Life from its roots, leaves, and seeds had been in that river and its headwaters. As a result, the waters bearing the life-giving residue contributed to the early humans living extraordinarily long lives. The Bible recorded people reaching the ages of seven or eight hundred years. One man, Methuselah, lived to be 969 years old.

Marian couldn't find fault with her dad's conjectures about the Tree of Life lengthening life spans. It made about as much sense as other speculations, like the climate theory, which purported that the healthy, wholesome climate of those early centuries extended life expectancies.

Whatever the case, Dad had followed every possible lead to discover what had become of the Tree of Life, had even traveled to remote parts of the world that were rumored to be the original Garden of Eden. He'd eventually concluded the garden had been destroyed by a catastrophic flood and buried under layers of sediment. As a result of the flood, remnants of the life-giving water sources had become so diluted that the average life span had drastically diminished.

If only Dad had stopped at that dead end. Instead, he'd researched every fable and lore regarding the Tree of Life, miraculous healings, and unusual longevity of lives. Some legends claimed that seeds from the Tree of Life had been brought onto Noah's ark, preserved during the flood, and passed down through generations of protectors. Other legends supported the dispersal theory, which said remnants of the Tree of Life were carried by the floodwaters to various parts of the world.

Her dad had meticulously studied every report including the tales by Herodotus, the mythical exploits of Alexander the Great, the stories of Prester John from the early Crusades, and the claims of Ponce de León during his explorations of Florida. All the accounts had one thing in common—fountains of youth that supposedly restored the life and vitality of anyone who bathed in or drank the water.

Her dad's library—now in shambles—contained every tale, every mention, every hint of miraculous water and anything else her dad thought pointed back to the Tree of Life.

After Marian started college, she hadn't kept up with Dad's research into the tree, hadn't wanted to anymore. He'd made no secret that he transferred to Mercer's Research and Development Centre in Canterbury in order to pursue additional leads regarding the Tree of Life in England. By that point, she'd realized his obsession not only had taken him away from her and Ellen but bordered on lunacy.

"At least two seeds from the tree ended up in England, Marian," he'd told her during one of her early visits after he'd moved to Canterbury. "An account written in Latin by some of the very first priests to arrive in England contains a detailed list of relics brought for safekeeping from barbarians attacking the Roman Empire. Two seeds are a part of that list."

Britannia—as it was then called—had been on the fringes of the ancient world, a faraway Roman outpost. Even today, Roman ruins were strewn about the country. The seeds on the list archived in the British Museum could have been any type of seed. The idea that they'd been preserved from the fruit that had once hung on the Tree of Life was preposterous and made Marian cringe every time her dad mentioned it.

Now with the safety deposit box in front of her—its steely gray interior containing only heaven knew what—she swallowed the apprehension plaguing her since her talk with Harrison in the hospital.

Marian shook her head. The box wouldn't contain seeds. It couldn't.

She lifted her hands to the lid only to realize her fingers were trembling. "Stop it, Marian. Do what you came for."

Slowly she lifted the top of the box. The chiming trill of her cell phone in her purse startled her. She dropped the lid into place, snatched up her phone, and saw Jasper's name and number on the screen.

She'd already ignored three of his calls, had let them go to voicemail. But somehow, at this moment, she needed to hear his voice—the voice of reason to ground her in reality, science, and empirical evidence. Jasper was every bit as logical as she was, and talking with him would calm her nerves.

She picked up his call. "Jasper?"

"Hi." His voice on the other end echoed with relief. "I was beginning to worry something happened to you."

"No, I'm fine. Everything's fine." Except that, really, nothing was fine. A deep part of her suspected nothing would be fine ever again.

"How's your dad?"

"The same."

"Have you found out what happened?"

"Not a thing."

He was silent a moment, and she almost thought she heard an exasperated sigh. "Let me fly over and help you."

"I can't let you do that . . ." Giving him permission to come would take their relationship to the next level. And she couldn't lead him on.

"I know how hard it is to be alone while you watch someone you love suffer." From everything he'd told her, his mom had run off shortly after his dad had been diagnosed with Lou Gehrig's. Since then, Jasper had been alone, watching his dad slowly deteriorate, unable to do anything to stop the disease.

"Thank you, Jasper. But you know I'm not alone. I have Harrison." She fingered the safety deposit box in front of her. She could picture Jasper at his desk, the one across from hers. He'd be leaning back in his chair, his lab coat unbuttoned, his protective eyewear pushed up to the top of his head making his hair stick up.

"You sure?"

About Harrison? She bit back her doubts, knowing they were unfounded. "I'll be fine."

Silence spread between them. She hoped she hadn't hurt Jasper's feelings. But she'd always been upfront with him that she wasn't ready for a relationship.

"So . . ." he said. "You don't sound like you're at the hospital. Where are you?"

She ought to tell him about the break-ins and the possibility someone was after another one of her dad's cures. But this was neither the time nor place. "I stopped by Dad's bank for a minute. Why?"

"No reason."

"You don't need to worry about me."

"Promise you'll let me know if anything changes?"

"Promise."

After ending the call, she turned her attention back to the box. She couldn't stall any longer. Sucking in a fortifying breath, she lifted the cover.

She wasn't sure what she'd expected—perhaps wads of rolled money or rare family heirlooms or even glittering jewels. Not that her dad had need of a secret stash of money or jewels. His fortune was established, and he had no need to be secretive about it.

Perhaps she really wanted to see the seeds after all. Or dried leaves. Or roots. Or something having to do with the Tree of Life. If Dad had left her tangible evidence, something to prove his life's work had been worthwhile, maybe she could forgive him for abandoning her and Ellen.

Instead, she found herself looking at a small flask and an assortment of papers.

What if he'd written down the formula for a breakthrough drug? Perhaps it was on one of the sheets.

She unfolded first one paper and then another only to find them to be pages torn from his books. One contained a picture of a strange Gothic-like sculpture at the top of a pillar and the other the floor plan of an ancient church.

She continued unfolding the rest of the sheets, discovering an odd assortment of articles and a typed-out list of Bible references. A final paper revealed her dad's short, messy handwriting with these words underlined at the top: "Speculations of Breaching the Time-Space Continuum."

A scan of the six points on the sheet only made her want to

toss up her hands in exasperation. She let the paper fall on top of the others.

"Oh Dad." Did he seriously believe in time travel—like going to the past or to the future? He was more deranged than she realized.

For a full minute, she stared at the papers scattered over the table, a keen sense of disappointment warring within her—not disappointment in Dad, but for her and Ellen and all they'd lost because he'd been lost in his own world. Marian had the overwhelming urge to crumple the sheets and toss them into the wastebasket by the door. The time he'd spent on his stupid research had been nothing but a waste. A complete waste.

After years, this was all he had to show? These were his most prized possessions? The things he had to lock away in a bank for safekeeping?

She fought back a sudden swell of bitter tears. He could have used his skills much more productively—like in being a father. Instead, he'd been pursuing mythical trees—and time-crossing possibilities.

She reached for the last item in the box—the flask. The dull metallic-looking artifact was very old. Not more than three inches tall, it was rectangular in shape and rose to a spout flanked on each side by arm-like handles. She fingered the intricate details carved into the flat surface of both sides.

It was too small to serve as a drinking vessel. Perhaps it had once been a relic worn as a pendant. She shook it gently and then tipped it over, praying it would contain something—anything. But it was empty. She raised it to her nose and sniffed but couldn't detect an odor or any other clue to help her understand why Dad had put it in his box.

Over the years of living in Kent, Dad had collected unique historical artifacts. That was no secret. As home of the famous Canterbury Cathedral, the area was steeped in history and folklore. Even though Marian hadn't studied history as much as her dad, she still loved the aura and rich cultural heritage of Canterbury.

She stuffed the items into her purse. Perhaps if she returned to Dad's house and sorted through the mess, she'd find evidence to help her understand why he'd put the flask and papers into the safety deposit box.

After she returned the box and stepped out of the bank, she scrolled through the contacts on her phone to find Harrison's number. She'd call him and let him know she wouldn't be returning to the hospital right away after all.

A man wearing a navy suit and mirror-like sunglasses collided with her.

"Pardon me." She took a step back. Was she becoming one of those people glued to her device, not paying attention to the world around her?

The man bumped her again, and this time, he grabbed her purse strap. "Give me your bag."

For a moment, she could only stare at his fingers gripping her purse. Was she being robbed? The idea was absurd, surreal.

"Now." The man's tone was steely. He flashed open his suit coat, revealing the handle of a gun sticking out of an inner pocket.

~ 4 ~

"I'M AN AMERICAN." Marian willed her voice not to tremble. "And I only have American cash."

"Just hand over your bag." Her attacker yanked at the strap. His hair was clipped short, and he was well groomed—certainly not the appearance of a man desperate enough to rob her in broad daylight.

The rational part of her mind warned her to cooperate, that nothing was worth the risk of getting hurt. On the other hand, she didn't want to lose the items from her dad's safety deposit box—not before she'd had the chance to investigate them more fully.

"I'll give you my wallet." She reached inside the bag.

"I want the whole thing."

Her fingers closed around the papers and the flask. She jerked them from her purse and at the same time let the strap fall from her shoulder.

Without his hold, she lurched away, trying to put as much distance between them as possible. Her assailant fumbled with her purse, digging inside, before glancing at her again and honing in on the papers and flask in her hand.

A warning clanged in Marian's head, urging her to run, to make a commotion, to do something to attract assistance. She stumbled back several more paces and then flagged down two women exiting a shop across the street. "Help! This man is robbing me!"

With his attention trained on the papers, the thief tossed her purse to the ground and stalked toward her with quick, certain steps.

The women had stopped, shopping bags in hand, but were either too entertained or too afraid to do anything but stare.

In her high heels, Marian spun and tried to sprint but was as wobbly and unsteady as a patient coming off anesthetic.

Her pursuer's footsteps pounded on the cobbled sidewalk behind her.

She spotted another group ahead. "Help!"

At the screech of tires on the pavement and the sight of a black Bentley headed directly for her, she froze. *This is it. I'm about to die.*

The Bentley squealed to a halt only inches away, and the back door swung open. "Get in!" Harrison's familiar voice shouted from the interior.

The thief's hand closed around her arm.

She swung her elbow backward as hard as she could. It connected with some part of the man's face, giving her the split second she needed to break away and dive into the car.

Without waiting for her to close the door, Harrison yelled at his driver, and the car roared away, sending her sprawling across the seat.

Harrison grasped her. "Hang on!"

She latched onto him as the Bentley careened down the street. The door swung open wider before banging closed. Only after they'd taken several sharp corners and were on a long stretch of road did she push herself up and take a breath.

"That was close." Harrison peered out the rear window.

She reached for her seat belt, but her hand was trembling too much to get the clip into the fastener. In her other hand, she still clutched the papers and bottle from the safety deposit box. Somehow, she'd also managed to hang on to her phone, but her purse and all her ID and credit cards were back on the sidewalk.

She blew out a shaky breath. "What's going on, Harrison?"

Harrison's gaze darted from one side window to the other and then behind them again. "That man is a security guard for Lionel Inc. Clearly, Lionel is after the items you just emptied out of your dad's safety deposit box."

Harrison was right. The thief hadn't wanted her purse or wallet. He'd been after the papers. "How did you know I'd be at the bank? And how did you know I was checking Dad's box?" For that matter, how had her attacker known she'd be there? She hadn't told anyone where she was going.

Evidently, everyone was keeping tabs on her.

Harrison gave instructions to his driver, a diminutive Asian man whose head barely reached high enough to see over the steering wheel. Then he shifted to face her, his expression grave. "I followed you, Marian."

So she couldn't trust Harrison after all.

As if sensing her suspicion, he held out a calming hand. "It's not like that, love. I asked Bojing to keep an eye on the comings and goings at the hospital." Harrison nodded toward his driver. "Two ticks after you took your leave, Bojing rang me on his mobile to inform me Lionel was indeed trailing you."

She sensed he was telling her the truth. Nevertheless, she clutched the wad of papers and the bottle tighter.

"Now after Lionel accosted you, it's quite apparent that whatever Arthur was working on was vitally important, and Lionel really wants to get their hands on it."

The image of the gun in her attacker's coat pocket seared her mind. Whatever Dad had discovered *was* important—so important people were willing to kill to get it.

"A few weeks ago, your dad said something." Harrison swallowed hard, his Adam's apple rising and falling. "At the time I brushed it aside. But now, with everything that's transpired . . ."

"What did he say?" She glanced out the front window to see that Bojing had turned onto Whitehall Road. He was jerking the wheel back and forth and nearly taking the curves on two wheels like a driver from a crime show, even though no one seemed to be following them.

"You'll think I'm a buffoon for repeating it. For considering there might be weight to it."

"Probably."

Harrison held on tightly to the leather seat with one hand and with the other tugged at his bow tie and collar as if they were strangling him. "He mentioned the ultimate cure can vibrate energy billions of times smaller than nuclei to a frequency and wavelength that can rejuvenate any illness."

"Yes, I've heard his theory." And she knew as well as Harrison the physics behind drugs, all about heat and friction and the vibration of particles that worked to kill targeted microscopic organisms.

Harrison cleared his throat. "This time he indicated the ultimate cure could possibly vibrate energy at such a frequency that it would have a strange effect on those who are healthy."

"A strange effect? Like what?"

He grabbed on to the door handle as Bojing whipped the car around another bend. "It could vibrate in such a way that people would have realistic visions of the past or future or possibly even cross time."

His words jolted her—along with Bojing's crazy driving—and her thoughts jumped to the paper from the safety deposit box. "As in breaching the time-space continuum?"

Chagrin crinkled his forehead. "I know, right? The whole thing is ludicrous. Preposterous, even. But I wouldn't bring it up except Arthur emphasized that healthy people having such wavelength vibrations would likely lose consciousness for the duration of their visions or time crossing."

"Lose consciousness?"

"What if he meant they would fall into a coma?" Harrison's serious eyes met hers.

Her thoughts pinged as a million neurons connected the dots. "So Dad developed his ultimate cure from remnants he finally found from the Tree of Life. He experimented with the new drug on himself and fell into a coma. And now while he's in the coma, he's supposedly crossing the time continuum?"

For several heartbeats, the gunning of the engine filled the space between them.

"Can you imagine? It's sheer madness." Harrison spoke the words first. Thankfully.

"It's impossible."

"Quite."

They lapsed into silence. Her dad's ramblings *were* impossible, weren't they? But what if he had ingested something to purpose-fully cause a loss of consciousness? "If Dad tested a drug on him-self, then why were the hospital labs negative?"

"Precisely. His urine or blood would show traces of something."

They'd both examined the initial lab reports as well as the additional test results. Arthur Creighton wasn't taking a single medication for anything. For a man in his early sixties, he was at his prime.

"I apologize, love." Harrison released a long, tired sigh. "There's no sense in fretting about it. I'm sure Arthur didn't mean to imply he believed in crossing time. That's a bit too deluded even for him."

Was it?

Marian loosened her hold on the items she'd found at the bank and set them in her lap. She riffled through the papers, pulled one out, and handed it to Harrison.

He unfolded it and began to read. "Speculations of Breaching the Time-Space Continuum. Preface: Although I could find no written historical records from anyone making claims of breaching the time-space fourth dimension, I found stories from those having such realistic visions and dreams of the past, that I've concluded movement through the quantum energy field is possible and those who pass through it have been too ignorant or afraid to confess it."

Marian read along silently as Harrison continued to read aloud.

"Number one: No evidence exists of people having visions/movements that overlap with their own time continuum; all visions/movements are of entirely different eras. Number two: It appears that people have visions or movement through the quantum energy field to a time period they affix in their mind; e.g. many claim to have visions of the crucifixion of Christ."

Harrison stopped reading, his expression one of incredulity. "This was in his safety deposit box?"

She nodded. "I guess speculating about breaching time wasn't too deluded for him."

"Apparently not." Harrison's attention dropped to the rest of the items on her lap, as if they might provide answers. He startled at the sight of the flask, which had tumbled onto the seat next to her. "Is that what I think it is?"

She picked up the container and inspected it. "What is it?"

"It's a pilgrim ampulla." His eyes widened behind his glasses. "During the Middle Ages when people took pilgrimages to holy shrines, they carried little flasks filled with holy water or holy oil."

"Like the pilgrims from Chaucer's *Canterbury Tales*?"

"Right. Like the thousands of pilgrims who came to Canterbury Cathedral to the shrine of St. Thomas. They purchased ampullae, badges, and other souvenirs."

She knew enough Latin to understand that *ampullae* was the plural form of *ampulla*. During her visits to Canterbury over the years, she'd heard the term, and she'd inevitably learned the history that made the cathedral so famous. Thomas Becket, the Archbishop of Canterbury during the twelfth century, had fallen out of favor with the king and was assassinated by four knights in Canterbury Cathedral.

For some reason, the pope canonized Becket, turning him into a saint. After that, people from all over England made pilgrimages to visit St. Thomas's tomb in the cathedral.

"So what's Dad doing with a pilgrim ampulla?" She turned the flask over, grazing the engravings on both sides.

"Arthur's got up to something. Do you mind if I have a look?"

She handed it to Harrison. If he could figure out why it was among Dad's most prized possessions, then more power to him.

Harrison turned on the flashlight of his phone, shining it onto the container and examining it from all angles. "If my hunch is correct, this is the St. Thomas ampulla that was stolen from Canterbury Cathedral three weeks ago when it was brought there for display with the Esztergom relic."

Marian raised her brow. "Why would Dad have a stolen ampulla? And what in the world is the Esztergom relic?"

"The Esztergom is thought to be a bone from the elbow of Thomas Becket. The bone has been on display at various cathedrals around the country, including Westminster and St. Margaret's Church. Even St. Michael's in Harbledown before arriving in Canterbury."

"You're kidding. How can anyone care about a piece of elbow bone from a dead archbishop?" In fact, how could anyone know if such a bone had once belonged to Becket? Maybe it came from another dead person and was passed off as Becket's with the hope of making money.

Harrison shrugged as though he didn't get the fascination either. "During the last Sunday afternoon of Becket Week, mass was held in the crypt of the cathedral. The ampulla went missing after that."

If Dad had taken it, how would he have managed such a feat? And more importantly, why? "Dad isn't a thief. He's eccentric at times, but he'd never steal something out of the cathedral."

"Sorry, love. The fleurs-de-lys decorating the edges and the details of Becket on both sides most certainly makes it a St. Thomas ampulla." Harrison studied the flask as if it was a long-lost treasure.

Though faded, the front had an engraving of angels flying over Becket. The back depicted the famous saint being attacked by the knights who killed him.

"How do you know this is the one stolen from Becket Week? There are probably lots of ampullae around the area."

"Actually, no. The *Kentish Gazette* ran a big article about the crime. Historians and museum curators know of only three original St. Thomas ampullae that still exist."

"Maybe this isn't an original." Even as she said the words, she had the sinking feeling Harrison was right about its authenticity. But she couldn't believe Dad had stolen it.

Harrison lifted the flask to his nose and sniffed. He tipped it over much the same way she had earlier in the viewing room at the bank. Then he attempted to peer down the narrow opening.

"The more I try to comprehend what's happened to Dad, the more complicated things seem to get and the less I understand of what he actually did."

Harrison scrutinized the container a moment longer before holding it out to her. "Rumor has it that the original ampulla held holy water, in particular holy water mixed with blood from St. Thomas Becket himself."

As she took the ampulla, a scoffing laugh begged for release. Water with blood from Becket was as foolish as his elbow bone. But Harrison continued before she could voice her sarcasm. "The holy water was thought to cure diseases. The monks bottled the water in ampullae like this and sold it to pilgrims."

Bojing slowed the Bentley, and ahead, Marian glimpsed Harrison's estate, Chesterfield Park. As the car drew to a stop in front of imposing iron gates, Marian tried to make sense of everything—particularly the facts that her dad might have drugged himself into a coma and had likely stolen an important relic from Canterbury Cathedral.

What had he been thinking? Maybe that was the problem. What if he'd developed a mental illness that had caused him to behave irrationally?

She exhaled her frustration. He hadn't sounded demented or irrational during their last phone call. Distracted, yes. But he'd been as sharp and intelligent as usual.

Bojing rolled down his window and spoke into the intercom. A moment later, the gates swung open to admit them. Harrison's driver directed the car down a long paved driveway that circled an elegant yard. With several flower beds in full bloom, the vibrant green grass made the stately palatial-sized manor stand out all the more.

Marian gaped as she usually did as they drew closer to the mansion built in Anglo-Italian style with its magnificent stonework, many large-paned cross windows, gated porch entrance with two arches and a cupola, and a striking hall tower on the east end. The manor was three stories high with a grandeur that was breathtaking.

Harrison had once explained that the original house had been built by the Durham family in the 1300s. King Edward III had awarded Sir Durham the land for daring deeds that had helped the English defeat the French at Crecy.

Apparently, the original structure had been much less lavish. After it had been ransacked during the English Civil War, it had been reconstructed and enlarged, especially during Victorian times. In the 1880s, the mansion had passed to the Burlington family, who were distant relatives of the Durhams. Harrison's grandparents and parents invested enormous amounts of capital into restoring the interior to some of its rich historical heritage.

For several decades, the Burlington family opened parts of the mansion and gardens to tourists. But after Harrison inherited the estate, he made it his private residence and ended the public viewing.

Bojing rolled the Bentley to a stop across from the entrance, and Marian tried to envision the house the way it had been in the 1300s, smaller, less ornate, but surely just as magnificent. Bojing exited the car, rounded to the trunk, and began removing Harrison's wheelchair. Harrison opened his door and pivoted in readiness for Bojing.

Marian gathered up the papers and ampulla and stepped out of the car to find that the evening had grown considerably cooler. She wished now she'd thought to bring a sweater. The sun had begun to fade, turning the sky a royal blue like the pieces of colored glass in the cathedral window. The vibrant blue reflected off the manor's stones, turning the gray to lavender.

Weariness overtook her. In addition to jet lag and sleep deprivation, worry and the strain of the attack were beginning to take a toll. She wanted to return to the hospital and be with Dad, but she had the feeling Harrison would insist she get a good night's sleep first here at Chesterfield Park, where hopefully she would be safe. She decided that she wouldn't argue with him. This time.

She closed the car door and faced the imposing porch entrance that was reminiscent of a gatehouse found on a castle, albeit slightly smaller in size. She fumbled with the ampulla and tightened her grip on it. She couldn't let anything happen to the relic until she figured out why Dad had it.

She brought the opening to her nose and sniffed again as she had earlier. What if the rumors were true, and it had held liquid of some kind? And what if Dad had consumed it?

Whatever fluid it had contained could have been quite old and had an adverse effect on him. Even if the hospital's blood tests hadn't revealed traces of anything out of the ordinary in his system, she was suddenly overcome with the suspicion that whatever had been in the flask was related to his coma in some way.

Knowing Dad, he'd likely poured the contents into a disposable tube and placed the ampulla into his safety deposit box to keep from being caught with the incriminating evidence. The hospital personnel had indicated he'd fallen unconscious in the main lobby shortly after he arrived, but they hadn't mentioned him having a container on him. Nothing of the sort had been in the plastic bag of his possessions. But if he'd had something, it could have rolled away, been tossed in the trash, or even kicked into a corner by a passerby.

Whatever the case, she wanted to know more about the liquid. She touched her tongue to the inner neck and licked it. She didn't taste any chemicals or compounds, at least any she could distinguish. But there was a slight grit. She stuck her tongue in and licked harder so that it came loose.

This time she closed her mouth around the sandpapery substance, and a strange rush, like a gust of wind, charged through her veins, down her body, and into her arms and legs. The gust was oddly warm in the chill of the evening. As the grit dissolved against her tongue, she heard a pounding gallop of horse hooves on the driveway.

Swiveling, she was shocked to find an enormous horse bearing down on her, its rider apparently not paying any attention to the vehicle in its path. She groped for the Bentley door handle. But her fingers only grasped air.

A glance out of her periphery told her the car was gone—that Bojing had already driven it away. How had the slight man assisted Harrison into his wheelchair and moved the vehicle so rapidly?

The thunder of hooves drew nearer, kicking up stones and dust with every step. And yet, wasn't Harrison's driveway paved?

She stepped back farther, out of the way, expecting to stumble into the tulip garden and the large manicured lawn. But uneven grass tickled her ankles. The stallion passed by, leaving a breeze in its wake that wafted across her cheeks and bare arms and brought the odor of horseflesh with a mixture of hay, mud, and sweat.

The rider bent low as though he'd been galloping at top speed for some time. As he reined in his beast, he slid off in a fluid motion, clearly an experienced equestrian. Perhaps he was another guest out riding for the evening, although Harrison's family had turned the original stables into a greenhouse decades ago, and Harrison boarded a couple of remaining horses at a neighboring farm.

The man straightened to his full height, and she drew back in surprise at the sight of his attire. He was wearing what appeared to be a flowing surcoat that was dark and coarse and rather gothic-looking, especially with the hood up. His scuffed leather boots hugged his calves and were laced with thick, strange twine.

Was he some kind of reenactor? If so, his costume was authentic—worn and weathered and certainly not clean. It outlined his broad shoulders and imposing size, which she guessed to be about six feet three inches.

He dropped the horse's reins and took several long, hurried strides toward the entrance, but then halted abruptly. Before she could blink, he swung around and was gripping a knife with a frighteningly sharp blade and pointing it in her direction.

She gasped and took another step back, wishing for the safety of the Bentley so she could open the door, leap inside, and lock the car behind her. But again, the vehicle had strangely disappeared and so had the tulip garden.

Why was this guest wielding a knife? Was he another attacker like the one outside the bank? A scream welled up in her throat and pushed for release.

The stranger's gaze collided with hers, and she found herself looking into eyes so blue they matched the brilliance of the evening

46

sky overhead. As beautiful as those eyes were, they were equally fierce and intense. Dark brows furrowed above them, matching the hair that showed beneath his hood.

With a square-shaped jaw covered in a layer of stubble and broad cheeks coated with the same, he was ruggedly handsome in a foreboding way. He bore an air of confidence and power and danger. As though sensing her fear, he lowered his knife, studying her face the same way she was his.

He didn't speak, but something in his expression attested to pain and sorrows of the deepest kind, haunted memories, and even self-loathing. Though she had no idea who he was or where he was from, the contradiction of his powerful outward strength and fragile inner spirit reached inside, touched her, and beckoned her toward him in an almost magnetic pull.

At a flicker of light in one of the manor windows, she glanced behind him, only to gasp again. Though the house was still three stories high, the long wings had diminished in length. The tower on the east end rose above the house, but the parapet and crenellations were simpler, as if designed for battle not beauty.

The center entrance consisted of a simple black iron gate and none of the fancy scrolling and intricate brickwork. Above it was a shield bearing a family coat of arms, one she'd never noticed there before. The surface field was crimson and the outer edge azure. A golden stag stood regally at the center.

"Marian?"

Harrison. She shifted toward the direction of his voice, but he wasn't there. All she saw was the yard. However, instead of the neatly trimmed lawn and blooming flower beds, the grass was long and scraggly beneath clusters of sprawling oak and gnarled yew. Where had the trees come from? The stone wall along the perimeter encircled the grounds and was much thicker and taller than the one they'd just passed in the car.

What was happening? Was she hallucinating?

She shifted to find that the fierce-looking man was still watching her. He held himself immobile, as though his slightest move would frighten her.

The gate behind him swung open with a squeal. "Sire?"

He lifted a hand, signaling the newcomer to silence, all without taking his powerful gaze from her.

A muscle in his jaw twitched.

If he was nothing more than a vision, then why did he seem so real?

5

"MARIAN?" Harrison's voice came from behind her again. Fingers circled around her hand and pressed her flesh. "What is it, love? You look as though you've seen a ghost."

She glanced down to find him in his wheelchair right beside her.

Her gaze shifted back to the horse and rider. But they had disappeared. She searched the manor entrance and driveway, but the man and beast were nowhere to be found. The trees on the lawn were gone, the grass was trimmed, and the side wings of the house stood in place. All the decorative architecture had returned, and the shield that bore the coat of arms was no longer in the spot above the center arch.

Had she seen a ghost?

She swayed and grabbed on to Harrison, suddenly so tired she felt as though she might collapse.

"Bojing, go get Drake." Harrison motioned to his driver standing next to the Bentley, which was parked in the same spot as before. "Inform him I need his assistance right away bringing Marian inside."

She wanted to tell Harrison she'd be fine, that she didn't need any help. But once again a breeze wafted over her, bringing with it the odor of horseflesh and the distinct sound of a neigh. The

49

lower manor window winked with light for several seconds then went dark.

What was going on?

She caught sight of the outline of a broad figure once more, but then he was gone and Harrison's butler, Drake, took his place and was hurrying toward her, out the door before Bojing could summon him. Immaculately attired in a suit, vest, and bow tie, Drake looked as though he'd stepped out of the 1850s like Harrison. With thin stooped shoulders and graying hair, the butler had always struck Marian as grandfatherly.

Before she could protest, he scooped her up into his arms and was carrying her as easily as a baby. He might appear old and weak, but his years of assisting and lifting Harrison had given him strength that belied his age.

"I can walk, Drake. Really."

"It's no trouble, miss."

"Jet lag is catching up to me." She knew she should wiggle to free herself, but a wave of exhaustion crashed over her, and she gave way to a yawn.

As they crossed into the entrance hall, she couldn't keep from peering around for a glimpse of the stranger. Somehow she sensed he was there, though she didn't see him. The hall was big enough to be a room in its own right. It had a shiny white marble floor and was lined with oak paneling milled from trees once grown on the estate. Most impressive, however, were the dozen columns that supported a center dome decorated with stained glass circles depicting local game birds.

One side of the entrance hall opened to the main drawing room, and the other side led to the staircase hall, which contained wide oak steps that rose to a balcony with more of the richly carved dark oak.

While Harrison steered his wheelchair toward the elevator, Drake carried her up the spiraling stairway past paintings of the long-deceased people who'd once roamed the halls of Harrison's home. At one of the guest chambers, a maid met them and ushered them into a large room with a marble fireplace taking up one wall and two long windows curtained with thick tapestries on another. A hall branched off into a boudoir complete with a private bathroom, walk-in closet, and a mirrored room that contained a settee, dressing table, and a jewelry armoire.

Drake deposited her onto the canopied bed with a lush blue spread and curtains. The color reminded her of the eyes of the man she'd seen outside the entrance.

"There you are, miss."

"Thank you, Drake." Marian yawned again, fatigue rushing in and making her tremble.

The maid tried to pry the papers and ampulla out of her hands, but Marian wasn't ready to let go. She wanted to examine everything again, especially the ampulla, and try to figure out what had just happened to her. But the thick heaviness of slumber settled over her. Her eyes closed, and even as she fought to stay awake, she fell asleep in an instant.

• ● •

Marian's lashes fluttered open. For several seconds, she couldn't make sense of where she was. But as she focused on the canopy overhead, images flooded her mind—the strange changes to Chesterfield Park, the large horse riding down the driveway, and the ruggedly handsome man with the knife.

"Marian? Are you awake?" Harrison spoke from her bedside.

She shifted to the sight of him, disheveled and haggard in his wheelchair, his dark hair mussed, his bow tie gone, and the top of his dress shirt unbuttoned.

Her fingers made contact with a silky bedspread before sliding to the satin nightgown she was wearing. Who had undressed her? The maid? And what had happened to the items from her dad's safety deposit box?

Her gaze darted around.

"They're right here." Harrison cocked his head to the bedside table to the stack of wrinkled papers and the ampulla.

She released a breath. "Thank you."

"How are you faring?"

"I'm fine. How long have I been asleep?"

"Twenty-four hours."

"What?" She rose to her elbows and glanced to the windows. The heavy draperies were half open, revealing the faded light of the evening and darkening sky.

"I was getting so worried about you, I debated phoning my doctor to come have a look, but then you roused and insisted you were fine."

"I did?" She didn't have any recollection of waking up. Apparently the past few stressful days and sleepless nights had caught up to her.

"I hope you're feeling better now?"

"Much." She stretched her legs, but then froze as she remembered why she was at Chesterfield Park in England to begin with. "Dad? How is he?"

"His condition is unchanged."

She dropped back against a mound of pillows, unsure whether to be relieved he wasn't worse or disappointed he wasn't better. Either way, she needed to get to the hospital and be with him again.

As though sensing her urgency, Harrison pressed her hand. "I've spent a few hours with him today and instructed the hospital staff to phone immediately if there's any change whatsoever."

"Thank you. I suppose you called Ellen?"

"I considered it, but there's too much danger here now. And I'm not keen on her walking into the middle of it."

"Good point." Marian was just glad she'd been the one attacked outside the bank and not her sister or Harrison.

"What happened when we arrived home yesterday?" Harrison's question cut through her haze. The dark circles under his eyes attested to his sleeplessness in the midst of her long hours of slumber.

Her thoughts flew back to when she'd stepped out of Harrison's car, the startlingly real encounter with the man, and then the exhaustion afterward.

Harrison picked up a gold-rimmed porcelain cup from the bedside table, blew on the steam rising from it, and took a sip. When he replaced it to the saucer, his expression was grave. "For a while, I couldn't keep from wondering if you were going to fall into a coma like Arthur."

She wanted to pretend the incident had been nothing more than a dream, but how could she deny what she'd seen, especially in light of everything she'd learned since emptying the safety deposit box. "I tasted some of the residue left in the ampulla."

Harrison sat up straighter. "What about it?"

"It caused me to have a vision."

"One of the realistic visions of the past Arthur mentioned?" Harrison nodded again toward the papers on the bedside table.

The sights, smells, and sounds of her experience lingered, perhaps had stayed with her during her slumber. Could she really describe what had happened as merely a vision? But what else could it have been? For several minutes, she described to Harrison the horse and man and old manor and surrounding yard. When she finished, Harrison watched her with wide eyes.

"I don't think I was just seeing it. Everything was so real, almost as if I was standing in the past." Did Harrison think she was crazy? She certainly felt like it. "What do you think?"

He was silent before expelling a breath. "I can only conclude Arthur's research is solid. The water in that flask was indeed original holy water. Since you're already healthy, the slight bit you ingested passed through you without any inhibition from illness or disease. Without the friction from the diseased cells, it began to vibrate at a frequency and wavelength that shifted you to another time. There's absolutely no other way to work it out."

For a heartbeat, she waited for Harrison's solemnity to dissolve into laughter, for him to say he was jesting and then launch into what he really thought based on solid empirical and scientific reasoning.

But his eyes didn't contain any mirth. And his lips didn't twitch into even the barest of smiles.

She stared up at the rich blue bed canopy, her brain working frantically to come up with another answer. "Surely as scientists, we can discover something more plausible, more realistic. Perhaps the drug from the ampulla has some kind of hallucinogenic property."

"Or perhaps it truly contained the holy water related to one of the two ancient seeds Arthur suspected came from the Tree of Life. Perhaps a water source came into contact with the seeds and gained properties that can heal illnesses."

"I don't know . . ."

"In trying to make sense of the ampulla and the healing water, I've done loads of researching." Harrison waved at the stacks of books piled on the floor around his wheelchair. "I discovered there are two primary locations in the UK for many of the miraculous healings that occurred over the centuries."

Her dad's library in his terraced home was nothing compared to Harrison's, which at one time housed over fifty thousand books. During past visits, Marian always wandered through the library looking at the built-in wall shelves with a sense of awe. Most of the books were as ancient as the house.

Harrison bent and retrieved the top book, a crusty volume with a spine curling up at the edges. "One of the spots is in Walsingham in Norfolk where there are several wells once believed to cause visions and heal illnesses. In 1061, a wealthy noblewoman by the name of Lady Richeldis de Faverches claimed the well water gave her three visions in which she saw the Virgin Mary and the house Mary lived in when the angel appeared to her in Nazareth."

"But what does this have to do with the ampulla and the healing water?"

"It's entirely possible one of the sacred seeds from the Tree of Life ended up in Walsingham and was eventually planted so that its life-giving properties infiltrated the ground and seeped into a natural wellspring. It would certainly explain the realistic visions as well as the many miraculous healings that occurred there."

"Supposed healings."

Harrison picked up another book. "*The Pynson Ballad*, thought to have been written in the 1460s. It documents the healings at Walsingham." He carefully turned the brittle, yellowed pages until he reached one marked by a sticky note. Then he began to read. "Many sick have been cured, the dead revived, the lame made whole, the blind have had their sight restored. Deaf-mutes, lunatics, and lepers have all been made well. People troubled by evil spirits have experienced deliverance. Also souls suffering from inner problems have found comfort. Every human suffering, bodily or spiritual, can find a remedy here."

Marian's own suffering soul warred within her. She didn't want to believe in such tales. But why would an ancient historian make it all up?

Harrison closed the book, discarded it, and rummaged through a different stack. "I know the healings sound strange, love. But everything I've read supports Arthur's theory."

If she hadn't experienced the realistic vision for herself yesterday, she would have scoffed at Harrison. But there was a part of her now that needed to understand the intricacies of her dad's research.

Harrison picked up the thick tome *St. Thomas, His Death and Miracles* and began paging through it. "This book documents the writings of two monks, Benedict of Peterborough and William of

Canterbury. They recorded over seven hundred miracles between the two of them in separate documents."

"In Canterbury?"

Harrison nodded.

"So you think the second seed from the Tree of Life ended up in Canterbury?" What was she saying? Did she believe in the seeds now too? Was she going crazy right along with Harrison and her dad?

"After Thomas Becket's death," Harrison said, "the monks began to sell holy water to the pilgrims. That's when the miracles started happening."

"What if they made up the miracles to sell more holy water?" Yes, she had faith God could intervene and perform miracles when he chose to. But she also believed too many frauds worked for their own benefit and fame just as much in the present as they had in the past.

Harrison flipped through more pages. "The accounts of the two monks are quite amazing. If they'd just wanted money, then why record hundreds when a dozen would have sufficed?"

This whole conversation was insane. "If a seed from the Tree of Life ended up in Canterbury, why wasn't it discovered earlier? Why at Becket's death?"

Harrison dug through the books again and pulled out another. "It's possible that like in Walsingham, the seed somehow ended up in the ground, distributing its life-giving qualities into a nearby underground spring. Thus the wellspring in Canterbury could have been in existence long before Becket's death."

He opened the brittle pages to a place with a sticky note. "I found the account of St. Mildred, an abbess in 690, who was rumored to have miraculous healing powers. It's possible she stumbled upon the Canterbury wellspring and used the water in mixing herbal remedies."

Marian was silent, trying to digest everything Harrison had

researched while she'd been sleeping. He seemed convinced the miracles recorded at Walsingham and Canterbury were somehow related to the mythical seeds from the Tree of Life.

"If there really were wellsprings that contained traces of residue from the Tree of Life, then why can't people be healed from the springs today? After all, people still make pilgrimages to the Shrine of Our Lady of Walsingham and to Canterbury Cathedral."

Harrison picked up his cup of tea and leaned back in his wheelchair. "I've made a study of that. And while I'm still a bit muddled, my guess is that things changed drastically when King Henry the VIII destroyed the holy places during his Reformation. He had the wells at Walsingham filled in completely with the rubble from the shrine. The entire place sat in disrepair for so long that perhaps the original wellspring dried up or was buried deeper in the earth so that it's no longer readily available."

"And the same happened to the wellspring in Canterbury?"

Harrison sipped his tea before responding. "Some say a natural spring exists beneath the crypt of the cathedral. Other speculations point to a wellspring at a priory which was a short distance away from the cathedral."

Marian stifled a yawn, surprised to discover she was tired again. "This is all very interesting, Harrison. But you know we sound like we're spouting nonsense from a science fiction novel, don't you?"

Harrison nodded somewhat sheepishly. "I feel as mad as I'm sure I sound."

She wanted to dismiss everything he'd told her as easily as she'd always tossed aside her dad's ramblings. But she needed answers. And right now, Harrison's propositions were certainly logical.

A gust of wind whistled in the fireplace at the same time the windowpanes rattled, startling her so that she pushed up from the mattress. Suddenly chilled, she pulled the covers up to her chin. The bedside lamp was on, but it didn't reach the corners of the large room. Out of the corner of her eyes, she thought she saw a shadow and movement near one of the curtains, but when she looked, nothing was there.

Did she need to accept the possibility she'd had more than a hallucination or vision yesterday? That her body had spanned two eras, and she'd stood directly in the past? If her father was right about the Tree of Life, then she couldn't overlook his speculations about breaching the time-space continuum, could she?

"I've been a complete cad for going on so long." Harrison frowned, powering his wheelchair in reverse toward the bell pull on the wall. "You need nourishment. I'll ring for the maid."

"Harrison, tell me the truth. Do you *really* think the residue shifted me to another time?" The idea made her skin prickle. She peered into the corner again, expecting to see more shadows or fluttery movements. But everything was motionless.

His wheelchair tire bumped the wall. He switched off the motor before tugging on the bell pull. "Full disclosure. I'm not an expert on the physics of time and space, but from the little I've studied, physicists agree that time is not sequential but is simultaneous."

"Not sequential?"

"Time doesn't happen in a straight line from beginning to end. Rather it exists in a block universe, where past, present, and future are equally real and present. Thus, those who claim to have had so-called ghost sightings may in fact have stumbled upon an overlap, putting two structures of reality together."

"If that's true, then people could overlap with the future too."

"You're quite right. Think about the prophets in the Bible who had glimpses of the future. The Apostle Paul claims to have been taken up to the third heaven, possibly outside of his body. And the writer of the book of Revelation is said to have witnessed the future happenings firsthand as they were unfolding."

She cracked a smile. "Are you sure you're not a physicist? You sound like you have it all figured out."

He smiled in return. "No, I'm nothing more than a deluded chemist."

A soft rap on the door was followed by a maid poking her head inside. "You rang, Lord Burlington?"

As Harrison gave instructions to the servant, Marian snuggled back into the pillows, relishing the softness of the bed and warmth of the comforter. Her eyes ached with the need for more sleep, and she almost closed them, except once again a movement by the window caught her attention.

This time when she looked, she didn't see a shadow. She saw the outline of a man standing and peering outside. The curtains were gone. Instead, long wooden shutters had been thrown open, revealing a starlit sky. An early moon gave enough light for her to realize she was looking at the man she'd encountered yesterday. The square jaw, muscled cheekbones, and strong nose were all the same. His head was devoid of a covering, revealing shoulder-length dark hair pulled back with a leather strip.

Unlike previously, she wasn't afraid. She knew now what was happening. But she was too utterly and completely fascinated by what she was seeing to do anything but stare.

He lifted a hand to rub his eyes, and the muscles in his arm rippled in the moonlight. Only then did she realize he was bare from the waist up, wearing pants that looked more like tights that ended at the knees. His chest was every bit as sculpted as his arms, broad and taut, with strength emanating from every bulging muscle.

Wow. He was gorgeous. In fact, he had the kind of body that belonged to a firefighter or boxer or hockey player. The kind of body that could turn heads and weaken knees. The kind of body that deserved to be on the cover of *Men's Health* magazine.

As though sensing he was no longer alone, he shifted away from the soft glow coming in the window, shrouding his face in darkness. She couldn't be sure if he saw her, but he remained motionless, and from the intensity of his stance, he seemed to be staring at her.

A breeze from the open window ruffled her unbound hair and brought with it an unfamiliar woodsy-smoky scent, as if someone was having a late spring bonfire. The chill in the air was distinct, unlike the warm coziness from moments ago.

The stranger stepped away from the corner. Though the darkness still veiled his face, the tenseness of his posture, the rigidness of his spine, the angle of his head were signs he was very much aware of her presence, that she was as real to him as he was to her.

"I've ordered a meal for you." Harrison's voice was faint, as though he was speaking from a distance. Could Harrison see the man too?

She shifted only slightly, but in that instant, the man disappeared.

Where had he gone? She stared hard, hoping her vision would clear, waiting breathlessly for him to materialize.

"You saw him again, didn't you?" Harrison's quiet question came from right beside the bed.

Only then did she realize she was sitting on her knees, her hands clutched at her sides, and her body stiff with anticipation. "He was in the room."

"Is he still here?"

She strained to see anything, even just a shadow, in the spot where the man had stood. But the curtains were back, the window was closed, the air was warm with only the lingering scent of Harrison's Earl Grey tea. "No. He's gone."

Harrison's expression was serious, and she had no doubt he believed her, although she wasn't sure why any sane person would.

~ 6 ~

ALL THROUGHOUT THE NIGHT and into the next day, Marian waited anxiously for another bizarre time overlap. She couldn't deny she wanted to experience it again, especially so she could catch a glimpse of the blue-eyed man.

Squeezing her eyes closed, she held her breath and waited a few seconds before opening them, hoping to spot him. But everything in Chesterfield Park's magnificent library was just the same as before, and Dad's papers remained scattered across the glossy mahogany table in front of her—the papers from the safety deposit box that she'd been studying for the past three hours since returning from visiting her dad at the hospital.

While out, she and Harrison retrieved her purse from the Canterbury Police Station. Though someone had rummaged through it, nothing had been taken. Then they stopped by Mercer Labs, and Marian investigated Dad's office, which had still been in complete disarray. She'd hoped to find solid evidence of something but hadn't.

Now after reading Dad's papers dozens of times, she was growing frustrated with herself. With a sigh, she moved away from the table and crossed to the windows. Not only did she love the library with its floor-to-ceiling bookshelves, but she loved the towering windows that overlooked the spacious back gardens of Chester-field Park. The sculpted shrubs, the flower beds in full bloom, and even the maze were visible from the library.

Sunlight poured over the wisteria that covered the stone walls and cascaded down sides of trees and bushes. The vibrant purple contrasted with the bright green of the fresh grass, new leaves, and full hedges. Even a special archway was covered in wisteria and ivy, creating a shaded canopy.

Her sights locked in on a man at the far edge of the garden, and her heart picked up its pace. Was he the man from her vision?

She leaned closer and watched the figure. He was kneeling, and when he straightened, she released a breath of disappointment at the sight of the weathered old face. It was only Harrison's gardener.

Her gaze strayed to the ampulla resting in the center of the chaos on the table. Should she taste more of the residue so she could experience another peek into the past?

Her feet seemed to have a will of their own, carrying her back to the table. Her fingers had a will of their own too. In an instant, the ancient vessel was in her hands.

She stared at the open mouth of the container. It had only taken a few grains. Did she dare try a few more? The rational part of her warned against it. Too many unknowns existed. What if this time she was stuck in the overlap longer? And what about afterward? Would she sleep again for twenty-four hours or had that happened because of how tired she'd been from everything else?

Did any of it matter?

Before she could rationalize further, she licked her pinky, stuck it into the bottle, and then rubbed it around, hoping some of the grains would stick. She scraped back and forth and all around, then finally pulled her finger out.

For a long second she stared at her skin. She couldn't see any residue. It was likely all gone. This wouldn't do anything.

Even so, her pulse sped faster as she stuck her pinky into her mouth. According to Dad's list of speculations about crossing time, all she had to do was picture the handsome stranger and she'd likely overlap with his era again—whenever that was.

She closed her eyes and attempted to visualize him. She only got as far as picturing his face when a strange warmth bathed her.

Her eyes shot open. Brilliant sunlight nearly blinded her, and a cool breeze teased her loose hair. Gone were the glass windows and walls of books. Instead, she stood outside the back of the house, except this was the smaller Chesterfield Park, the one without the spacious side wings, the one in which the library wasn't yet a part of the manor.

She took in the simplistic flower beds without any of the modern brick edging, the dirt paths instead of the marble walkways. To the west where the greenhouse was supposed to be, a low structure built of gray weathered boards and a slate roof with wide double doors filled the space. It had to be the barn.

Her pulse thrummed with sudden excitement. This couldn't be just a hallucination. It was too realistic. Had the holy water residue again worked within her in such a way that she'd breached the time-space continuum?

Any good scientist would want to test for herself the reality of her experience. But how?

An array of purple and yellow posies danced at her feet amidst spindly grass. She stooped and plucked a posy, bringing it to her nose and drawing in the scent of light sweetness. She ran her fingers over the petals, feeling the velvet. Nearby, several bees swirled among a patch of clover, their buzzing the only sound in the yard. Bending again, she broke off a blade of grass and then stuck it into her mouth, crunching it between her teeth and tasting the earthiness.

All evidence from her five senses pointed to the reality of her standing in the past. She straightened and took a small step. If she was having a hallucination, how would she be able to move?

Again she glanced around at her surroundings, this time taking in the thickly wooded area that bordered Chesterfield Park on the opposite side of the imposing brick wall that she'd seen from the front of the mansion. Overhead a hawk circled, its long wings outstretched. It resembled one of the birds in the dome in Chesterfield Park's hallway room, one she'd never seen in the busy metropolitan Canterbury area during any of her visits.

"Should I have the maid make a coffee?" a voice called to her.

No, she silently pleaded to the vision. *Don't go away yet*. But even as she tried to cling to the outdoor scene, the library surrounded her once again.

She tried to conjure the quiet garden, but the soft hum of Harrison's wheelchair told her she was in the library. When she dared to look, she was sitting in a chair at the table, her head resting upon her arms amidst the scattered research.

Had she fallen asleep? Fatigue clouded her head, and her eyelids felt heavy with slumber. With a yawn, she stood and stretched.

"Or I can have her lay out tea?" Harrison drew nearer.

She peered out the windows. The greenhouse, with its glistening glass rooftop, graced the yard, and the gardener stood where she'd last seen him.

Had she really stepped outside into the past? It had all happened so quickly that it could have been just a vision.

The same exhaustion she'd felt after her first ingestion swept over her. She wavered and leaned against the table to keep from collapsing.

"Marian?" Harrison's voice was edged with concern.

If the residue caused the minuscule energy particles within her to vibrate at higher frequencies, then it stood to reason the use of such energy would tax the body.

She fought the drowsiness even as she groped at a nearby chair, needing to sit. Something fell from her hand and fluttered to the floor. As she lowered herself back into the chair and glanced down, every function within her body silenced.

It was the posy.

A shiver raced up her backbone.

"Marian love, what's happened?"

She retrieved the delicate flower, brought it to her nose, and breathed in the faint fragrance again. It was real. Totally real.

Trembling, she held it out in her palm to show Harrison.

He drew closer, his brows slanting as he took it in.

"Do you grow posies in any of the gardens?" She already knew the answer. She was well aware that Chesterfield Park's gardens contained only elegant and cultivated species of plants, not wildflowers.

As she relayed her experience, Harrison didn't touch the posy but instead stared at it reverently.

When she finished, he released a low whistle. "Well done, you. This posy is a massive deal. Absolutely massive. Precisely what we needed to confirm the holy water does more than just give visions."

She gazed in wonder at the tiny piece of the past that had come with her. Gently she placed it on the table, expecting it to disappear but praying it wouldn't.

"All the more reason to keep sorting out Arthur's tricky clues." Harrison swiveled in his wheelchair to face the disarray she'd left on the table. "Any luck?"

"I've read each paper over and over, but I'm no step closer to unlocking their mystery." Harrison had read through them too, although reluctantly, insisting he didn't expect her to share the information with him. She'd assured him she needed his help, that Dad had probably expected her to show him the contents of the safety deposit box and seek his input.

"Knowing Arthur, I daresay he has a specific reason for each and every item he left you."

"Why couldn't he spell it out and make this easier?" She yawned and fought away the fatigue still hovering over her, beckoning her to slumber.

"Because he knows you're every bit as bright as he is and will figure it out in two shakes."

"You had more faith in his research than I ever did."

"I could listen to him easier because I wasn't the one he was neglecting for the research." Harrison's soft comment hung suspended in the air, inviting her to unburden her hurts.

She shuffled several sheets. Harrison should know by now she wasn't as expressive as Ellen. Dear Ellen had never had any trouble baring her soul, especially to Harrison. But Marian . . . she'd never had the luxury of giving way to her emotions, not when she needed to stay strong for Ellen and Dad. Besides, she always had so much to accomplish and never enough time to wallow in self-pity for more than a few seconds.

Harrison pointed to the sheet listing ten different Bible verses. "I see you've written out each of the verses using the King James Version."

"Yes, and not surprising, they all have to do with the passing of time." She rubbed her hands over her arms. Even with a crackling fire on the hearth and the floor heaters pumping out air, the library contained a chill that had required her to don her gray cashmere sweater above the ruffled silk blouse she was wearing with her flared dark jeans.

"What do you think they mean?" she asked. "And why did he choose these specific verses?"

"Perhaps to show that the Creator supports the fluidity of time and isn't bound by the past, present, or future?" Harrison picked up the next paper, a diagram of a Gothic-looking stone head with a beard, mustache, long curly hair, and a protruding tongue. "How about this one? Did you discover anything about it?"

"A little." She pulled her phone out of her pocket only to see Jasper had called two more times. She'd answered his first call earlier in the morning, and he'd been anxious when he hadn't heard from her yesterday. She'd told him about the near-robbing and her need to hide away and catch up on sleep at Chesterfield Park. But she'd refrained from mentioning the strange visions and the ampulla.

As a fellow distinguished scientist, Jasper would never understand what was happening to her. How could he, when she was having difficulty explaining it, even to herself? He'd probably tell her she was under too much pressure and volunteer again to come over and be with her.

For now, she'd keep ignoring him, at least until she could come up with a plausible excuse for what was going on.

Instead she pulled up the internet page that described the statue head. "It's the carved capital of one of the columns in Our Lady crypt of Canterbury Cathedral."

"That's what I thought." Harrison studied the black-and-white drawing. The page had been ripped from one of Dad's books, *Archaeologia Cantiana*, Volume 13, written in 1880. Plugging the title into an advanced internet search had easily given her access to the book, which contained a detailed discussion of the architecture of Our Lady, the central chapel beneath Canterbury Cathedral.

She'd learned the stone head was at the top of column F on the north part of the underground chapel. All the other pillars had carvings too, mostly of monsters, dragons, and other mythical creatures. Out of them all, why had Dad chosen the human head?

She retrieved another sheet from the table. "Dad also ripped out the page containing the floor plan of Our Lady." The yellowed paper was from the same book, and she'd easily located the position of column F on the diagram.

Although she'd once walked through the crypt during a tour, she hadn't taken much interest in the columns that held up the chapel's ceiling and lent support to the structure above it. Compared to the more spectacular architectural feats elsewhere in the cathedral, the crypt had paled in comparison. Now she wished she'd paid more attention.

Harrison placed the page with the carved sculpture next to the floor plan. "What message is Arthur communicating through these two pages?"

"What does this particular column in the crypt have to do with his research?"

"That's the million-pound question, isn't it?" Harrison began to power his chair around the table toward some of the other papers.

"Dad didn't need to be quite so mysterious with what he left." In fact, he could have told her more when they were on the phone the other day.

Even as her frustration mounted, she knew he wasn't totally at fault for his evasiveness. She'd made it clear in recent years that she was no longer the little girl who worshipped the ground he walked on and believed everything he told her. She'd snubbed his conversations about his research often enough that he'd spoken of it less over time.

Harrison came to a stop at the opposite end of the table. "With Lionel Inc. going after you so aggressively, it's quite possible they've known about Arthur's Tree of Life theories for some time. Even if not, Arthur wouldn't want a discovery of this magnitude falling into the wrong hands."

Did Lionel suspect that the holy water could not only heal but also enable a person to cross over time? And what would they do with the holy water if they accessed it? Maybe that's why Dad had been so secretive, because he didn't know the long-term ramifications.

Harrison picked up two other pages from the table. One contained several paragraphs about the Priory of St. Sepulchre, founded in 1100 in Canterbury on St. George's Street.

The other sheet discussed in more depth how the monks sold the holy water to pilgrims visiting Canterbury Cathedral, water the St. Sepulchre nuns provided from a wellspring somewhere on the nunnery grounds. Harrison read the paragraphs, his eyes narrowing with each word.

When he finished, he placed the two wrinkled papers side by side on the table. "If I had to hazard another guess, I'd say Arthur hoped to see into the past—or cross over there—so he could work out the location of the original spring at St. Sepulchre."

"That's what I was thinking. But after a quick online search for the history of St. Sepulchre, I learned Canterbury's Archeological Trust excavated the old convent about ten years ago. They unearthed a cemetery but found nothing more than the skeletal remains of nuns, along with tokens from a Roman graveyard. There's no mention of a discovery of a wellspring."

"Quite right, but archaeologists aren't looking for wellsprings. Such an excavation would require much deeper digging with specialized equipment."

Her thoughts ticked in an unending rhythm, just like the ticking of the pendulum in the large longcase clock in the corner. "So do you think Dad's still living in the past?"

Harrison's attention shifted to the posy. "As mad as it sounds, I think we have to give him the benefit of the doubt until he proves otherwise."

She fingered the small flower, the living proof something was different about the holy water, that it had life-giving qualities that defied explanation, that maybe it had indirectly originated from the Tree of Life from the Garden of Eden—or at least from one of the seeds.

Even if she was beginning to grasp the importance of her dad's discoveries, she still had so many questions. "How can a body be in two places at once?"

"It's highly unlikely a body and soul could straddle two eras indefinitely. My guess is that he's at risk for losing his life in one or both places."

As fascinating as it was to think of her dad stepping back in time as she had, not only was he in a life-threatening coma in the present, but who knew what kind of dangers he might face in the past. "I hate that he's put his life in jeopardy, Harrison."

"Don't worry, love." Harrison's voice rose with bravado even though worry creased his forehead. "Knowing Arthur as I do, I'm sure he planned out every move before setting his plan into motion."

If her dad had indeed traveled back in time, then he'd been in the past for almost five days, likely to some point in the Middle Ages when Canterbury's St. Sepulchre—the source of the holy water—was still in existence. How would a modern man survive in a place so radically different?

"We need to bring him back." Her sights shifted from one full bookcase to another around the room, as if they held resources that could help her. "Whatever he's doing isn't worth the possibility of him dying."

Harrison nodded at the piece of paper containing Dad's scribbled thoughts regarding time crossing. His expression was somber. "Read numbers three and four on his list."

She'd already read the list numerous times, but she reached for the sheet anyway. "Number three: People seem to recover from their visions or movement into the past at varying levels and lengths of time."

"Number four: There are no indications full recovery can always be made. I speculate that if a person dies while having the vision or movement into the past, then the body remaining in the present will also die—and vice versa."

Harrison pressed his lips together and stared at the sheets, tapping his long fingers against the table. "What if we need to track down more holy water and give him another dose?"

She touched the ampulla. "So you think another dose will heal him?"

"If the old tales are true, then the holy water has the capability to heal the sick. Certainly coma falls into that category."

"Could we try the granules from this ampulla?" She grazed the worn engraving on the flask. "The residue is powerful. Maybe it would be enough to heal him."

"I don't think so. But we can always give it a go."

God had probably created the Tree of Life with a chemical compound with unique physiological properties, making it a one-of-a-kind substance not found anywhere else except in that tree. She and Harrison could speculate all they wanted on what such a compound was capable of doing, but the truth was, they were likely only skimming the surface. They couldn't know anything for certain until they found more and began testing it.

Was that what her dad had intended for her to do? Find more holy water? Revive him? So that then he could direct them to the location of the wellspring which would allow them to do further experimentation on the water?

Her pulse surged with a new sense of anticipation and energy. "You said there are only three of the St. Thomas ampullae left in the world—well, two now, since we have this one. Can we locate the others?"

"Such a task is doubtful. Arthur likely attempted to acquire them from various museums and didn't get anywhere. But hopefully, he's left us clues for how to find more holy water some place."

Harrison powered his wheelchair, backed away from the table, and steered toward the door. He gave a few brief instructions to Drake, who bowed and then hurried away.

"Ready?" Harrison fiddled with his bow tie, tightening it into place. "Time to get on with it, then."

"Where are we going?" She began gathering up the papers.

"We need to work out a way to save Arthur. And since his clues seem to be pointing us to the crypt of the cathedral, let's have a look and pray we'll find the answers we need there."

~ 7 ~

"THE CATHEDRAL CONSTABLE won't be able to stall our stalker for very long." Harrison glanced over his shoulder toward the entrance. With the permanent ramp at the north door, the crypt was handicap accessible—a positive facet of their investigation of Our Lady under the cathedral.

The negative was that their stalker might suspect they were looking for something in the crypt and try to interfere—or steal whatever information they found. *If* they found something, and Marian fervently prayed they would.

They'd been followed almost from the moment they'd pulled out of Chesterfield Park. It only confirmed that Dad had truly been on to something important, perhaps even world-changing.

"We need to hurry." She strode the rest of the way down the ramp around Harrison and an older couple ambling slowly along. Drake followed closely after her, his steps echoing ominously.

Even though column F wasn't labeled as such, she'd studied the crypt diagram and had nearly memorized the floor plan on the ride over. She headed directly to it and found the carving of the man with the tongue sticking out just the way it had been drawn on the page from *Archaeologia Cantiana*.

With brightly lit candelabra lamps hanging from the arched

ceiling throughout, she had no trouble seeing the details of the carving. She rose onto her toes and ran a hand across the sculpture. Rough edges mingled with stone that had been worn over the centuries.

Think, Marian. Think, she silently chided herself. Why the man with the tongue? Tongues help with talking, chewing, swallowing, and tasting.

Maybe the clue had to do with the eyes. She poked the raised circles, ran her fingers across the eyebrows, down the beard, over the curled hair. Her mind raced with medical facts about each one. But nothing gave her any hints about why Dad had singled out this column with this particular architectural capital.

She glanced at the ramp that led back to the entrance. Their stalker would be in the crypt any second. She had to figure out the answer now.

Why had Dad left the information about the crypt? Why the cathedral? Because it was one of the few landmarks in Canterbury that had managed to exist from the past to the present? When so many other medieval structures had been destroyed by man, fire, or rot, this cathedral, this crypt, these columns, this capital had stood the test of time to endure.

"Maybe he's sending a message." If he wanted to communicate from the past to the present, he'd leave a note in a place that existed in both eras. If no one had discovered and removed his message over the centuries, it would be hundreds of years old, perhaps disintegrated with age, depending upon what material he used. Nevertheless, she needed to locate it. Quickly.

Communication. Mouth.

She skimmed the sculpture's mouth and tongue, then prodded and poked at it. It wiggled, but only slightly. There had to be a secret hiding place somewhere, even if only a tiny one to fit a slip of parchment. She pulled harder, and it moved again, but not fast enough.

"Drake," she hissed over her shoulder. "Help me move the carving."

Harrison's butler cast a frown toward the crypt entrance before reaching up and taking hold of the tongue. He wrestled with the carving for several moments before the stone groaned and the whole head began to slide forward like a drawer away from the pillar until it came off altogether, revealing a space about three inches wide by two inches high—bigger than she'd anticipated.

A tiny thrill whispered through her. How had her dad known this hiding place existed? For a second, she allowed herself to admire his exceptional intelligence in a way she hadn't in a long time. But at a commotion in the entrance hall, she reached up and tugged loose the objects inside—two ampullae and an old watch.

The cathedral security man wouldn't be able to detain their stalker for long—though Harrison had slipped him cash to try.

"Quick put the head back." Even before the words left her mouth, Drake was already fitting the sculpture into its original place.

Heart hammering, she stuffed the findings into her purse and hurried away from column F toward Harrison, who was peering into St. Gabriel's Chapel and studying the bright fresco painted on the walls.

She barely reached him when a man stalked down the ramp. His gaze shot around until it landed upon Harrison and her.

In several long strides, Drake crossed to her and put a hand on her elbow in a protective gesture while at the same time sending a warning look toward the newcomer.

"Did you get the clue?" Harrison powered his chair toward the next exhibit.

"Yes." As much as she wanted to peek into her purse and examine the articles, she resisted the urge.

"Good on you."

She slowed her steps to accommodate him, even though everything within her wanted to flee out of the crypt to the waiting Bentley, especially as the stalker began to wind toward them through the columns. Surely he wouldn't confront them with so many people around. Likely he was just keeping tabs and waiting for them to reveal something important.

The man didn't appear familiar. In a black leather jacket and dark jeans, he was shorter and stockier than the person who'd attacked her outside the bank. Were both working for Lionel Inc.? Or were multiple companies trying to get their hands on Dad's information?

"Act like a tourist so he doesn't suspect you've found something already," Harrison whispered with a forced smile. "Take some snaps with your mobile."

She feigned interest in the Jesus Chapel at the eastern part of the crypt and began taking pictures like other visitors of the vaulted ceiling with its intricate decorations.

As Harrison stopped to examine artifacts, she responded with what she hoped was the appropriate enthusiasm. But with every step she took—even with Drake by her side—she could sense the stalker behind them, watching their every move.

With the man following them, would she have to forgo seeing the Miracle Windows up above in Trinity Chapel at the very front of the cathedral? The exquisitely beautiful stained glass had been created in the late twelfth century and told stories of people who'd been healed by drinking the holy water at Canterbury Cathedral.

She'd once believed people in the Middle Ages had contrived such tales to entertain themselves. Like the one about Adam the Forester, who'd been shot in the neck by a poacher trying to steal a deer from the king's forest. The first scene in the stained glass depicted Adam with the arrow sticking out of his neck. In the next scene, Adam was lying in bed drinking holy water containing

Becket's blood. In the concluding roundel, Adam stood healed, giving his thanks at Becket's tomb.

Now after everything she'd learned from her dad's research, she was anxious to see the stained glass windows again—windows that immortalized the healing quality of the holy water. Did they testify to the power of the ultimate cure more than anyone truly understood?

They worked their way around the crypt only to find that the stalker had positioned himself near the ramp, blocking their exit. Did he suspect she had items in her purse and intend to grab it again?

"How are we going to get out of here?" she whispered.

"Bojing is pulling up." Harrison and Drake exchanged a look filled with a gravity that sent a chill through Marian. "Get on to the nave and exit through the door in the southwest transept."

They were standing in front of the stairway that led up to the main floor of the cathedral. "I'm not leaving you down here by yourself."

"Once you head up, I'm quite certain the unwelcome riffraff will abandon his post. And I'll be out in a jiffy."

Because the stalker would be pursuing her. She tried not to shudder at the thought.

"Marian love, promise you'll go directly out?"

She cut him off with a curt nod. "I'll do it, so long as you promise you'll get out safely."

"I'll manage fine." Harrison squeezed her hand. "Now go."

She didn't waste any more time with platitudes or assessing the plan. The fact was, her dad was risking his life for this venture, and now she needed to do her part.

Swallowing her trepidation, she lunged up the steps, taking them two at a time with Drake's footsteps clamping behind her. When she reached the top, she didn't pause but dodged sightseers, darted past tour guides, and dashed across the nave toward the outer door, the exit sign guiding her.

A shout echoed through the lofty openness of the cathedral. She glanced behind Drake to see the stalker in the black leather jacket along with another man. They'd spotted her and Drake and were starting after them.

Even though the grandeur and majesty of the ancient church always astounded her, she couldn't stop to take it in. Her heart thudded a warning that she had to keep going, that her dad's research was at stake.

The sharp popping of gunfire echoed in the air. Why were her stalkers shooting? To intimidate her into stopping? Clearly they didn't want her to leave without the chance to confront her.

Her body tensed. Any second she might feel the stinging bite of a bullet entering her back. But she ducked her head and kept running. Her footsteps slapped hard against the tile. Her breathing grew more ragged.

An ancient-looking door loomed ahead. She was almost there. More shots rang out.

She cringed and hunkered lower. With a final burst of energy, she threw open the door. Late-day sunlight blinded her for only a second before she caught sight of the Bentley waiting at the curb, the door open, Bojing sitting in the front seat, hands already tightly gripping the wheel.

"Faster!" Drake's voice called out behind her, and she found herself being swept along with his hunched frame shielding her. When they reached the car, he none-too-gently threw her inside before lunging in and slamming the door behind him.

Bojing stomped on the gas, and the tires pealed as he raced away. Several bullets pinged against the car. One hit the back window, cracking the glass and leaving a shattered web.

Drake yanked her down and covered her body with his.

The car careened back and forth at top speed, and Marian struggled to hang on to the seat and not slide onto the floor. A few moments later, when the Bentley steadied, Drake cautiously lifted himself and peered out the back window. She raised her head and began to sit up, but he pushed her back down. "Stay low."

Something dripped onto the seat by her face. At first, against the black leather, she couldn't tell what it was. But then she rose to her elbows and examined Drake, taking in the bright crimson darkening his coat sleeve. "You've been shot."

He watched out the back window, his face a mask of determination. "Just a surface wound, miss. Nothin' to be fretting about."

The bullet could have killed Drake. Or her. At the thought, her blood turned to ice, and her breath froze in her chest. Suddenly, she wished she wasn't in Canterbury and was instead home in Connecticut, safe in her lab, doing her work in isolation and oblivion.

What had she gotten herself into?

She tried to gasp in a breath. But the car jerked again. "Hold tight!" Bojing shouted in a clipped Asian accent. "We've got company!" Beneath her, she could feel the car accelerating, swaying back and forth as Bojing took one turn after another at death-defying speeds. As with when he'd helped her escape the thief outside the bank, she didn't know how he could see out the front windshield, much less maneuver the car so swiftly. But he seemed to know what he was doing. Or at least she prayed he did.

She finally peeked up to find that they were flying down a country road. "Aren't we planning to get Harrison?"

Neither Drake nor Bojing answered.

Dread pooled in her stomach. "Please tell me another driver picked him up at the crypt. Or that he's catching a cab."

Drake stared straight ahead, his face pale and taut. Bojing shook his head.

She leaned back, fighting a wave of panic. "Did something happen to him?"

Bojing glanced at his side mirror. "I had to circle around for a few minutes to get them off my tail. By the time I made it back to the north entrance, I didn't see him there. Only his wheelchair."

"Oh no! Do you think they kidnapped him?"

"Looks like it."

She drew in a sharp breath, her lungs suddenly tight with the need to weep.

The gates of Chesterfield Park loomed ahead. They were already open, and the instant Bojing crossed through them, they began to swing shut.

As they closed with a resounding clang, she had the desperate urge to turn around. How could she hide inside when Harrison was in danger?

She raked her gaze from Bojing to Drake and back as the car halted in front of the manor entrance. "You need to go back and look for him."

Drake opened the door, winced, then stepped out and began to round the car.

"We can't leave him at the mercy of those people," she said loudly enough for both men to hear.

Her door jerked open, and Drake reached for her.

"We have to do something." She held herself back. "We can't just let them take Harrison." But what could they do except call the police and report the incident? Hopefully, the cathedral constable had already done so.

"Miss." Drake's tone was gentle. "Lord Burlington made us promise we'd bring you here straightaway. Those were his wishes."

She swallowed her rebuttal at the image of Harrison powering up the crypt ramp, knowing full well he'd put himself at the mercy of dangerous thugs. She sagged against the seat. *Oh, Harrison. What have you done?*

This time as Drake made an effort to help her out of the car, she didn't resist. She went with him numbly, mutely, and trembling with each step.

"Not to worry, miss." Drake paused inside the front entry room. "They might bully the lord up a bit. But they wouldn't dare hurt him in a bad way, eh. Not Lord Burlington."

She managed a slight nod before stumbling forward. Although Drake meant his words as reassurance, they only stirred her fear.

One thing was certain. She could no longer doubt her dad or his theories. And she was sorry she ever had.

~ 8 ~

SHE SHOULDN'T have allowed Harrison to go with her inside the crypt. She should have made him wait with Bojing.

Marian stared past the tapestries out the bedroom window. Every external light that existed on the grounds of Chesterfield Park was on, pushing away the darkness of the evening hour. The sprawling front gardens were lit by ground laser lights. Beams all along the stone wall surrounded the estate. And on the road near the front gate, the headlights of several police cars added to the blazing display.

She should feel safer with the lights, security cameras, heavily locked doors and windows, and police presence. But her insides hadn't stopped quavering. In the short time since she'd arrived in England, she'd been stalked, robbed, shot at, chased, and almost killed. As if that wasn't enough, she'd crossed back in time. Three times.

And now, Harrison had been kidnapped. Bystanders at the crypt entrance had confirmed it to the police when they'd arrived at the cathedral. Unfortunately, the security guard had rushed to the nave at the sound of the gunfire and hadn't been outside to intervene.

It hadn't taken long for the news of Lord Burlington's abduction to spread and for reporters to converge upon the estate. Drake had gone outside and had answered all the police and news reporter questions.

Of course, the police had needed to speak with her too. But neither she nor Drake had revealed the real reason why they'd been inside the crypt. They'd remained vague, telling the investigators that Mercer's competitors were likely harassing them for information regarding one of Arthur's drugs.

The police were waiting to escort her to the hospital so she could spend time with her dad and give him the holy water. She was ready to drive over as soon as the physician finished tending to Drake's wound. She told Drake she would go by herself, that he should rest. But he was insisting on accompanying her.

She let the thick curtains fall back over the window and padded in her stocking feet across the hardwood floor to the canopied bed. She stopped at the edge and stared down at the items she'd retrieved from the crypt. Two ampullae filled with holy water. And not just any ampullae. The flasks contained the pictures of St. Thomas, identical to the one that had been in the safety deposit box.

The ampullae had been shocking enough, and at first she'd thought her dad had located the other two that existed in museums. But at the sight of the Rolex that had been with the flasks, her shock had risen to a new level.

She picked up the watch from the bed and ran a thumb across the scuffed glass front.

It was the same Rolex in the plastic bag the hospital staff had given her—the same shape, size, style, and with the same engraving of love from her and Ellen on the back. But instead of shiny silver with an equally shiny, sleek wristband, the watch was dusty, corroded, and had stopped working—almost as if it had been tucked away in the hiding spot in the crypt for hundreds of years.

She'd retrieved the bag of Dad's possessions from her purse

and dumped it out. The Rolex was still there, as were the ancient-looking coins. Even so, the evidence pointed to only one conclusion: her dad had placed the ampullae into the crypt and had added his Rolex. Perhaps he'd determined parchment couldn't withstand the passing of time the same way a watch could. Or perhaps he'd wanted her to know beyond a shadow of a doubt he'd gone to the past.

Whatever the case, both flasks had been corked tightly, and she'd had a difficult time unsealing them. But once the corks were out, she'd been able to see the liquid inside. She estimated that each contained approximately a tablespoon, which wasn't much. She couldn't afford to lose a single drop. Since the corks had crumbled after removing them, she'd had to re-seal the flasks with rubber tops she'd found in Harrison's home lab.

She'd bagged the cork pieces, having no doubt they contained residue from the holy water. In the morning, she planned to examine them under a microscope in Harrison's lab. She wished she had time to do so before administering a dose to Dad tonight. But she couldn't waste time.

Even though Dad's message from the past wasn't entirely clear, she suspected he'd meant for her to use one of the flasks of holy water to heal him of his coma. But what about the other ampulla? Did he want Ellen to drink it to see if it would heal her?

Thankfully, she'd soon be able to ask her dad the questions that had multiplied with each passing hour. At least she hoped once she administered the holy water, he'd recover from the coma quickly. She couldn't be sure what would happen after the substance filtered through his system. Perhaps it would take some time for him to regain consciousness.

She returned the watch to the bed and skimmed a hand over the wrinkled papers that he'd left for her. The clues were making more sense now than the first time she'd read them.

She picked up the time-travel speculation sheet. "Number five:

After studying historical examples of people experiencing visions, I'm convinced a person is able to envision/move to the same period on multiple occasions. Number six: Additionally, from what I'm able to decipher, the day and hour of the visions/movement correspond to the same day and hour on the various time-space intersections."

Inadvertently, she'd tested rules five and six and found them to be true. Each of her visions—or crossings into the past—had corresponded to the same time frame. When it had been evening in the present, she'd experienced evening in the past. With May in the present, she'd witnessed May flowers in the past.

Was this the type of information Harrison's abductors were after? Did they know about the ampullae? What would they do to Harrison in an effort to elicit the knowledge they wanted?

A shudder worked its way up her spine.

More likely they were after the drug for its ability to heal, not because it caused time crossovers. If the holy water had the power to heal—as depicted in the cathedral's Miracle Windows—and if the properties could be replicated, the impact would be astounding. What if the water could not only heal VHL but all other serious genetic diseases? What if it could heal cancer or AIDS or diabetes?

If so, the holy water would easily turn into the most potent drug in the entire world. The person who took credit for the discovery could become the wealthiest person on earth—and possibly the most powerful. He could control the world, and there was no telling what would become of humanity.

Maybe that's why God had placed the angel at the Garden of Eden—to keep people away from the Tree of Life? Not to prevent them from having something good, but to protect them from something that had the potential to ultimately destroy the world?

She released a shaky laugh. "You're taking this whole thing too far, Marian. Settle down and think rationally."

Her phone on the bedside table buzzed. It was probably Jasper again. She considered ignoring his call. But after brushing him off all day, she didn't have the heart to let his call go to voicemail again. Besides, with all that had happened, she could use a friendly ear.

She grabbed her phone only to discover a Kent number lighting up the screen.

Her heart jumped in her chest. Harrison. Maybe the police had located Harrison.

She answered quickly. "Hello?"

"Is this Marian Creighton?" The voice on the other line was serious, subdued.

"This is she."

"I'm phoning from Kent and Canterbury Hospital." The person hesitated for several seconds—several seconds that caused Marian to shut her eyes as if in doing so she could prevent the news.

"I regret to inform you that your father, Arthur Creighton, is dead."

● ● ●

The syringe in Marian's hand shook. A glance toward the closed hospital room door told her she was still alone and no one would witness what she was about to do.

Her dad's face was waxy, the life drained away. A strand of his gray hair had slipped over his forehead, but she didn't have the heart to comb it back. Instead, she willed him to open his eyes and look up at her.

Even though he had a full head of gray hair, his rounded face was youthful in appearance—without wrinkles or age spots. He was too young to die. Too intelligent. Too ambitious. He still had so much to give to the world.

And he had too much explaining yet to do, too many questions to answer, too much work remaining with all that he'd uncovered with the holy water.

At the rise in voices in the hallway, Marian focused on the syringe.

After the police had provided an escort to the hospital, she'd asked the doctors and nurses if she might have a moment alone with Dad to say her good-byes. Now, even with Drake positioned outside the closed door, she guessed she had only a few minutes before the hospital staff returned.

Besides, she wasn't safe. Whoever was trying to steal her dad's research had made it clear they intended to get it one way or another. They would know she'd left Chesterfield Park at the late hour to drive to the hospital, and there was no telling what they might attempt.

She tried to still her trembling fingers, but the long point of the needle continued to wobble. "You have to do this, Marian. It's his only hope."

Without second-guessing herself any longer, she thrust the needle into his shoulder and squeezed the liquid into his vein. A tablespoon didn't take long.

She flicked the side of the bottle and then rattled it to make sure every last precious drop of the holy water had gone into her dad, that nothing remained. Then she withdrew the needle, placed it back into its container, and stuffed it into her purse out of sight.

Thankfully, Harrison's home lab was stocked full of every imaginable item a scientist might ever need. If only she hadn't needed the syringe under these circumstances . . .

She released the breath she felt like she'd been holding since she'd gotten the phone call from the hospital an hour ago. Then she pressed her fingers against Dad's external jugular vein. "Please work your miracle."

Her soft plea faded into an eerie silence. After the constant whirring and beeping of the life-support machines and monitors, now the only sounds were the voices in the hallway and the distant bell at the nurse's station.

The physicians hadn't been able to pinpoint an exact cause of death. They wouldn't know anything specific until Dad had an autopsy—which she hoped they wouldn't need.

"Come back to me, Dad." Her voice wobbled with unshed tears, tears she wouldn't let herself release yet.

If her dad's speculations about breaching the time-space continuum were correct—point number four on his list—then something must have happened to him in the past to cause his death there, which in turn had ended his life in the present.

She had no idea if the residue from the Tree of Life was able to bring someone back from the dead, someone who'd been gone for an hour and thirty minutes according to the time of death written on his hospital chart.

The excerpts Harrison had read to her from the *Pynson Ballad* about the wellspring in Walsingham and from the monks' recordings from Canterbury hadn't mentioned people reviving after they died.

However, with so many mysteries yet to unlock regarding the holy water, they simply didn't know its capabilities. It might have the power to do more than even her dad had imagined.

"Please, Dad. Please." The pulse beneath her fingers was cold and lifeless. She adjusted her touch, probing for the protruding vessel on the other side of his neck. She pressed against it and watched the timer on her phone. It ticked off thirty seconds, then sixty, and finally ninety.

She felt nothing. Not even the slightest twitch in his flesh.

What if it took hours for the holy water to work? Or days?

She shifted her trembling fingers to Dad's mouth and hoped she'd feel the breath of life there, all the while trying to ignore the reminder that the tiny granules she'd ingested had worked in her system instantly.

She pressed his lips but couldn't detect even a whisper of warmth. His expression and body position hadn't changed from earlier in the day when she'd visited. Everything about him was rigid, as if frozen in time.

Tears stung at the backs of her eyes. "Dad, I don't know if you can hear me. But I believe you now. And I need you to return and finish the work you started. Or at the very least, tell me what to do next."

Watching his face, she prayed and waited for his eyelids to flutter, his nostrils to flare, or the muscles in his jaw to twitch. Anything. Another minute passed, then two. And an ache formed in her throat.

She lowered herself to the chair next to his bed, her legs suddenly weak. She reached for his hand and grasped the unresponsive digits in her own. Regret and sadness combined, swirling together, dissolving into one another.

"Oh, Dad, I'm sorry. So sorry . . ." Her voice choked, and warm tears spilled onto her cheeks. She was sorry for so much, mostly that now she'd never be able to have a better future with him where they could be close and happy.

That's all she'd ever wanted—to be a family like they were before Mom got sick. Since he'd been nearing the fulfillment of all his years of research into the ultimate cure, maybe he would have been happy again, maybe he would have wanted to be with her and Ellen, maybe he would have made the time to love them.

But now . . .

A soft tap on the door told her the time was up. She'd been too late to rescue her dad. Now, she'd used up one of the precious flasks of holy water for nothing. Not only had she failed to save her dad, but she'd failed him in his most important research.

"Miss Creighton?" A kind voice came from the door, now open a crack. The attending physician peeked through.

She swiped at the tears on her cheeks but couldn't make her voice work to respond.

It was time to call Ellen. Marian couldn't avoid involving Ellen in the chaos in Canterbury any longer. She had to tell Ellen Dad was dead. Of course upon hearing the news, Ellen would catch the first flight to England. The minute she arrived, Marian would have her drink the last ampulla of holy water. Hopefully, it would cure her of VHL. Perhaps then, Dad's death wouldn't be in vain.

9

BLEARY-EYED after a sleepless night, Marian wrapped the comforter about her shoulders against the early morning chill that permeated Harrison's home lab.

Her phone call with Ellen after returning from the hospital had been emotional and difficult. Marian had cried silent tears right along with Ellen's heartfelt sobs. Even though they'd often commiserated over Dad's obsession with his odd theories, Ellen had never harbored the same bitterness for his absence in their lives. Instead, Ellen had the capability of loving with her whole heart, unconditionally, in a way Marian hadn't been able to.

Even so, the pain of the loss sank deep in Marian's chest, a sick, dead weight along with guilt for not finding the ampullae in the crypt sooner, for not reviving him before it was too late. Now she and Ellen had no one left but each other.

At least Ellen was on her way. Within twelve hours, Marian would be able to hug her. And if all went as planned—if the holy water really was the ultimate cure—then by this time tomorrow, Ellen would no longer have tumors on her kidneys.

Marian stared at the last ampulla in front of her on Harrison's desk. The glow from the desk light illuminated the workspace, which was now littered with all the equipment she'd gotten out.

Sighing, she reclined in the wingback chair she'd dragged over to the desk. Her sights traveled to the ancient coat of arms on the wall next to the window, the same shield that had been above the entrance to the manor in her first time crossing, with the crimson background, azure trim, and golden stag standing tall and proud. She guessed the heraldry belonged to Harrison's family.

"Where are you, Harrison?"

She'd been in Harrison's massive lab for the past hours studying the cork pieces with a high-powered microscope while waiting for the police to update her regarding the search for Harrison.

But she hadn't heard anything, and she hadn't been able to find traces of anything in the cork other than the usual water molecules consisting of one oxygen atom and two connected hydrogens.

Deep down she'd guessed that would be the case. Her dad wouldn't have crossed into the past if he'd figured out a way to replicate the holy water. He wouldn't have needed to. The lack of a solute within the water macromolecules explained why no formulas, tests, or even a hint of progress toward a new development ment existed in any of Dad's stuff.

If neither of them had been able to find a trace of recognizable compounds in the water, then she could only speculate that the properties of the Tree of Life weren't of this world. What other explanation did she have?

Marian tried to ignore the prick at her conscience, the one growing stronger with each hour since Dad's passing, the one urging her not to let his lifework stop here, that she had to take up where he'd left off.

She wanted to give Ellen the holy water from the last ampulla. But at this point Marian didn't know for sure if the water would truly heal Ellen. Even though the old stories pointed to that capability, her dad hadn't tested the curative properties of the holy water on anyone. She and Harrison had speculated that he'd wanted to find the source of the water first.

Should she do the same? Ellen wasn't deathly ill yet. Hopefully, she still had many months—maybe years—ahead. After all, their mom had lived into her late thirties.

Marian sat forward and plucked at a sticky note on Harrison's desk—one of dozens having to do with Von Hippel-Lindau. She'd been surprised to discover how much research into VHL Harrison was doing so privately. His tests were extensive and detailed and every bit as thorough as her own. She guessed he was researching for Ellen, just like she was.

He was a good man.

Tears pricked her eyes, just as they had every time she thought about not only her dad but also Harrison. What were his captors doing to him? Although he was still young and strong and healthy, being without his wheelchair would limit his ability to escape.

Marian pushed back from the desk and stood, rolling and kneading her aching shoulders that had been slumped in one position for too long as she'd peered through the microscope. The slit in the curtain told her it was still dark outside, that dawn hadn't yet broken. Even though she was tired, her mind was too awake and alert to allow her to slumber.

One thought persisted above all the others—she could go back in time and save her dad. If her dad's time-crossing speculations were correct, she had the ability to envision any year outside her own lifetime. But even if she knew what year her dad had chosen, she wouldn't be able to return to earlier this week to intercept and help him. She was still bound by the hour and months.

Instead, she could visualize the May one year earlier and leave a note for him in the crypt, a warning to be more watchful. She doubted it would revive him in the present. But at the very least, she could prevent the death in the past, couldn't she? That was better than losing him completely.

In crossing into the past again, this time more extensively, she'd also be able to do her own research into finding the original source of the holy water. When she revived from her coma, then she could begin excavations and testing.

If she revived . . .

She shoved that thought from her head. She would revive. She had to. After all, she was resourceful and smart. She'd locate flasks of the holy water to leave in the crypt like Dad had done—one to revive her out of the coma and one to heal Ellen. With so many recorded healings, she suspected the flasks were a dime a dozen in the Middle Ages, that she'd probably be able to purchase them at the cathedral. No doubt that's what her dad had done with the coins he'd taken with him.

However, before she could even think about drinking the holy water and going back to warn her dad, she had to discover what year he'd traveled to. With determined steps, she headed up to her bedroom. The mansion was dark and silent, the long hallways spooky. At any moment, she half expected a thief or stalker to jump out, point a gun at her, and demand to have the ampullae.

When she reached her bedroom and stepped inside without a confrontation, she released a tense breath. The bedside lamp was still on and her papers scattered across the bed where she'd left them after she'd gotten the call from the hospital that Dad was dead. Before running off, she should have put the papers in Harrison's home safe as he'd advised. But she'd been too distraught—was still distraught.

Clutching the blanket closer to ward off the early morning chill, she couldn't hold in a shiver. At the same time, a yawn pushed for release. Reflexively, she pressed her hand against her mouth in an attempt to stifle it.

The moment her fingers made contact with her lips, warmth blew through her and spread along the length of her arms and legs. She knew immediately what was happening, and she eagerly touched her fingertips to her tongue, hoping to ingest more of the residue left there from handling the corks.

She could feel her pulse accelerating, her blood heating, and her heart palpitating. The breeze blowing in her veins was lighter than the gust she'd had during her first vision, but it was there nonetheless, making her eyes hazy for an instant before clearing.

The light from her room was gone, as if someone had flipped the switches. Now darkness shrouded her. Even so, she could see the outline of a canopied bed, only it wasn't the same bed anymore. It was smaller, and the tapestries thicker, more luxurious. While she couldn't tell what color the material was, one glance at the mattress told her it was occupied.

A breeze came in through the open windows. It was cold and curled around her legs and brought with it the damp scent of earth and woodsmoke that she'd experienced previously.

A shaft of early morning moonlight entered the room and fell across the bed. There, tangled in the covers, was the man she'd seen before, his arm draped casually across his eyes.

Her breath caught. Before she could think or move, his hand darted out and encircled her wrist in a pinching grip. The movement was so sudden and unexpected, she released a tiny yelp.

In an instant, he was out of bed standing only an inch from her, his fingers tightening like a chain. She flexed against him, amazed to find that his touch was solid, his hand warm, his calluses rough.

"Who are you?" His voice was low and harsh, but she wasn't frightened, though she knew she ought to be.

How should she answer him? Maybe it was better if she said nothing.

This time, he was clad in white linen undershorts that looked like boxers—only with a drawstring at the waist. His upper body was once again bare. Up close, there was no mistaking the chiseled beauty of his form, and she could feel the heat radiating from his torso, see the rise and fall of his chest, and hear his ragged breaths. Although the darkness shrouded the blue of his eyes, the intensity and power of his gaze pierced to her soul as it had before.

A deep part of her quivered at the realization she was having such an encounter. But another part of her couldn't believe he was real, and that disbelief emboldened her so that she lifted a hand to his face and grazed the stubble.

The scratchy texture felt authentic. But still, she couldn't be touching him, could she?

She skimmed his jaw and then his cheek. Dampness made a line down his rough skin. Had he recently shed tears? If so, why?

He did nothing to stop her. In fact, he released his grip on her wrist and dropped his hands to his sides, his breathing hoarse and rapid. The tension of his body told her his sleep was haunted by unspeakable terrors, nightmares that brought silent tears to his cheeks. She didn't know this man or what had happened to him, but she had an overwhelming need to console him.

Maybe this was why their paths kept crossing, because she was meant to see him and offer him a measure of solace. Besides, she might never see him again after tonight, so it wouldn't hurt to make the most of this moment.

Before her rational side could urge her to use caution, she shifted her hand to his other cheek. She glided over his scruff until she felt the warmth of the lingering tears. With her fingertips, she brushed them away.

He leaned in so that she felt his breath near her forehead. But somehow she sensed his restraint, that he wanted to touch her in return but was forcing himself to hold back. Maybe he thought by moving he'd frighten her or make her disappear.

Whatever the case, his reserve again gave her a liberty she wouldn't otherwise have taken, and she allowed herself to caress the hard line of his jaw, wishing she could somehow soothe him and take away the tension.

She willed that he'd feel her strength reaching out to him, holding him up, and alleviating his nightmares. She wanted to say something, but before she could speak, he was gone.

The bedside lamp cast its glow upon the papers still scattered over her bed. She stood at the edge, her mind spinning, trying to process what had happened. Disappointment tightened her chest. She wanted to linger with him a few moments longer, not only to comfort him but to discover more about him—at the very least learn his name.

After their encounters at Chesterfield Park, she believed the manor was his home. He likely claimed this room as his own. But what era was he from? The glimpse she'd had of the manor from the outside suggested an early time, certainly before Elizabethan or even Tudor-Jacobean times when the architecture had become more elaborate.

For several heartbeats, she waited, hoping for another glimpse of the stranger, a sound, a scent, anything. But the room remained unchanging.

As with the other times she'd crossed into the past, exhaustion swept over her, and she wanted to drop down onto the mattress. But she didn't have time to sleep. She had too much to do to get ready if she hoped to travel back in time and attempt to rescue Dad. Even so, she had to rest. If she didn't, she suspected she'd collapse.

With a yawn, she lowered herself to the edge of the mattress and pictured the smaller bedframe set lower and tried to imagine that she was sitting in the past again. How was it possible she kept seeing the same man in the same era?

Perhaps her dad's crossing was creating some kind of time-space overlap, so that whatever past period he'd visited was somehow bumping into the present causing her to go there too.

But what period was it?

She guessed the late 1100s or early 1200s after the death of Thomas Becket when the miracles associated with the holy water were still being recorded.

Her attention shifted again to the papers on the bed—specifically to the sheet with the Bible references about time. What if that's where she'd find the date, somewhere amidst all the numbers? Why else had her dad left the verses, unless they contained another clue?

Picking up the sheet, she smoothed a hand over the verses she'd written out.

Romans 13:11: *Knowing the time, that now it is high time to awake out of sleep*. Was this a clue telling her she needed to wake her dad from the coma?

Psalm 31:15: *My times are in thy hand*. Was this one indicating that Dad was relying on her?

Of course she could speculate on the meaning behind each of the ten verses. Her dad had likely specifically picked them to tell her a message. But did they also convey a time in history?

As she read the verses again, she studied the number patterns, searching in particular for a year near the time of Thomas Becket's death in 1170, the period when the holy water contributed to all those healings the monks had recorded.

She added, subtracted, multiplied, even divided. She tried to formulate a reason for accepting one verse over another based on themes. But nothing came to mind. The only oddity was with the verse in Ecclesiastes. The first thing she'd noticed was that it had been abbreviated while the others hadn't.

Eccl 3:82: *A time to love, and a time to hate; a time of war, and a time of peace. A time to be born, and a time to die; a time to plant, and a time to pluck up that which is planted.*

The second issue was that none of the chapters in Ecclesiastes had contained a verse 82. As she'd read through the chapter earlier, she'd surmised that Dad had been referring to verse 8 or verse 2 or perhaps both. So she'd written out each to be safe.

Of all the references on the list, the Ecclesiastes passage was also the only one where he'd spaced the book name closer to the numbers, almost as if everything was connected—Eccl3:82.

1382.

Her heartbeat stumbled before racing forward. That was it. He'd gone back to 1382. And he was telling her that he'd gone *to pluck up what had been planted* from the Tree of Life.

What had happened in 1382 to make it significant? Why hadn't he chosen a time closer to Becket?

Perhaps the crypt hadn't yet been completed in the 1100s. Maybe he'd needed to locate an era when the crypt was not only finished but safe in order to ensure the ampullae he hid there would survive to the present day.

In truth, it didn't really matter why he'd settled on 1382. That's where he'd gone. Where he'd died. And now she needed to go back to May of 1381—a year earlier—and attempt to intervene in some way.

She had a sudden and overwhelming urge to touch her fingers to her lips again and travel back to the blue-eyed stranger. He was only inches away, alive, warm, and breathing. She sensed he was dangerous, but something about him drew her nonetheless.

No. She quickly stuffed her hands into her pockets. The next time she traveled to the past, she would do so intentionally and with a plan. First she had to research the year 1382 and develop a solid hypothesis for why her dad had selected that particular time. And then she had to get ready for her own departure to the year 1381. That needed to include writing out some kind of explanation for Ellen.

She wouldn't be able to disclose everything. If the note fell into the wrong hands, she'd jeopardize the details of the ultimate cure, everything Dad tried so hard to keep hidden, probably from people who'd abuse the information.

Maybe she should wait to enact her plan. Until the police located Harrison and she had the opportunity to discuss it with him. Or until Ellen arrived. Or maybe she should call Jasper and finally explain what was going on.

"They won't understand and will just try to talk me out of it." That's what she would have done with Dad if he'd revealed his plans. She suspected even Drake and Bojing would try to stop her.

She started to gather the pages on the bed, but she paused over a sheet torn from a newer book than the others. The top of the sheet was titled "Pilgrimages During the Middle Ages."

She'd already read the article several times. The author noted that after a long period of silence in Canterbury, a slew of supposed miracles occurred in the late 1300s, the last ever to be recorded there. But he claimed the leaders falsely invented the miracles in order to entice more pilgrimages as a means of filling the Church's coffers.

What if the resurgence of miracles hadn't simply been Church propaganda? What if something really had caused a reappearance of miracles in the late 1300s? Like the rediscovery of the holy water?

She extricated her phone from her pocket and typed in a search for the year 1382 in Canterbury, England. At the sight of the results, her mouth dropped open.

There had been an earthquake in Kent on May 21, 1382, with an estimated magnitude of 5.8. It had a great enough force that the shock was felt in London. Interestingly, the earthquake interrupted a synod of religious leaders who had convened at Blackfriars in London to challenge the writings of John Wycliffe, accusing him of heresy for translating the Bible from Latin to English.

The earthquake damaged the Canterbury Cathedral belfry, dislodged the bells, and sent it crashing to the ground. It also caused severe structural damage to other churches, manors, and castles. Perhaps the shifting of the land had allowed a dormant spring at St. Sepulchre Priory to bubble to life.

She scrolled to the bottom of the article, noting that an aftershock had occurred May 24 with a 5.0 magnitude. Her dad had gone back five days ago on May 21. He'd probably timed his visit to occur right after the chaos of the earthquake to have the greatest chance of locating the wellspring that may have sprung to life after years of dormancy.

Obviously he'd found holy water someplace—if not from the cathedral then maybe from the wellspring. He'd had time to put those ampullae into the crypt. Then the aftershock hit.

What if somehow he'd been hurt during that second earthquake and it led to his death? After all, most of the structures of the Middle Ages wouldn't have been built to withstand such tremors.

Whatever had happened, now she was more convinced than ever she had to go back. She couldn't allow her dad to die somewhere in the past, not if she still had any chance of helping him. And not if she still had a chance to carry on his life's work and find the ultimate cure.

~ 10 ~

THEY WERE BEING FOLLOWED.

Marian glanced out the rear window and caught a glimpse of the silver Range Rover that had trailed them since they'd pulled out of Chesterfield Park.

"This is nuts, eh," Drake muttered from his spot next to Bojing in the front of the Bentley. "Foolhardy."

She didn't blame Drake for his caution, especially because the police still hadn't discovered Harrison's whereabouts. In fact, the local daily news reports had spoken of little else but the ongoing search for the abducted Lord Burlington.

Even with the danger, she had no choice but to venture out. She'd gone first to her dad's terraced house on St. Peter's Lane with the excuse that she needed to pick out his funeral outfit as well as gather more of her own clothing. Drake had positioned himself outside the front door and had given her five minutes. The house had been in the same state of disarray as the first time she'd visited it. So, she'd easily located the ancient coins scattered on the dining room floor.

She pressed a hand against her skirt and the pouch of coins now in her pocket. She wasn't sure what items would travel with her to the past. But since Dad had apparently been able to take whatever he'd had on him when he'd lapsed into the coma—like his watch—she hoped the same would be true for her.

Her already taut nerves stretched tighter. Was she doing the right thing? The question ricocheted through her mind as it had a hundred times over the past hours while she'd prepared to leave.

Drake's gaze darted to the rearview mirror. "You got what you wanted, miss. Let's get on to Chesterfield Park straightaway."

"Only one more stop. I promise." She pulled her phone out of her purse and scrolled through her photos. She halted at the picture of her, Ellen, and Dad together last Christmas. Harrison had taken the photo at Chesterfield Park in the spacious drawing room in front of a twelve-foot-tall Christmas tree.

Dad was in the middle, his hulking frame dwarfing her and Ellen. His gray hair was unkempt, his smile slight, and his eyes distant, as though his mind was a thousand miles away. Marian touched his face, guessing he actually had been a thousand miles away in the past. He'd probably already known at that point his plans to cross time, had likely been waiting for May when he could steal the St. Thomas ampulla relic when it came to Canterbury Cathedral.

"Good-bye," she whispered. Even though she had every intention of returning to the present, she needed to see the picture of them one last time. Just in case she didn't recover . . .

She didn't want to think about that happening. But going back a year before Dad was risky. There was so much that could go wrong, including not being able to find more holy water—especially if Dad had gotten it from the opening of the wellspring after the earthquake and hadn't been able to purchase it from the cathedral. It was possible that before the earthquake the flasks sold at the cathedral hadn't contained the miraculous holy water and had only been an imitation. Even if that was the case, surely the original St. Thomas ampullae were still available. She was resourceful and would find them. Like her dad, she would search for two—one to revive herself from the coma and then one to heal Ellen.

Clicking off her phone, she slipped it back into her purse. She'd do whatever she had to for as long as it took, until she found a way to save Dad and Ellen.

Poor Ellen. She was in for a shock when she arrived in Canterbury.

Marian had written a note to her sister regarding everything that had transpired, her current plans to save Dad, as well as instructions for how to bring her out of the coma. She'd placed the information in Harrison's safe, along with all the items from Dad's safety deposit box. Then, Marian had luxuriated in a long, hot shower—likely the last one she'd have for a few days.

After studying several descriptions of medieval clothing, she'd considered trying to find a costume shop for an authentic medieval gown. But she hadn't wanted to chance drawing even more attention to herself.

Instead, when she'd reached her dad's house and her wardrobe there, she dressed in what she hoped was a modest outfit—a flowing white skirt that nearly touched her ankles, summer sandals, and a silky coral long-sleeved blouse covered with a cashmere shawl. She also wore the tear-drop pearl necklace her mother had given her.

Marian peered past Bojing and Drake to find that the Bentley was nearing the St. George's Roundabout. Her stomach fluttered, and she pressed her hand against it only to realize her fingers were trembling.

"Pull off onto Canterbury Lane near St. George's Tower." The old square tower constructed of stone stood at the edge of a shopping plaza. With its arched gates, crenellated parapets, and leaded glass windows, it was a remnant of bygone eras, a lone guardian rising tall above the street. A clock jutted out on one side, upheld by a gargoyle, its grotesque face issuing a warning—but of what, she'd never known.

"What's here that you want?" Drake's voice was edged with suspicion.

"I need to check on an old landmark. That's all." She reached for the ampulla she'd previously tucked in the folds of her skirt on her lap. Her shaking fingers fumbled at the plug from Harrison's lab. After a long second, it popped loose.

Bojing was slowing the Bentley for the turn, and even though Drake was scowling and staring out the rearview mirror, he didn't protest.

As the car turned, Marian caught sight of the old city wall ahead past shopping centers. This was it. She only had seconds left.

"Whatever happens to me," she said to Bojing and Drake, "take me back to Chesterfield Park and not to the hospital. I need to be at Chesterfield Park."

Then, before either of the men could reply and before she could talk herself out of her mission, she lifted the flask to her lips, tipped it up, and emptied the scant drops of liquid onto her tongue. *I need to go to the year 1381*, she silently chanted. *1381.*

Her last thought was that the holy water was tasteless. Then the world went black.

• ● •

Complete and encompassing silence greeted Marian. Had she somehow become suspended in the time-space continuum between the past and the present?

A moment later, the soft scuff of footsteps nearby confirmed she'd arrived someplace—although she had no idea where.

She struggled to open her eyes, but her lids were heavy, her head groggy, and her body lethargic. Beneath her, the ground was hard and cold.

The footsteps drew nearer and stopped beside her. Someone knelt, the movement bringing the waft of dust. Gentle hands slipped behind her neck, lifted her head slightly, and then pressed a grainy rim against her mouth.

Marian's tongue was dry and stuck to the roof of her mouth, but she found that she could part her lips, eager to quench her thirst.

A warm liquid slipped into her mouth tasting of honey and sage. She took several sips of the sweet mixture before the mug lifted and she was lowered back to the ground upon a pallet of some kind. Her fingers at her sides made contact with coarse linen that was filled with a thin layer of something stiff. Was it straw?

Her eyes flew open to the sight of a dull gray ceiling. She shifted her head to take in walls of the same plain color, nothing on them except a simple wooden cross. The room was small enough to be a closet with a narrow rectangular window that allowed in some light, but not enough to ward off the shadows.

Her gaze came to rest on a woman kneeling next to her, a clay cup in her hands. The woman was draped from head to foot in layers of black and white. A nun.

Marian's heart sped with anticipation. Did the presence of this nun mean she'd ended up in St. Sepulchre Priory on St. George's Street? The nunnery no longer existed in present-day Canterbury, so she'd had no way of knowing exactly where it had once stood, only a guess from the excavation records. But if she was here, then it would appear that her calculation regarding the location had been correct.

She studied the cell-like room again, noting the cracks in the wall, the spiderweb in one corner, and the barrenness. Even if it wasn't pristine, overall it was clean.

She'd done it. She was in the past. And not just fleetingly. This time, her body felt firmly connected in some unexplainable way.

What about the present time? What had happened after she'd ingested the holy water in the back seat of the Bentley? Had Bojing returned her to Chesterfield Park as she'd asked? Was she even now lying in a coma similar to the one her dad had experienced?

Gentle fingers brushed at Marian's forehead, drawing her attention back to the face of the nun hovering above her—a thin but pretty face framed by a tight white wimple, which extended below her chin and covered all of her neck. A long black veil was attached to the coif and draped over the woman's head, flowing down her back. She also wore a white habit that was adorned with a black scapular and woven belt.

"Where am I?" Marian's voice was strangely hoarse.

The nun glanced over her shoulder at the open door before leaning in to Marian and whispering, "The infirmary of St. Sepulchre's." Marian nodded, but before she could ask another question, the nun continued. "I found you near the back gate of the priory this morn."

"So I've only been here a few hours?"

"All day, my lady. The bells shall soon ring for Vespers."

If Marian remembered the terminology correctly, Vespers was the evening prayer hour, usually spoken around 6:00 p.m.

The nun offered her another sip of water, and the warm liquid soothed Marian's dry throat. "Thank you for helping me."

The nun nodded and smiled. Her eyes were lovely and gentle, framed with long lashes. "My lady . . ." She stalled, clearly waiting for Marian to fill in the details of her name.

Marian hesitated. She didn't have to be a historian to know that women's roles had been vastly different in ages past, that most had very little independence and rarely traveled anywhere alone.

Though Marian was fluent in French, she didn't want to risk pretending to be French since England was at war with France in the 1300s in what had become known as the Hundred Years' War.

Instead, during her planning, she'd decided if anyone questioned what she was doing alone in Canterbury, she'd inform them she was from a noble English family who'd been living in Denmark and that she'd run away from them. Hopefully, that would account for her accent as well as her ignorance of social customs. From the little she'd gleaned during her quick research, Denmark had been largely influenced by the Church in much the same way as England with similar standards of living.

"I'm Marian Creighton." It couldn't hurt to give her real name, could it?

The nun's brows furrowed. "Creighton . . . I have not heard this family name. From where do you hail? Your accent and your garments—they are foreign." She nodded to the neatly folded pile of clothes at the head of the pallet.

Marian's fingers flew to her body beneath the blanket. Someone had attired her in a flowing robe—perhaps a habit similar to the one this nun wore. She patted her thigh. Her pouch of coins was gone, and she prayed it was safe in her stack of clothes.

"I don't remember much of what happened." Marian's mind spun as she searched for the right words, anything that would make her entry into Canterbury in 1381 sound believable. It was 1381, wasn't it? "What day and year is it?"

"The year of our Lord thirteen hundred eighty-one, on St. Augustine's day."

"St. Augustine's day?"

The nun's forehead remained wrinkled, and a new worry filled her eyes. "Can you not recall the circumstances that brought you to us or the date?"

Marian shook her head. She didn't want to lie, but what other choice did she have at this point?

"Then you have lost your memories. I have heard of such a malady happening before. I knew of a lad who was kicked in the head by his goat—"

More footsteps in the hall outside the door brought the nun's conversation to a halt. She clamped her lips closed and ducked her head.

The footsteps paused by the door. "Sister Christina?"

The nun rose and kept her head bowed, as though in deference to the newcomer who filled the door with her short, squat frame. "I thought I heard voices." The newcomer didn't speak above a whisper, but the censure in her tone fairly shouted. The wrinkles in her portly face identified her as an older nun.

Sister Christina shook her head and answered by making motions with her fingers—apparently some kind of sign language.

The older nun gave a curt sign in return, which caused Sister Christina to scurry off without so much as a good-bye. Only then did the older nun enter the room with slow, measured steps. Her rounded face contained none of the kindness or compassion Sister Christina had shown. Instead, her lips were pursed sternly, and her expression was severe.

"I see that you have awoken." The whisper was faint.

Marian nodded, again not sure how to reply. She supposed the less she said about herself, the better.

"I am Prioress Margery." She watched Marian as though expecting some sort of response.

Worry wormed through Marian. Should she rise to her knees and bow? Kiss the woman's hand? What exactly was appropriate?

The prioress's frown deepened at whatever breech of etiquette Marian had committed. "Have you come of your own volition, or did your family bring you to us?"

The question confused Marian.

The prioress's eyes narrowed. "Then Sister Christina is correct. You have indeed lost your memories?"

"It would appear so," Marian whispered back. She would survive better if she pretended to have forgotten her past. Then she wouldn't have to worry about giving wrong information.

The older nun stared with unrelenting curiosity as though attempting to identify Marian, the same way Christina had. Then her gaze went to the pile of Marian's belongings. "Since your family appears to be one of some means, we shall do our best to discover who they are and their intentions regarding your stay here."

Distant bells began to ring, and at their sounding, Prioress Margery pivoted and exited the room using the same slow steps as before.

When the scuffling faded down the hallway, Marian sat up, letting the wool blanket fall away. Her head spun, and she blinked back several waves of dizziness.

Her vision cleared, and she tugged at her gown. She was indeed wearing what appeared to be a nun's outfit, a loose-fitting white garment, but without any of the black trimmings. Her body felt strangely unencumbered. She wiggled, and mortification washed over her. Someone had taken off her bra and underwear and had placed a thin nightgown-like garment on underneath the robe.

She groped for her stack of clothing and searched through it. Her fingers came into contact with her lacy undergarments folded and at the bottom of the pile next to her sandals. But she couldn't find the pouch of money or her pearl necklace.

Dizziness hit her, and she pressed her hand against her forehead to ward off a wave of panic. She'd been awake for less than five minutes, and already she was in big trouble. She was penniless in 1381.

$\sim$ 11 $\sim$

How could she possibly survive without money?

Marian scrambled around the pallet and blanket to see if the pouch and jewelry had become tangled in the bedding. What if the items hadn't crossed time with her? The possibility was too awful to consider.

She reached up and felt her ears. The pearl studs still were there. If the earrings had stayed with her, then surely the other things had as well, which would account for the prioress assuming she was wealthy.

Marian stood, and the robe-like garment fell down to cover her bare feet. It was ten sizes too large, and without her undergarments, she felt entirely bare underneath.

Quickly, before anyone else passed by her room, she donned her panties and bra. She considered changing back into her skirt and blouse but then decided against it. She'd garner less attention if she remained in the nun's clothing, at least for the time being while she searched for her coins and pearls.

During the hunt, she could also explore St. Sepulchre for the location of the wellspring. If the water source wasn't available until after the earthquake that happened next year in 1382, then she would start searching for St. Thomas ampullae that contained the original holy water.

She picked up and unfolded the head covering someone had left beside the pallet. It was a simple piece of cloth, but as she draped it over her head, she wished she had access to a YouTube video with directions for attaching it correctly.

Once she secured it as best she could, she slipped on her sandals and padded to the door. Since she'd slept for the majority of the day, she couldn't waste another minute. After all, she only had one week. That's what she'd told Ellen in the note—to wait a week before checking the column head in the crypt. If Ellen went every day, she'd only put herself in danger and chance giving away the hiding place.

Although Marian wasn't sure how the whole exchange process worked, she hoped Harrison's theories about the nonlinear, overlapping of time held true, and that whatever day she placed the holy water in the crypt would line up with that same day in the present.

Marian peeked into the hallway, glancing both ways down the long corridor. Seeing that it was deserted, she tiptoed a few steps to the open door of the room next to hers. It was identical, containing nothing but a straw pallet on the wood floor. Each of the closet-like chambers down the rest of the hallway were the same.

The last room was bigger than the others but was locked. Through the barred window on the door, she could see shelves lined with clay jars and colored glass vials for tinctures, cordials, and ointments. A worktable stood at the center, holding a balance along with mortars and pestles of various sizes. The pungent aroma of garlic, sage, rosemary, and other herbs blended together and filled the air.

Was this an apothecary? Or at the very least the part of the infirmary where the nuns kept their herbs and medicines?

She almost smiled at the wonder of what she was seeing and

smelling. She was most definitely in another era. She held out her hands and wiggled her fingers. Then she pinched her arm, just to be sure she was there in the flesh and not merely having a vision.

The cool dampness of the hallway, the mustiness in the air, the scratchiness of her robe. The sensory details were too real for a hallucination or dream.

While her body lay unresponsive on a bed in the present, she was definitely alive and experiencing the past. She didn't know how such a thing was possible, but she was doing it.

She rattled the apothecary door. Then she stood on her toes to inspect the shelves better, hoping to glimpse the outline of a St. Thomas pilgrim ampulla. But without a light to dispel the darkness of the coming evening, she couldn't see the contents clearly enough. Maybe she'd have to wait until morning to convince Sister Christina or one of the other nuns to allow her inside.

With excitement humming through her, she started down another long hallway, passing by what looked to be a dining room on one side and a simple schoolroom of sorts on the other. She paused to peer inside both of them. Not a person was in sight.

Where was everyone? Perhaps they'd all gone to the chapel for Vespers.

Yes, that was it. Nuns were required to attend the services. And their absence gave her the perfect opportunity to snoop without anyone being aware of what she was doing.

Picking up her pace, she continued down the passageway, searching for her money and pearls as well as ampullae. Even with the growing shadows, she could see that each room was sparsely furnished without material comforts or decorations . . . and not a sign of her belongings.

Perhaps the prioress had confiscated her valuables under the assumption that they would provide payment for her room and board. With each passing minute, the thrill at being in the past began to fade under the steady but growing urgency thudding in her chest.

A low and rhythmic chanting in Latin wafted down the hallway and grew steadily louder as she drew nearer to a set of double doors. The nuns would likely soon finish Vespers and exit from the chapel. What would they say if they found her wandering around the nunnery? On the other hand, she only had several more rooms left to explore. She could finish if she hurried.

She poked her head through the open door on her left to discover it was a storage room of some kind, containing blankets, pallets, extra habits, a few washbasins, and a stack of towels. Everything was plain-colored and made of coarse linen or wool, certainly a far cry from the fluffy cotton and patterned material of modern towels and sheets.

She veered across the hallway, opening the door of the opposite room. The chamber was windowless, but enough evening light remained in the hallway to fall upon the few rudimentary pieces of furniture—one of which was a desk-like table.

Was this an office of sorts? Perhaps belonging to the prioress?

Marian crossed to the desk. Amidst what appeared to be stacks of thick parchment, ink bottles, and quill pens, her hand brushed against a lumpy pouch.

Her money.

She snatched it up and skimmed the rest of the table in an effort to locate her pearls. Down the hallway, the chanting had ceased.

Should she take the coins and leave? Perhaps she could find a nearby inn to use as a home base for the week where she might have more independence than she'd have at the nunnery.

Or perhaps she ought to stay. After all, she was inside the convent where she was safe and could investigate every possible location of the original spring that had been used to fill ampullae with holy water. If she didn't find anything, she could always move on then.

First, however, she had to secure her money. She left the office-like room, crossed to a nearby exit, and made her way outside as quietly as she could. A quick survey in the twilight revealed high stone walls that surrounded the convent. A smaller shed-like building sat to one side. An outhouse was placed well away from the main building near several rows of raised garden beds, with a thick stand of trees and brush beyond.

With hurried steps, she made her way toward the raised beds. Maybe she could hide the pouch somewhere among the trees, under a stone, or in a hollow of a log. She needed to work swiftly and return to the confines of the little room inside the convent before anyone noticed she was missing. Then in the morning by the light of day, she'd investigate the building and grounds again.

She ducked under a branch and squeezed past twigs that clawed at her robe and head covering. She pushed through the overgrowth until she reached the far convent wall. Down the wall a dozen paces was a door. Was this the back gate of the convent Sister Christina had mentioned?

Marian edged her way along the wall to the door. It was crafted of rough planks that were curved to fit an arched opening in the wall. A long wooden beam barred anyone outside from coming in. But it wouldn't prevent her from going out—when she was ready to visit the cathedral.

She wanted to take a peek on the other side and get a glimpse of how Canterbury looked in 1381. But the sightseeing would need to wait for another day. Instead, she made swift work of hiding the bag of coins beneath two stones before returning the way she'd come through the dense copse of trees.

When she reached the main building, darkness had begun to settle. She found the door near the chapel and reentered the building. The hallways were as quiet as before, and she could only assume everyone had retired to their rooms for the night. As she crept along, she only had to hide once—in the empty dining room—as someone passed by.

Finally reaching her room, she lowered herself to the pallet and pulled the wool blanket over her. The thin straw-filled mattress provided little cushion, and she turned first one way then another, trying to get comfortable on the hard ground. She hadn't slept on a floor since her childhood when she'd had sleepovers with friends. Even then, she'd had an air mattress to lie on in her comfortable flannel sleeping bag.

Here the ground was cold, the straw in the pallet was abrasive, and the blanket smelled stale. She couldn't keep from wondering who had used it before her and when it had last been laundered.

She had no pillow either, so she wadded up her discarded skirt and blouse underneath her head. Lying on her back, she stared through the darkness. Without her alarm clock, laptop cord light, or flashing cell phone alerts, the blackness was almost suffocating.

The silence, too, was overwhelming. No whirring of the heating unit, no distant thrum of highway traffic, and no buzz of outdoor lights. Gone was the chatter from a TV or the strains of Harrison playing his violin. It was as silent as death. Silent enough to hear footsteps padding down the hallway a short while later.

As the steps neared her room, she made herself lie completely motionless and pretend to be asleep. The person paused in the door, stood for a minute, then retreated the way she'd come.

She had no idea yet who might be friend or foe. But one thing she did know was that in the morning, she needed to start developing friendships if she had any hope of making her trip to 1381 successful.

• ● •

Marian's restless sleep was broken by the ringing of a bell in the middle of the night and again at dawn. She didn't know much about the routine of nuns, but she suspected the bells were the summons to more prayer in the chapel.

By the time faint light permeated Marian's tiny room, she was stiff and cold. The wool blanket and the layers of her robes hadn't been warm enough to stave off the chill from the May night.

"Just pretend you're camping, Marian," she whispered, trying to ignore the ache in her shoulders and back from sleeping on the hard ground.

Her full bladder finally prodded her up from the pallet and out of her room. Her only option was to find the outhouse near the raised garden beds, but the thought of having to go outside in the coldness of the early morning brought swift longing for a warm, cozy bathroom, with its bright lights and warm running water.

"It's just for a week," she told herself as she opened the door at the end of the infirmary hallway which led to the convent yard shrouded in the grayness of dawn. She hurried across the grass, which was damp with dew and breathed in crisp morning air laden with the scents of soil and the ever-present aroma of woodsmoke.

At the foulness of the outhouse, she breathed through her mouth. How could anyone ever learn to function without toilet paper and a flushable toilet? After she finished, she wished she could wash her hands or at the very least scrub with one of her scented sanitizers. Instead, she wiped her hands in the wet grass and dried them on her robe.

Slipping back into the convent, she stopped short at the sight of a shadowed figure waiting by the door to her room.

"Lady Marian," came a rushed whisper.

Marian's stomach growled in response, reminding her that she hadn't eaten anything since yesterday's breakfast. At the very least, she could settle for a cup of coffee. They did have coffee in the Middle Ages, didn't they? When exactly had the caffeinated brew been invented?

She searched the far reaches of her mind to remember that piece of trivia and had the vague recollection that coffee-drinking had come much later.

She'd miss her dark-roasted one-cup from her Keurig this morning. No swinging by Starbucks. Not even a cheap, flavored coffee from the gas station. She'd have a caffeine headache later in the day and should have thought to tuck some Excedrin in her money pouch.

"Lady Marian." An urgency in the nun's voice pricked Marian.

Through the darkness still permeating the hallway, Marian couldn't see clearly, but the outline of a thin, pretty face told her it was Sister Christina, the same nun she'd met yesterday.

"Good morning."

"'Tis not so good." Sister Christina glanced over her shoulder to the opposite end of the passageway that led to the chapel and the prioress's office. "You are in grave trouble."

"Trouble?" Little did this woman know what kind of trouble Marian would face if she didn't find any ampullae.

"Prioress Margery has misplaced your dowry." Sister Christina's voice was so hushed it was almost inaudible. "However, instead of searching for it, she has decided to make accusations of thievery."

"My pouch of money?"

"The prioress is accusing you of stealing it."

"How can I steal something that belongs to me?" Marian wanted to laugh at the absurdity of the accusation.

But Sister Christina was wringing her hands, clearly distraught. "Perhaps if you leave now, you could escape her—"

Sister Christina's words were cut off by the patter of footsteps. They both turned to see Prioress Margery's plump frame rounding the corner, followed by four other nuns with their heads bowed and hands tucked into their sleeves out of sight.

"Go." Sister Christina's tone was desperate.

Should she run? Marian glanced at the door she'd entered only moments before. She couldn't go yet. Once she left, she'd have no guarantee of getting back inside, and she needed to check the priory for holy water before moving on.

She would have to face the prioress and what appeared to be her posse. Surely she could speak reasonably with everyone about the bag of money and make them understand she hadn't stolen it.

The prioress halted in front of her and wasted no time in getting to the point. "Your dowry is missing."

"It's not a dowry." Did a noblewoman's family give a dowry to the Church when she entered a convent to symbolize her marriage to Christ? Somehow the recollection rang true, but that wasn't Marian's case, and she needed to convince the prioress of it.

"It's money I brought for my journey. That's all. I don't intend to stay long and will pay you—"

"Since you have lost your memories, your claims are completely untrustworthy." The prioress held a simple iron candleholder containing a stubby yellowish candle that emanated an acrid odor and cast long flickering shadows across the walls and down the hallway. It also made the woman's face appear hard and her gaze unrelenting.

What could Marian say to contradict the prioress? She couldn't suddenly pretend to have her memories back, not so soon after asserting she'd lost them. "I know enough to understand the bag of money is for my expenses and not a dowry."

"You have no way of knowing that. With the significant sum, I have no doubt your family intended it to be payment for your new life here. You shall tell me where the bag is at once or suffer the consequences of thievery."

"The money is mine." Marian pulled herself to her full height and stared back at the prioress, unwilling to let this medieval woman frighten her. "I can pay you for room and board, but I need the rest."

The prioress nodded just once, which set into motion the nuns behind her. The nuns rounded the prioress and came toward Marian. It wasn't until they reached her that they removed their hands from their robes to reveal coarse twine.

"You're planning to tie me up for taking what is rightfully mine?" Marian tried to step back. But the nuns closed in, preventing her escape. Before she could fight or even raise her hands in defense, the nuns grasped her arms and wrapped the twine around her wrists like pros, obviously having performed the task before.

"This is ridiculous." Marian wrenched her hands in an attempt to free herself. "You can't hold me against my will—"

The prioress's palm slammed against Marian's cheek, cutting off her words and her breath. Pain sliced across her jaw and cheekbone, making her eyes sting.

The prioress's hand remained lifted, ready to strike again. "I shall give you one more opportunity to inform me where you put the dowry money."

"It's not dowry money—"

The prioress slapped Marian's other cheek with such force it caused her head to jerk painfully. Then the prioress nodded toward Marian's room. "Lock her away."

The four nuns kept their gazes trained on the floor as they dragged Marian into her room. Against her shouts, they tied a gag around her mouth, forced her to her knees in front of the cross on the wall, then filed out silently, closing the door behind them. When a lock clicked into place, Marian stared at the closed door, her face smarting and her wrists burning.

Being trapped in a tiny cell and accused of stealing her own money hadn't been part of her plan for the morning. It hadn't been part of her plan in any form.

She attempted to move her hands, but at even the slightest effort, the twine dug into her wrists, making her cry out, except that the rag tied around her mouth was so tight she could hardly breathe.

What in the world had she gotten herself into? And how was she going to get out of the predicament?

She lifted her eyes up, and her gaze snagged upon the simple wooden cross. She hadn't prayed—really prayed—in a long time.

She hadn't wanted to need God. Hadn't wanted to need anybody's help. But if God didn't help her this time, she didn't know who else could.

Throughout the lonely day, she alternated between kneeling, praying, and pacing. By the time the shadows had begun to lengthen with the coming of the evening, her mouth was parched and her stomach ached from hunger.

When the door rattled, she held her breath, hoping to see Christina carrying water and food. But the nuns who had attended the prioress earlier stood in the passageway. Two of them stepped into the room and took hold of Marian's arms.

She tried to ask them to remove her gag and give her something to drink, but her voice came out garbled. As they guided her forward and out of her room, she craned her neck for the sight of Christina. Where was the friendly young nun?

The nuns led her outside into the large yard to a center patio-like area. Overhead the sky was turning violet, the wispy clouds like lace. The air was cool, and although a smoky scent wafted around her, it was pleasant.

The moment they freed her hands of the twine, she'd bolt away, retrieve her money, and escape from this place. But instead of unbinding her, the nuns pushed her down to her knees in front of a post and repositioned her hands so that she had no choice but to hold the post.

Around her, the yard grew silent. Other nuns had gathered a short distance away, and they stared at her with a somberness that set her on edge. At a jerk of her gown and brushing aside of her hair, Marian stiffened. She glanced over her shoulder in time to see a stick swinging down toward her. The rod connected with her shoulder and back with such force, a scream tore from her dry throat. The gag muted it, but in the silence of the yard, it echoed nonetheless.

Oh Lord Almighty help her. They were beating her.

As the cane fell against her back again, Marian arched in an effort to avoid the blow and the pain. But it slashed through her, causing blackness to descend. Her only prayer before she slipped into oblivion was that God would take her out of this nightmare and return her to the present where she belonged.

~ 12 ~

PERSPIRATION MADE A STEADY TRAIL down Sir William Durham's backbone beneath the well-fitted cotehardie that buttoned down the front and ended at his hips, falling over his breeches. The May afternoon wasn't especially warm, but his body pulsed with an urgency to return home.

He drove his faithful stallion hard, and his three squires did likewise with their steeds. Of course, they had their arming swords as well as their large battle swords and could combat any peril they might encounter, even if they wore no armor. Nevertheless, Will didn't want trouble.

At the reports of the uprisings in Essex, Will had cut short his tactical meetings in Dover on the coast. So had most of the other knights after they'd received word at midday that the royal official, Bampton in the Essex village of Brentwood, had been forced out of town on the tip of arrows.

The word was that Bampton had only been attempting to collect the unpaid poll taxes in Brentwood. The royal official had called a peaceable meeting of the surrounding villages. But tempers had escalated, and the men of the community had refused to cooperate. Eventually they'd chased Bampton off.

Will hadn't necessarily been rankled by that particular news. It

123

was the third poll tax within the past four years, and Will agreed—as treasonous as that might be—the newest levy to pay for the war against the French was both brutal and unfair. Some protest against the taxes was to be expected.

What he didn't like was the unrest spreading across the southeast part of the country, making its way toward Kent, toward his home, toward his sons.

"The horses are needing respite and refreshment, sire," one of the squires called as the Canterbury city walls rose steadily before them.

Will wanted to growl out his objection. His family estate was not far from Canterbury. They were almost there, and he wouldn't relax until he rode through the gates and saw both Phillip and Robert alive and well.

However, he bit back his grumbling and instead gave a curt nod. He might be hardened from war, but he wasn't so callous that he'd make the horses suffer needlessly. Therewith, he could use the opportunity to visit his sister and warn her of the turmoil. Already Canterbury had been stirred by the recent preaching of a priest by the name of John Ball. Ofttimes after Sunday mass, when people exited the service, Ball preached to them about the unfairness of being bondmen without rights and the need to go before the king and state their cause.

The Archbishop of Canterbury had imprisoned Ball for three months for such unlawful preaching but had been under increasing pressure from his parishioners to release the man. Whence last Will had ridden through Canterbury and the surrounding countryside, John Ball had been preaching again and inflaming the people, even though the archbishop had forbidden it.

Will's gaze strayed to the field at his left flank, the dark loam, rich and thick, freshly plowed and tilled. Men, women, and children alike dotted the land, tunics tucked into belts revealing their bare feet. Men wore snug-fitting coifs and women broad-brimmed straw hats. From all appearances, they seemed peaceable enough. In fact, none of the laborers they'd passed during their journey had appeared to be revolting.

As they neared the walls of Canterbury, instead of entering through the Riding Gate, he steered them toward St. George's. There, they passed by the cattle market where the stench of manure was strong and the bleats of weaning calves rose in the air.

He surveyed the double towers on either side of St. George's palisade, noting they were manned. Even so, the gate was wide open, the town seemingly without a care. He could only shake his head at the idiocy of the city guard. The walls had been refortified in recent years to act as a defense against the French, not to make the city look pretty.

Didn't they understand that because Canterbury was close to the coast as well as on the road to London, that if the French invaded, Canterbury would be one of the first towns attacked?

For that matter, any troublemaker could enter and wreak destruction.

With a shake of his head, Will guided his stallion through the gatehouse. Ahead, the fish market displayed strings of perch, trout, and salmon on open racks, and the odor of fish drying in the warm sun wafted toward them.

The market wasn't as busy now that Lent was past, and they easily maneuvered through the carts and stands of husbandmen and tradesmen selling wares. The long whitewashed wattle and daub walls of St. Sepulchre Priory stood out amidst the other weathered, gray businesses that lined the narrow street. The convent wasn't large, but it had been home to his younger sister for nigh ten years. She'd gone in as a girl of ten, a mere postulant. Last year, she'd finally taken her vows.

Will wasn't allowed to visit oft, as the prioress kept the women under her charge to a strict regime. But because of his continued donations, the prioress allowed him some leniency.

He reined alongside the tall arched gate that led inside the convent grounds and rang the bell to alert the women they had visitors.

The nuns moved slowly, and it took long minutes ere he and his squires were admitted. While a lay sister brought water for their horses, Christina came out to greet him, directed them to a shaded nook, then offered a simple fare of cheese, oatcakes, and frothy ale.

"Lord have mercy." Christina's face blanched as she turned away from a commotion in the courtyard. "I do wish the prioress would let that poor young woman be."

Will shifted on the bench where he sat to find two nuns dragging a woman by her arms out of the convent toward the center of the courtyard. The swirling of habits prevented him from seeing the woman fully, but she appeared limp, almost lifeless, as they hauled her toward a post used for punishment purposes.

He took a sip of his ale, grateful to be quenching his thirst, but still needled with the urgency to be on his way home.

Christina swiped at her cheeks, and Will realized she was crying. Although he hadn't seen his sister often since he'd been off to war in France, she still held a special place in his heart. She was the tender one, the sibling who had always understood him better than any other, the one to give him comfort when no one else could.

Even if she was gentlehearted, she rarely shed tears. And the sight of them now made him sit up and glance again at the disciplinary action unfolding before them.

The limp woman wore a habit and veil, but since she didn't wear a scapula he guessed she was only a novice. "What is her crime?"

"The prioress has accused her of stealing the dowry money given to the convent by her kin."

As the nuns hefted the woman against the post, her veil fell away, revealing hair that was the same russet as his finest gelding.

His pulse lurched, and he stood abruptly, heedless of his trencher toppling into the grass. The luxurious red-brown fell over her shoulders in beautiful waves. The same color hair as the woman from his dreams.

His heart pounded hard against his chest like the stampede of warhorses. He'd been troubled with nightmares since his first campaign in France long ago. But over the past year, the nightmares had become so frequent he could hardly sleep—ever since he'd failed Thomas, ever since Thomas had taken the brunt of the torture and excruciating death in his stead.

From the moment he'd returned to Bergerac to pay the ransom and had come across his brother's scattered bloody remains, he'd had no peace. Slumber brought him no comfort, didn't give him even a brief respite from the pain of the loss. Rather, sleep only made the nightmares worse. Until this week. Until his nightmares had been interrupted by a beautiful woman.

As the nuns situated the woman's bound hands to a hook at the top of the post, her russet hair fell across her face like a tangled curtain.

Was it truly the same woman? The one who'd wiped the tears from his cheeks—tears he hadn't known were there. She'd given him strength and comfort and a sense of peace he hadn't experienced in a long time. Surely this couldn't be the same person.

Yet his muscles tightened with the need to know. "Who is she?" His tone was harsh, menacing, the one that made people around him cringe.

But Christina could see past his hard exterior and answered him with the trust and love she'd always given him so unconditionally— even though he didn't deserve it. "Her name is Lady Marian Creighton. She came to us three days hence, alone, with only a pouch of money. The prioress assumed the coins were from her family as a dowry to the convent. Lady Marian claimed otherwise and took the money out of the prioress's office. Although Marian has since returned the pouch, the prioress hasn't yet relented in her punishment for the offense."

Will tried to digest the situation.

"Please make them stop hurting her, Will. She doesn't deserve it."

Christina's quiet statement was all Will needed to prod him into action. With swift strides, he approached the nuns, who had produced a rod the size of a walking stick. He had no doubt they intended to beat the limp woman's back, probably already had on several occasions.

Oblivious to his approach, the nun raised the stick to bring it down across the woman's shoulder. Will snatched it and snapped it in one motion. The startled nun released a squeak before scuttling away.

He tossed the stick to the ground, unrelenting in his fierce glare at the two nuns who'd been given the task of administering the discipline. They cowered into their habits as though they could hide within the folds. Their limbs visibly quaked and lips trembled.

He wasn't proud of his ability to intimidate. In fact, he wasn't proud of much. But in this case, if his gruff demeanor protected an innocent woman from further unnecessary discipline, then so be it.

"Inform the prioress I demand to have words with her."

The nuns bobbed their heads and backed away. He suspected they were as much pawns in the discipline as the woman herself was. Nonetheless, he despised them for their lack of courage.

"Anon." The one word was more menacing than the last, but he didn't care. He turned away from the women, who were scrambling to do his bidding, unsheathed his dirk, and in one quick flick cut the russet-haired woman free from the post.

She slid to the ground onto her side, and the hair fell away from her face. His pulse slammed to a halt at the sight of the smooth creamy complexion, dainty chin, high cheekbones, and full lips of the same woman he'd seen in his dreams.

Was she alive? He lowered himself to one knee and pressed his fingers to her lips, feeling for the warmth of her breath. At the soft burst, his pulse sputtered back to life and began to rage with the force of an advancing regiment in battle formation.

He slipped his arms beneath her, but the moment he made contact with her back, she cried out in pain.

"She has already been beaten badly." Christina spoke from beside him. "The prioress has been especially harsh with her."

Will lifted the woman again, this time more gingerly. Even so, she moaned. He had no wish to cause her further distress, but she clearly couldn't walk on her own. For a surprising instant, he considered mounting his stallion and spiriting her away from Prioress Margery.

However, if Lady Marian couldn't tolerate his gentle steps now, how would she survive a jostling ride to the manor house?

He had no choice but to leave her at St. Sepulchre to recover. But ere he departed, he'd make clear his wishes regarding her care.

He started forward. "Lead the way to the infirmary."

With wide eyes so like his own, Christina nodded and headed to a side door. Will followed her inside, even though convent rules forbade his presence. Christina led him a short distance to a cell and indicated for him to deposit Lady Marian onto the pallet.

As he knelt beside the thin pad and lowered her, she expelled a sigh, and her eyelids fluttered open to reveal eyes the dark brown of a richly fermented brew. They radiated agony. But they also connected with his—just as they had in his dreams. Other noblewomen didn't dare meet his gaze, were too daunted by him. But this woman had no fear, and he felt the tug of her gaze all the way to his innards.

He was surprised again when she lifted her hand and cupped his cheek. Although the movement made her wince and suck in a sharp breath, she didn't look away. "Thank you." Before he could respond or even manage a nod, her hand fell away from his cheek, her eyes closed, and her head lolled into unconsciousness.

Urgency rose in his breast. "Help her, Christina. You must help her."

Christina cocked her head, as though to question his passionate plea.

He sat back on his heels, the questions roiling through him too.

His sister squeezed his shoulder. "I shall do everything I can, William." She would earn the prioress's disfavor by giving aid to this woman, but threats of retribution wouldn't stop Christina from doing what was right—which was one of the many qualities he appreciated about her.

Will stood and straightened his shoulders with renewed determination. "Have no fear. Ere I depart, I shall ensure your safety along with that of your patient. No harm will befall either of you."

Christina nodded but was working to divest the woman of her habit. She'd pulled the loose-fitting garment away from the woman's back, revealing numerous purple and blue welts. At the sight, an oath slipped from Will's mouth. "Saint's blood."

The marks crisscrossed the pale, beautiful skin all the way down to the low dip at the base of her spine. Even with the swollen discoloration marring her back, the outline of her form was exquisite and womanly and showed her to be very desirable.

Christina tugged the habit lower toward the woman's buttocks but stopped and peered up at Will pointedly. "I shall be able to tend her wounds more efficiently with privacy."

He averted his gaze and backed out of the room into the hallway, fighting a wave of embarrassment. He hadn't been interested in any woman since Alice died two years ago. As much as his mother had encouraged him to remarry, as much as Lord Percy had pressured him for a union with his youngest daughter, he'd rebuffed their endeavors, claiming he was yet in mourning.

Not that he'd had a close relationship with Alice, since he'd been gone to war for most of their ten years of marriage. But she'd been good to him whenever he'd been home, and she'd been an excellent mother to his sons. He had no complaints about her.

Nonetheless, he hadn't grieved her loss the way a better man would have. He could blame his lack of remorse on his distress over what had happened with Thomas. But the truth was, he'd never known Alice well enough to miss her in life or death.

He wouldn't deny he had carnal needs like every other male. But he abhorred the practice of pillaging and raping after a battle as many of his companions were wont to do. Even with the availability of poor French wenches in every town and village who were willing to sell themselves, he always resisted the urge, no matter how strong.

He gave a curt shake of his head and stepped farther from the cell and the beautiful red-haired woman. The problem was that it had been too long since he'd allowed himself to think about a woman. And now his urges were causing strange dreams and desires. In fact, the dreams of this woman had been so realistic that at times he'd even felt her touch.

Maybe he needed to finally consider taking a new wife. Before he went mad altogether.

At the pad of footsteps from the next hallway, he tensed and braced himself for confrontation. Within a moment, Prioress Margery rounded the corner, a number of nuns trailing behind her.

Keen dislike pierced him as it did whenever he was required to speak with this woman. He spread his feet slightly and crossed his arms.

"Sir William." She halted in front of him and dipped her head in deference. Her retinue paused a dozen feet behind her, keeping heads down and hands hidden. When the prioress raised her eyes, they contained a disdain she'd never been able to hide, likely because he'd intervened on Christina's behalf in the past.

"Shall we step outside, sire?" She motioned toward the door at the end of the hallway.

Although she was tactfully suggesting that he remove his presence from the convent, he didn't budge. "You will cease the discipline of Lady Marian."

The old nun's lips pursed together, her fleshy jowls shaking.

Will lowered his voice to the volume he used to incite fear. "If I discover you have brought further harm to the lady in any form whatsoever, I shall report your abuse to the archbishop." He wanted to threaten to do everything to her that she'd done to Lady Marian, but he bit back the clipped words. He wouldn't harm a lady ever, not even a tyrant like the prioress.

"You will also allow Sister Christina to tend to Lady Marian until I retrieve her ladyship." He knew naught about Lady Marian's situation, where she'd come from, why she was at the priory, what her future plans were, or even if she needed retrieving. But the prioress didn't need to know that.

The prioress's small eyes gleamed sharply, but she lowered her head in a nod. As much as it pained the woman, she would do as he commanded. She had no other choice.

He spun on his heels and strode with firm footsteps down the corridor. He held himself rigidly, vowing to return within a sennight to check on his sister and Lady Marian. But as soon as he was mounted and riding again, he thrust all thoughts of the women from his mind. He had too many other concerns, too many battles, too many demons. And he didn't need any more.

~ 13 ~

DESPERATION NEEDLED MARIAN AWAKE. She opened her eyes and pushed herself to her elbows on the pallet in the cold infirmary cell.

She'd been inside St. Sepulchre's Priory for six days, which meant she had only one to go until Ellen checked the Canterbury Cathedral crypt for a supply of holy water. The last three days had passed quietly, with Sister Christina coming in to feed and tend her every couple of hours. It had been blissfully uneventful compared to the first three days of her stay . . .

Marian shuddered with such force it sent pain shooting through her bruised body from where she'd been beaten across her shoulders and back. And not just one beating. But two.

Of course, when they came for her a second time, she disclosed where she'd hidden the pouch of coins. But even after she informed the prioress, they marched her out to the courtyard and beat her anyway.

After they tossed her back into her cell, she lay on the floor, hardly able to swallow the sips of water Sister Christina gave her. She wasn't even able to lift her head to look at the cross on the wall. All she could do was pray she'd make it out of the living nightmare of 1381.

When the nuns arrived at her cell on the third afternoon, she wasn't able to resist as she had previously. She was too weak and passed in and out of consciousness as they hauled her into the yard and hooked her to the post.

It was only then she understood the magnitude of what she'd done by coming to the past. She'd been stupid to think she could handle being in a time so foreign to her own, when rulers like the prioress wielded unrestricted power, when justice wasn't always served, when corporal punishment was unrestrained, when women lacked the same rights as men, especially a foreign woman abandoned by her family—which is what they assumed of her.

How naïve she'd been to believe she could save her dad when she couldn't even save herself.

While she hung on the post waiting for her third beating, she'd braced herself for the first blow across her back but was suddenly cut loose. The next thing she knew, strong arms were carrying her. The touch was so gentle, so careful.

Nevertheless, she passed out again only to awake with *his* face above hers and those intense blue eyes peering down at her. Certain she was delirious, she reached out to touch him, to thank him, and he felt so real. The stubble on his cheeks was scruffy, the strength of his jaw hard against her hand.

Had she only dreamed him? Or had he been there?

Marian pushed herself up further, wincing at the ache in her backside. Afternoon sunlight streamed in through the high window, illuminating the starkness of the chamber.

She couldn't go on lying around. She had to get up today no matter how much it pained her, and she had to locate holy water. All she wanted to do was find enough to get home safely.

The soft footsteps and swish of robes told her Sister Christina was coming again. The kindhearted nun had been her only friend since arriving at the nunnery. But she remained resolutely silent since their first meeting.

Whenever Marian attempted to converse, Sister Christina cocked her head toward the hallway, as if to say they were not alone. The fear in the young woman's eyes kept Marian from persisting, even though she had a hundred questions. Marian understood such fear all too clearly now, and she had no wish to subject the sweet woman to the prioress's wrath.

As Sister Christina entered the room bearing a steaming mug, Marian's stomach rumbled. Even if the fare was only broth, she was grateful, although she would have given just about anything for a big cobb salad with a toasted whole grain bagel. And coffee. She missed coffee. If one good thing could be said of her beatings, at least the pain in the rest of her body had dulled the throbbing from her caffeine-deprivation headaches.

With a smile of greeting that lit her eyes, Sister Christina gently helped Marian sit up the rest of the way and then lifted the steaming mug to her lips.

"Thank you," Marian whispered and then allowed Christina to help her.

As Marian swallowed the last drop, she laid back against the pallet. Christina started to pull up the woolen blanket that covered the oversized undershirt Marian was wearing, the only stitch of clothing they'd allowed her.

"Would you help me get dressed?" Marian grasped the young woman's hand before she could get away. "I think I should try to walk around today, don't you agree? And regain my strength?"

Sister Christina nodded in acquiescence, which sent a breath of relief through Marian. Perhaps she could encourage the young woman to take her into the apothecary. Marian had to make use of the time up to discover something, especially if she had any hope of getting holy water to Ellen by tomorrow.

After Sister Christina helped Marian don a habit, the young nun brushed the tangles from Marian's hair, plaited it, and then covered it with a long veil. In spite of Marian's request to gain access to the apothecary, Sister Christina silently led her outside. As they shuffled slowly along the yard near the ivy-covered wall, Sister Christina tucked her arm through Marian's to hold her up.

Marian lifted her face to the sun and let the rays warm her skin. After the days inside the unheated room on the cold floor, Marian hadn't thought she'd ever be warm again. But the sunshine was pleasant, its presence as constant in the past as the present.

The scent of cherry blossoms hung in the air, mingling with the sweetness of daffodils and rosebuds growing in abundance along the walls. She breathed deeply, drawing in the fresh air.

Was it already almost June? If she calculated correctly— which was hard to do without the calendar app on her phone— tomorrow would be June 1. So much had happened since she'd left her lab in Connecticut. What must Jasper be thinking now that she was in a coma? Had he flown to Canterbury to be with her?

How was Ellen dealing with everything? By now, she was settled in at Chesterfield Park, maybe even at Marian's bedside at this very moment, gazing at her comatose face. It was strange to think her sister was only an overlap of time away, so close and yet so far.

Had Ellen believed Marian's notes about crossing time, or had she decided Marian was insane? And had the police found Harrison yet? Marian could only pray the investigators had uncovered the culprits and locked them away so Ellen wouldn't have to face any threats.

The other nuns working around the yard appeared occupied with specific tasks, some weeding the herb beds, one tending grapevines, and still another inside a shed-like structure organizing its contents. They worked silently so that only the hum of insects and the occasional trill of a bird filled the enclosed yard.

She and Sister Christina had ambled away from the others. Thankfully, they didn't have the worry of anyone else drawing near and disturbing them, since the other nuns kept their distance from

Marian—likely having no wish to earn the prioress's displeasure for fraternizing with her.

Marian tired much too soon and was relieved when Christina led her to a secluded stone bench and they sat down.

"I can speak a little bit out here." Seated next to her, Christina spoke softly, her head bent. "If we are quiet and careful."

"Are there any ancient wells or springs on the grounds of St. Sepulchre?"

"My lady?" Sister Christina's whisper contained surprise.

Marian supposed she should have started with introductions. But she didn't have any time to waste, not when the whispered conversation wouldn't last long and might only afford her a few precious moments to glean information.

Marian nodded in the direction of the only well on the grounds standing near the convent. "Are there any other old wells? Dried springs? And if so, where would I find them?"

"I do not know. But if you have need of a drink, I can draw from the well—"

"No, I'm seeking an ancient well. The water from it was once bottled and sold to pilgrims."

"Then you are a pilgrim visiting Canterbury?"

"I've heard of the holy water and would like to purchase it—so that it can heal my sister." She wasn't exactly lying. She did want the holy water for Ellen too. But of even greater urgency now was her desire to return home safely.

"Some of your memories have returned?"

Marian gave herself a mental slap. She was supposed to have amnesia. How could she have forgotten? She needed to be more careful lest she alienate her one ally. "I've begun to remember a few things."

"That is good. Praise God." Sister Christina's whisper was laced with such sincerity that Marian sat for a few minutes in silence, fighting her guilt at deceiving this kind woman.

Finally, she forced herself to probe again. "Can you help me find holy water?"

"Yes, it is sold at the cathedral to pilgrims."

"I need holy water from the original well here at St. Sepulchre that was used not long after St. Thomas Becket was murdered."

Sister Christina was silent for a moment. "Do you think the old holy water is blessed more so than the present water?"

"Do pilgrims still report miraculous healings?"

"No." Sister Christina's whisper was barely audible.

"Then I must find the old."

Before Marian could figure out how to convince Sister Christina to help her further, the young nun's head snapped up, and she stared in the direction of the convent gate, listening intently. The other nuns had halted their work to do the same.

In the distance beyond the nunnery came the sounds of shouting and singing.

Sister Christina's fingers tightened around Marian's arm, and she pulled her up from the bench. "Something is amiss. We must hide."

The clamor was growing louder with every passing second.

"Come. Make haste." Sister Christina's command was urgent, and she tugged Marian toward the heavily wooded area behind the raised beds, the same place Marian had gone the first night at the convent when she'd hidden the pouch of money.

With faces reflecting unease, the other nuns raced toward the building, paying no heed to Sister Christina or her.

"What's happening?" Marian stumbled to keep up with Sister Christina, who was now practically running.

Sister Christina didn't answer but plunged into the dense hawthorn, fighting through the spiny twigs, dragging Marian with her. They hadn't gone far before Marian stumbled and bumped her bruised shoulder. She tried to hold in the pain, but somehow a cry escaped.

"I am sorry, lady." Sister Christina squeezed her arm but didn't slow her pace or relent until they were deep in the woods near the wall. Even then, Sister Christina pushed Marian to the ground and began to cover her with brush and sticks, the scent of soil and disintegrating leaves thick in the air around them.

"What are you doing?" Marian was too winded and in too much pain to resist.

"Our habits." Sister Christina gasped for breath. "They stand out too much. We need to disguise ourselves. Blend in."

Sister Christina removed both of their veils and shoved the white cloth beneath a pile of dead leaves. Then she situated herself next to Marian and began to cover herself as well. Marian could see that Sister Christina had taken them to a slight dip in the ground that was framed by a downed tree on one side and a pile of brush on the other.

Once they were hidden and their labored breathing subsided, they lay unmoving. New noises echoed in the air—screaming and crying along with the sounds of breaking, splintering, and crashing. A cold dread settled in the pit of Marian's stomach, and she closed her eyes. More trouble.

She replayed the research she'd conducted on the year 1381. Of course, her internet search had been brief since she'd been in a hurry during her last hours. But from what she'd read, the only major event of 1381 in England had been Wat Tyler's Rebellion, which had eventually become known as the Peasants' Revolt. When she'd skimmed the article, she noted the uprising had happened in mid-June. She'd concluded such an event wouldn't affect her since she'd be gone by the time it occurred.

But at the escalation of the destructive noises outside the convent wall, she squirmed further under the brush surrounding them. What if historians had somehow gotten the dates wrong? What if the Peasants' Revolt had happened earlier?

Sister Christina resituated some of the leaves and brush. "At his last visit, Will warned me of the unrest."

"Then the poor are rebelling?"

"At least causing trouble."

The cold knot in Marian's middle cinched tighter. Perhaps she hadn't done her research on the 1381 rebellion carefully enough. No doubt the problems had been stirring throughout the country in the weeks leading up to the actual revolt.

Whatever the case, things were not looking up for her. In fact, things only seemed to be getting worse.

They hadn't been in their hiding place for long before the sounds of pillaging and looting moved into the nunnery grounds. Smashing and screaming came from inside the convent, and Marian was surprised when Sister Christina's trembling hand slid into hers. Marian shifted enough to see tears streaking the nun's cheeks and her eyes radiating with fear.

Marian had never seen Christina without her head covering and wimple, and the sight of the light brown hair was strange. It was cut short in what could almost be described as a bob, but it was blunt and plain without any of the layering that would help frame Christina's face more fashionably.

Marian squeezed the woman's hand but then froze at the shout that came from the edge of the woods. Loud male voices seemed to be arguing about whether to search the copse.

Please, God, please. Make them go away, Marian silently prayed. While their hiding spot might camouflage them from a distance, anyone walking nearby would surely see their faces and some of the white of their habits still peeking through the brush.

For what seemed an eternity, Marian hardly dared to breathe, until finally the noises seemed to pass away to a new part of the town, leaving an eerie silence in its wake.

"Do you think we're safe?" Marian started to push herself up, but Christina stopped her.

"Will strictly instructed me to hide in the woods until he came for me."

"Who's Will?"

"My brother."

"What if he doesn't come?"

"He will." She said it with such confidence Marian could almost believe Christina's brother to be a superhero of some kind.

"Should we at least go check on the others?"

"We need to obey Will. He knows best."

Marian was too sore and weak to manage on her own and so could do nothing but lie under the brush with Christina, praying that somehow someway she would escape unscathed from this new predicament.

The dip in the ground where they lay was like a shallow bowl, and Marian couldn't keep from speculating what had caused it—perhaps an underground spring? The branches of the ash tree overhead pointed to it like God's finger at the top of the Sistine Chapel. Her dad had always said ash trees were believed to have mythical properties. In fact, legends abounded of sacred ash trees next to life-giving wells.

For a while, she plied Christina with questions about the history of the priory and where old wells might have been located. She attempted to give Christina her theory about the possibility that one of the old wells had healing qualities because of its relation to the Tree of Life. And although Christina listened to her without any scoffing, the young nun was no more knowledgeable about old wellsprings than Marian herself.

Finally, Christina conceded that of all the land within the confines of St. Sepulchre Priory, the spot where they were hiding was the logical place for an old well.

The location would do Marian no good at the moment since she wouldn't be able to excavate it to see if a spring existed. However, she attempted to piece together exactly where it was on St. George's Street in the present. While it was difficult to get her bearings, she overlapped the present layout with the past and suspected the spring was near the modern St. George's clock tower, if not located entirely underneath it.

Through the rest of the afternoon and into the evening, Marian pretended ignorance of her past life and allowed Christina to do most of the sharing. She was relieved Christina didn't lapse into her usual silence but kept up a steady stream of whispered conversation.

She learned Christina was the youngest daughter of a landed knight who had gained favor from Edward the Black Prince for his brave deeds during a major battle with the French that the English had won in large part because of Christina's father. Her grandfather had also been a valiant knight, and the late king had rewarded him for his service by giving him an estate.

Christina admitted she'd rarely seen her father while growing up, but she didn't seem the least disturbed that he'd been gone so frequently—unlike Marian, who'd resented every minute of her dad's absence.

Christina had one older sister who was married and had half a dozen children. She hadn't seen her sister since she was ten, and again didn't seem bothered by the distance or lack of relationship. After losing two other brothers, Christina clearly cherished her remaining brother, Will. Her mother was still alive and resided with Will, who had inherited their father's title and estate. From what Marian gathered, Will had two sons aged eight and six, Christina's nephews whom she rarely saw.

"Did you always want to be a nun?" Marian whispered as darkness began to settle around them, casting shadows that moved with the wind, which whistled and creaked in the trees overhead.

"I had no choice." Christina spoke without a trace of bitterness. "My father was not able to provide a substantial dowry that would allow for a good match for both of his daughters. Therefore, he deemed I should be safe and happy here instead."

"And are you? Safe and happy?" Marian had seen little joy

among the nuns. And certainly they weren't safe—if this current dilemma was any indication.

"Yes, I am content. I could ask for naught more than a life of service and worship to God."

Confinement within the same four walls day after day, wearing clothing identical to everyone else, eating bland food, and hardly ever speaking? Marian almost snorted. How could anyone find contentment in such a life?

At the snap of a nearby twig, Marian's response froze.

Christina's fingers found hers and squeezed a warning to remain silent and motionless. But she couldn't stop herself from lifting her head. There, near the wall a dozen paces away, were two cloaked men, dirks outstretched as they surveyed the woods. Were they peasants searching for nuns?

A new sense of panic swelled within Marian. Maybe women in the Middle Ages were accustomed to lying down and doing whatever they were told without question, but after suffering from the prioress, she wasn't about to let herself be captured.

Marian bent near Christina's ear. "We need to sneak away. Now."

~ 14 ~

"HUSH," CHRISTINA HISSED.

The cloaked figures parted ways, each branching deeper into the woods, their steps soundless as they wound through brush.

Marian searched for any other intruders but saw no one else. "If we make it to the gate, then we'll slip into town and find a new place to hide."

When one of the cloaked figures halted and shifted his head their direction, Christina clamped a hand over Marian's mouth. The man tossed back his hood but made no other move.

Christina's hand immediately fell away, and she sat straight up, letting the brush scatter around her. "Will." The relief in her whisper was so encompassing that Marian felt it all the way to her aching bones.

The man veered toward them until he reached Christina. He dropped to one knee beside her and drew her into a tight embrace. "Thank the saints."

He held her for a long moment before pulling back and examining her. "Are you unharmed?"

"Yes. I took shelter in the woods, just as you instructed." Christina turned to Marian and tugged her up. "I have Lady Marian with me."

Will shifted, and only then did Marian see his face—the broad cheeks, square jaw, strong nose. And the eyes. Those piercing, sorrow-filled eyes. Darkness prevented her from seeing the blue. But she knew they were as bright blue as a dusk sky. He was the man she'd seen in her visions. And he was also the same man who'd rescued her from the last beating.

"It's you." She was unable to control the amazement in her voice.

He searched her face before scanning her arms, neck, and torso—as though he was making sure she wasn't hurt.

The other cloaked figure was now making his way toward them. Christina glanced at him but then apparently recognized and dismissed him at the same time. Instead, she rose to her knees and assisted Marian to hers.

All the while, Marian couldn't take her eyes from Will, from his ruggedly handsome features, the unshaven stubble, his dark hair tied back at his neck, and his fierce expression which made him look every bit like a warrior.

Did he recall seeing her when she'd traveled briefly to the past before? She wanted to ask him, to discover what he'd experienced on his side of the time-space continuum. But she sensed she might put herself in danger if she admitted to having met him previously. What if they decided she was a heretic and burned her at the stake?

For now, it was best to leave her ties with the future unmentioned, along with her prior time crossings.

"Lady Marian, this is my brother, Sir William Durham." Christina waved at her brother. "Sir William, may I present Lady Marian Creighton."

Will hadn't taken his intense gaze from her, and she felt the heat of it seep down into her chest. "How do you fare, lady?"

"I'm doing better, thanks to your rescue from another beating."

He bowed his head slightly in acknowledgment of her gratitude.

"Then the prioress has respected my command to cause you no further ill?"

"She has." Christina's adoration for her brother was unmistakable in her voice and expression. "They all fear you, Brother."

"Good."

"We durst be on our way, sire." The other cloaked man was peering around the dark woods. Under the shadow of his hood, his face was ruddy and coarse. His hair was all one length and clipped in a rounded fashion, his bangs falling flat across his forehead.

Will stood and assisted Christina to her feet before reaching for Marian's arm. She attempted to push herself up, but her aching body and stiff joints wouldn't cooperate, and she found herself having to rely upon his strength more than she wanted.

She couldn't keep from admiring the power of his build, the thickness of his arms, the rippling muscles in his shoulders, his physique and manliness that were entirely different from any guy she'd ever known.

"You are still weak." His tone was hard, unrelenting. Yet it reverberated through her, stirring her awareness of him even more.

"I'm fine." But once she was standing, her knees could barely hold her, and to her chagrin, she began to crumple back to the ground.

Before she could protest, she found herself being swept up into his arms. His broad chest enveloped her, and it took a second for her to identify the tightly bound rings of metal as chainmail beneath his cloak.

The warmth of his breath brushed her forehead, and his arm pressed underneath her leg and against her backside. She didn't consider herself to be a prude. But somehow his hold felt too bold.

"You don't need to carry me." She wiggled to free herself from his grasp. But the motion made her more aware of his arm positioned so intimately. "I can walk on my own."

He'd already begun to stalk toward the gate. "If you wish to make it out of Canterbury unmolested, I advise your cooperation."

"I cannot leave the convent, Will." Christina's loud whisper trailed them.

"Only until the rebels move on."

"What has become of my sisters?"

Will shook his head, and in the shadows of the deepening night, Marian caught sight of the sharp anger lining his face, an anger that made her heart flip in dread. Had some of the women been killed? Raped? Taken as hostages?

As though sensing what Will's silence meant, Christina's voice trembled when she next spoke. "Can we not bring them to safety as well?"

"Those who remain have locked themselves in the cellar." Will lifted the bar across the back gate and opened the door cautiously.

Christina didn't speak again.

As they moved out of the convent grounds, part of Marian wanted to stay at the nunnery. Now would be the perfect time to search for ampullae while everyone was scared and hiding away. But the other part of her cautioned against remaining. She'd already made the mistake of underestimating the danger of the Middle Ages, and she couldn't do so again. She would need to come back and resume her search once the rebels had moved on.

With a deathly silent tread, Will carried her down a grassy path that led to what appeared to be a main road. Upon reaching the street—which she assumed to be St. George's—she gaped at the sight that met her. To her right was the old city wall—except it wasn't old anymore. It towered high above the ground. The stones were neatly chiseled, and the crenellations rose to their full height. In place of the modern-day roundabout stood a city gate, St. George's Gate, with imposing castle-like turrets on either side of a gatehouse. Even in the fading light, she could see the entire structure was truly magnificent.

A horse with its rider passed through the gate and galloped down a dirt road into what appeared to be open country. Trees, rocks, and rolling hills sprawled out where the cinema and supermarket should have been.

To the left, the town of Canterbury nestled within the walls. With its tall, tottering homes crowded together on cobbled streets, it was unrecognizable from what it had become in her lifetime. Without street lamps, car headlights, traffic signals, or even the neon lights that emanated from business signs, the town was strangely dark.

Chills skittered up her arms. Only a tablespoon of holy water was all that was standing in the way of her experiencing an entirely different world—a world of electric lights, fast-moving vehicles, modern brick buildings.

The street in front of them was deserted and littered with debris, smashed furniture, ripped bedding, overturned food bins. The front door and main gate of St. Sepulchre both hung wide open, the windows of the chapel were cracked and broken, and what appeared to be sacred relics and other holy items were strewn all around.

The need to explore and find holy water pulsed harder at the sight of the Canterbury Cathedral spirals rising into the pink and orange splashes of clouds in the darkening sky. But before she could make up her mind on whether to stay, Will was already striding toward a narrow side alley, moving off the street into the shadows.

The stench of human waste and rotting garbage assaulted her, and she pressed her face against Will's cloak. The scratchy wool brushed her nose and his scruffy chin grazed her forehead. Although his garment had the scent of wind and smoke, it was a far cry better than the alley.

From the shadows came a soft snorting breath, and Marian made out two horses. The only time she'd ever been on a horse had been at camp when she'd been a young girl. Riding around a paddock on the back of a gentle mare had done nothing to prepare her for the kind of swift horsemanship she would need tonight.

"We must be off at once." Will spoke to his cloaked companion. "Thad, you take Christina out Dover Road. And I shall ride with Lady Marian out Rheims Way."

At the mention of the familiar road that led to Chesterfield Park, Marian guessed that's where Will was taking them. Of course, his living in the manor made perfect sense in light of previously seeing him there. Even if Harrison's house wasn't where she needed to be to complete her mission, at least it would be familiar.

"Sire, I'm reluctant to split ways." Thad reached for the reins of one of the horses. "Would we not be safer together? If trouble assails us, I could speak up for you."

Will shook his head curtly. "We shall only attract attention more readily together."

"They will have compassion on me, as I am one of them. But you? They thirst for the blood of the nobility. If they catch you, they'll have no mercy this night."

"We go our separate ways." Will's voice was low and bode no further argument.

His companion nodded and bowed slightly to Will. "Ready, Sister?" He offered Christina his cupped hands as a step to the stirrup.

Even in her cumbersome habit, Christina had no trouble mounting and was situated in the saddle before Marian could manage to figure out how it was done.

"Go," Will whispered harshly. "And Godspeed."

Thad swung up behind Christina, and in an instant, they were gone, the pounding of hooves fading away to silence.

"Ready, lady?" Will's voice rumbled near her cheek.

"Yes, but I should warn you that I'm not—" Before she could finish, he thrust her up onto the saddle, a stiff leather seat that was wide and difficult to straddle in her habit. The white linen crept high, exposing her legs, exactly why most women had ridden sidesaddle. She started to adjust herself, but suddenly Will was behind her, and she had no room to move with both of them squeezed together.

His thighs hugged her tightly, and at the intimate contact heat flooded her cheeks. He reached past her to grip the reins, his presence boxing her in and overpowering her.

Should she slip down? But where would she go? She had no one else she could rely on.

No, this was her best option. Although she felt the brush of his chest behind her, she sat stiffly and was grateful when he held himself as aloof as the quarters would allow . . .

Until he urged his horse forward. The jostling nearly knocked Marian from her perch, and she fumbled to grab on to the pommel. He easily caught her, wrapping one of his hands around her waist and guiding the reins with the other. The firmness of his hold told her he had no intention of letting go.

So much for maintaining personal space. She didn't want to be so aware of the pressure of his arm against her side and stomach, but her senses were keenly alert to everything in this strange time period—particularly to everything about him.

Once past the city gate, she again gazed at the countryside with wonder. Even in the descending darkness, lit by a glorious array of stars overhead, the barrenness of the rolling land spread out for miles. Gone were the businesses, homes, roads, and the sprawling urban development. It was silent and empty in an almost apocalyptic way.

A breeze blew against her, the chill welcome against her heated skin. The pounding of the horse hooves echoed loudly. If they were at risk, why didn't he urge his horse to a softer and quieter tread? And why take the open road? Why not try to ride cross-country where they wouldn't be seen or stopped by peasants who thirsted for their blood?

At the remembrance of the cries and screams from the afternoon, she shuddered at the prospect of facing any peasants, blood-thirsty or not. Will brought his cloak forward, draping it around her, likely thinking her shudder was from cold and not realizing it was from fear.

She lifted her chin. She had to be brave. After all, she was a smart and self-sufficient woman. She would survive and get home. Somehow.

Each bump of the horse jarred her aching body and reminded her of how Will had saved her from further punishment at the hands of the nuns. She wanted to speak to him, but now that she was with him again, she felt strangely shy. Was it because of their proximity? Or because he was more handsome than she remembered?

For heaven's sake. She wasn't an awkward teenager trying to gather up the courage to speak to a boy. She was a grown woman and accustomed to talking with men all the time. She could certainly manage a conversation tonight. "I didn't have the chance to thank you for saving me the other day."

For a moment, he didn't reply, and she wondered if he'd failed to hear her above the clopping of the horse. "The prioress wields her power too freely." His voice was low near her ear again, and the deepness of it wound through her blood.

As with her visions of him, something about him pulled her in. Not only was he entirely too attractive physically, but she wanted to know more about him. "How is it that once you freed me, the prioress no longer tormented me?"

He didn't answer.

Christina hadn't spoken of what Will had said or done to the prioress, but his efforts had protected her. "Apparently, you also wield your power freely?"

She meant for her question to tease, but his body turned rigid around her. "I would that my power be used for good and not evil." His tone was brittle. "Was I mistaken to assume your punishment was undeserving?"

"No. The prioress had no right to my money. I only took back what was mine in the first place."

"It was not meant for your dowry?"

"Not to St. Sepulchre. My jewels and money are my own." Although she doubted she'd ever see them again.

At the eerie quietness of the countryside, a strange foreboding began to churn within her. Who knew what lurked in the shadows, behind the boulders, or in the patches of shrubs and trees they passed?

"If your kin did not give you over to the priory"—his voice less menacing, more curious—"then perhaps they wished to wed you to a man you could not abide?"

She shook her head. She didn't want to deceive Will, yet what could she say that wouldn't make her seem utterly crazy? For now, she needed to keep the pretense of amnesia. "I wish I knew what happened after I was separated from my traveling companions, but my mind is blank."

Once she spoke the lie, she loathed herself for it but figured it wouldn't matter too much since she intended to leave just as soon as the opportunity arose and would never see him again.

"Mayhap you have a husband and children waiting for you somewhere." His tone took on an edge again, and she knew he hadn't believed her.

"I remember a few things." She attempted to keep her voice steady and confident. "And I know I've never been married."

"At your age?"

"I'm not that old." She supposed for the Middle Ages, twenty-eight meant she practically had one foot in the grave.

"A widow?"

"No. I've told you, I've never been married."

"Then you must be escaping from a betrothal to someone you do not wish to marry." His statement came out an accusation.

"And if I am, perhaps it's for the best." Before he could pry further, she decided to change the topic. "What demons are you trying to escape?"

"Lady?" Surprise tinged his voice.

"I imagine you're running away from something that happened in your past?" When he stiffened, she realized she'd landed upon the truth and suspected his wounds went deep. "You've been hurt by someone or something, haven't you?"

Several heartbeats passed before he responded in the low tone that told her he was angry. "You speak too boldly, lady. Let us ride in silence."

• • •

Through the darkness, Will surveyed the surrounding area, noting every stray cat, every overturned stone, and every moving shadow. Although they were almost past the Canterbury town walls, he remained vigilant. The circuitous route he'd chosen had taken them away from the city, away from rebels who might be camped outside the town gates. Even so, he wouldn't rest until they were back within the confines of Chesterfield Park.

The anger within his breast swelled again as it had earlier when he'd first received news of the attack against Canterbury, specifically against the cathedral and abbeys. All the ride into town, he'd mentally lashed himself for leaving Christina and Lady Marian there, could only picture them the way he'd found Thomas.

He'd wanted to crush something—or someone—and was glad he hadn't encountered any rebels on the trip to the priory, or he would have taken out his rage upon them.

Even now, remnants of the terror still pumped through his blood. Thank the Father in heaven, Christina always obeyed him and had acted quickly to hide in the woods, taking Lady Marian along as he'd bidden her.

His stallion caught a dip in the road, jarring them. Lady Marian released a stilted whimper, and he suspected she was attempting to disguise her pain, that the ride was much more difficult on her battered body than she was allowing.

He eased the reins, trying to gentle the pace.

From the moment he'd seen her in the woods with Christina, his pulse hadn't stopped its strange rhythm. Even now, his body betrayed him with the whisper of desire whenever he considered how close she was and how beautiful.

On the other hand, her bold way of conversing vexed him. She was much too forthright. Maybe she wasn't running away from an unpleasant betrothal as he suspected. Maybe her intended had sent her away for unleashing her tongue too oft.

"I'm sorry." The sound of her voice startled him. "I shouldn't have asked you about your past."

He'd expected her to remain silent, to follow his command, or at the very least to be intimidated by it. But his stern mannerisms obviously failed to frighten her.

"Perhaps we can both agree to let the past remain in the past. After all, it has no bearing on our current predicament." Her back inadvertently brushed against his chest.

He could sense she was losing the strength and stamina to maintain a semblance of distance from him. As a lady, of course she was concerned about propriety, but with her wounds, he ought to give her leave to recline and assure her she had nothing to fear from him, that he was a man of honor.

"Let's start again," she said before he could speak. "I'll only ask you questions about your present, like how old are you? What you do for a living? Those kinds of things."

Another jostle of the horse sent her against his chest altogether, and this time she didn't attempt to reposition herself and instead relaxed lightly against him.

The pressure was a form of torturous pleasure.

Strands of her hair had come loose from the simple plait she wore down her back. The silky threads brushed his cheek. Ere he could stop himself, he leaned his nose into her head and breathed in her scent. He caught the faint whiff of something sweet, almost fruity.

He couldn't deny this woman of his dreams fascinated him even more so now that she was real. And he was relieved all over again that she'd been with Christina during the attack on the priory.

"So how old are you?"

He shifted so that his nose now touched her ear. "You will not do as I bid and stay silent?" His whisper surprised him by coming out more teasing than menacing. His reaction would have embarrassed him except she responded with a rapid intake of breath that stirred the desire already coursing through his blood.

"It would be more fun to pester you with questions." Her answer was low and breathy.

He moved his mouth to her ear. "Nine and twenty."

She drew in another sharp breath but didn't move. Instead, she leaned in almost imperceptibly, enough for him to sense he affected her as much as she did him.

A grin twitched at the corners of his lips. But then, just as suddenly, he scowled. He hadn't smiled in over two years and didn't deserve a moment's happiness. Not after what he'd allowed to happen to Thomas.

He lifted his head and scanned the road ahead as well as each passing landmark.

"So you're twenty-nine. What do you do for a living?"

"A living?"

"Your occupation."

He still wasn't exactly sure what she meant. "Surely, you must know I am not a bondman or laborer. I am well-born." His sister would not be in the priory if she were not a noblewoman. At the moment, he would not be afraid for her life nor would he fear for his family's safety if he were but a simple yeoman, husbandman, or even tradesman.

"And what exactly does a *well-born* man do all day?"

Did he detect sarcasm in her tone? He bristled. Did she think he was pompous and lazy? "I am a knight, and I serve the king. In the past ten years of war, I have only been home five times."

She was quiet, as though pondering his words.

His mind flashed with images from his life, the years he'd spent in France on one military campaign after another. The young boy of nineteen had left full of enthusiasm and energy and optimism. He'd wanted to be like his father—brave and strong and dedicated.

After a decade of fighting, he'd proven himself to be just as brave and strong. But dedicated? To what cause? The doubt had surfaced more and more over the past year even though he'd fought against it.

"That must have been difficult to be away from home for so long." Lady Marian spoke so softly he almost didn't hear her.

Had it been difficult? Maybe at times, especially when he'd come home to gather the ransom and had to leave Thomas behind in a French dungeon. But he supposed he'd borne his duties the same as any other man—with honor and pride and determination.

"Do you have to go away and fight in France again?"

"Yes." He didn't know when the young king, at the beckoning of his ambitious uncle John of Gaunt, would commence another campaign in France. After the failure of the siege of Nantes earlier in the year, King Richard was eager to prove himself and protect Calais in the ongoing battle to retain ancestral land in France.

"How long until you leave?"

"I cannot say for certain, but 'twill not be overlong now." He'd already been home for two months, the longest reprieve he'd had.

"Your sons must miss you whenever you go."

He wasn't sure how she knew about his sons but reasoned Christina must have gossiped about him. "My sons are strong and brave. Erelong, they will be fostered out and trained to be knights. Though I have already provided them with tutors and a swordsmaster."

For several moments, she said naught more. Had he spoken something offensive? He considered himself to be a decent father. Some fellow knights treated their sons harshly, thought doing so would train them to be tough. But Will had always believed respect and kindness went much further in developing character.

"I can see you are a good man." She gently pressed his arm.

The words and touch had a strange effect on him, comforting and warming him in the same moment. Just as her touch had affected him in his dream.

She leaned her head back against his shoulder as if that was the most natural thing in the world for her to do, as though she already trusted him.

For a short while, she asked him questions about the bondmen and the growing conflict and what might happen next now that they'd attacked Canterbury. He was surprised at her insights and interest, and did his best to answer her forthrightly, growing more fascinated by her with every passing moment.

Although he'd remained occupied with other matters over the preceding days, unbidden thoughts of her had crept into his conscience, especially at night in his chamber. Now that he was with her again, he had the desire to wrap both arms around her and to envelop her with his body, soul, and strength.

Normally, he had a self-control that was as hard as his metal plate. But he was weak with the swift longing to know her more, to taste of her sweetness, to breathe in her scent. The wanting scared him with its intensity, so unlike anything he'd ever felt for Alice.

He tightened his grip on the reins and held himself back.

"I can't thank you enough for coming tonight. I don't know what I would have done without both you and Christina." She had an unusual way of speaking. She was English, but had she grown up in a foreign country?

"Your accent. You are from the Low Countries, are you not?"

"I guess you could say that."

"And your kin?"

She didn't respond for a minute. He could sense her inner struggle with what to reveal to him and how much she could trust him.

He was the one prying now when she'd asked to leave the past behind them. He cleared his throat, needing to reassure her that she was under no obligation to speak about anything too painful. After all, he hadn't.

But she spoke first, her tone edged with sorrow. "I'm on my own now."

His arm rested lightly across her middle to keep her from bouncing too needlessly. Thus far, he'd kept his hand balled into a fist to avoid touching her improperly. But now he uncurled his fingers and positioned them at her hip, relishing the curve. He closed his eyes for just a second to ward off the shower of desire that rained through him at the contact.

Saints help him. He'd gone much too long without a wife to desire this woman so powerfully.

He fisted his hand again and chided himself. The matter was settled. He would take a wife before he left for France. He would give his mother leave to make arrangements for him as she wanted.

The short hairs at the base of his neck stood, warning him of danger. Ere he could reach his sword or dirk, several ruffians appeared from out of nowhere. His stallion reared with fright.

Although he fumbled frantically to stay atop his mount, he'd been too preoccupied with Lady Marian and hadn't maintained a solid grip on the reins. As he fell backward, all he could think was that he'd do anything to keep Lady Marian safe.

~15~

AMIDST SHOUTS OF MEN and the frightened squeals of the horse, Marian found herself slipping off. Somehow Will managed to hold her, and as they made impact with the ground, he braced her fall. Even so, the hard jolt wrenched the breath from her lungs and sent pain through her already sore body.

What was happening? Were they being attacked?

A boot connected with her ribs. "What do we have here?"

In an instant, Will stabbed his dirk, and her attacker's agonized scream rent the air. Through the darkness, Marian tried to make sense of exactly what Will had just done. When she righted herself, she glimpsed the handle of his dirk buried deep into the peasant's boot, pinning his foot to the ground.

Her stomach lurched with queasiness, and she pressed a hand to her mouth. Although she'd known Will was a seasoned knight, the reality of who he was hit her. He was a trained warrior accustomed to killing others—who, in fact, made a regular job out of it.

Will sprang to his feet and planted himself in front of her, legs spread, his sword unsheathed. "If anyone touches the lady again, you will die."

From what she surmised, at least a dozen men surrounded them. Without torches, they were shrouded by the night. But she could still make out their simple garb and rough features, along with crude weapons—hoes, axes, knives, and other sharp objects.

Dread trickled through her at the possibility they might be the same peasants who'd attacked the convent. Even with his sword, how would Will be able to fight them all?

His broad back faced her, his cloak tossed aside revealing chainmail. She wished she had a knife and could stand next to him, but she doubted she'd be able to do anything other than get in his way. Even so, she unraveled her tangled habit and stood, ignoring the new aches that shot through her body.

"I am Sir William Durham." Menace radiated from his body and tone, making him a formidable foe. From the exclamations and whispered oaths, the peasants clearly knew Will's name as well as his reputation. "I mean you no ill will. Let me pass."

The man with the dirk in his foot groaned, but no one came to his aid. While Marian didn't want the man to suffer needlessly, she hoped the inaction meant the others were sufficiently afraid of Will and would do as he commanded.

"Whose side are you on?" One of the peasants stepped forward, a gray-bearded man wielding a two-pronged haymaking fork. "Ours or theirs?"

Before Will could answer, horse hooves pounded behind them. A moment later a rider reined in on the outskirts of the circle of peasants. "Hold your weapons!"

In the faint starlight, Marian recognized Will's companion from earlier. Thad. But he was alone now, without Christina. As if noticing the same, Will visibly tensed.

"Sir William Durham is my master." Thad's voice rang out. He'd thrown back his hood, revealing a humble but earnest expression. "I've pledged him my fealty. He is fair and honest and kind, not only to me, but to all his vassals."

Another murmuring arose.

"He's renowned for his feats of valor in battle." Thad spoke hastily, clearly attempting to sway the group before hostility broke out. "We would do well to have a friend in this strong warrior rather than a foe."

Marian moved out of Will's shadow to his side. His raised sword remained unswerving, ready to cleave anyone in half if they made the wrong move. From their frozen stances, they must have realized that too.

"If he is on our side," called a younger man with a bold white scar running the length of his face, "then why is he helping a nun?"

For a heartbeat, Thad didn't answer. And suddenly Marian was relieved Will's servant had the foresight to leave Christina behind.

"She is my betrothed." Will broke the silence. His jaw flexed, and Marian marveled that he could state a bold-faced lie so calmly.

"A nun, your betrothed?" The same man released a guffaw.

"I'm not a nun." Marian stepped forward, deciding if Will could act, she could add authenticity to his fabrication. Out of the corner of her eye, she could see him shake his head curtly, as though cautioning her to stay silent. But she pretended not to notice him. "I was staying at St. Sepulchre Priory until our wedding could be arranged."

At her pronouncement, the men eyed her with suspicion and grumbled to each other.

Apparently she needed to be more convincing. She drew in a fortifying breath and spoke again. "Since Sir William expects to leave for France any day, we hope to be married as soon as possible. So if you will let us be on our way, we would appreciate it."

The volume among the peasants escalated. Thad exchanged a look with Will, a grave one that said the two would fight their way free if need be.

What had she said wrong? A shiver raced up her spine.

"If 'tis a wedding you want," shouted the older man with the hay fork, "then we durst give you one."

The others rumbled their agreement, and within seconds, their voices turned boisterous—a new sense of excitement inciting them.

This wasn't going well. In fact, it was going from bad to worse. She tried to catch Will's eye, nodding at him to say something—anything—to make things right. But he wasn't looking at her, was instead exchanging terse words with Thad.

"Father John's up the road." The proclamation echoed in the night air. "Methinks he can perform the wedding!"

The men cheered at the suggestion.

"No!" Her protest resounded above the commotion. As the men quieted and stared at her again, her mind raced to find an excuse. "It's just that we want to be married in the presence of family—and—and in a chapel."

"Are you saying we're not your family, milady?" The question was drenched with spite from a man on the perimeter of the crowd. "That we're not good enough to be witnessing your vows?"

Before she could think of a way to get herself out of this new dilemma, Will spoke. "Do not heed her words. She is only a woman and knows not what she says."

Irritation rolled in to replace her panic. Although she didn't know him well, he hadn't struck her as being chauvinistic. Was she wrong?

As though sensing her ire, he grasped her arm and guided her so that she was out of sight behind him. "I welcome you to witness our exchange of vows. All of you. But once I have wed the woman, I shall take her home to bed straightaway."

The peasants burst into raucous laughter and lewd jesting.

With a fresh burst of exasperation, Marian jerked to free herself from his grip. His gentle squeeze stopped her. Was that a signal he was only playacting? She surely hoped so. Whatever the case, she knew he was asking her to cooperate if they hoped to leave this group peacefully.

Amidst more laughter, the men lowered their weapons, their animosity dispelling as they started down the road.

Will retrieved his dirk from the foot of the peasant who'd kicked her. After sheathing his weapons, Will turned to her and encircled her waist. As he lifted her toward the saddle, he leaned in, his body brushing hers. "This is the safest course."

His nearness, the hard length of him, the strength of his hold—everything about him made her weak so that she could only nod, somehow rendered mute. Then he gently deposited her in the saddle sideways. He didn't join her atop the horse, but instead led the magnificent creature by the reins as he followed the peasants, their voices raised in song and laughter.

Leading his horse too, Thad walked alongside Will. Every now and then, they exchanged terse words, as if arguing. But Marian couldn't hear anything above the ruckus the peasants were making.

After walking a short distance, they came upon what appeared to be an encampment of peasants not far from Canterbury's city walls. Several large fires crackled and spewed flames and sparks high in the air. Men loitered around them, the loot from their raids strewn in piles and spilling from bags. Food, wine, garments, belts, blankets.

The men were eating and drinking in celebration. The waft of roasting meat mingled with the heavy, almost stinging, aroma of smoke. By the light of the fire, Marian was able to distinguish the clothing—the long hose that hugged their legs, the tunics that fell to below their thighs, and the strange variety of hats including one that resembled a hood with a long dangling tail.

A few women mingled about, tending large pots or turning spits. Most appeared older and haggard, as worn as the frayed tunics and cloaks they wore.

Everything fascinated Marian and yet sent trepidation through her at the same time. The sights, sounds, and scents told her this was real, that she wasn't simply dreaming this in her coma-induced state.

She remained on Will's horse as he stalked off with his purposeful stride. Thad held the reins of both horses, and she wanted to ask him where Christina was. But she prayed that soon enough they'd be on their way, and she'd be reunited with the young nun. Just as soon as Will managed to find a way to convince these peasants that a wedding wouldn't be necessary . . .

As she waited, her backside grew stiff, and she shivered in the dropping temperatures. She hugged her arms over the habit and shift underneath. What she wouldn't give for the smooth leather seats and heated interior of the Bentley. And the speed. Even if Bojing's driving had been crazy, at least he'd been able to whisk them away from danger.

After speaking at length with a different group of peasants, Will returned, his expression unreadable—except for the ever-present tension and determination. He spoke again to Thad in low tones before looking up at her. "My lady." In the flickering glow from the flames, she could see that his gaze was somber and yet resigned.

"Are we ready to be on our way?"

He shook his head and reached for her, his hands spanning her waist, gentle and strong at the same time. "We are to be wed now."

"You're joking." The words came out louder than she intended.

He situated her on the ground.

"I thought we were pretending." She stepped away from his steadying hold but bumped into the horse. "I didn't think you were serious about going through with the charade."

With one long step forward, he ate up the space between them, so that she found herself boxed in by his towering frame on one side and warm horseflesh on the other. "I see no reason to deny them what they want."

"I do." She almost shouted, but at the warning mirrored in his dark eyes, she swallowed her frustration and forced herself to think rationally and speak calmly. She must have misunderstood him. He couldn't possibly think they should get married. It was too preposterous to even consider. "We can't get married."

"We can and shall." His statement was confident as though the decision was a foregone conclusion. "Since you are on your own and cannot return to your kin or St. Sepulchre's, I shall avail you with my protection. As my wife."

Speechless, she stared up at his darkly handsome face, the thin scar above his eyebrow lending him a formidable aura. Since she'd hinted she was running away from a bad betrothal, she couldn't contradict herself now. Besides, she had no money, nowhere to go, and no one else she could turn to. This strange suggestion of marriage might be her only means of survival. If she turned him down and walked away, she had no idea how she'd make it through the night. In fact, with these bands of peasants roaming the countryside carrying a vendetta against the nobility and clergy, she dreaded to think what might happen if she ventured out on her own. As much as she wanted to hang on to her independence, she felt trapped.

Will lifted a hand to her face and combed back a strand of her hair, surprising her with his gentleness. "I shall not force you into a union."

His fingertips were coarse against her temple, but his touch was infinitely soft. "We're strangers."

"No more or less than any other woman I might consider taking as my wife."

They truly were from different worlds. This was an era when love and romance weren't always considered important in making marriage matches.

"I don't understand." She fumbled for a response. "Why would you want to marry me? What benefit do you receive?"

He dropped his attention to his boots as though to hide his embarrassment. "It is past time for me to take another wife."

"Why not some other lady? Surely you can find someone more suitable."

"There are others."

She suspected his other prospects had to do with dowries and land and how each family could benefit from the marriage. She had nothing to offer him. And besides, she was going home just as soon as she could manage it. "You must choose someone else."

His gaze shot up and met hers. The connection was instantaneous and powerful, one that never failed to magnetically pull her in. "I would have you." His voice was low, and something in it blazed a trail through her belly.

"Why me?" Did he remember her from the visions? Did he recognize her and feel as though they already had a bond too? She drew in a breath and waited for his answer.

She expected some kind of explanation, some statement of her attributes, or at the very least that he had no reason. But he said nothing. Instead, his hand snaked to her back at the same time that he swooped down. His mouth caught hers. Not gently or sweetly or carefully. No, his lips were sure and strong and commanding, sweeping her up and squeezing the air from her lungs.

The urging pressure of his mouth against hers seemed to awaken her to a deep and consuming hunger of her own. She found herself pressed tightly to him. Within seconds, she could think of nothing but her desire for this man, the desire to know more about him, spend time with him, and go on kissing him.

He broke away, abruptly releasing her and taking a step back. "That is why."

Her breath came rushing back much too quickly. Her knees trembled, and she was glad for the long robe that hid her reaction.

"You cannot deny you feel likewise, lady."

She couldn't deny it even if she'd wanted to. Her lungs wouldn't cooperate, and her mind was too scrambled with desire and confusion.

When he held out the crook of his arm toward her, she clasped her hands together. This was his proposal of marriage. If she denied it, she suspected he was too honorable to offer again. But how could she possibly accept? It was ludicrous to contemplate getting married after less than a week in the past when she'd lived for twenty-eight years in the present and had never considered it.

Now, here she was. Weak-kneed from a kiss with a man she barely knew. She couldn't deny the chemistry. He'd made clear he'd felt it keenly too.

But physical attraction wasn't enough of a basis for marriage.

"I vow to be a good husband to you, Marian." He spoke sincerely, as though sensing her question. His eyes were filled with the same kindness she'd noticed before.

When she'd been beaten, he'd shown compassion toward her. His instructions to the prioress had kept her safe at the nunnery. He'd helped her escape from the convent when doing so had put him in great danger. He'd protected her from the peasants who'd attacked them. And he'd vowed to kill on her behalf.

From what she'd witnessed of him so far, she guessed he'd make some woman a good husband—a woman from the Middle Ages, not her.

Yet, what if marriage to this wealthy nobleman was an answer to her problems? Did she dare go through with so audacious a plan? She would not only have his protection, but she'd have his money and his resources. She could ride back to Canterbury whenever she wanted, visit the nunnery or the cathedral without sneaking around. Such trips would surely be within her rights as a nobleman's wife.

What did she have to lose? After all, if she had her way, she'd find holy water as soon as tomorrow and be gone within a day or two. At the very least the marriage would get them out of their current predicament without putting them into more danger.

The thoughts whizzed through her head in the span of a few seconds. Before she could talk herself out of marrying William Durham, she slipped her hand into the curve of his arm.

He didn't move except to glance at her fingers tucked there before looking back at her face. "You are certain, lady?"

She swallowed the rational protest that threatened to choke her and lifted her chin. "Shall we?"

• ● •

Kneeling beside Marian in the grassy field, Will could feel her fingers tremble against his, betraying her uncertainty, although throughout the short ceremony, she'd remained outwardly composed.

John Ball, the priest, stood above them and was almost done reciting the last of the prayers that would officially unite them as man and wife.

Thad had warned Will not to go through with the wedding, had claimed he was being rash. His manservant had implored him to do things aright—post the banns, wait the customary period, and have a loyal priest of the Church marry them, not one who preached and prayed in the common tongue rather than Latin.

In hushed tones during the walk to the peasant camp, they'd discussed the possibility of fighting their way free—if need be. But Will hadn't wanted any bloodshed this night. Not so close to his doorstep. Not when doing so would make him an enemy to these rebels and put his kin and home at greater risk than they already were, especially when he'd leave for France erelong.

He would appease them with this simple act. 'Twas not much. And if Marian was running away from an arrangement to a man she didn't want, perhaps someone cruel, then he'd prove to her she'd chosen aright with him.

Will had no doubt she would have survived a cruel match—she

had an inner fortitude that could not be easily broken. Yet, she was too kind to be matched with a harsh man.

Not only had he noticed Marian's kind spirit, but he liked her quick wit and their ability to talk so easily. He'd never been smooth-tongued, especially with Alice. Their brief times together had been filled mostly with silence. He blamed himself for not taking more interest in her and putting her at ease. Perhaps with a more forthright woman, he would do better this time.

The firelight flickered over Marian's face, highlighting her elegance and grace and beauty. She was exquisite. Her auburn hair was stunning, especially in contrast to her pale skin. Her brown eyes had the power to captivate him, make him forget about himself and his nightmares, even if just for an instant.

He could admit he'd been attracted to Marian from the first time he'd seen her—even before, when he'd imagined her in his dreams, felt her touch, and experienced a strange peace within her presence. But now after kissing her, the delectable taste of her had seeped into his blood, and he didn't know how he'd remove that taste without draining himself completely.

Maybe his first declaration about their betrothal had been an excuse to protect her. But once he'd offered the suggestion, he knew it was exactly what he wanted. He wanted this woman of his dreams to be his. And why tarry? Why give his mother opportunity to object? Why give Lord Percy cause to interfere?

Once he was wed to Marian, there would be naught anyone could do to change it. After all, he had an army of yeomen and freemen as witnesses to the marriage.

Will didn't have to look at the men gathered around to know most were grinning like drunken fools. They relished the chance to see a nobleman taking his wedding vows. They would talk of this night for years to come.

As John Ball made his final proclamation, Will rose and assisted Marian to her feet. From the slowness of her movement, he could tell she still nursed wounds. Nevertheless, as she stood to her full height, which only came to his shoulders, she held herself regally.

"You must stay and celebrate with us." Ball smiled widely, revealing the jagged gaps where teeth had been knocked out—likely in beatings he'd endured during his arrests. Even if Will didn't agree with Ball's methods and preaching, he wouldn't begrudge the man sympathy for the hardships he'd endured.

Ball was skeletal and his skin an almost yellowish color. His time in prison had wasted him away, but his expression exuded hope and determination. 'Twas easy to see why the rebels flocked to him.

"My deepest gratitude. But I must hasten away with my bride." At the chorus of protest, Will added, "To my marriage bed."

The ensuing roar of cheers was exactly what he'd expected. The proclamation, as before, made Marian squirm with discomfort and brought a spark of indignation to her eyes. But Will wasn't embarrassed in the least. He relished the prospect of the coming night with her. Even so, he hoped she understood he'd had no choice but to speak the words. If the onlookers believed he was in a hurry to bed his wife, they would easily forgive him and release him to be on his way.

Amidst vulgar well-wishes, Will hoisted Marian onto his stallion and mounted behind her. This time, when he wrapped his arm around her middle, he didn't hesitate to rest his hand on her hip. She was his now in the sight of both God and man. He had every right to touch her. Although she didn't resist, she held herself stiffly again, as she had when they'd first started the journey.

Once they were out of sight of both the city and camp, Will kicked his mount into a gallop, and Thad did likewise, except his manservant circled off to backtrack and retrieve Christina where he'd hidden her. Will prayed they would encounter no more trouble the rest of the ride home. All he wanted was to ensconce Marian inside the walls of Chesterfield Park. It was his sacred duty to ensure her well-being. That realization pounded through him with each beat of the hooves.

He wouldn't deny his decision had been impulsive, but now that they were bound, he would gladly accept the full weight of his responsibility to her. She was his to love, honor, and protect, and he'd do so to the best of his ability. Even though his remaining days home were numbered, he endeavored to win her heart. He could do nothing less.

~ 16 ~

A SENSE OF HOMECOMING fell over Marian as Will led her through the front doors of Chesterfield Park.

The entrance was much smaller than the one in Harrison's modern home, the walls whitewashed, and the floor scuffed wood planks. It smelled musty and damp and contained a chill. Nonetheless, it was familiar and safe.

Straight ahead, the hall opened into what appeared to be a long dining room. She guessed it was the main room of the manor, like the great hall one would find in a castle. The light from a hearth fire and several sconces revealed timbered rafters, trestle tables running the length of the room, colorful tapestries hanging from plastered walls, and imposing swords and shields above the door.

A slender woman in the great hall moved toward them, her footsteps muted by the layer of rushes strewn on the floor. She wore a linen headdress and brown tunic tied with an apron. Although her face was plain, she offered them a lovely smile, even as she glanced behind Will anxiously.

Will nodded at her. "Thad will follow shortly."

"Then he is unharmed?"

"Indeed. And bringing Christina."

Relief flickered through the woman's unassuming eyes, before she shifted her focus to Marian. Her brows lifted in question. "I see you have rescued another?"

"This is my wife, Lady Marian."

"Your wife, sire?"

"You have not heard amiss."

The woman's eyes widened, her shock so obvious Marian couldn't quell the flutter of doubt that took to flight in her stomach, as it had done often since she'd risen from taking her vows. Had she done the right thing in marrying Will? What would happen when she was inexplicably whisked back to the present? Making rash decisions was so out of character from her usual analytical, methodical, decision-making process. She pressed her hand against her middle to stop the uneasiness but then swayed.

In the next instant, Will scooped her up, his dark brooding gaze assessing her as sharply as it always did. "You are weak and tired. We shall wait for proper introductions until the morrow."

"I guess I am worn out." She was unable to find the energy to make him put her down. Not that she particularly wanted him to release her, not when she liked the strength of his arms surrounding her and the hardness of his chest against her cheek.

"You will attend Lady Marian." Will spoke curtly to the young woman.

The servant managed to close her mouth and proceeded to dart into action. From one of the tables where she'd apparently been sitting with her mending, she retrieved a tallow candle in its holder. She held it out at arm's length and let its glow light the way through a side door to a narrow staircase that led to the second floor. While not the large spiraling carved oak stairway that graced Harrison's Chesterfield Park home, it was in the same location.

The woman guided them up the steps to the second floor. She started down the hallway, but her footsteps faltered, as though she didn't quite know where to go.

"To my chambers." Will's voice was straightforward, unashamed.

But Marian felt herself flush at the thought of going directly to Will's bedroom, especially in light of the suggestive comments he'd made to the peasants. He couldn't possibly think they'd share intimacies. Not when they hardly knew each other. He'd surely been blustering to appease the men. At least she hoped so. Because she had no intention of having a real marriage. The union was a means to accomplish what she'd come to do. That's all.

Although the corridor didn't have a balcony, Marian recognized it as the same hallway in Harrison's home. The layout and spacing of the doorways were the same. Even before the servant stopped in front of Will's room, Marian knew which one was his. It was the guest room she'd occupied. That would account for why she'd seen Will there two times.

Leading the way inside, the maid set to work lighting other candles and sconces, bringing the dark room to life. A side door was closed, but Marian suspected it led to a dressing room, regrettably without a modern bathroom. A chamber pot near the bed told her how she'd be relieving herself at Chesterfield Park—not the way she preferred, but she supposed it was better than an outhouse.

The canopied bed was the same she'd seen in her vision, a smaller version of the one she'd slept in. Rather than blue, it was cloaked in a deep burgundy and surrounded by thick bed-curtains. The soft candlelight made the finely embroidered linen shimmer like wine in a crystal goblet.

Will lowered her to the bed, its mattress feather-stuffed and in a rope-slung frame. Though sagging, it was much more comfortable than the pallet at the nunnery.

Her eyes drooped in fatigue. Drowsiness rushed through her aching, battered body. Had she only left the infirmary that afternoon for her walk with Christina? After hiding for hours, fleeing on horseback, and then being accosted by peasants, it seemed ages ago.

"Sarah will assist you, my lady."

Marian lifted her lashes to find Will standing above her. His granite expression had softened and the raw pain that usually haunted his eyes was replaced with worry. Although he didn't ask her how she was doing, she could sense the question.

Mustering energy, she lifted a hand and grasped his. "Thank you. For everything."

He captured her hand with both of his. Then he bent and pressed his lips against her knuckles. He held his kiss there for a long, sweet moment, letting his breath and the warmth of his lips linger.

Her pulse skittered wildly. And she couldn't keep from thinking about his kiss at the peasant camp, the way it had charged through her with such power and passion. She didn't know why his merest touch or his kiss should affect her so much. But she couldn't deny she'd liked the kiss earlier. And she couldn't deny she liked his kiss on her hand now.

When he straightened, he released her and took a step back. He met her gaze as he had at the camp, his eyes repeating what he'd said then—that he desired her and knew she felt the same.

That he could read her so easily was mortifying. She closed her eyes to keep him from seeing any other feelings. She sensed he was a man who didn't play games, who said exactly what he thought, and would expect the same honesty from her.

The prospect of such openness frightened her. She'd always been content with surface relationships where she never had to reveal her pains, frustrations, and fears. But somehow with this intensely magnetic man, she'd exposed herself, made herself vulnerable, given him a glimpse inside. In letting down her guard, she'd unleashed an attraction she didn't know how to wrestle back. It was out there, and only seemed to fight against her efforts to contain it.

"Bring my wife aught she needs." Will spoke quietly to the servant.

"Aye, I'll take good care of her, sire."

Although Will's stride was muted by the rushes on the floor, Marian could tell he was leaving the room. She lifted her lashes to watch him go, admiring everything about him from his purposeful stride to the hair pulled back into a ponytail at his broad shoulders. His wounded soul, his dangerous demeanor, his dark rugged looks—together they were an explosive combination, one that could easily ignite desire in any woman.

Except she couldn't be that woman. She couldn't let herself feel anything for him. She hadn't come to the past to get caught up in a relationship, especially not one like this.

No, the best course of action was to maintain her distance from him.

He paused at the door and slid a glance her way, almost as though he'd known she was watching him. He held her gaze for an instant, long enough to strike a spark in her belly again, like metal against flint. He gave her a curt nod, then left the room.

Once he was gone, Marian released her breath and silently chastised herself. Only then did she realize the servant woman, Sarah, was watching her with a look of wonderment widening her eyes.

She rapidly dropped her sights. "Milady."

Marian could only imagine what Sarah must be thinking, likely questioning why Will had married her. Marian had neither the energy nor the will to justify herself to this stranger. In fact, what she really wanted was a few moments alone to compose herself. "Would you be so kind as to find something for me to eat? I've had almost nothing all day and am famished."

"Aye, milady." Sarah dipped her head and then exited the room.

Marian settled back into the sagging mattress, closed her eyes, and for the first time since arriving to 1381 she felt out of harm's way and perhaps hopeful. Tomorrow, she'd begin her search for the ampullae. But for tonight, she could rest in peace. A wave of exhaustion fell over her, giving her no choice but to succumb to a deep black sleep.

• • •

A soft caress against her cheek woke Marian. She couldn't make her eyelids open, but she relished the familiar touch. And the familiar lemony-lavender scent of the shower gel and body lotion Ellen wore.

"I have emailed or phoned every cathedral, church, and museum in the UK, but no one knows the whereabouts of the last two St. Thomas ampullae." The voice with the British accent sounded like Harrison's. Swift and profound relief bubbled up. He was safe and home again. How and when had that happened?

The fingers stroked Marian's forehead, pushing back her hair. "We need to check the hiding place in the crypt today."

Ellen? Marian tried to open her mouth to speak but couldn't move so much as a breath. At the same time, she attempted to lift her eyelids again and force herself up from the mattress. But she couldn't do anything. It was as if her body was a block of ice, immovable in the slightest.

The only thing working was her mind, and it was flying.

"Her note said to wait one week." Ellen's voice was laced with weariness. "Today is exactly one week."

Had it been seven days? Yesterday had been her sixth day in the past. If she'd slept for hours, then it made sense that she'd awoken on the seventh. But how had she been able to return to the present, and why wasn't her body cooperating with her mind?

She wanted desperately to see Ellen, to look upon that beautiful face of her sister above her, to squeeze her in a hug and tell her that she loved her. She wanted to admonish her not to worry, to rest and take care of herself so she wouldn't make herself sick.

The solidness of a modern mattress pressed beneath her, and the crispness of a sheet covered her. A tube in her nose, likely the nasogastric tube, was providing nourishment. And there was also an IV in her arm.

"I don't want you to go to the crypt, Ellen." Harrison spoke firmly. "In fact, I absolutely forbid it."

Yes, she echoed Harrison. *Don't go. I'm here.* She focused all her attention on her mouth, praying it would open, so her words would find release. But no matter how much she willed her frozen body to work, it wouldn't.

"Someone has to go——"

"I will." Harrison's tone was low and resigned.

"Not after what they did to you."

Who were *they*? What had they done? Marian's heart raced. Again she worked to pry her eyelids up, her mind shouting at Harrison and Ellen not to go, not to put themselves in danger, not when she hadn't hidden anything there yet.

"Why did she pick the crypt?" Ellen's fingers slid down into Marian's.

Marian wanted to squeeze back, even if only minutely. Surely Ellen would feel the movement and know she could hear them. For a second she focused all her thoughts and energy on her fingers. *Move.* She commanded, then pleaded.

But there was nothing.

Apparently coming out of a coma took some time. She should have known better. Surely it was only a matter of time before she could make some indication to her sister and Harrison that she was with them.

Harrison released a tired sigh. "I understand your frustration, love. But when so many other places have been torn down or wrecked from wars and the passing of time, the crypt has remained relatively unchanged since the Middle Ages."

"But this place." Marian could picture Ellen waving one of her elegant hands at the room. "She could have hidden something here."

"This has always been a private residence. She would have no way of knowing if she could gain access. Whereas, the cathedral was open to pilgrims and had hundreds of visitors converging upon it every year. She'd have a much easier time getting into the cathedral than Chesterfield Park."

Marian couldn't wait to tell Harrison how wrong he was—that she'd made it into Chesterfield Park before the cathedral. Of course, both he and Ellen would be horrified to learn of the circumstances she'd experienced. But she would enjoy seeing Harrison's reaction when she informed him of all she'd learned about his family home.

In doing so, she'd have to explain that she'd married Sir William Durham. They'd think she was crazy for doing so. And she was, wasn't she?

Her thoughts returned to Will. He'd driven his dirk through a peasant's foot and nailed it to the ground with no remorse. With drawn sword, he'd been ready to battle a dozen peasants, and would have slain them without hesitation if they'd challenged him. He was a fierce warrior who had likely killed countless men.

Yet, in stark contrast to his warlike demeanor, he'd carried her like she was a crown jewel. He'd deposited her on his bed with such tenderness. And then he'd kissed her hand . . .

Warmth speared her middle and spread outward to her arms and legs. She would miss him. Even though they hadn't been together long, she liked him, more so than any other man she'd ever met.

What would he say when he found her unresponsive? Her pulse stumbled at the thought.

The hand encompassing hers was comforting. Thick calluses pressed against her tender skin. Her eyelids fluttered. She must be regaining her movement, sooner rather than later. She lifted her lashes and found herself staring at a burgundy canopy.

She shifted her gaze to see a dark head bent over her hand. It was Will sitting in a tall-backed chair next to her bed, holding one of her hands between his. His broad shoulders were slumped and his head bent, as though he were praying.

What had happened? Where was Ellen?

For a frantic second, she scrambled to conjure her sister and Harrison again. They were there. Only a slight overlapping dimension of time and space away. She had to return to them.

A soft pressure against her hand stopped the runaway thoughts and brought her back completely to the moment, to the realization that Will's lips were pressed to the back of her hand. His breath was warm and bathed her skin.

His kiss was long and lingering before he lowered her hand back to the bed. Even there he kept his hold, head still bent, weariness radiating from the droop of his shoulders.

How long had he been at her side?

She gently squeezed his hand.

His head snapped up, and his tortured eyes met hers. What haunted this man? What had happened to him to cause such heartache?

She had the sudden and intense longing to ease his pain, to comfort him, to turn that agony to peace. What could she do to help him?

She offered him a smile, at least as much of one as her lips would allow.

He released a tense breath, and his grip around her hand tightened. "How do you fare?" He studied her face before assessing the rest of her body.

"I'm just fine." She pushed up to her elbow. Someone had changed her out of her habit and put her into a thin shift.

He swallowed hard before speaking again. "We could wake you to no avail."

Had she fallen into a coma for a slight time? Somehow she'd been able to travel back to the present, or at the very least had envisioned it. But how could she explain that to Will when she couldn't understand it herself? "I'm sure I was just very tired. After recent events."

"Naught ails you in particular?"

Just disappointment that she hadn't returned to the present after all. "No, nothing ails me." As soon as the words were out, her stomach gave an angry rumble.

Will glanced toward a corner of the room where Sarah stood, wringing her hands anxiously. "Fetch Lady Marian a meal."

Sarah nodded her assent and scurried out the doorway, her hurried steps echoing in the hallway.

"I'll get up," Marian said. "I can manage for myself."

"You must rest." Will spoke the words as if she had no other option.

"What time is it?"

"Past midday."

Half the day was gone. She tried not to panic. Even if she hadn't found the ampullae, she needed to place something into the crypt to let Harrison and Ellen know she was all right. She couldn't let Harrison go there today for nothing.

"I would like to get dressed." She tried to push herself higher in the bed but only fumbled against the sagging mattress.

Will reached out to steady her, releasing her hand and instead grasping her upper arm. His fingers were warm through the thin linen. "You are still too weak."

She wasn't a weak woman, and she'd prove it to him. "I'd like to meet your family today."

"You will meet them erelong."

"And Christina. I want to make sure she's all right."

"She fares well and has already been in this morn to sit by your side."

Marian was running out of excuses. She didn't relish the idea of going back outside the gates of Chesterfield Park. But she had no choice. She had to communicate with Harrison. Today. Perhaps she could leave him a clue that she was looking for a new hiding spot.

Yes, she could locate a place here in Chesterfield Park, a nook or cranny somewhere within this original structure that had remained from 1381 until the present.

But where? She'd have to probe the room and see if she could locate a loose floorboard, area in the wall, something. Then she'd need to find a way to let Harrison know she'd changed the spot. Was there an item from the house, a small heirloom she could place in the crypt, signaling Harrison to search his home?

Whatever the case, she couldn't rest in bed all day.

As though sensing her growing determination, Will's jaw flexed. Something in the steely lines of his face told her he was accustomed to giving commands and having them followed without question.

But he'd quickly learn she wasn't like most people he ordered around. Even if she was currently in the Middle Ages where women had fewer rights, she wasn't about to stand back and let Will or any other man rule her life.

"I really must get up." She swung her legs over the edge of the bed and let the covers fall away altogether. A moment of dizziness assaulted her, but she caught herself.

As she began to stand unsteadily to her feet, Will grasped her and brought her easily down onto his lap. She wriggled and tried to stand back to her feet, but Will's arms slipped around her waist, drawing her further into his embrace.

Suddenly, she was conscious of their nearness, of the fact that her shift was tangled around her legs, exposing her knees and lower thigh, that its scooped neckline hung low, giving Will a slight view of her cleavage. It was less than her swimsuit would have revealed, but at Will's quick intake of breath, she guessed she was showing more than men during the past were accustomed to seeing.

He spread his fingers flat over her stomach. Through the thin linen, his touch scorched her. His other hand drifted into the unbound hair that hung down her back. His fingers wound into the thickness until lost there.

Every breath he took was louder than the last and echoed in her ear, pumping into her blood, sending heat to the tips of her toes and fingers. When he pressed his face into her hair and breathed in a deep gulp of air, her arms went around him as if they had a life and will of their own. She shifted her head and brushed her cheek against his, finding pleasure in the scrape of his unshaven scruff with her skin.

His jaw rippled against her, and he tilted his head enough that his lips found the pulse in her neck beneath her ear. As his kiss landed there, she couldn't hold back a gasp. Or another, as his mouth slid lower to her collarbone.

How could this man do this to her? Make her forget about everything but him? Because she couldn't remember what had been so important to make her climb out of bed.

A startled gasp resounded from the doorway. "Oh my."

Marian jumped and would have broken away from Will in mortification, except he didn't release her. Instead, his hand against her stomach pressed tighter, holding her in place. At the same time he brushed a thick wave of her hair off her shoulder, exposing more of her collarbone where her nightgown had slipped down. His lips caressed the spot, before he spoke in a growl. "Be gone, Christina. Can you not see we are occupied?"

"Christina?" Marian sat forward and glimpsed Christina cloaked from head to toe in her usual apparel. The young nun had cast her eyes down, but her face was the flaming red of autumn leaves, especially in contrast to the tight-fitting white wimple that outlined her face.

As Marian pushed against Will's chest to free herself from his seductive embrace, a low protest rumbled in his chest. His eyes were glassy with unsated desire and his expression taut. Yet, he released her, albeit reluctantly.

She scooted from his lap and stood—or at least tried to. Her legs were too weak to support her weight. As she faltered, Will lifted her and laid her back into the bed. As he flipped the coverlet over her, his attention shifted to her lips. Her stomach barely had time to clench with anticipation before he captured her mouth.

His kiss was hard and swift and shot through her like a gun blast.

He broke the kiss abruptly, this time before she was sated. "Stay in bed, wife." He spoke in a low tone that told her he would accept nothing less than complete obedience. Then he strode out of the chamber, passing Christina without a word.

The moment he was out of the room, Marian expelled a breath—half from desire and half from frustration. Why, oh why, had she allowed herself to kiss him again? On the other hand, what harm could come from a few stolen kisses?

A warning inside told her to be careful. Will wasn't the kind of man she could kiss and then abandon. He felt things deeply and personally. His worry at her bedside this morning was proof of that. When it was time for her to go, she'd hurt him—perhaps badly.

All the more reason to get out of bed and search for holy water.

Christina tiptoed across the rushes, her face still flaming. Marian could only imagine what the young nun thought of her. She probably considered her a hussy, making out with her brother after knowing him only a day.

"I'm sorry," Marian started. "I didn't mean to—well, you know . . ."

Christina didn't respond except to dip her head lower.

"You probably think the worst of me."

"Oh no, lady." She glanced up then, shaking her head. "I could never think that. I admit I was surprised to hear about your hasty marriage the past eve. But I rejoice to see William happy again."

What had she done to make Will happy? As far as she could

tell, she'd only made his life more complicated. "Wasn't he happy with his first wife?"

"He was content enough. And he would have laid down his life for Alice."

Alice. Marian rolled the name around silently. Had she been pretty? Rich? Funny? What had Will loved about her?

"But Will and Alice were young when they met, and he was gone for such long periods of time." Christina sat down in the chair Will had vacated. "I fear they never had the chance to see if love could bloom."

Marian had the sudden unpleasant vision of Will in this bed-chamber with another woman. He'd likely lain in this very bed with his wife.

"Now that my brother is older and more mature, he knows his mind well. He realized you are the woman he needs, and he wasted no time in claiming you."

"I'm the woman he needs? How so?"

Christina smiled and looked up from her clasped hands. "You are strong-willed and determined and unconstrained. You will be good for him."

"I see." Marian didn't have the heart to tell Christina that she wasn't good for Will. In fact, she'd only cause him grief.

Sarah entered the room carrying a tray. Christina rose to help Marian sit up in the lumpy, uneven bed, and then Sarah placed on her lap the tray containing a bowl of steaming porridge, bacon slabs, dark bread, and watery ale.

As she ate, Christina chattered nonstop, just as she had yesterday in the woods. And Marian couldn't help but think that a woman as lively and talkative as Christina didn't belong in a convent. She clearly had bottled her words for so long that now she needed to express them. She rambled on about Chesterfield Park, about its history, about the grounds, the stables, the flowers, and even the chapel.

Marian didn't mind, and tried to remember every detail so she could tell Harrison. He would be delighted to know about the original owners of the manor, how the house had looked, and what it had contained. After she finished the meal, a drowsy contentment overcame her.

As Christina took the cup out of her hands and situated her into the pillows, Marian yawned, suddenly too tired to do anything. As much as she needed to get to work saving herself and her family, she knew her body wouldn't cooperate until she allowed herself to recover.

$\sim$ *17* $\sim$

"SHE'S AWAKE, MILORD." Sarah's statement broke through Will's quiet reverie in his antechamber.

At midmorning, he'd been assessing the ledgers and attempting to figure out how he could raise money to support himself and his men on the next campaign. The king would expect him to not only contribute toward the general warfare needs, but also to support the men at arms he brought with him.

He could not take more from his vassals—although he guessed most other noblemen would resort to the extortion when the time arose. To do so would grievously hurt the people who depended upon them even more than they'd already been hurt.

Sitting back in his chair, he expelled a sigh. He had not yet discovered a different means of funding the war efforts. Neither had Thad, who stood next to his desk, a frown marring his young face.

Other than the writing desk, chair, and cabinet against one wall where he kept his ink and ledgers and documents of importance, the room was sparsely furnished. The small door behind him led down to a vault where he kept the family's valuables. The door remained locked at all times, and only Thad knew where he kept the key.

Sarah hesitated, clasping her hands and waiting with head bowed.

"Instruct my wife that I wish her to remain abed today."

"Aye, I have done so."

"And . . . ?"

"She is already up, milord, and has insisted on getting dressed."

"Inform her that whatever she puts on, I shall personally divest ere I toss her back into bed."

A slight smile tugged at Sarah's lips as she closed the door and took her leave.

Will had the sudden image of unlacing Marian's gown and half hoped she'd persist in disobeying so he might follow through with his threat.

"You do realize Lady Marian is not submissive." Thad spoke as quietly and seriously as always. As his steward, Thad steadfastly kept his ledgers and accounts in working order whilst Will was away. The man was trustworthy and reliable, and they agreed on nearly every financial matter.

"Yes, I realize this about her." Submission was equated with being a good wife. But Will couldn't deny Marian's feisty spirit was one of the things he liked about her.

Will had no doubt Thad loved Sarah devoutly. But watching them together, one would never surmise the two were married. In fact, Will guessed that's how his marriage with Alice had been—how most marriages were. If affection and tenderness existed, the expression of them was private.

But for a reason he couldn't explain, he was unable to keep his passion for Marian relegated to the bedchamber. She was intruding upon his thoughts at all times of the day and night—like now, because she utterly fascinated him. She had from the first moment he'd seen her in his dreams, standing in front of the manor at dusk, her glorious hair aflame from the setting sun.

He couldn't deny he was eager to join her in bed and consummate their marriage. The waiting had likely made his thoughts of her run more rampant. But after her first unresponsive night when he'd been unable to wake her, he'd chastised himself to be patient and allow her time to recuperate from the beatings she'd sustained at St. Sepulchre.

After he'd insisted she rest in her chambers yesterday, he'd bedded down in the great hall last night, pushing back his desire for her once again, especially after the view he'd gotten of her slender legs and womanly shape. She was more comely than his weak flesh could withstand. He understood now why some men went to such lengths for their women, why they ended up sacrificing so much, why they sometimes even made fools of themselves.

It was clear the right woman could wield great power over a man—at least Marian seemed to have enchanted him. One soft gasp, one word of gratitude, one lift of her lashes, and he became like melted tallow.

Just thinking about her reaction to his kisses sent heat twisting tightly through his gut. She hadn't been passive, hadn't simply tolerated his advances—as Alice had done. She'd responded with an ardor that had taken him by surprise and yet had pleased him.

Yes, he sensed Marian's naivety and innocence. But he also sensed a deep well of emotion within her that if nourished and cherished would match his own.

Thad picked up one of the ledgers and placed it with the others in the cabinet behind the writing desk. "If you regret your decision, you still have time for an annulment—since you have not yet consummated your union."

"She is my wife. I shall keep her, whether I have bedded her or not."

"But Lady Felice—"

"I rule Chesterfield Park, not my mother." Even as he spoke the words, he realized Thad was only trying to protect him. His mother hadn't been pleased to hear the news of his marriage to Marian since they knew almost naught about her.

"How could you despise my plans with Lord Percy?" Lady Felice's eyes had flashed with resentment toward Will as she'd spoken to him yesterday when he finally allowed her to enter his antechamber. "You have given up a beneficial arrangement."

A beneficial arrangement that would have brought Chesterfield Park a dowry, wealth he could have used to assist his war efforts.

"And for what?" Lady Felice released a scoffing laugh. "To feed your lust?"

He wanted to lash back but restrained himself. "I have done what is expected of me in many ways. In this matter, I shall do as I please."

"If she has run away and her kin is powerful, they may decide to take revenge upon us for thwarting her union to the man of their choice. What shall we do then?"

"She is mine now." He felt the truth of his statement all the way to his bones. Even if they had not become one flesh yet, he could not—would not—relinquish her. "If anyone wants to take her away from me, they will have to fight me."

"And what if her kin—or her betrothed—come for her while you are away in France?"

The very idea made his blood run cold. If something like that happened, even if Thad sent him a missive anon, such a letter wouldn't reach him for weeks—if not months. By the time he returned to defend Marian and his home, he could very well be too late.

Every time he departed, he felt as if he was leaving his kin at the mercy of fate. He'd never liked knowing the people he loved were defenseless and powerless without him there. Yet, what choice did he have? What choice would he have now?

He was at the mercy of the king—a boy king, no less. King Richard was only fourteen years old, having ascended to the throne after the death of his grandfather, King Edward III. If only Richard's father, the Black Prince, had lived, then England would have a solid and sound sovereign. As it was, the crown had gone to the Black Prince's oldest son, Richard. Now with the recent unrest in the countryside, the boy king could hardly keep peace in his own lands, much less control lands abroad.

Will pushed his ledgers aside and stood. Even with the shutters thrown back to the summer day, the small room off the great hall was stuffy. It didn't help the day had dawned warm, and that without a cloud in the sky, it might prove to be the hottest yet.

Thad cocked an eyebrow, as though attempting to decipher what about Marian made Will decide to abandon all sound reasoning.

No one else would be able to understand the visions he'd had of Marian, the bond he already felt with her, the way her presence soothed his tortured soul. If they believed he was merely lusting after a beautiful woman, so be it. They would not be amiss. He did desire her.

However, his need for her went much deeper than physical. He couldn't explain why, except that in his dreams she'd touched his wounds and brought him comfort he hadn't known existed. Maybe with her, he could finally find solace.

* * *

Marian smoothed her hands over the silky royal blue gown that reminded her of Will's eyes. Sarah had helped to lace up the sides with strings that formed tight x's across her ribs.

While it was fancy enough to belong to a fairy tale princess, Marian had only worn it for five minutes and was already hot and ready to take it off. Having belonged to Alice—as did all of the garments she'd been given—the sleeves were long and the train dragged across the floor. If the heavy linen wasn't enough, Sarah had insisted she wear a shift underneath. The long shirt-like garment took the place of her bra and panties, which were long gone, probably burned by someone who thought they were scandalous and of the devil.

"You look lovely, milady." Sarah stepped back and assessed Marian with a smile. "'Tis quite clear why the master is taken with you."

"If he's so taken, he shouldn't have confined me to my room today." It had been frustrating enough that she'd slept all of yesterday and missed the week deadline of getting ampullae into the crypt as well as the opportunity to find and inform Harrison of a new hiding place. Today, she'd felt mostly stronger and better, her bruises were finally dulling, and she hadn't wanted to rest any longer. But every time she'd gotten up, Sarah or Christina had insisted on guiding her back to bed.

She had no doubt Harrison had returned to the crypt to look for the ampullae. Not only had she put his life in danger again, but she'd likely worried him out of his mind.

Of course, she'd attempted to make her mind connect to the present. But no matter how hard she'd concentrated or visualized Ellen and Harrison, she hadn't been able to see them. If only she could figure out what had triggered the last connection, she might be able to duplicate it.

In the meantime, she could only hope Harrison and Ellen would realize she was still looking for holy water—or would begin to once she regained her strength. She'd indicated in the original note she'd left in Harrison's safe, that if there wasn't anything in the crypt after the first week, they should look again exactly one week later.

Certainly in the next week, Marian could persuade Will to take her back to Canterbury so she could search St. Sepulchre as well as go to the cathedral. And if Will refused, then she'd find a way to sneak out and go on her own. But at the moment, with the passing of the first week's deadline, the urgency had subsided.

"Will is stubborn, isn't he?" Marian tugged at the low bodice, trying to shift it higher. Though she hadn't seen him since yesterday, he'd relayed instructions through the servants that he wanted her to continue recuperating. She'd finally sent him a message that she was done resting and intended to join the family for dinner in the great hall. She would have gone down whether he acquiesced or not, but thankfully he had.

"He wanted to be sure you are not taxing yourself, milady." Sarah guided her to a stool in front of a dressing table. Once Marian was situated, Sarah began combing her unruly hair. Marian was glad not to have a mirror. She could only imagine how terrible her hair looked after days without a shower, flat iron, or any hair products whatsoever. She guessed she looked as horrid as she felt. And smelled.

She'd asked for a bath, but Sarah had indicated that because of the amount of work and time required to draw and heat water, they only prepared baths when several members of the household were available to use the same water.

Marian breathed in past the restricting laces upon her ribs and caught the whiff of lingering body odor. "Maybe you could find perfume or something sweet-scented to help me smell better?"

"Aye, milady. I shall fetch you oil of lavender." Sarah's fingers were cool and deft in her hair, and Marian closed her eyes as she allowed the kindly maidservant to hopefully work some kind of magic. Perhaps tomorrow she'd ask for a pitcher of water and at least give herself a sponge bath.

Sarah coiled her hair into braids decorated with ribbons then covered the back of Marian's head with a sheer veil. By the time Sarah finished her ministrations along with applying lavender oil, Marian felt more put-together.

The maidservant led Marian down the hallway to the stairs and into the great hall. Marian was surprised to find that people were already sitting at the trestle tables, which were covered in white linen and set with polished pewter and glass goblets banded in silver.

The brass candlesticks at the centers of the tables were lit, and strains of light from the fading evening sun descended through the high narrow open windows, adding to the glow. A man sat on a stool next to the hearth, playing a harp and singing, though no one seemed to pay him any attention. Servants bustled about the tables, pouring wine and ale from jugs.

Marian followed Sarah across the fresh rushes, hoping she wouldn't stumble in the uncomfortably tight pointed leather slippers she was wearing. Her heartbeat gave an involuntary sputter of nervousness, especially as the voices quieted and the guests focused upon her. Marian tried not to fidget but to walk with all the confidence of a modern woman. Because that's what she was. Wasn't she?

At the head table, Will was reclining in a carved oak chair and speaking in low tones with a gentleman seated next to him. As though sensing the change in the mood of his guests, Will shifted. At the sight of her, he pushed back in his chair and rose.

She could see that he'd taken time with his appearance. Although his chin and jaw were still dark with a layer of stubble, he'd tamed his hair. He wore a light blue tunic over clean woolen trousers. The blue served to highlight his eyes, making them brighter and more beautiful than she remembered. Those eyes fell upon her, taking her in, and brightening with an appreciation that made Marian's pulse trip like that of a middle school girl at her first dance.

He rounded the table and strode toward her. Upon reaching her, he took her hand, lifted it to his lips, and placed a tender kiss upon it. "My lady." He spoke in a low tone meant for her ears alone. "You are lovely."

She wanted to stay irritated at him for his insistence on her resting today, but she sensed he'd only had her best interest at heart. Besides, he was too handsome and his wounded eyes were as deep and irresistible as always. She couldn't prevent a surge of attraction from whispering through her and reminding her all too acutely of the feel of his hands in her hair and his kisses upon her neck.

The truth was, she'd never met a man like William Durham, a

man who shook her to the very core. Because he was so raw and real, he forced her to be likewise, which was daunting. She was used to hiding behind her experiments and statistics and filling her life with finding a cure for Ellen—partly because then she didn't have to face the emptiness left by her mom's death, her dad's distance, and Ellen's impending death. But here in the Middle Ages she had nowhere to hide.

Will didn't relinquish her hand and beckoned her with his eyes to accompany him to the table. His expression told her that she could trust him, that she'd be safe with him, and that he'd cherish her to his dying breath. The revelation both frightened and drew her at the same time.

As they moved forward together, she was conscious of all eyes upon them. These people regarded her as the lady of the manor now, a privilege and an honor. What if she said or did something wrong? After all, she didn't know the first thing about being a lady. Surely it was only a matter of time before someone recognized she didn't belong, accused her of being an imposter, and pointed out she couldn't be a noblewoman from an English family living in the Low Countries.

She decided her best mode of survival was saying as little as possible, especially around all these people. So she nodded as Will made the introductions to various cousins and relatives and other visitors. When he reached a stately woman with Christina's eyes but none of the warmth, Marian realized this was Will's mother even before he introduced her as such.

Lady Felice eyed Marian critically. "My lady, I finally meet the comely maiden who caused my son to abandon all reason and pursue his carnal instincts instead."

"Mother." Will scowled at the regal and darkly beautiful woman who held her head high and defied him with one slanted glance.

Under Lady Felice's assessment, Marian tried not to shrink even though she guessed the woman could see past the fancy updo and gown to the reality of who Marian was—the gritty, grimy, unwashed layer.

Will took a step toward his mother. "Lady Marian is my wife." He spoke the words softly, but the menace in them was sharp. "If you do not respect her at all times, you will force me to remove you from Chesterfield Park."

Marian cringed. While she appreciated Will's sticking up for her, his words would only cause more animosity. What mother would ever take kindly to being usurped by her daughter-in-law? "I'm sure we'll get along just fine once we get to know one another." She offered Lady Felice what she hoped was a warm smile.

Lady Felice didn't spare her a glance. Instead, she lifted her chin just enough for Marian to see Will in that movement, for her to understand where Will had inherited his pride and stubbornness.

The anxiety weaving through Marian threatened to rise up. But she quickly pushed it down. Why worry when she wouldn't be in the past much longer? If all went as planned, she had only a week before she'd revive and return to her own time period away from the scrutiny of these people and this woman who didn't like her.

Will tucked Marian's hand securely into the crook of his arm and led her to the head table where he'd been sitting before she arrived. He pulled out the chair next to his and helped situate her before lowering himself to his spot. The doting coming from Jasper would have irritated her, perhaps even smothered her. Why, then, didn't she chafe under the attention coming from Will?

When he sat next to her, the servants took that as their cue to begin bringing in the first course of their meal, carrying platters of meat and bowls of soup, the steam filling the air with the rich aroma of onions and beef.

Marian made small talk with the woman next to her, an older relative of some importance. But the woman didn't seem inclined to speak long and after a few moments of stilted conversation turned her attention to Will's mother, who made a point of snubbing Marian too.

"Do not pay heed to my mother," Will said as a servant finished filling their goblets with wine.

"She gave me quite the compliment." Marian tried to make light of the moment. "Apparently, my beauty has great sway over you. One glance at my body and you're at my beck and call."

He stabbed a large piece of roast with the tip of his knife.

"If I bat my eyelashes at you, what will you do next? Grant my wish for a bath?" She smiled at him and then batted her eyelashes coquettishly.

He didn't grin, but his lips twitched just slightly, as if he wanted to smile but wouldn't give himself permission.

"Or if I pucker my lips every so often like this"—she pressed her lips into a pretend kiss—"then maybe you'll grant my wish to ride into Canterbury tomorrow."

His gaze shifted to her lips and lingered there.

Her mind went immediately to work remembering exactly how his lips felt on her skin.

Oh, heavens above. She couldn't go there, couldn't look at his lips in return. She dropped her attention to the piece of juicy meat before her and feigned interest in it. Obviously, flirtatious banter didn't work with Will. The air was already charged enough between them, and she couldn't afford to let any more sparks fly.

"Anyway, thank you for defending me to your mother. That was very kind."

He swallowed a bite and then nodded. "She will accept my decision and respect it."

Marian didn't think so. The woman clearly blamed her for snaring Will—probably believed she'd enticed him. And why would Lady Felice like her? Marian was a nobody. Without a dowry. Or land. Or connections. She couldn't fault Lady Felice for questioning why her son had made such a reckless match to a stranger. Marian would have done the same had their roles been reversed.

"Where are your sons?" Marian attempted to cut her roast into smaller pieces.

Will raised one brow as if confused by her query. Now that she thought about it, there were only adults in the room. Perhaps children ate separately.

"It's just that I'd like to meet them." Marian spoke hurriedly to cover her faux pas. If she'd been a historian and more familiar with customs in the Middle Ages, perhaps she would have been better equipped to blend in. As it was, she was reminded all over again how inept she was.

"I shall introduce you to my sons on the morrow." His slightly cocked brow still questioned her. Did he doubt she wanted to meet his sons? She'd never considered herself to be the maternal type, hadn't ever had a longing for a baby like many women her age who were married.

But looking at Will, at his striking profile, at the strength he exuded, she was curious to see him with his boys, to watch them interact, and to discover more about him in the process.

"And will you give me a tour of Chesterfield Park?"

"You may ask Sarah to do so." He bit off a piece of meat from the end of his knife.

She hadn't expected his dismissal. "I want *you* to give me the tour." The words escaped before she could stop them. She'd already decided she didn't want to hurt him, and the less time she spent with him the better. Yet one day together wouldn't harm anyone, especially if she kept things platonic between them.

His chewing slowed, and he gave her a sidelong glance she couldn't read.

"How will we get to know one another if we don't spend time together?" she said.

"We are together now."

Strangely it wasn't enough. "Yes, but I would like to hear your perspective of your home and your land and see it through your eyes."

He lowered his knife to his trencher and shifted so he was studying her face. His blue eyes were keen and searching for the truth.

"Let's spend all of tomorrow together." She was surprised by how much she wanted it.

His expression filled with hesitation. Men and women had vastly different spheres in the Middle Ages. And she could almost hear him ask the question: What would they find to do all day together? She wasn't quite sure either. She was a workaholic and rarely took vacation days. But certainly they could find plenty of activities to fill their time.

"Don't worry." She tried for a coy smile. "I promise I'll make it worth your while." As soon as the words were out, she realized how suggestive she sounded and wished she could reel them back in.

He held her gaze, and something hot flared in his eyes that sent a warning down to the tip of her toes. "Very well, lady. But know this: I shall hold you to your promise."

Her pulse charged forward erratically, and she focused on her trencher lest he see his effect upon her. Had she done the right thing in making this arrangement, or had she made another foolish move?

Inwardly she chastised herself. *Stay smart and focused, Marian.* She had to make the most of every opportunity to understand the logistics of crossing time and figure out how to save herself and her family.

Her day with Will would be to that end. She would use the time to better understand the past, the people, and the customs—from a scientific perspective. It could be nothing more than that.

~18~

WILL STEPPED FURTHER into the darkened chamber. The bed curtains were open, revealing Marian's sleeping form. She was sprawled out, her hair unplaited and spread out in wild abandon.

His gut tightened at the thought of burying his fingers there.

He unlaced his hose and let them drop to the floor, and then he slid his shift over his head, letting it pool on the floor too. After two nights of allowing her to recuperate, he'd tarried long enough. In fact, after sitting next to her all throughout the eve, watching her eat, listening to her talk, glimpsing her smiles—he'd enjoyed her company much more than he'd imagined he would. And he'd been disappointed when his time with her had been cut short.

When two neighboring knights had arrived after dinner, he'd closeted himself in his antechamber with them. They'd relayed news of the unrest that was quickly escalating, bearing reports of looting and destruction and murder. The rebels now traversed the countryside, slaying not only clergy and those in service to God but helpless lawyers, judges, and other officials, and they were burning all records—as if such heinous deeds could bring an end to the unfair taxes.

His fellow knights were worried because some bands had also

attacked noble homes, demanding the knights join their cause or face death. They were being led by a man called Wat Tyler, who apparently had vengeance and death at the forefront of his agenda.

The news had been discouraging. If the marauders came to Chesterfield Park, the additional guards he'd posted along the manor walls would hopefully deter an attack, for he had no intention of joining the rebels and supporting their needless destruction and violent murders. He could only pray his recent gesture of goodwill, giving them a public wedding, would suffice to keep them at bay.

His fellow knights had also carried word that some of the neighboring lords and knights were considering combining efforts to squelch the rebellion. Will had known what such an effort would entail—seasoned knights like himself in plate armor charging on warhorses against rebels with inferior weapons. It would be a bloody battle with too many lost lives. He'd decided he would refrain, pray for peace, and rise to warfare as a last resort.

The meeting had lasted long into the night. After his friends had finally spread pallets in the great hall, Will had taken his leave and ascended to his chamber, anticipation mounting with each step.

He wished for moonlight to come in through the open shutters so he could gaze upon his new bride more fully. She'd been stunning earlier, so much so that she'd nearly taken his breath away every time he looked at her.

His wife. This ravishing woman was his wife.

He lowered himself onto the bed and stretched out next to her. She didn't move.

He turned to his side so he was facing her and held his breath, waiting for her to rouse and sense his presence beside her.

In the quietness, her breathing was low and even with the rhythm of sleep.

His fingers easily found her hair, and he combed through the silky strands. He brought a fistful to his nose and breathed her in. Just the slight contact was enough to send a burning trail through him.

He slid closer until he felt the exquisite length of her body against his. With his nose buried in her hair, he wrapped an arm around her middle.

She would surely awaken now and would welcome him. He'd not been amiss in sensing her interest in him. She might not have the same deep need he did, but every time he'd touched her, she'd responded with a barely concealed passion that he was eager to unleash.

He pressed a kiss into the back of her head. But even as he waited for her to stir, he was unwilling to disturb her rest. Her back rose and fell steadily against him. He didn't have to look to guess she still retained her bruises.

He gentled his hold, and the same peace he'd experienced during his visions stole back through his chest—rare peace, one that gave him respite from the nightmares that haunted him.

Closing his eyes, he expelled a long breath, releasing for just a moment the self-loathing that was his constant companion. He didn't understand why or how this beautiful woman could soothe him in a way naught else could. But he wouldn't fight it.

Within seconds, his own breathing steadied to match hers. With his arms around her and his face pressed into her hair, he fell into a deep, dreamless sleep.

● ● ●

Marian awoke to the strange feeling she was hovering between two worlds. She tried to reach out and grasp Ellen. She could sense her sister's presence even if she couldn't hear anything. But the solid pressure against her back and warm breath against her neck jolted her out of her sleep.

Her eyes flew open to see the light of dawn streaming in through open shutters. The room was cloaked in shadows and the house quiet. She still wasn't used to such utter silence, waking without the hum of an air conditioner or the beep of an alarm clock.

She started to stretch then froze. She wasn't alone. A large muscular body curled against her, an arm slung haphazardly across her waist. She didn't need to look to know Will had joined her in bed.

Embarrassment crashed through her, quickly followed by indignation. How dare Will do so without her permission? They hardly knew each other. How could he even think about sleeping with her?

She supposed during medieval times, coupling was seen as more practical than romantic. Even so, she hadn't expected him to jump into bed with her so readily. Apparently his suggestions to the peasants about bedding her had been more serious than she'd realized.

She expelled a tense sigh. But of course he was serious. He didn't know she was planning to leave, that their marriage was fleeting. He was only doing what any husband during his time would—going to bed with his wife. In fact, he'd probably been more patient than other men might have been in the same situation. He'd given her time to rest and recover before taking his rightful place in his bed.

Whatever the case, she had to figure out a way to stop things from progressing any further. It was not only awkward, much too soon, and inappropriate, since theirs was a temporary relationship, but it was also dangerous. Without birth control, she had no idea what the ramifications would be if she happened to get pregnant during the time crossing.

She tried not to squirm but was anxious to put some space between them. She lifted his arm just slightly, so she could escape from his hold. But the moment she touched him, his breathing against her neck changed, and she knew he was awake.

For a long moment, she didn't breathe, and he didn't move.

Finally, he bent in to her neck and pressed his lips there. The touch was so tender that it filled her with a strange, unquenchable longing for more.

She bit her lip. She had to move away. Now. And the only way she would be able to keep him at bay was by being honest with him. At least as honest as she could be under the circumstances.

"Will?" She shifted under his arms so she could see his face in the amber morning light.

"Hmmm?" he mumbled sleepily, his eyes still closed, his fingers skimming up her arm, already sending delicious shivers over her skin.

"Will, wait." She scooted away. "We can't, well—you know."

At her declaration, his eyes opened and found hers. His were murky with sleep and desire. He didn't need to respond for her to know his answer. She would have to do a better job explaining herself, or he'd pull her back against him with no thought of sleep.

Her mind raced to find an excuse. She was only in the past momentarily. She'd be leaving by the end of the week. She didn't consider herself really married to him—at least permanently. "We have to wait . . ."

Her words faded away as his fingers trailed higher to her neck and then to her cheek where he brushed her hair back. His fingers were soft and gentle and altogether too enticing.

He would think she was crazy if she revealed that she'd crossed back in time. She couldn't do it, not yet, not here, maybe not ever. But she had to think of some way to plausibly explain why she couldn't share intimacies with him. "You see, where I come from, men and women spend time getting to know each other. They talk a lot and build a friendship—and they court—before becoming more intimate."

His fingers moved through her hair again, to her neck where his thumb caressed her pulse. It was thumping fast. "We are wed.

We need no other reason." His low, thick tone was nearly her undoing.

"But what of love?" She forced the words quickly. "Shouldn't love exist between a man and woman before they share themselves?"

He reached for her, this time more forcefully, and brought her against him. "The day we wed, I promised to love you." His whisper was warm against her forehead. "And I never break my promises."

He kissed her, moving from her forehead to her temple. She closed her eyes to fight against the pleasure of his touch. It would be all too easy to give in to this man. He was as noble and good and tender as he was fierce and rugged and tough. What would it hurt to allow herself this stolen moment of loving? She was technically married to him.

But as his kiss moved to her ear, and his hands slid down the length of her arm to her hip, a warning rang loud and long in her head. Before he could stop her, she rolled out of his grasp and jumped out of bed. "Please, Will." She stood at the edge, her chest rising and falling in rapid bursts.

His brows furrowed, in anger or frustration, she couldn't tell. Then he propped himself up on his elbow and looked up at her. His middle was tangled in the coverlet, but his chest and legs were bare, making her suddenly realize he was naked except for his linen drawers.

"I need time to get to know you better." She scrambled for coherent words. "Could I have one week?" She'd be long gone in a week. At least she hoped so.

"A sennight?" His voice was incredulous, almost angry. "I have already given you three nights."

There was a part of her that couldn't believe she was actually having this exchange, this bargaining over sleeping with a man she'd rashly married. It was likely the strangest conversation she'd ever had. But she had to try to maintain boundaries. Not only for herself but for him for after she left.

"Seven days." She squared her shoulders, trying to muster her inner reserves. "We can spend the time getting to know each other and becoming friends."

He didn't say anything, and for long seconds she didn't dare look at him. Finally, she chanced a peek. He was lying on his back, his arms crossed behind his head, and he was studying her. Thankfully, his anger seemed to have dissipated. More than anything, he seemed puzzled, almost curious.

She was close to convincing him and couldn't give up yet. "I have heard that relationships based upon friendship are stronger and more fulfilling." At least that's what she'd seen between her mom and dad. They'd shared everything—talked ceaselessly, made time for fun, and laughed often. She supposed that's why her dad hadn't handled Mom's death well. He'd lost not only his wife but also his best friend.

The muscles in Will's biceps bulged and his long, bare legs stretched out, crossed casually at his ankles. He was beautiful. Every single inch of him. She swallowed hard and stared down at her own bare feet.

"Three more days."

Her gaze shot up to find that he wore an amused look. "That's hardly long enough—"

"My days here in Kent are short."

She mentally calculated the time. She had five days left to find holy water and get it to the crypt. Five days before Ellen and Harrison would go back to the cathedral once again. Five days before she could return to the present.

"How about five days?" She prayed that would indeed be enough time.

"Very well. Five, unless I woo you first." His voice hinted at a challenge that sent a flutter of warmth into her belly.

As if the matter was settled, Will flipped the coverlet off his body and stood, heedless of the fact she was standing there and that every rippling part of his body was exposed to her.

With a rapid intake of breath, she pivoted so that her back was facing him. She listened to the slide of linen against flesh, and only when his footsteps started across the room did she turn.

Fully clad, he was nearly at the door and seemed intent on leaving.

"Remember"—she wanted to hold on to him but knew she shouldn't—"you promised to spend the day with me."

Gripping the door, he paused. "I shall send for you."

"Where are you going now?" The question came out breathy and too eager.

"I visit the chapel every morn." He spoke quietly without meeting her gaze, as though he was embarrassed by this acknowledgment.

"I'd like to go too." Once the words were out, she realized how true they were, not just so she could be with him but because something tugged at her heart, a need for peace and help that went beyond herself, something she hadn't allowed herself to feel in a long time.

Will lifted his head, surprise widening his eyes, revealing his deep haunted wounds. She had the feeling he was about to say no, that this was one place he went by himself.

"Please?"

Opening the door a crack, he hesitated. After a moment more, he reached for a cloak hanging from a peg on the back of the door and held it out to her. "Don this first."

She smiled, crossed to him, and took it willingly.

He swung the door wide and waved her through. Once they were in the dark hallway lit by a single smoking sconce, he started ahead of her. Before he could move beyond her reach, she slipped her hand into his.

At her touch, his steps faltered. He glanced down at her hand, and for a second she wondered if she'd been too bold.

But then his fingers closed around hers more firmly, and she shoved aside the warning that she was allowing herself to become too invested. Surely becoming friends with this man wouldn't hurt anyone, would it?

~ 19 ~

WILL'S HEART THRUMMED with a new feeling he couldn't quite describe. All he knew was that his chest was filled with warmth and fullness and satisfaction like none he'd ever known.

Marian sat across from Phillip and Robert, her head bent over the chessboard, her expression intent. The glow from the hearth fire lit her pale complexion and highlighted the spark in her eyes, the one that said she took the game seriously and was determined to win.

Both sons had his dark hair and blue eyes, but Phillip was the stockier of the two. At eight, the boy was past ready for fostering out. In light of Alice's death, Will had put off the move longer than he should have. Now, he had no more excuses and needed to make the arrangements soon, ere he left again for France.

After his sons had patiently explained the rules of chess to Marian, they'd taken turns playing with her. He was proud of how intelligent both of the boys were already. Every time they glanced his way at the head of the table, their young faces seemed to seek his approval. Even now, Phillip raised his brow at him, beseeching whether to allow his new mother to win the game or whether he should challenge her.

Will shook his head curtly. He sensed Marian would desire to win fairly or not at all. She'd caught on rapidly, and with enough practice she would soon beat Phillip in her own right.

Phillip nodded and then made his next move, one that took Marian's queen. Marian caught her bottom lip between her teeth, an unconscious habit that sent heat to Will's gut every time he witnessed it.

Her fingers tapped against her king. Her soft, graceful fingers. He could almost feel them twined with his. He'd not understood her gesture the first time she'd placed her hand in his. But when they'd knelt together in the chapel yesterday and she'd kept her hand wrapped with his, he'd taken comfort from her hold, felt somehow bolder with her by his side.

When he'd poured out his transgressions before the Almighty Father, the burden hadn't weighed quite as heavily as usual. Upon rising from prayers, she'd squeezed his fingers. And when he looked down into her eyes, she smiled up at him, her beautiful eyes radiating acceptance and reassuring him that no matter what he'd done, the mistakes he'd made, she could see beyond them to the man he wanted to be.

After she dressed for the day and after they broke their fast, he gave her the tour of the house and grounds she wanted. She seemed to know her way around, almost as if she'd been there before. She even greeted the flowers in the garden like long-lost friends.

Upon her insistence, they watched his sons in their sword and jousting drills. At her encouragement, he joined the swordsmaster and was surprised to find how much he enjoyed training his boys and wondered why he'd never done so before.

She planned a noon fare in the garden—something she called a picnic—and invited Robert and Phillip to join them. The boys were as surprised as he was, but they weren't able to resist her charm as she led them to a secluded and shaded section directly under a canopy of ivy.

As Will laid back on the blanket she'd spread on the ground, he watched her through half-lidded eyes. Her face was animated as she told the boys stories about ships that could sail in the sky and some that could even carry men all the way to the moon. He loved how she enthralled the boys, how she genuinely liked being with them and treated them like young men and not children.

She would be a good mother to his sons as well as the children they would conceive together. He held in an exasperated sigh at the thought of the promise he'd given her—that she could have five days to get to know him. Part of him didn't understand why it should matter. They could still learn about each other even after they consummated their marriage, couldn't they? They had their whole lives to learn about each other.

However, even as his irritation surfaced from time to time, he only had to think of Alice, of the separate lives they'd lived, of the distance he'd felt even when they were together. Already with Marian, in so short a span, a connection drew him like a wave to the shore.

Mayhap if he took the time to understand her over the next few days, they would share a closeness even when he was gone off to war, a bond that could foster fondness in both their hearts through the passing of time and distance.

This morn, she'd met him in the chapel for prayers again. Afterward, she needed only to smile up at him for his reserves to weaken so that he all too readily agreed to her request to spend another day with him. She wanted to observe Robert and Phillip's lessons as their tutor worked them through arithmetic and science. Will hadn't needed much prodding to oversee the tutor and ascertain his worth.

Throughout the morn, more than anything, he learned how

well-educated Marian was, along with how much she relished explaining concepts to his sons. He found her intelligence fascinating and enjoyed observing her as much as he had his sons.

Even now, with the chessboard spread out on the table, he owned freely that he'd savored the time together more than he thought he would—not only with her, but with his sons. He couldn't recall when he'd been with them for more than a few minutes at a time. They were shy around him, perhaps even afraid of him. And he'd decided earlier today, he'd avail every opportunity henceforth to show them they had naught to fear.

With a steady drizzle forcing them to remain inside, Marian hadn't been daunted. She'd insisted on learning chess. Now as the rain pattered against the shutters and roof, the gentle rhythm filled the great hall.

"Checkmate," Phillip said solemnly.

Marian studied each of her remaining pieces and then sighed. "Yes, you have beaten me."

"'Tis only your first day, my lady." Little Robert spoke as solemnly as his big brother. "With practice, you will improve."

"Do you think so?" She leaned across the table and brushed back a stray strand of damp hair from Robert's cheek.

"You are already much better at it than I was my first time." Robert glanced at Will as though seeking approval for his answer. He nodded at the boy, whose chest puffed out with pleasure at Will's acknowledgment.

Marian studied each of the boys before rising to her feet. "It's my turn to teach you a game."

They climbed off their bench, eagerness lighting their eyes.

"Have you heard of hide-and-seek?"

They shook their heads.

She explained the rules and finished with an excited smile, as eager to play the game as they were.

Phillip looked around, already searching for a place to hide.

"So, we can hide anywhere within the ground level. But we cannot go to the chambers above?"

"Right."

"No going in the chapel." Will stretched his legs out in front of him and reclined in his chair. "Or the kitchen."

The boys nodded.

"I'll count to fifty," Marian said, "while you hide."

With wide grins, they scampered away. She turned her gaze upon Will expectantly.

He met hers as directly as he always did, loving that she wasn't intimidated by him in the least.

"Shoo." She waved at him. "You have to hide too."

"Me?" He released a scoffing laugh.

"I suppose you're right." She cut him off, her eyes baiting him. "I'd find you too easily."

At her challenge, he rose from his chair. She didn't know him well if she thought she could find him. He'd become an expert at espionage missions, learning to see but not be seen.

As he started away from the table, her lips curved into a self-satisfied smile, and he realized she did know him well enough to guess he'd take her challenge, that he was too proud to refuse.

He veered toward the open door of his antechamber and hid a smile of his own. Two could play this game. Maybe she'd goaded him into hiding, but he'd relish the chance to show her she couldn't get anything past him.

Once he secluded himself, he leaned against the wall and listened to her, first finding Robert and then Phillip. Their shouts and laughter echoed all the way into his antechamber, Marian's sweet laughter mingling in.

When was the last time he'd heard his boys laugh? When was the last time he'd played a game with them? If ever?

"Shall we help you find Father, my lady?" Robert asked.

"No. I don't want him to think he can outwit me." She spoke loudly, for his benefit, no doubt.

Another smile twitched Will's lips. But he smothered it, crossed his arms, and waited. Patiently.

She came, just as he expected, to the half-open door of the antechamber. It squeaked as she pushed it wider, and her soft-slippered steps entered. She stopped halfway into the room, and he could picture her scanning every corner, lit only by the gray daylight coming in the half-open shutters. It took only a few seconds for her footsteps to resume toward the inner vault door he'd left adrift.

She tentatively peeked inside, her eyes wide. She searched the darkness until her sights honed in on him. "I've found you."

He reached for her hand. "You have." He drew her through the door and across the landing toward him. With a decisiveness that would let her know this had been his intent all along, he roped his arms around her and brought his mouth down on hers.

He smothered her gasp in the crushing kiss he'd wanted to give her all yesterday and today. He was ready for her, and he wasn't ashamed for her to know it. He supposed he half expected her to tolerate his kiss for a few seconds ere she struggled to put an end to the forbidden pleasure and remind him of his promise to remain chaste for five days.

So he was unprepared when she lifted on her toes, wrapped her arms around his neck, and melded her lips with his. As she met him kiss for kiss, fervor with fervor, her passion only stirred his. That his wife shared his desires, wanted to be with him, and enjoyed kissing him as much as he did her—he'd never imagined he'd experience such a relationship. And it was made all the sweeter because of the beauty of their day together.

He halted, pulling back a fraction so their ragged breathing mingled. Was this one of the benefits of becoming friends first? Would it add depth and passion to their marriage?

When he'd wed her that night in front of the rebels, he'd vowed to love, honor, and cherish her. He'd meant what he said. He would consciously choose to love, honor, and cherish her for the rest of his earthly life. They were not feelings to come and go at a whim. Instead they were actions and decisions he would make regarding how he treated her.

Nevertheless, was it possible he might actually *feel* love for her? No doubt he desired her. But could this rush of emotions be the beginning of love?

He gentled his hold and then pressed his lips to her forehead to restrain himself.

She leaned into him, as if sensing his shift in mood. "You outwitted me after all." Her voice contained a smile.

He kissed her forehead again. Had he really outwitted her? Was that even possible when she held such power over him?

"You didn't show me this room during our tour yesterday."

He hadn't considered it before. But now that they were here, he would show her. If something ever happened to him in France, if he didn't come home, he wanted her to know this was here, that she would never want nor worry for her future.

He retrieved a torch from the great hall and the keys from their hiding place. When he ducked back inside the low doorway, he led her down a narrow stone stairway. Breathing in the dampness of the earth and the stones, he felt the chill of the air increase as they descended. At the bottom, he unlocked the chain that bolted shut a thick oaken door.

The slab scraped and squealed as he strained to open it. He didn't go into the vault oft, only to take from the treasury when he left for war or to add to its contents when he returned.

Once inside the stone chamber, he raised the torch high and hooked it through a wall bracket. The light illuminated chests and boxes scattered about the dirt floor.

"This vault was a part of the original house that once stood here."

She passed ahead of him, fingering the chests and moving to the wall to study some of the artifacts hung about—ancient weapons, rusted armor, and the family coat of arms—all placed there by his grandfather and father as a testament to their courage.

"I thought Chesterfield Park was the first manor built on this location."

"This land was owned by an archbishop who fell out of favor with King Edward III. The king was eager to reward his best warrior for his deeds of valor at the Battle of Crecy, and so he knighted my grandfather and gave him the land."

Several recessed ledges had been carved out of the walls and still contained relics and other religious items the archbishop had considered valuable.

"My grandfather used his spoils of war to tear down the archbishop's residence and build a manor fit for a knight."

Marian was studying the contents inside one of the recesses. Her eyes widened and her face paled as she pulled something out. It took him a moment to identify what she held—a small rectangular flask with carvings on the outside.

"You have an original St. Thomas ampulla?" She swished it, testing for liquid inside, and then she held the item as though it was as precious as gold.

"A pilgrim ampulla. The monks sell them at the cathedral."

"But this is one from the time of Thomas Becket. It's what I've been looking for."

Only then did he realize her fingers were shaking. In fact, her whole body seemed to be trembling.

"Do you have another?" She peered into the recess again.

"Why is this ampulla important to you?" He was reminded of how little he knew about this woman. He'd suspected she'd been running away from an unhappy match and had taken her dowry and fled to safety at the priory. Whilst Christina claimed Marian

216

had lost her memories, Will suspected Marian had only said so to protect herself.

Marian didn't respond to his question about the ampulla but instead dug deeper into the hole.

He knew that she'd heard him. He crossed to her and waited for her to finish. When she straightened and turned, he swiped the ampulla from her hand.

She tried to snatch it back, but he easily held it out of reach. She strained after it, and when she realized she wouldn't be able to get it from him, she folded her arms across her chest and scowled.

"Answer me, Marian. Why is this flask important to you?"

A dozen replies rippled across her features. He could see her tossing out one after another, trying to find a way to placate him.

"The truth." His tone was low and demanding.

Her brown eyes were the darkest he'd ever seen them. She held his gaze before her shoulders finally slumped. "It's for my sister."

He could sense she'd told him the truth but only partially so. "And . . ."

"She's dying, and the holy water will cure her."

Tension eased from Will's body—tension he hadn't known was gathering. He wasn't sure what he'd expected her to reveal—perhaps something more dangerous and foreboding. This news of her sister, whilst tragic, was easy to accept.

"Please, Will." She peered at him earnestly. "I made arrangements to deliver two ampullae to a special hiding place in the crypt of Canterbury Cathedral by the end of the week. My sister will be counting on me to have them there."

Many believed in the power of the holy water and oil to bring about healing. 'Twas why so many ventured to Canterbury every year on pilgrimage, to find relief from ailments of both body and soul. While he'd never encountered such healing for himself, he would not discount it for others.

"Where is your sister?" He would help Marian with her mission if it would bring her peace of mind. "Mayhap I can deliver the ampulla to her directly."

Marian dropped her attention, hiding her eyes again. "She's in a place we cannot go."

A place Marian did not wish to disclose? It was possible this sister had traveled with Marian from the Low Countries and was nearby. Living in a convent, perhaps? Quarantined in a secluded cottage? How could he convince Marian she could trust him with the location?

He returned the ampulla to her, and she again held it reverently. "If I put the ampulla in the secret hiding place in the crypt, it will get to her."

"You are certain of this?"

She nodded. Her eyes radiated trust and vulnerability as she described to him the carved column where there was a space small enough to hide something. "It's just that I need to find one more ampulla," she finished.

"I shall purchase another for you at the cathedral."

She crossed to the next recessed ledge and began feeling inside. "I need to find an original, one with specific pictures of Becket."

"If it is holy water, what difference does the container make?"

She stuck her arm deeper into the recess. "The original St. Thomas ampullae were filled with water from a spring at St. Sepulchre, a spring that had true curative properties. The holy water that is now used for filling the ampullae does not have the life-giving residue." She spoke so matter-of-factly that he knew he would not be able to sway her. The only thing he could do was help her.

He began searching through the numerous nooks and crannies within the vault. After scouring the room, he was surprised when she released a happy squeal. "I've found another."

She grasped a second flask with the same engraving of St. Thomas, and she sank to the floor. Her smile held such relief that he could not help but wonder if this had been her true motive for coming to Canterbury and not an unsuitable match as he'd believed.

"Can we go to the cathedral today?" She studied the newfound flask. "I'd like to put these in the crypt."

Will didn't respond. She must know he wouldn't ride out in the rain this late in the day, especially not with the unrest throughout Kent.

When she glanced up, her eyes were wide and beautiful and filled with such expectation he could feel himself weakening. He helped her back to her feet and steadied her.

"I must put them in the hiding spot as soon as possible."

As he began to comprehend her plan to accompany him, he shook his head curtly. He'd never permit her to put herself in peril. "I shall deliver them for you, mayhap at week's end." Or after he'd gained further reports on whether the rebels had ceased their looting and destruction.

"I need to go. What if you can't find the hiding spot?"

"You are not going." He spun on his heels and walked toward the door. "It is too dangerous."

As he expected, she followed after him. "Please, Will." Her hand on his back stopped him. He didn't turn and instead remained facing forward. He didn't want to look into her eyes and chance losing his ability to say no.

He steeled himself, knowing he would anger her. But her protection and safety were worth the wrath. "I forbid you from leaving."

"You have no right to forbid me."

"You are my wife. I have every right."

"You can't dictate my life."

"You will entrust the mission to me or not at all."

With that, he exited the vault, holding the door open for her. She hesitated, as though trying to grasp his decision. Finally, she stalked past him, her eyes flashing with anger, her shoulders rigid, her chin aloft.

She'd challenged more of his decisions in the short time he'd known her than anyone else ever had. And he found his own ire rising along with a shot of hot desire. How was it possible she was the most infuriating woman he'd ever met as well as the most beguiling?

~ 20 ~

WOULD WILL WANT HER to accompany him to chapel today as he had the past two mornings? As much as she wished she could stop longing for him, she'd done little else but think about him most of the night, replaying the passionate kiss he'd given her while playing hide-and-seek. Her body betrayed her by yearning for another just like it.

Marian rolled to the edge of the bed and forced herself to sit up. Dawn had already broken, and the rain had stopped.

Even so, her mood was as damp as the humid air that permeated the bedroom. She should be excited, even relieved, that she'd found two ampullae here at Chesterfield Park. The discovery had been more than she'd hoped for.

Yet, somehow, she couldn't muster the same enthusiasm she'd felt yesterday when she'd first chanced upon the holy water. She'd had all evening and night to think about the implications of her find and the fact that she had three days left. Only three days left to be with Will.

Each moment with him had been more real than if she'd been living in the present. Every sound of his breath, every touch, every beat of his pulse—everything about him was more vibrant than anything she'd known before.

And each hour she spent with him seemed to draw her further into his life and the year 1381 so that there had been moments, especially during the past two days, when she'd forgotten she didn't belong.

It scared Marian to think she'd lost track of time. Nevertheless, she loved spending every second of every day with Will. And with his sons. They'd readily accepted her, had none of the wariness she'd expected of children who were gaining a new mother. She supposed they'd already had two years to grieve their own mother. In addition, they respected Will enough to honor his decision about taking a new wife.

Marian sighed and pushed back a thick lock of hair. Should she have done the same with his decision regarding traveling to the cathedral? It was just that she wasn't used to anyone ordering her life, telling her where she could or couldn't go. And she was beyond frustrated knowing the cathedral was less than a fifteen-minute car ride away, yet she had no way to get there.

There was still the possibility of sneaking out and walking to the cathedral by herself. But if Will had decided even riding with him would pose too many dangers, then was she really willing to take the chance alone?

Although she chafed under his overprotectiveness, the long night had given her plenty of time to think about her predicament and to conclude she was left with no choice but to trust him.

At a soft rap on the door, Marian's pulse spurted forward, and she stood. After avoiding her the previous evening, had Will decided to seek her out? Did he miss her too?

The door opened a crack, and Sarah poked her head in. Upon seeing Marian, she opened the door further.

No Will again. Marian crossed her arms over her chest to ward off a chill filled with disappointment.

Sarah gave quiet instructions to someone behind her, and then before Marian realized what was happening, a kitchen boy carried in an enormous wooden tub followed by two strong men each hauling cauldrons of steaming water.

Marian stared in confusion as they dumped the hot water into the tub. After they departed, Sarah emptied two pitchers of what appeared to be cooler water into the wooden tub before motioning to Marian. "A bath, milady."

"Oh, heavens above." Marian's skin was already tingling in anticipation. After ten days of nothing but sponge baths, the thought of immersing her entire body into the water filled her with a sense of bliss.

"Sir William ordered it brought up for you."

Will had done this for her? In spite of their argument? Tears sprang to her eyes.

Watching her reaction, Sarah smiled. "He may be stubborn, milady. But he will love you to his dying breath."

Marian had to swallow hard to dislodge the tight lump in her throat. "Where is he now?"

"Readying to leave."

Her heart gave an erratic thump. "He's leaving? Where's he going?"

"He did not say, milady."

To Canterbury. Marian glanced at the bedside table. The leather pouch where she'd stowed the ampullae was gone. Will had crept in or had one of the servants retrieve it for him. Hopefully, he wouldn't see the note she'd penned to her dad, warning him of his impending death. The note was carefully wrapped along with the ampullae in layers of an old blanket. If he did read it, what would he think? Whatever the case, she was relieved he was willing to carry the ampullae to the crypt.

"Has he left yet?" Marian crossed to the door, anxious to see him, to thank him, to bridge the rift that had opened up between them.

Sarah glanced out the window. "Not yet."

Marian slipped into the hallway and ran toward the stairs that would lead to the great hall. Thankfully, Sarah made no move to stop her. Only when Marian started down the steep steps did she realize she was barefoot and donned in her thin nightshift. For only a second, she considered returning to her room for a cloak, but at the sound of Will's voice below, she made her feet move faster.

In the entryway, she caught sight of him through the arched doorway striding toward a waiting horse. "Will. Wait."

He stopped and circled around. His expression was grim, his eyes ringed underneath with dark circles, and his lips pressed into a hard line. Yet he was ruggedly handsome, more so with each passing day she was with him.

She had an overwhelming urge to fling herself into his arms and to kiss him and tell him she loved him. But surely she didn't love him and was only grateful for his kindness. She stopped short and stared at him, suddenly mute.

He seemed to be resisting meeting her gaze, looking slightly beyond her for a long minute. When he finally dropped his sights and looked into her eyes, his anger was gone. Yes, his determination was still there. He still had no intention of letting her go with him, no matter what other tantrums she threw. But he wasn't upset at her.

"The bath," she whispered. "Thank you."

He nodded and gave a slight bow. Then he spun and continued striding toward his squires already atop their steeds and a groomsman who held the reins of his horse.

She wanted more than a nod and a bow. And she wanted to give him more than a thank-you. Before she lost courage, she bolted after him and wrapped her fingers around his bicep. "Will?"

He froze.

His name on her lips was an invitation. For a second she was afraid he might reject it. Then he slowly pivoted, and when he was facing her again, she launched herself against him, wrapping her arms around his waist and pressing into him as though it might be the last time she'd see him.

His arms closed around her fiercely then, without hesitation. And he pressed his face into her long, wild hair.

She breathed in his woodsy scent. This was where she wanted to be, in a place she never wanted to leave. Against him. In his arms. With his strength and life pulsing around her.

Love burned through her. The words pushed for release. How was it possible to love this man already?

His arms slackened, and he began to pull away.

She clung to him and lifted her face to his. It was another invitation, and he read it well. He angled down and seized her lips, like a warrior laying claim to his prize. His kiss was powerful and spoke to her—saying all the things he couldn't—that he cherished her, wanted her, and would do anything for her.

He broke the kiss as forcefully as he started it, swung up on his mount, and rode away without looking back.

She watched him until he disappeared. Only then did she tremble. It came from deep within—a trembling that warned she was heading toward disaster and that if she didn't stop herself from falling in love with William Durham, she would be the cause of untold tragedy.

• ● •

Marian sat in the tub until her skin wrinkled. The water, steeped with thyme, was soothing. And the soap, unlike the hard modern bar, was soft and oily and scented with musk and cloves.

She was embarrassed to have Sarah in the room with her while she was naked, and at first turned down the offer to wash her hair. But once Marian started the process, she found it was cumbersome in the small tub, and having Sarah's assistance was essential, especially for the rinsing process.

Sarah seemed to think nothing of the awkward situation,

helping Marian dry off and then assisting her into a gown, this one an emerald green that was as soft as velvet and flowed like a summer brook.

Marian still couldn't get used to not wearing undergarments. What did women do when they had their periods? How in the world did they manage without underwear and adhesive pads?

Even though, hopefully, her period would hold off until she returned to the present, she brought up the question to Sarah as the young servant ran a comb through her hair. "What would happen if I began to menstruate?"

Sarah paused, the comb deep in Marian's thick wet hair. "Menses? Do you mean your courses?"

Marian nodded. She was getting better at using medieval words but still had much to learn.

Sarah gently pulled the comb the rest of the way through Marian's hair before answering, clearly choosing her words carefully. "Do you suspect the master's babe already grows inside you?"

Heat spilled into Marian's cheeks. "Oh no, that's not what I meant. I only wanted to know what I would wear to stanch the flow of blood."

Sarah began the process of braiding and coiling Marian's hair with deft fingers. "'Twill not be long, milady." Her voice was low and soothing as though attempting to offer Marian comfort. "You are still young and will have many babies."

Many babies? As if that was the sign of her success as a woman? Marian wanted to protest but realized she would be foolish to do so. Already she was foolish to bring up so personal a topic. "Tell me more about you, Sarah." Time to change the subject. "How long have you been married to Thad? And do you have children?"

Again Sarah's hands stilled.

Marian waited. Had she crossed an invisible line? She guessed nobly born women didn't interact so personally with their maidservants. But proper or not, Marian wanted a friend, someone she could talk to. Lady Felice and her retinue disdained her. Christina had secluded herself in her chambers until she could return to St. Sepulchre. Sarah was the only other female who made any effort to engage her—though she likely had no choice.

Marian wished she could assure Sarah that she wasn't a noblewoman, that there weren't any differences between them, that in the eyes of God they were equal. But she realized it would be hundreds of years yet until class distinctions held less sway.

Marian tried again. "Thad seems like a kind husband."

"He is very good, milady." Sarah's hands resumed their grooming.

"And he's a good father?"

Several slow strokes of the comb followed before Sarah answered. "I wist that he would be. But I have not yet borne him any wee ones."

During Marian's years as an intern before working with Mercer Pharmaceuticals, she'd spent part of her time testing infertility drugs, and now her mind raced with all the possibilities of medicines. If only she could recommend something to Sarah. Of course, the problem might not lie with Sarah at all, but with Thad. But without modern labs or medicine, there was no way to know. Or to help them.

"I lose my courses," Sarah continued slowly. "I oft feel the flutter of the new life. But my womb will not hold the babe for long."

Sarah was plagued with miscarriages? Marian's heart fell. She searched for words of comfort, but before she could think of something to say, a commotion outside the open window at the front of the manor caused both of them to startle. The voices were boisterous and angry and reminded Marian of the disturbance she'd heard the day the peasants had attacked St. Sepulchre.

Sarah rushed to the window and peered out before pressing a shaking hand against her mouth.

"What is it, Sarah?" Marian rose from her dressing table.

"Rebels are here, milady." Sarah's voice was hollow with fear. "A very large group of them at the gate."

Marian crossed to stand beside Sarah peering at the growing horde. The shouting and the clamor increased, and Marian prayed the gate would hold the peasants at bay. As some began to climb over the wall, Marian hoped the men Will had left behind would be able to fight them off.

But as more peasants dropped over the wall, she could see that the guards would soon be outnumbered and cut down. What if rather than fighting, they opened the gate, allowed the peasants inside, and attempted to broker peace?

As if one of Will's guards had drawn the same conclusion, the gate began to swing open from the inside. Within seconds, the peasants swarmed through, shouting their victory.

For a moment, all Marian could hear were the screams of the nuns trapped inside the priory as the peasants attacked. What would they do here at Chesterfield Park? Loot and destroy? Rape and murder?

She glanced around the room, wanting to find a hiding place, somewhere she could be out of harm's way. But as swiftly as the desire came, she just as swiftly swept it aside. She was the lady of the house. She had Robert and Phillip to consider along with all the others in her care. If she didn't attempt to make peace with the peasants in Will's absence, who would?

Marian strode toward the door. "Where are Robert and Phillip?"

"They were with their tutor." Sarah raced after her.

"I must keep them safe, Sarah." Her chest pounded with the need to go to the boys. They would surely be frightened. If she could whisk them down to the vault and hide them there, they would be out of harm's way until Will returned.

If Will returned . . .

What if he'd ridden into this mass of marauding peasants? What if she'd sent him out to meet his death?

A shudder crept up her back. He would have been here, if not for her insistence on taking the ampullae to Canterbury today. He would have known what to do to calm the angry men, or at the very least, he and his men at arms would have been present to defend the place and protect his sons.

Now, everyone was in danger. Because of her.

"Robert? Phillip?" Her voice and footsteps echoed with desperation in the long corridor. She picked up her skirts, annoyed with the thick material for tangling in her legs. As she descended the stairs and stumbled into the great hall, she stopped short at the sight that met her.

In the middle of the room, two rebels held Robert and Phillip with knives pressed to their throats.

~ 21 ~

DESOLATION AND DESTRUCTION met Will wherever he rode. The low burn of anger in his chest had fanned into a fire by the time he finished in town and started toward home, his squires close on his trail.

Didn't the rebels know their raiding and looting would only hurt them? Didn't they understand that abandoning their labor in the fields would bring hardships and starvation once winter settled?

At least workers had begun repairs at St. Sepulchre and most of the nuns were restored. He'd given the prioress a donation toward the rebuilding of the gates, gaining her promise that this time she would have them constructed of iron and kept locked at all times.

When he'd made his way to the cathedral, the devastation within had been worse—especially in the archbishop's chambers. He'd heard that the Bishop of Canterbury had not been present in town when Wat Tyler and John Ball had entered. If so, the bishop's head would have been at the end of a pike at the forefront of their calamitous parade.

Will had received no opposition at the cathedral since the monks were distracted and busy bringing order back to the chaos. Even so, he instructed his squires to stand guard at the entrance whilst he went below.

He was surprised to find Marian's hiding spot exactly where she'd described it. As he stuffed the ampullae and strange note she'd penned to her father into the small space, he wasn't able to halt the barrage of questions. How had Marian known about this hiding place? How was her father involved? Where was she really from?

He didn't want to have any doubts about her, wanted to trust her completely. But as before, he had a premonition something was not as it ought to be. He'd intended to be patient and allow her to reveal her past in her own timing. However, maybe he needed to probe for more information. At least then, he could prepare himself for repercussions that might arise.

Amidst his inner warring, his pulse warmed at the remembrance of her standing before him that morn, the early light reflecting off her bed-tousled hair, highlighting its deep brown and red. Of course, rushing out to him in her thin shift and uncovered head had been naught short of scandalous.

But her delicate features had been tense with the need to see him. And that realization, more than anything, burned a slow trail through him all day. She'd defied all properness and modesty to come to him. She'd been unashamed of her desire to see him. And she'd willingly accepted his embrace and kiss.

He'd known the kiss was her apology along with her acceptance of his decision. And it had contained the depth of her feeling for him—something he was still trying to comprehend. Yes, he could admit his fondness for her was growing, different from the physical attraction that came easily. Was it possible she was experiencing the same kind of fondness for him?

The soggy ground slowed his mount. The mud in the beast's hooves was thick and heavy. As he crested the rise of the hill, he motioned to his squires and slowed the horse, intending to dismount and pry loose the sludge. But as he tugged the reins and brushed a hand over the stallion's withers, appreciating the powerful muscles of its neck and shoulders, a wisp of smoke in the distance snagged his attention.

The black curl drifted upward like a coiling adder. And it came directly from Chesterfield Park. The beating in Will's chest silenced, and a deadly calm fell over him. Something had happened.

With a sharp jab to the horse's flanks and a quick flick of the reins, he urged his mount to gallop. The closer his home loomed, the harder he pushed the stallion, moving well ahead of his squires. With each pound of the hooves, his chest pounded harder, until it hurt painfully.

The visions of Thomas's body filled his mind's eye. The vultures perched on his brother's sightless head, the putrid body pieces in the ditch. The moment he'd recognized his brother amidst the decimated remains, he'd fallen to his knees and vomited until he'd had naught left.

He hadn't been there to protect Thomas. And now, what if he was too late to protect his family? His wife. And his sons.

"God have mercy." His breath came in quick spurts. Nausea crowded his throat, and he tasted bile at the back of his tongue. "God have mercy."

As he charged through the open gatehouse, another thought assailed him. Someone among the ranks of his household must have betrayed him and opened the gates wide to a roving band of rebels. Who had done it?

He unsheathed one of his swords, his body rigid with the need to kill the one who had been disloyal. The grounds swarmed with men, looting his storehouse and stables and home. But even as he charged forward, his sword swinging at anyone close enough to feel its blade, his mind cautioned him against too much bloodshed, at least until he determined what had become of his kin.

At the manor entryway, he dismounted, slashing away the rebels who converged upon him in an attempt to capture him. He entered the house with long, angry strides, the blood on his weapon a warning that he would kill if need be.

As he stalked into the great hall, he repelled several more men. With curses, they fell back.

"Sire." A familiar voice called out a warning. He spun to see Thad, his steward and friend, standing next to a stranger, who clearly, with in his simple garb, sun-bronzed face, and plain chaperon-style hat, was no nobleman. Yet, he held himself with the bearing of a leader, his expression hardened, as if he'd witnessed so much heartbreak that he'd lost his heart altogether.

Thad's young face compressed with worry lines, and his gaze darted behind the stranger.

Will followed the glance, and his chest seized. Two men stood at Marian's side. One was pinning her arms behind her back, and the other held a knife to her throat, which she'd arched in a desperate act to keep her skin from being nicked. But already blood trailed down her pale neck and pooled in the hollow at the base of her throat. Surprisingly, her eyes were calm, even angry. On the floor behind her, Phillip crouched low, shielding Robert in his arms.

"Sir William, welcome home." The stranger offered a smile that didn't reach his eyes. "We've been waiting for you."

Will sensed half a dozen men closing in around him. He lifted his sword in warning.

"If you be putting down your weapon"—the stranger glanced toward Marian—"then we will be putting down ours. But if you choose not to . . ."

Marian released a pained gasp, and the rebel holding the knife grinned as fresh blood trickled down her neck.

Instantly, Will's dagger was in his hand, aimed at the man's heart and ready to throw.

"Wait!" Thad stepped forward, his expression wreathed with urgency. "They're here to seek peace. They mean you no harm."

You. Not *us.* "So you are the one who betrayed me." Will spat at the man who'd been his most trusted companion.

Thad shook his head, then cocked his head to the corner where Sarah stood with the other women, amongst them Will's mother and sister. Thad's eyes said it all. Whatever he'd done had been to protect Sarah and everyone else. Now Will must do likewise for the people he loved.

"Please, sire. 'Tis Wat Tyler. And he's here to recruit you to be the sovereign captain."

Wat Tyler? The leader of the rebellion?

Will examined the stranger again, taking in the smattering of gray at the man's temple, the leathery lines in his forehead and at his eyes, and the sorrow—deep sorrow—etched into those lines. He didn't know much about this man except hearsay from the knights who'd visited him earlier in the week. One of the rumors was that his daughter had been indecently assaulted by a poll tax collector. Seeing the sadness in the man's face now, Will could almost believe it was true.

Even so, Will's fingers tightened around his dagger, its lethal tip aimed at Marian's captor.

Wat looked at it pointedly. "You've a brave wife, sire. She insisted that if we must be hurting someone, it be her and not your sons."

Marian didn't move. Every muscle in Will's body tensed with the need to set her free. Could he impale her captor before the man slit her throat open?

"I've been hearing you're a mighty warrior." Wat's voice echoed in the now-silent hall. "I be supposing you can kill my man Jack clean through quicker than a bat can fly. But my man Chester. Now he's a fair shot with the arrow." Wat nodded to the side of the room where a youth had his bow taut and arrow notched. It was aimed at Marian's heart.

Will's muscles twitched with the need to slay both rebels at the

JODY HEDLUND

same time. But with only one dagger, he was at a disadvantage. The truth was, if he wanted to save Marian and his sons, he would have to play along with this crowd of miscreants—at least for the time being.

Slowly, Will lowered his blade and used it to point to the trestle table closest to the hearth fire. "Let my wife be, and I shall sit down and share a drink with you."

Wat didn't smile, but the tight lines at his mouth relaxed. He nodded at Marian's captor, who released the pressure of the knife and shoved Marian behind him.

Marian knelt and gathered Robert into her arms. The little boy came to her willingly, clinging to her and burying his face into her bosom. Phillip lifted his chin at the rebels, as if to say they would have to kill him first before he let anything happen to his brother.

The boy's ferocity reflected Will's except that his encompassed both of his sons. And Marian. She kissed Robert's head and held him tightly before meeting Will's gaze. Her eyes reached out to him and seemed to tell him she was strong, not to worry about her, that she would take care of his boys.

In that instant, he knew he loved her, that the emotion building within his breast was not mere fondness. It was love. He loved her more than he'd ever loved anyone or anything.

Although Will would never agree to be the sovereign captain of these rebelling ruffians, for now he would do whatever was necessary to protect the woman and the family he loved.

• • •

Marian's neck stung painfully, but she bit back her complaints and focused instead on Robert and Phillip throughout the long night. Although Phillip had been brave for a boy of eight, he finally curled up against her with Robert and slept.

She tried to stay awake so she could listen to the discussion between Will, Wat Tyler, and several of the other leaders within the group. But eventually she gave in to sleep too.

She heard enough to understand that Will had no choice but to go along with Wat. Although Will argued eloquently and presented a multitude of considerations against becoming their captain, Wat Tyler remained steadfast in his insistence. The rebel leader didn't say so, but it was clear that Will would join their cause or lose his family.

Apparently Wat had seen what Marian had when Will had stormed into the great hall with his sword drawn, effortlessly cutting down anyone in his path. Will was mercilessly determined to save his family. He'd do anything to keep them from harm. He'd kill anyone. He'd sacrifice his own life. And he'd even align himself with his enemy.

Maybe Wat had known all that ahead. Maybe that's why he came to Chesterfield Park. And maybe that's why he cornered the boys and her first.

Whatever the case, Marian sensed she and the boys would be safe as long as Will did exactly what Wat asked of him. At first she found a measure of comfort in the realization that Will would go to any lengths to protect them.

However, that comfort had dissolved into fear as she'd begun to understand why Will was able to sacrifice himself so willingly. Yes, he was noble and honorable and placed their needs above his own. But ultimately, he loathed himself, didn't believe he deserved to live. Such self-hatred pushed him to a recklessness that could someday end in his death.

The very prospect chilled her to the bone.

In the morning, Sarah roused Marian. Around them, the men were rolling blankets, strapping on weapons, and preparing to be on their way. The air was sour with the stench of so many unwashed bodies, and after just one day, the sweet scents from her bath were gone.

Sarah, who had tended her wound, now silently pressed a bundle and a leather jug into her arms, as she did to each of the boys. Then, the same peasants who had guarded them all through the night forced them to their feet and hustled them outside. Ahead, Will was mounted on his horse next to Wat Tyler, speaking with the man in hushed tones. Outfitted in his padded gambeston and chain mail, Will had his weapons in hand and a squire on the horse next to him.

She paused and waited for Will to see and acknowledge her. But he was apparently too consumed with his conversation to give her notice.

Thad assisted her onto a horse and placed Robert in the saddle in front of her, thankfully giving the boy the reins. Marian had seen Robert ride, and at six he was much better at handling the horse than she was. In truth, he was an expert compared to her.

If only Phillip could have his horse. She strained to see him among the group of men on foot. Upon glimpsing him, she gasped. Someone had stolen his pack and jug. And now his hands were tied behind his back and a rope wound around his neck. He held his chin high, and his mouth was set with the same determination she'd seen in Will's expression. Clearly he planned to bear the situation with dignity and courage—just as his father would.

Even so, indignation swelled within Marian's chest, especially at the sight of the coarse hemp already chafing the boy's fair skin. Boys his age were supposed to play Little League baseball, build forts in the woods, and watch *Star Wars*. Weren't they?

Marian started to slide off her horse, determined to take Phillip's place, but Thad forced her back up.

"Let me down." She glared at him. "I'm planning to walk."

"My lady." Thad didn't relinquish his grip upon her, his splotchy face growing redder. "Sir William wants you to remain on the mare with the young lad."

"I want Phillip to ride instead."

"Sir William insists."

As though sensing the commotion, Will's gaze shot her direction. The stark desperation in his stunning blue eyes rent her heart in half. She could only imagine his agony at seeing his son bound so viciously.

He shifted his gaze to Thad and nodded curtly.

Thad produced a rope and started to unravel it. "If you try getting down, the master's instructed me to bind you to the horse."

The words gave Marian pause, and her sights returned to Will. But he'd already nudged his horse forward, his stiff back turned to her, the matter settled. How could he let his son endure such humiliation and pain without making an effort to stop it?

"No telling what they might do to you, lady." Thad's eyes beseeched her to comprehend his meaning. "But they durst not harm the lad."

With a sickening lump forming in her stomach, she nodded. She finally understood. As a woman, she was dispensable, worthless, and in much more danger. Will was doing his best to protect her, and she needed to trust his wisdom and decisions.

Thad roped their bundles onto the saddle before patting the horse's flank and stepping back. Even though Thad had allowed Wat Tyler into the manor, Marian understood he'd only done so to avoid bloodshed and protect everyone. Now he took his place among the men of his own rank, as much a prisoner as Will.

As they started out the gates of Chesterfield Park, Marian glanced behind to the magnificent stonework, the large windows, the entrance with two open arches, and the hall tower on the east end. While not as sprawling or magnificent as the modern home, it was still impressive.

And it felt like home. It had been a safe and comfortable place amidst the dangers and disorder of 1381. Now she was being thrust out into the middle of a rebellion. From her previous research into the uprising, she knew the outcome already. The revolt wouldn't last more than another week before it was squelched.

In the meantime, however, thousands of people—nobility and peasant alike—would be slaughtered.

Marian could only pray, desperately, that Will and his sons wouldn't be among those who died. And that she wouldn't be either.

~22~

Marian huddled against Robert and Phillip in the darkness. Even though the June night was balmy and the sky studded with stars, she couldn't get warm. She'd been shivering off and on since the horde had stopped earlier in the evening.

After four days of being on the road, the peasants had steadily gained more followers until the ranks swelled beyond what her eyes could see. If she had to guess, she would say at least twenty—if not thirty—thousand had congregated, with more arriving every hour, not only from Kent but also from Essex, Sussex, Staffordshire, and Bedfordshire.

Robert had predicted they were heading toward London. And he'd been right. The boy had been an astute guide as they made their way slowly to Rochester and Rochester Castle, which Wat Tyler had taken without a fight. The lord, a knight by the name of Sir John, had been forced to join the peasant ranks the same way Will had, with his family held hostage.

Now they were only a few miles southeast of the capital on Blackheath, a sprawling hilly area covered for miles around with peasant camps. The air was hazy with smoke and the scents of a thousand meals being cooked in the open. The raucous noises of celebration had been ongoing for hours, especially from the pillagers who returned from looting London.

Earlier, Wat and the other leaders of the revolt had sent Sir John by the River Thames to the Tower of London to bear tidings to the king. He'd been instructed to ask King Richard to come out to Blackheath and negotiate peace with the rebels. Sir John returned with news from the king that he would visit Blackheath in the morning and meet with the leaders.

In the meantime, the rebels had threatened to burn the suburbs around London and then conquer the city by force, slaying all within if the mayor didn't open the gates.

Faced with so many armed men, the city officials had no choice but to give in to the demands. Wat Tyler, the priest John Ball, and others had led thousands throughout London. Reports had begun to trickle back regarding the destruction, particularly the slaying of rich merchants, noblemen, men of the court, as well as clergy. The rioters had broken in to the king's prison and set free the criminals, who had then joined in the killing and looting.

All evening, Marian prayed that Will, wherever he was, would remain unharmed. She'd seen him only at a distance during the long days of riding toward London. The jostling of the crowds, the sheer masses of people, had separated them. But thankfully, as the ranks had swelled and as they'd drawn closer to London, the peasants had become too preoccupied to pay attention to Phillip, a lone boy among the many hostages they held. Marian had persuaded Thad to cut the boy's binding loose, and, although afraid of the repercussions, Thad had finally done so.

Will had tasked Thad with guarding them, and the young steward hadn't strayed from their sides. Even now, Thad sat in front of them, his hand on his sword pommel.

It was June 9. She'd been in 1381 for fifteen days. While the two weeks had seemed to last an eternity and had been filled with one life-threatening danger after another, in some ways she felt as though she'd just arrived, especially when it came to being with Will.

If Ellen or Harrison had gotten into the crypt yesterday and found the ampullae Will had hopefully been able to put into the hiding spot, then she might very well be taking a hot shower and sipping a cup of coffee soon. At the thought of indulging in the two luxuries, she should have been excited. Instead a strange trepidation slithered through her.

What would happen to her body here in 1381? Would she fall into a coma on Blackheath? If so, how would a 1381 comatose body survive without IVs, NG tubes, and antibiotics to ward off infections?

Without modern medical advancements, a coma in the Middle Ages would most certainly lead to death. How long would she have before dying? A few days? A week at most?

When first crossing time, she hadn't considered—hadn't really cared—what became of her past body once she returned to her real life. But here, with Robert and Phillip, she couldn't keep from worrying. They would be frantic if she suddenly fell into an unconscious state.

With the imminence of going back to the present, she'd begun to more carefully examine all the angles of the return process. When her comatose body died in 1381, would she also die in the present time? She suspected her modern body would terminate at the same time her 1381 body did. After all, on her dad's list of speculations, he'd indicated a death in the past or vice versa would result in a corresponding death in the other time era. She'd already concluded that's what had happened to him.

If her 1381 body was doomed to die, that meant even if she fully awakened in the present, she wouldn't have long to live. Unless . . . There had to be an *unless*. Surely the process of crossing back into time wasn't fatal for everyone. After all, there were records of people who had lived to tell about their visions. She could only speculate that meant they'd discovered a cure.

The ultimate cure . . .

Of course. Those early accounts were from people who had access to the wellsprings. They'd likely had the holy water to draw them back to reality and additional water when they started feeling ill as their comatose body in the past began to die.

That meant, once she awoke in the present, her body would require another dose. Was that why her dad had put two ampullae into the crypt? Had he known he would need two in order to survive? One to bring him out of the coma and another to sustain his life?

If she gave one of the ampullae to Ellen, Marian wouldn't have the two doses she would need herself. That meant her only hope for saving both Ellen and herself was to find the old wellspring in the area where St. Sepulchre had once stood. What if St. George's Tower, the old square tower at the edge of a shopping plaza, was truly the place? What if it had been built to guard the well? Maybe the gargoyle holding the clock was issuing a warning not to disturb the spot.

Even if it was really the location of the old well, there were no guarantees. Besides, how would she and Harrison begin investigating and digging without drawing attention from the competition who was bent on stealing the miracle cure from them?

Marian squeezed her eyes shut, wishing she could as easily squeeze away all the disturbing thoughts. Robert's hair tickled her chin, and she snuggled him tighter.

The distant shrill screams and the accompanying vicious laughter sent a shiver through Marian. Robert slipped his hand into hers and lifted his head from the crook of her arm. "I promise to protect you, Mother."

It was the first time he'd called her anything beside "my lady." And his declaration brought stinging tears to her eyes. "You have already." She worked to get the words past her constricting throat. "You are a brave and good man like your father."

He laid his head back down, apparently satisfied that all was well. Marian pressed a kiss into his dust-coated, uncombed hair, and he released a small tired sigh. On the other side of Robert, she caught Phillip watching her.

Phillip was decidedly more reserved and solemn and nodded at Marian. "You are brave and good likewise, my lady. I see now why my father chose you. If I find a wife half as beautiful and kind as you, I shall indeed be fortunate."

"Thank you." Again, tears pricked Marian's eyes. Though the ground was hard and cold and her body ached all over and they'd finished the last of the food Sarah had packed for them, somehow Phillip's affirmation took away every thought of discomfort—even if just for a moment.

Suddenly, she hated the fact that she could be jerked out of 1381 away from these boys, away from her duty to take care of them, perhaps without even being able to say good-bye.

She wanted—no, needed—to be able to say good-bye to Will. How could she leave without seeing him one more time, without looking into his eyes, hearing his voice, and maybe even tasting his lips? The idea of never speaking with him again wrenched her heart. She closed her eyes to fight against the need for him that welled up within her more and more often lately.

Shouts and laughter once again pierced the air. If the long grass hadn't been crushed against her cheek and the scent of soil so strong in her nose, she would have been tempted to think this was just one long nightmare she was experiencing. But the warmth of Robert's small body, the soft pressure of his breathing, and the crackle of a nearby fire proved this was all very real.

"Father." Phillip's whisper cut through the night.

Marian's eyes flew open to see Will hovering above the boy, who was now kneeling.

"You have done well keeping your mother and brother safe." Will rested a hand on the boy's head.

Phillip nodded, drinking in not only the sight of his father but his praise.

Firelight flickered across Will's face. His expression was grim, his eyes sadder and more haunted than Marian had ever seen them.

Robert stirred and opened his eyes. At the sight of his father, he released Marian and sat up. It was clear he wanted to bury himself against his father's chest. But he held back.

"And you, Robert," Will said. "You did well guiding the horse for your mother."

Robert straightened and smiled.

Will ruffled the young boy's hair but didn't smile back. Instead, his gaze shifted to Marian. Even in the dark, his eyes were intense and hungry and desperate all at once. She could sense he needed her. She wasn't sure exactly how, but that thought sent a quiver through her belly and a sudden keen need to be with him too.

He didn't say anything to her. He didn't have to. When he held out his hand, it was enough. She took it and let him help her to her feet. After the past days of riding, her beautiful emerald gown was filthy, her hands and nails crusted with grime, and her face likely streaked with dust. But at the moment, nothing seemed to matter except that Will wanted to be with her.

He led her to a spot a dozen or so paces away from Thad and the boys, into the shadows and out of the light of the flames. It wasn't private. She could sense the boys' eyes upon them with each step they took. And yet, she felt no shame or embarrassment as Will lay in the grass and pulled her down. He draped his cloak over them and then drew her against him, wrapping his arms around her so that he was holding her much the same way he had the night he'd slept with her.

One arm encircled her waist, and the other slid up to her neck. She realized he wanted her to free her hair, and she quickly loosened her braid. As soon as her hair was free, he buried his fingers and face there with a soft groan that rumbled through her all the way to her toes.

She expected him to kiss her, was ashamed at how much she wanted his kisses. But within moments, she could feel the even rise and fall of his chest and knew he was asleep. She guessed he hadn't slept much since they'd been captured. And now, with the rebel leaders occupied for the night, maybe he'd decided to finally allow himself to rest.

Her eyes closed in exhaustion too. For the first time since the peasant mob had descended upon Chesterfield Park, she felt safe again. She was where she wanted—no, needed—to be. She laid her hand over his and intertwined their fingers. And she prayed she would have at least this last night with Will before she had to leave him.

• • •

The crunch of grass awoke Will. Through the slit in his eyelids, he glimpsed Thad adding more fuel to the fire. From the way Marian relaxed against him, he knew she was still asleep. A glance in the direction of his sons told Will they slumbered too. And a peek at the sky overhead informed him he'd slept several hours and had another hour or so ere dawn broke. Several hours of unbroken, dreamless sleep. It only happened with her.

A quietness had settled upon Blackheath. After the frenzy and fighting of the past eve, most of the rebels had likely passed out from intoxication or exhaustion.

From what he'd seen and heard, the rebels had torn asunder Marshalsea prison in Southwark along with Fleet and Newgate prisons, so that now not only were the bondmen ravaging London, but so were countless murderers, thieves, and rapists.

The rebels had attacked numerous palaces and abbeys, demolishing the buildings and burning priceless books and paperwork in the streets. Then they'd moved on to ransack the Tower of London with a list of hated nobles and officials that they demanded be executed. Will was glad he'd been there to prevent the rebels from slaying some of the royal family, including the king's half sister.

Even though Will had tried to protect whomever he could, the rebels had hunted down and beheaded as many of those nobles as they could find, putting their heads on pikes and parading them around the city before affixing the heads to London Bridge. The bloody display had been all the permission the masses had needed to continue the looting and bloodshed far into the night.

It hadn't mattered that King Richard had issued charters announcing the abolition of serfdom and had promised to administer justice. The rebels hadn't been satisfied. And Wat Tyler intended to make more demands of the king at the meeting on the morrow.

Will had decided this meeting was his chance to do something decisive. So he'd sent a secret message to Walworth, the mayor of London, to be prepared for action. He'd also informed Thad that if his efforts at helping the king failed, he was to take Marian and his sons forthwith to the Continent for safekeeping.

As if sensing his wakefulness, Marian's fingers tightened in his, offering him fortitude. Just the feel of her alone was enough to calm his spirit. After the senseless killings and violence he'd witnessed earlier and with what was to come in the hours ahead, he needed the balm of her touch, the quietness and peace of her body, her soft, steady presence to hold his nightmares at bay.

She shifted so that she was facing him. In the darkness, he sensed more than saw that she'd opened her eyes and was attempting to study his face. "Sleep longer." Her whisper was faint so only the two of them could hear it.

"You sleep." He drew her head against his chest and pressed his lips into her hair.

She snuggled against him. Any other night he might have been aware of how enthralling her body felt against his, how much he still longed for her. But his mind overflowed with images he'd seen in London earlier—images of the gruesome torture and death everywhere he'd gone. With each new corpse he'd stumbled upon, he'd pictured Thomas, until he'd thought he would go mad if he had to look at one more headless body on the street.

"What is it?" she whispered.

He tightened his arms around her. For a long moment, he just held her, drawing succor again from her.

"Will, tell me what haunts you."

He shook his head.

"Please. Then I can help bear the burden. You won't have to carry it alone anymore." Her breath was warm upon his neck, her voice filled with a plea.

Could she really want to hear about his troubles?

Part of him cautioned against revealing those deep wounds. The pain and heartache were his cross to bear. At the same time, he longed to share with her in a way he hadn't with anyone else. He wasn't sure what about her beckoned him to open himself up. Maybe it had to do with the vow he'd made to spend time getting to know one another.

Still he hesitated. "I do not want to trouble you—"

"Don't hide this from me. I want to know about every part of you, even the hardest parts."

What about the parts she was hiding from him? He wanted to know that too. He wanted complete honesty, no matter what may come of it. But maybe that kind of openness had to start with him.

"Very well," he whispered. "I shall share. But then you must share also."

"Share what?"

"The truth about your past."

She was motionless for several heartbeats, then nodded.

He released a breath and dug his fingers in her hair, as though that could keep him from sinking into the despair that sought to suck him down like quicksand every time he relived the past.

"I did not want to take Thomas with me to Bergerac, but he was young and eager, much like I had once been."

The garrisons had been camped outside Bergerac, surrounding the French town. The winter had been particularly cold, and the army had grown restless. Smaller groups had made raids into the countryside as a means of foraging for food and supplies. Will eased his conscience by telling himself the army depended upon such raids for survival. If innocent men, women, and children were killed during the confiscation of goods and securing of supplies, it was all a part of the brutality of war.

Even as he excused the killing, Will understood that taking food from poor French people ensured their death anyway, by starvation rather than by sword.

"I never let Thomas out of my sight." Will shivered as he recalled the cold of that winter. "But he was ill, supplies were low, and we were hungry. Thomas was too weak to go anywhere, and I tasked my squire with watching him. I left to lead a raid of a church tower rumored to contain a large supply of food."

The newer soldiers always were more susceptible to the diseases that were rampant in the army camps. Will hadn't worried about Thomas, had known his brother simply needed time to adjust to the starkness of life on campaign.

Unfortunately, the forage had been farther away and lasted longer than Will expected. Even now, regret pummeled him as he pictured the flames licking the church tower. Families had locked themselves inside to evade the English soldiers and protect their fortress. At the threat of the fire and the first flames, Will expected the people to come outside and surrender themselves and their goods.

But the French had decided they would rather die than face the English. In hindsight, Will could understand why. They'd heard the stories of having to offer *patis*—money for protection—which so few of them had. Without the payment, many captains brutally beat, chopped off the ears of, or even strangulated their prisoners.

The townspeople hadn't known Will wouldn't do those things to them.

Whatever the case, the winter foray hadn't produced the supplies the English army had needed and instead resulted in languishing death for innocent people. Will had watched helplessly as the structure was erelong engulfed in flames, the screams and cries of the dying inside fading to silence in the crisp winter day.

He'd ridden away, discouraged with the futility of the war, the weight of needless deaths upon him, and with very little to show for all the destruction. After two days of hard riding, they arrived back at the encampment around Bergerac only to discover chaos and more bloodshed.

The French captain, Arnaud de Cervole, had attacked during the moment of weakness, when several contingencies—in addition to Will's—had been away pillaging. Cervole slaughtered those too weak to defend themselves and took some of the noblemen as prisoners.

"Thomas was captured." Panic welled in Will's gut, the same way it had the day he'd gone into his tent only to find his squire dead and Thomas gone. Marian's hand rose to his chest, to his heart. The steady pressure and warmth brought him back to Blackheath, to the June night, to the sweetness of having her there in his arms even if they were both captives.

"I sent missives to Cervole pleading with him to take me in Thomas's stead. But he would not harken and demanded one thousand gold francs for Thomas's release. I returned home with all haste, emptied the coffers at Chesterfield Park, and crossed the Channel." Will closed his eyes against the memory of the frantic race to procure the ransom and get back to Thomas, the days of sleeplessness and bone-weary travel.

His throat tightened, and suddenly he didn't want to talk anymore. He wanted to stand up and punch something.

Marian lifted her face away from his chest. Her breath hovered above his mouth. And then her lips brushed his. Tentatively and yet tenderly. Her kiss contained understanding and heartbroken-ness—as though she felt his pain in every part of her being.

Her lips moved to his cheeks, eyes, nose, almost as if she was giving him a benediction that offered forgiveness and absolution for everything he'd ever done. When her lips returned to his, he was ready for her, ready to receive her blessing. Maybe he'd never be able to let go of the burden of Thomas's death. But her accep-tance, regardless of his mistakes, had loosened the straps of the heavy weight.

He could not kiss her tenderly just now. His need for her swelled too forcefully. He captured her mouth and did not tame himself. He kissed her until the heat and the passion consumed him and made him forget about Thomas and the war with the French and even the fact that he was a prisoner and would go into battle today.

He wasn't sure if he would have stopped himself from taking her fully, except she pulled away and buried her face against his chest—in embarrassment or discomfort, he wasn't sure. Even if they were secluded and covered, they weren't alone. And this was neither the time nor place to make her wholly his. That would need to wait for when they were alone, and he could cherish her as she deserved.

For long moments, he held her tight, willing his pulse and breathing to return to normal. She, too, seemed to be fighting to bring herself under control. And that thought pleased him.

He lifted a silent prayer of gratitude that God had brought her to him. In the same breath he despised that he must leave her today to go into battle. Although he'd always believed he was ready to die—that in dying he could somehow atone for his mistakes at Bergerac—he was no longer so certain. He wanted to spend every night in Marian's arms. He wanted to taste of her kisses every day. And he wanted to remain like this—baring the deepest parts of their souls with one another.

If he lived beyond today, he prayed God would make a way for them to be together without so many months of separation.

He brushed a kiss against her forehead.

"I guess it's my turn," she whispered.

He wanted to tell her she didn't have to share about her past. He suspected in doing so, the truth might disrupt this beautiful peaceful moment, and he wasn't ready to let go of it.

She struggled to put some distance between them. As much as he wanted to hang on to her, he loosened his grip.

She seemed to search for the right words to say and her body grew more rigid. "If I tell you the truth, you'll think I'm insane."

"Test me."

She drew in a deep breath. "I'm from another time and place."

~23~

MARIAN WAITED FOR WILL to respond, and when he didn't, she repeated herself. "I'm from a different time and place."

"Yes, you're from the Low Countries."

"No. I'm from America. It's a place vastly different from this."

"America?" He seemed to test the word. "I have never heard of this region."

Of course not, since over a hundred years still needed to pass before Christopher Columbus would discover it.

"You wouldn't know of it." She drew in a breath to fortify herself for what she must say next. "Nor would you know of my time, a time yet to come."

"Yet to come? As in the future?"

"Yes." What more could she tell him to clarify? Probably not much. Her muscles tensed in expectation of his reaction—frustration, disbelief, ridicule.

But he surprised her by stroking her hair again. "So you are an angel of some kind?"

Of course Will would seek to spiritualize what she was saying rather than attributing it to science, especially since angels and saints played a prominent role in the traditions and lore of the

Middle Ages. "No, I'm not an angel. But I suppose you could liken it to that."

He continued to gently caress her hair. "I cannot deny what you say is unusual. Yet, I find everything about you out of the ordinary. Including the visions I had of you ere your arrival."

So her first few crossings to the past *had* occurred in 1381. She wasn't sure what had drawn her to that year even before she knew anything about Will. But somehow she was inextricably intertwined with it. Was it possible providential forces had guided her to Will at this point in time so she could help him heal?

Whatever the case, she knew now Thomas's death had been the source of his nightmares and restlessness during those instances she met him.

"'Twould seem God has destined us to be together," he whispered.

She couldn't respond—couldn't tell him that she was leaving and would never see him again.

"Is *America* where your kin live?"

She shook her head. How could she explain that her dad was a world-renowned pharmaceutical scientist in Canterbury but had just recently died—or would die after the earthquake of 1382. And how could she explain that Ellen was a pediatric missionary nurse to orphans in Haiti, especially because Haiti didn't exist yet either. "My family is scattered in different places."

"Thus, you are estranged from them?"

"In some ways I am. But I do love them. Very much. And I want my sister Ellen to get better more than anything else."

As though sensing she felt as deeply for Ellen as he had for Thomas, his arms tightened around her. "So you are not escaping an unhappy betrothal?"

Her thoughts turned to Jasper. "There was a man who would have liked more—"

"And you would have had him in return?" An edge crept into Will's voice.

"Do I detect jealousy?"

"Did you care for him?"

She couldn't keep from smiling and teasing him. "He's very handsome."

"You do not desire him as you desire me." His voice was stubborn, and she was tempted to banter a little bit longer . . . until his fingers skimmed up her backbone.

In the growing dawn, she could see his face more clearly. His blue eyes were expectant and beautiful, waiting for her answer, and wouldn't be satisfied until she spoke the truth about how she felt.

She lifted a hand to his cheek, brushing the scratchy stubble. She had no idea what the upcoming day would bring or how much longer she would be a part of Will's world. But she suspected that today would be her last in 1381, that the past few hours with him must be her good-bye. Somehow, Ellen and Harrison hadn't been able to get inside the crypt yet. But surely they would soon. And once they retrieved the ampullae, they would waste no time in giving her the holy water.

Yes, this was her good-bye to Will, the special time with him that she'd hoped for. "William Durham." She studied his face, the scar above his eyebrow, the permanent sad crinkles at the corners of his eyes. "I have never loved a man. Until you."

It was true, down to the depths of her being. She'd fallen madly and passionately in love with Will in a way she never had with anyone else. And she doubted she'd ever love anyone else as much ever again.

At her declaration, his lips began to curve into a rare smile. But before she could see it fully realized, Thad stood above them, his expression urgent. "Sire, they're back."

Will pulled away from her and was on his feet before she could make sense of what was happening. He began speaking with Thad in low tones while his squire assisted him with his plate armor.

As she sat up, she wrapped his cloak tighter, suddenly cold. She noticed then that the boys were sitting up also, watching their father, taking in everything he said and did.

If only she and Will could go on forever in their private world where it was just the two of them whispering and kissing. Where she was the center of his world and he had nothing to do but lavish her with his attention. But that could never happen, no matter how much she might long for it.

As Will tugged on his gauntlets, his squire finished fitting the sabatons over his boots. Thad held his shield as well as his bascinet containing a visor hinged in at the front. As Thad held out the bascinet, Will dropped his voice. "Vow you will sneak them away and do as I've instructed."

Thad nodded gravely.

Them? Did Will mean the boys and her?

Marian rose to her knees. She tried to recall again the information she'd read about the end of the Peasants' Revolt. But she'd only skimmed the articles, had never expected she'd be sitting here in the middle of the revolt, a prisoner of war.

What if a battle occurred on Blackheath today? Was that what Will was referring to? If so, he'd be a part of the combat.

A terrible premonition settled over her.

Will didn't say good-bye. As he stalked toward the growing commotion, he looked over his shoulder first at his sons and then at her, almost as if he wanted one more glimpse before he marched off to his death.

When he disappeared from sight, she cupped a hand over her mouth to catch a cry of despair. She wasn't sure what he had planned, but suddenly she knew their time together last night had been the only farewell he would give. And now she might never see him again.

● ● ●

With each passing hour of waiting, the tension inside Marian twined tighter. From the somberness on the boys' faces, she suspected they realized as she did that this day would hold much heartache and pain. She tried to eat some of the fresh bread and cheese Will had brought them, but her thoughts were too anxious.

When the masses around them began to rally and move toward the River Thames, Thad encouraged them to do so as well. They hadn't gone far before several of the peasant men who had held them captive on the ride to London appeared and forced them to move beyond the others.

Marian attempted to walk with a modicum of dignity even though her feet ached with blisters from the too-tight pointed shoes. If only she'd had a comfortable pair of sandals. And a lightweight summer dress. The heavy velvety material of the skirt and tight laces of the bodice were almost unbearable at times, especially during the heat of the summer day. Yet, none of the other women seemed uncomfortable wearing such heavy layered garments, and Marian could only guess their bodies were acclimated since that's all they'd ever known.

On one side of her, Phillip strode with his chin angled up. Robert held her hand and trudged on the other. London loomed ahead, an endless stretch of slate and thatched rooftops along the Thames. She hadn't expected the city to be as metropolitan and big as the modern London, but she was surprised nonetheless at the rows upon rows of tall homes packed so densely.

They stopped a short distance away from what appeared to be an abbey. "St. Bartholomew's Priory," Thad whispered in answer to her question. Thousands of peasants had congregated along the western end of the priory, bearing polearms, battleaxes, pikes, and swords. The king and a regiment of his men-at-arms had positioned themselves to the east.

Marian searched for Will among the peasant ranks, but amidst the confusion and throngs of people, she couldn't spot Will's dark, foreboding form. It wasn't until their captors pushed them forward to the front of the crowd that Marian realized what was happening—the leaders of the rebels were meeting with the king.

A distance away in an open grassy expanse, bright blue and red hues of clothing and standards marked the presence of nobility and royalty. The knights were decked from head to foot in plate armor and were heavily armed with swords and sharp pikes that would easily decimate the peasants. Their warhorses, too, were intimidating, massive beasts that stood at least fifteen hands high, fitted with armor like the warriors astride them.

She could easily picture Will as one such warrior, her mind spinning back to the tale he'd shared of his time in France, of losing Thomas. Will was a man who loved deeply and who also felt the pain of loss deeply. Even though he hadn't declared his love in response to hers, she'd felt his passion and knew he cared for her.

Marian glanced to the sun overhead to gauge the time. It was past noon by now. Without a cloud in the sky or a tree to offer shade, the heat had begun to bake through Marian's gown, plastering it to her sweat-slickened skin. After walking several miles, her mouth was parched.

As though sensing her discomfort, Phillip held out the leather jug he'd slung over his shoulder, the only one with any water left.

"You and Robert drink first." She combed damp strands from Robert's flushed face.

"No, lady." Phillip pushed the jug into her hands. "'Tis for you."

Before she could argue, several riders broke away from the peasant ranks and began to make their way across the grassy knoll toward the king's men. Her heart leapt at the sight of Will among them in his plate armor but holding his bascinet. Astride his horse, his presence was fierce and imposing, especially next to Wat Tyler, who appeared frail on a little horse. Several other armored knights accompanied the rebel leader, including Sir John from Rochester.

When the peasants behind her roughly pushed her and the children further to the front of the ranks along with Sir John's wife and children, she understood that once again they were pawns in a dangerous game. These men would slit their throats if Will and Sir John and the other captive knights failed to cooperate.

Upon reaching the king, Wat and his band of men dismounted. A dagger in hand, Wat only half bent his knee in front of the king. Then, as though equals, Wat took the king's hand and shook it forcibly. Marian wasn't versed in the etiquette reserved for royalty, but even she realized Wat's familiarity with the king was disrespectful and excessive.

Although a strange hush fell over the crowd around her, they were too distant to hear the conversation going on between Wat Tyler and a distinguished gentleman that several peasants around her whispered to be Walworth, the mayor of London.

After some discourse, a flask was brought forward and handed to Wat Tyler. He drank for several moments, reminding Marian of how thirsty she was. She swayed slightly, and Phillip caught her arm.

"Please, lady." He offered the jug to her again. When he uncorked it and pressed it to her lips, she couldn't refuse.

The liquid was tepid and tasted of leather, but it quenched the burning in her throat. As she lowered the container and started to thank Phillip, the surrounding crowd began to clamor and draw their weapons.

Marian glanced again to where Wat Tyler stood with Will and the others in front of the king. But instead of the peaceful meeting, Wat was lunging at the mayor with his dagger, stabbing him in the stomach. The blow knocked the mayor backward.

Marian drew in a startled breath, expecting that the mayor would crumple. But he quickly recovered, throwing aside his cloak to reveal a hauberk of chainmail, apparently prepared for the attack. The other men on both sides drew their weapons, and in an instant they were engaged in hand-to-hand combat. Amidst the swinging swords, Marian sought Will, her heart thudding with fresh dread.

Instead of fighting against the king's men, Will spun and struck Wat in the side. The peasant leader staggered. One of King Richard's royal knights took advantage of the weakness and thrust his dirk into Wat's chest and side with a burst of rapid jabs.

Crimson rapidly seeped through Wat's garments. He staggered and then dropped to his knees. For a moment Marian couldn't believe what she was witnessing, that this battle was unfolding before her.

This was no Hollywood movie or History Channel documentary. This was reality. The peasant leader was bleeding, and the men were killing one another.

The awful truth was that Will had just placed himself in mortal danger. Now that he'd taken a stand with the king, the entire peasant army would turn on him, especially once they realized he was responsible for attacking Wat first. Already the men around her were shouting, raising their weapons, and leaving her and the boys behind in their impatience to join the conflict.

A hand enclosed about her upper arm and yanked her backward. She started to struggle but then realized it was Thad. "Come quickly." His voice was low and urgent.

Grabbing both Robert and Phillip, she followed Thad as they fought their way through the surging, angry crowd. Thankfully, no one was paying attention to them. She suspected that had been Will's plan all along, to have Thad usher her and the boys away the moment the peasants were distracted by the fighting. Maybe he'd even designed his attack to be a diversion so she and the boys could escape undetected.

Although part of her longed to stay and discover Will's fate, she had to do whatever she could to keep his sons safe from any vengeance the peasants might seek for his role in the fight.

Marian waited for someone to recognize her as Will's wife and to force her back to the battle. But others were attempting to leave too, perhaps some, like them, who'd been coerced into coming and now hoped to make a getaway.

By the time they reached the edge of the crowd, she was breathing hard and shaking. She bent over at the waist to suck in deep breaths, but Thad dragged her along, forcing her to keep moving.

When they came to a secluded knoll, Thad dropped a coin into the hand of a dirty urchin who'd been holding the reins of two horses. The boy scampered toward the gathering, clearly eager to discover what was going on. Marian wanted to shout after the child to return with news, but he was gone before she could formulate the words.

Thad hoisted her into the saddle behind Phillip, and she barely had time to grab on to the boy to keep herself aloft before he kicked the horse in the ribs and raced away.

Thad followed close behind with Robert, the pounding hooves as wild as her heartbeat. They pushed the horses continually harder until they were riding at a frightening speed. All she could do was shut her eyes and pray—not only for them, but for Will.

~24~

MARIAN COULDN'T RISE from the bench to help the servants with the packing. After the hours of fleeing from London, she was desperate to know what had happened to Will and wasn't sure whether her legs were trembling out of worry or exhaustion.

Never again would she complain about how texting and social media were taking the place of real conversations. If she'd had the capability to text, she could have discovered how he was doing right away instead of going endless hours with no idea.

And she'd also never again complain about long car rides, not after galloping more than thirty torturous miles on the back of a horse. The heat of the day had parched them, but they'd pressed forward regardless and had only stopped once out of compassion for the horses.

When they'd arrived at Chesterfield Park at dusk, Marian had collapsed onto the ground and hadn't been able to get back up. Thad had carried her inside. And now he and Sarah and the others rushed around, preparing to leave.

Christina had returned to St. Sepulchre during their absence, but Will's mother, Lady Felice, had greeted them. Upon hearing the news of Will's treachery against Wat Tyler, her face had paled,

and she'd wordlessly begun assisting Sarah with stowing everything of value they could fit into chests and bags.

"Where are we going?" Marian forced herself up so that she
could help, unwilling to sit back any longer.

Thad was shoving large quantities of food into a grain sack,
his straight bangs plastered to his dusty face. "The master has
entrusted me with seeing you to the coast for your transport to
the Continent. You'll find safety with a friend in Amsterdam."

Amsterdam? From an aching place deep inside, she couldn't
bear the thought of going to Amsterdam or returning to the present day without making sure Will was all right. "I'm not leaving."

"You must." Thad spoke as if the matter was already settled.

"I won't go anywhere without Will."

"When 'tis safe for your return, I shall send word."

"Lady Felice may go with the boys, but I'm staying here and
waiting for news of Will."

Thad halted in his efforts to stuff more food into the already full
bag and frowned. "The master gave me explicit instructions—"

"I will not go." She used her most decisive tone and held his
gaze until he dropped his.

He wiped at the perspiration trickling down his temple. "The
rebels may come looking for revenge, and if they find you here,
they'll show no mercy."

It didn't matter whether she was here at Chesterfield Park or
running away to Amsterdam, she would soon be in a coma. She
was surprised she hadn't yet fallen unconscious but was grateful
at the same time.

Even so, she couldn't keep a new worry from sifting through
her, the dread that something terrible may have happened to Ellen
and Harrison to keep them from going to the crypt. She'd also
considered the likelihood that the ampullae had somehow fallen
into the wrong hands, that Harrison had retrieved them as planned
but had been robbed on his way out of the crypt.

Thad was watching her, frustration etched on his ruddy face. He'd already failed his master once in allowing the rebels inside Chesterfield Park. Even if he'd had no choice but to do so, she'd witnessed his despair in having to let Will down. Now, tasked with seeing to her safety, he was loath to fail Will again.

"If the rebels come looking for me, then you can hide me in the vault and tell them I've left with the others. They won't expect me to have stayed behind."

"'Tis not what the master wanted. He made me swear an oath I wouldn't rest until I see you and his sons safely launched at Dover. If you don't go, word will spread that only Lady Felice and the lads fled."

"Send Sarah in my stead. She'll pretend to be me."

At her words, Thad straightened and glanced at his wife, who was clomping down the stairway.

"She will be safer with them, especially once the rebels learn of your role in aiding the escape of Sir William's family."

Thad didn't respond. Instead, he watched his wife move across the great hall toward the open chests. She placed more items inside, folding them tightly to make room for all they'd need.

In the descending night, the sconces cast a glow across the room, coating everything with a honey-colored glaze. While Marian missed being able to turn on lights at the flip of a switch, she could admit there was a beauty to the simplicity of her life here. In the ease of modern conveniences, she often failed to notice the little things like the violet shadows in a room at sunset or the soft whispers of the wind against the open shutters.

Marian took a sip of the ale Sarah had brought her and found she even relished the bitterness of the watery drink against her tongue. "Sarah is levelheaded and will be able to help Lady Felice take care of the boys."

Thad lowered his head and stared with unfocused eyes upon

the bag before him. Finally he nodded. "The master will cut off my ears for allowing you to stay."

Will would do nothing of the sort, although she had no doubt he'd be angry, more with her than Thad. "He'll realize soon enough you could do nothing to sway me."

Thad smiled ruefully. "You are indeed a strong woman, lady."

Within the hour, under the cover of darkness, she tucked Robert and Phillip in the back of the wagon next to Lady Felice and Sarah and kissed the boys good-bye. Thad gave her a strict warning not to open the gates for anyone and to stay inside until he returned on the morrow.

After watching them ride away, she made her way upstairs to her chamber, realizing her cheeks were wet with tears and that she already missed the boys. Even though she hadn't known them long, somehow after the past days of trying to survive together, she'd let them in her heart and allowed herself to love them like they were her own. She would miss them terribly when she returned to her other life.

A different maid attended to her needs, helping her wash away the grit of the past days, brushing her tangled hair, and bringing her a clean shift. Once finished, Marian tumbled into bed and fell into an exhausted sleep.

Marian wasn't sure how long she slumbered when a commotion outside awoke her and sent fear skittering across her skin. With her pulse tapping a slow drumbeat of dread, she tiptoed barefooted through the corridors. Thad's warning not to allow anyone inside the gates echoed ominously, especially when she realized the clopping of horse hooves was drawing up in front of the manor—that someone had allowed the visitors to enter, perhaps someone sympathetic to the peasant cause.

Once in the great hall, she picked up her pace, hurrying several frightened women servants ahead of her toward Will's antechamber.

Before she could reach the room, the thick front door banged open, hitting the wall with a thud that reverberated down to her bones. Marian stumbled. They weren't going to make it into the vault in time.

A half a dozen men barged through the entryway with the clanking of armor and the heavy tread of boots. In the dim glow of the moonlight streaming through the high open windows, she could see the intruders were heavily armed.

Since she wouldn't be able to outrun them now, she could do nothing else but face them with dignity. She clasped her trembling hands together and stepped forward into a shaft of moonlight. "Who are you and what do you want?"

At the sound of her voice, the men halted.

"She is here as you predicted," someone said.

"I am Lady Marian Durham." She spoke the words with as much authority as she could muster and was surprised at how naturally her new name rolled off her tongue. "Tell me why you are barging into my home in the middle of the night."

The men didn't move, except for one, who shouldered his way to the front. Even in the dark, she recognized the outline of his muscular body, the intensity of his demeanor, and the fierceness of his stance.

Her heart tumbled over itself, and relief rushed in like a gust and swept away her fears. She started across the room, tears stinging her eyes. He was alive and safe and here. She rapidly closed the distance, the need to be in his arms greater than her need for another breath. She started to throw her arms around him, but he captured both of her hands in a bruising grip.

"You disobeyed me, wife." His voice was hard and angry.

She winced. She'd expected him to be happy to be reunited but should have known he'd be upset at her blatant disregard of his orders to leave with Thad. Even so, she wouldn't cower. "Sarah is disguised as me. Thad will spread the rumor that I've left with the others, and no one will suspect otherwise."

Will's hold loosened. He swayed, and one of the other knights steadied him. "You have lost a great deal of blood, sire."

Somewhere behind her, servants had begun to light the sconces, which brought to life Will's ruggedly handsome face covered with dust and blood. He still wore pieces of his plate armor but had shed much of it—likely so it wouldn't slow him down during his ride.

"Everyone is safe?" His eyes were glassy.

"Yes, we're all fine. The boys were very brave."

He yanked off his glove, lifted a hand, and touched her cheek, as though to make sure she was indeed standing before him alive and well. She leaned in to his calloused fingers, but before she could melt into his caress, he crumpled to the ground.

"Will!" She dropped to her knees beside him.

"He was wounded during the melee, my lady." One of the knights knelt next to Will. She recognized the thin man with the silver hair and pointed silvery beard as Sir John of Rochester. "We warned him against riding this far, but he insisted on coming. He would not be swayed otherwise. I am astonished he lasted this long before succumbing to his injuries."

"How badly is he hurt?" She glided her hands over Will's arms and chest, searching for signs of his wound.

"I am afraid 'tis severe, my lady."

As her fingers skimmed along his side, she grazed a slick, sticky spot. "He needs a doctor."

"I already took the liberty of sending one of my squires for my surgeon. He is very skilled, the best in all of Kent."

Will needed to go to the emergency room in an ambulance where he could receive immediate care by experts, not languish here waiting for a doctor from the Middle Ages to show up without access to modern equipment, sterilization, or antibiotics.

"Help me carry him up to his chamber," she said with mounting frustration. "We must tend to his wounds until the doctor arrives."

Sir John and two of the squires lifted Will, and she led the way to his room, where they laid him on the bed. Marian began to help the servants free him from the rest of his armor and garments, ordering others to bring hot water, soap, and clean towels.

She gave instructions for several different herbal salves, praying the servants would be able to locate what was needed to provide a healing balm, ordering them to ride to the apothecary at St. Sepulchre if need be. She might not have access to modern medicine, but at least she knew enough to create something that might help—even if just a little.

As they peeled away the last layer of Will's blood-soaked garments, she sucked in a sharp breath. He'd been stabbed in several places. The puncture in the fleshy part of his upper arm had severed muscles and oozed crimson even though Will had attempted to staunch the flow by tying a piece of his shift around it.

Another wound in his lower back was long and jagged and would need many stitches. But it was the gash at his right side that worried Marian the most. The blade had gone deep. Without an MRI scan, she wouldn't know what had been damaged—a kidney, liver, gallbladder, perhaps part of his large intestine, depending on the angle the blade had entered.

She suspected Will was bleeding internally, but without proper surgical instruments, she had no way of helping him. Even though she'd taken numerous medical classes over the years, she was definitely no surgeon.

Later when the surgeon arrived, Marian rose from the side of the bed where she was keeping vigil. She'd been administering herbal water as often as she could get Will to swallow the bitter decoction, and she'd plastered poultices to his wounds. She was beyond frustrated at the length of time it had taken for the surgeon to arrive, silently lamenting that she couldn't call for a medevac to fly Will to the best medical facility money could buy.

The surgeon took one look at Will's wounds and shook his head gravely as though he didn't hold any hope. Marian attempted to explain what she believed to be the problem and urged the surgeon to cut Will open and perform surgery—at the very least attempt to sew his insides together and stop the internal bleeding.

But the gray-haired surgeon only peered at her with pursed lips and flaring nostrils as he laid out an assortment of crude instruments.

Marian ordered a servant hovering nearby to bring her boiling water so she could sterilize the instruments first. As the servant rushed to do her bidding, the doctor shook his head. "My lady, you must leave the chamber. There is naught more you can do for him except to pray."

"I intend to stay and help you with the surgery."

"Surgery will not save him."

Without the proper instruments, anesthesia, and antibiotics, the surgery might only make things worse. But they had to try, didn't they? "What are you planning to do?"

"Since the wound is so deep, I am left with no option but to cauterize it." He picked up an iron poker instrument.

Chills crept up Marian's back at the image of the red-hot tool searing Will's flesh in an attempt to seal the wound and blood vessels shut. He'd face excruciating pain and would likely continue to bleed internally. "There must be some other option."

"My lady." The surgeon's voice became testy. "Sir William may succumb to his injuries, but 'twill most certainly be so if you do not allow me to do what I was called here for."

"You were not called here for this." She didn't realize her tone had escalated until someone touched her elbow from behind. She swung to find Sir John standing there, his kind face etched with compassion and sadness.

"My lady, my surgeon is a good man. He will do all he can for Sir William."

Marian tried to quell the frustration and panic climbing from her stomach to her chest and throat. Will was dying. She glanced again to his pale face, to the slow rise and fall of his chest, to the lifeblood already draining away.

"If you will allow me, my lady," Sir John was saying, "I shall accompany you to the chapel and together we shall beseech God to spare Sir William's life."

"If we hope that God will spare my husband's life, then we must find another way to help him."

"Sire." The surgeon addressed Sir John. "Please usher this woman from the sickbed. We are wasting time."

Sir John took her arm more firmly.

"No!" She jerked away from the knight. He was only trying to do what he thought was best for Will, but surely even rudimentary surgery would be better than the cauterizing.

"You are distraught, lady." Sir John spoke gently. "And rightly so. Your husband is a courageous man. If not for his brilliant plan today, we might all be dead. As it was, he brought about the end of the rebellion, and for that we are all in his debt. If he perishes, it will be with great honor for having saved his king."

Sir John's news brought tears to Marian's eyes again, and this time they escaped and ran down her cheeks. "I can't lose him. I love him too much to let him die." How was it possible to love someone so deeply? She'd never imagined she'd love a man as thoroughly and completely, never thought she'd need someone as much as she needed him. But she did in a way that almost frightened her.

"And he loved you. Even though the king offered to have his best physicians and surgeons tend Sir William, your husband asked permission to return to his home so he could check on your safety. He would not rest or stop until he knew for himself you were alive and unharmed."

She wiped away more tears. How had he ridden any length much less the journey from London with such wounds? How had

270

he been able to stay conscious? She could only imagine the pain he'd suffered over the course of the past hours. "He's stubborn."

"He spoke likewise of you." Faint mirth tinged Sir John's words.

The surgeon lifted the iron out of the fire. It glowed orange-red.

Marian couldn't let Will die, couldn't bear to think about life without him. They'd had so little time together, and she was suddenly greedy for more, so much more.

She had to find a way to save him. Her mind raced with all the possibilities and landed on only one. There was only one thing left to do.

"Sir John, will you take me to Canterbury Cathedral?"

~25~

MARIAN RAISED THE CANDLE toward the capital of column F. At the top, the stone face of the bearded man stared back at her with beady eyes. It was as formidable in the past as the present, just less worn with time.

She touched the protruding tongue but then stopped. Was she doing the right thing?

During the galloping ride with Sir John, she'd prayed with each beat of hooves that the ampullae would still be in the crypt. She was still puzzled by the overlap of the past and present and didn't know how the transmission of ampullae worked.

The one thing she did understand was that if she took one out, she had no guarantee of finding more holy water to leave for Ellen and Harrison. In that event, she might be stuck in the past, maybe forever.

Was this the life she really wanted?

Her fingers trembled against the rough carving. Did she want to stay in the 1300s without all the modern conveniences she relied upon and loved? Could she give up her career, the one she'd worked so hard to obtain? What about never being able to see Ellen again?

Yet how could she leave Will behind? Her entire body tightened with protest at the thought of not being with him.

Even though her heart warred within her over her future, she knew without a doubt she couldn't let Will die, not when she had a means to possibly save him. When she'd asked to ride to the cathedral, Sir John had clearly humored her out of respect for Will. And he'd also honored her request to instruct the surgeon to wait for the cauterizing until they returned.

She glanced through the dank cavern over to the narrow steps at the far end that led to the nave. The underground crypt was smaller and darker than the modern structure with only one entrance—the one she'd fled up when she'd escaped from Lionel's thugs.

Sir John waited for her at the top, giving her the privacy she'd requested. His title and prestige as well as his bribe had persuaded the monks to allow them in at this early hour of the morning, though they'd been preparing for Lauds and hadn't wanted to be disturbed.

The kindly knight had understood her urgency and had likely felt it too. They'd had to wait for the groomsman to saddle fresh horses and then had ridden the distance into town, galloping through the quiet moonlit countryside on a circuitous route to avoid any angry peasants who might be fleeing from London.

During the ride, Sir John filled her in on all the events that transpired after she left Blackheath with the boys. He informed her that upon seeing Wat Tyler attacked, the peasants lifted weapons to fight against the king's men.

However, in a valiant effort to avoid further bloodshed, the king encouraged the peasants to disperse. With their leader stabbed to death and fearing the worst, many ran off. Those coerced into joining the rebels, like Sir John, made their true allegiance known. Walworth, the mayor of London, cut off Wat Tyler's head, displayed it on a pole, and returned to London with the king's troops to restore order on the streets.

No doubt Sir John was in a hurry to return to his own family and assure himself of their safety and protection. But out of gratitude to Will for his bravery in the recent battle as well as out of respect for the king's request to assist Will, the neighboring knight was doing all he could to ensure Will's survival.

With precious seconds of Will's life ticking away, Marian set aside her reservations. She placed the candle on the floor and tugged at the tongue of the carving with both hands. To her relief it scraped forward—even if only a fraction. She wiggled and hefted until it came out. Will's loosening from earlier in the week had likely saved her much hardship in taking it out today.

The candlelight was smoky and dim, providing little illumination of the cavern. Nevertheless, she could see the small black hole in the column. She rose on her tiptoes and probed within the hiding place.

She grazed the engraved patterns of the ampullae and brushed against the parchment note she'd left for her father. Everything was still there.

She closed her fingers around one of the flasks and removed it. Then before she lost courage, she unsheathed the small dagger she'd taken from among Will's weapons. With the sharp tip, she carved the letters E and C into the ampulla. This flask was for Ellen. She absolutely wouldn't allow Ellen to use it on her. Ellen had to drink it and cure herself.

With a final cut on the ampulla, she blew the dust away, fingered Ellen's initials one last time, then returned the container to the hiding place. She pulled out the other one, slipped it through the folds of her gown into the pouch tied underneath.

Her fingers connected with a piece of clay she'd broken off a bowl. She'd already carved onto it a crude replica of St. George's Tower and the clock sticking out the side. She hoped Harrison would understand her message—that perhaps the tower stood as a protection over the old life-giving spring that had once been in St. Sepulchre.

She was certain with his wealth and family's powerful connections, he'd be able to gain access to the tower and find a way to drill deep underneath the ground. If he ever managed to find the location of the original spring—if it still existed somewhere down there—then perhaps he could carry on Dad's work.

She placed the clay piece into the hiding spot and then shoved the carving of the head back. She wedged it in as tightly as she could and held up the candle to make sure it was secure.

She had no idea what was keeping Ellen and Harrison from the crypt, but their delay had now changed the course of her life.

For better or worse, she would remain in the past.

● ● ●

By the time Marian returned to Chesterfield Park, the sky was a tangle of pink and orange. The stars were gone and morning birdsong rose in the balmy air. The chirps and twitters would have been a sweet sound had she not been driven with anxiety to know whether Will had lasted the hours she'd been on her mission.

After dismounting, she rushed ahead of Sir John, speeding through the corridors until she barged into Will's chamber. The surgeon had fallen asleep in the chair next to the bed. At her appearance, he startled awake.

"Is he still alive?" she asked breathlessly, crossing to the bed.

Sir John entered a moment later, and the surgeon rose hastily, attempting to appear dignified as he bent to assess Will.

Marian didn't wait for his prognosis. Instead, she reached for Will's hand. It was limp and lifeless and dropped back to the bed. She pressed two fingers against his wrist, feeling for a pulse. A sluggish throb met her touch.

She bit back a sob of relief. He was hanging on.

Her fingers fumbled in her skirt in her haste to free the ampulla. When she pulled it out, the surgeon stepped back. "St. Thomas water?" His voice contained a reverence she hadn't expected.

She nodded and pried at the cork gingerly, unwilling to lose a single drop of the liquid inside.

The surgeon's eyes rounded with wonder as he studied the front engraving, the one of Becket and the angels flying over him. She had no wish to see the other side where Becket was being stabbed to death.

"Where did you find it?" the surgeon asked.

She didn't want to give away the hiding place in the crypt or spread news about Chesterfield Park's vault. So she chose her words with care. "Sir William's family had it among their treasures."

The answer seemed to satisfy the gentleman. He stood back and waited as she finished unplugging the ampulla. Like Sir John, the surgeon accepted the possibility of miracles and the supernatural so much more readily than she ever had. She supposed the age of modern science and medicine had eroded the need for miracles.

She leaned in toward Will. His features were chiseled with pain even in his slumber. She slipped a hand behind his head but then glanced at Sir John and the surgeon. "Would you help me hold up Sir William?"

As they raised Will into a sitting position, his head lolled back. Beneath the dark layer of unshaven scruff, his skin was the same gray as the ashes on the hearth. His lips were pale too, and his breathing shallow and ragged.

Her stomach knotted with love for this man, for his courage, his determination, and his willingness to sacrifice himself for his king and family. He inspired her to want to live with more courage and passion.

She lifted the spout to his lips. "Hold his head steady. He must drink it all."

Sir John and the surgeon followed her instructions carefully. As she tilted the flask into Will's mouth, she dribbled the holy water in tiny increments, making sure he swallowed each minuscule amount before she tipped in more.

Like the ampullae her dad had discovered, this one contained only about a tablespoon. Once it was gone, she rinsed inside with water and then poured the additional water into his mouth too. She repeated the process several times, hoping to get every molecule of the holy water into Will's system.

When she was sure not even the slightest drop remained, Sir John and the surgeon lowered Will back to the bed. Then the three of them stood by his side, waiting for a miracle.

Marian wasn't sure what would happen. But she couldn't keep from thinking of the stained glass windows at Canterbury Cathedral bearing testimony to the fact that miracles could happen. Whether as a result of the residue from the Tree of Life or whether through God's intervention, she had to believe it truly was possible for God to heal when he chose to.

They watched wordlessly, but Will's face remained pale and lifeless. He didn't move except to struggle to breathe.

Marian's legs felt suddenly weak. What if the holy water didn't work to revive him? What if he was already too close to death? Worse yet, what if the liquid inside the flasks wasn't the authentic holy water? Not only would Will die, but Ellen would too.

Sir John's arm steadied her. "I beg you to sit and rest, lady. This has been a trying night, and you have done all you can for now."

She nodded and allowed him to help her into the chair beside the bed. She couldn't take her sights from Will's face, watching for signs of returning color, anything to signal he was reviving. With no more mention of the cauterizing, Sir John and the surgeon eventually took their leave with the promise to return soon.

As she sat next to Will, she reached for his limp hand. Deep sorrow weighed her down. She'd never expected to fall in love with the man of her dreams in 1381. But now that she had, she wanted no one else. He was her one and only. And without him, she didn't know where she belonged.

• ● •

A strange calm sifted through Will, the kind that settled over him whenever he was lying on the cold, hard ground on his back next to a fire, staring up at the stars.

Was he in heaven? Would he be reunited with Thomas and be able to tell him how sorry he was he'd left him sick and defenseless that day outside Bergerac?

Will attempted to open his eyes and sit up, but he couldn't move. He tried to make his mouth work to call out for his brother, but he couldn't speak.

At the soft shudder of a breath nigh his cheek, his pulse quickened. Marian.

Was she entering heaven with him? As much as he wanted her to live and have a happy life on earth, he wouldn't complain if they entered paradise together.

His mind spun back to the battle with Wat Tyler and the initial thrust he'd made. In attacking Wat first, he'd taken the brunt of the wrath of Wat's accomplices. They'd come after him with a vengeance. Nevertheless, they'd been no match for the well-trained knights and king's men who had rallied to Will's aid and cut them down.

He rejoiced the rebel leader was slain and the revolt squelched. But in striking first, he'd made himself a target and had also put his kin in danger. All the whilst he'd ridden away from London, he'd worried Wat's men would go after his wife and children, that they would find his family and torture them in reprisal.

Even though Thad had given his word that he'd aid his family's escape from London to Amsterdam, his steward was no warrior. He wouldn't be able to fend off a mob of bondmen bent on destruction and revenge.

Thus, even though his companions had warned him against such hard travel in his wounded condition, he'd pushed onward through the pain. When he'd ridden up to Chesterfield Park and was greeted by dark windows and calm silence, he'd allowed himself a measure of relief. Until he walked in and saw Marian . . .

Her soft breath brushed his cheek again and stirred anger in him. She ought to have gone into hiding as he'd instructed. She wouldn't be safe anywhere near him. Even if the rebels hadn't sought reprisals yet, they very well could regroup and come looking for him. And when they came, they'd have no qualms about ripping him apart limb by limb and displaying his severed parts all throughout the countryside. He shuddered to think what they might do to her.

He needed Thad to take her far away until the tempest of unrest subsided. But even as his anger roiled about his gut, he breathed her in and lifted a prayer of gratefulness God had spared her.

He prayed for himself too, that God might spare him, though he didn't deserve it. He could no longer deny he longed to live, desperately so, because he couldn't bear the thought of being torn asunder from Marian forever.

He wanted a lifetime with her, a lifetime of getting to know the fascinating and beautiful woman who'd arrived into his life so unexpectedly but so powerfully. He wanted the chance to deepen their relationship. He'd tasted of what that might look like, especially the night on Blackheath when he'd opened up to her about Thomas's death. The sharing hadn't been easy, but when it was done, he'd felt a bond with Marian that went beyond any he'd known before.

"Marian," he whispered and was surprised when his voice worked.

She drew in a quick breath. Her fingers pressed his wrist and then his neck. They were warm but trembling.

Again, as before, he tried to open his eyes. This time his lashes rose, and he found himself peering up at her face. She was sitting in the chair next to his bed. The room was bright with daylight highlighting the dried streaks that ran down her cheeks, the paths of her tears. Tears for him?

He lifted his arm and realized he could do so easily. It stung with the pain of one of his wounds—although not nearly as excruciating as he'd expected it to be. He mentally touched each of his injuries. None of them hurt the way they had during the ride home. How was that possible? He'd suspected one of his wounds, the one he'd taken to his side, had been a fatal blow. The dagger had pierced deep into his innards. But even that particular injury felt warm and tight.

Marian was watching his face expectantly, her long hair hanging over her shoulders and resting upon his bare and bandaged chest.

He lifted his fingers to her cheek and caressed it with his thumb. "You disobeyed me." His voice was raspy and harsher than he intended.

Tears swelled to the brims of her eyes, and she smiled tremulously. "Go ahead and be mad at me. But I couldn't leave you."

He wouldn't tell her, but he was glad she was there, even if she was still in danger from anyone who came seeking revenge. His arm grew weak, and he had to drop it to his side. "The others?"

"Thad returned at midday. They made it to Dover and began the crossing without any incidents."

Relief rolled through him with the power of a spring storm on the open sea, and he had to close his eyes even though all he wanted to do was stare at Marian's face.

She pressed her hand against his forehead. "How are you feeling?"

"Weary." He touched his side. Linen covered the wound, but the burning torture was no longer present.

Her fingers slid into his hair, and the touch was cool and soothing. "I didn't think the holy water was working, but your color is better and pulse stronger."

His eyes flew open and collided with her big brown ones. "What holy water?"

"Sir John took me to the crypt, and I retrieved one of the ampullae you put there."

Will hadn't believed the holy water could work miracles, had assumed the water was a token of faith, something to comfort the dying. But at the absence of the pain that had racked his body for the past long hours, was it possible he'd been mistaken?

Was it truly miracle water after all? If so, then it was a rare gift—a gift Marian had bestowed upon him at the expense of saving her sister. "What of your sister's life?"

"The other ampulla is still there for her."

"Then she has no need of two?"

Marian shook her head and didn't meet his gaze. "She'll live if she drinks just one."

She was withholding something from him. His relief fled, leaving a churning path of worry in its wake. "Who was the other ampulla for?"

For several slow breaths, she hesitated in answering. Finally, she dropped her sights to his. "For me." The resignation and sadness in her eyes brought a fresh wave of pain—this time to his heart.

"Are you ill?"

"In a way. But it's nothing to worry about now."

He couldn't make sense of what she was saying. But one thing was certain. She'd sacrificed herself for him. "You must avail yourself of the ampulla in the crypt, and we shall seek another for your sister."

She shook her head. Her eyes contained a determination that told him her answer. She would not abandon her sister even if it meant she must die in the process. He understood how she felt. How could he begrudge her this desire when he'd once felt likewise about Thomas? If he'd been able to exchange his life for Thomas's, he would have done so faster than a hare could slip into its hole.

"Then we shall begin the search for another ampulla. There must be more."

"Perhaps." Marian's fingers combed through his hair, once again soothing him.

Something was amiss. He could sense it. But another wave of weariness crashed over him, and his eyes drooped closed.

She cupped his cheek. "All that matters is you're alive."

He wanted to protest that she mattered too, and that he couldn't imagine living without her. But drowsiness descended upon him as thick as a heavy coverlet, and he could do naught but yield to a deep and healing sleep.

~26~

MARIAN KEPT HER VIGIL at Will's bedside all through the rest of the day. He slept so soundly that when the surgeon returned to check his wounds, he barely stirred. Marian had been awed just as much as the surgeon to see the once jagged bloody gashes now fusing together, the skin clean and pink with very little scabbing or scarring. Not only would Will live, but he wouldn't have any permanent damage.

She marveled that the holy water had the power to cure so thoroughly and completely. She shouldn't have been surprised by the healing. After all, she'd already experienced the effects of the holy water for herself with its amazing ability to transport her to another time period.

But by watching it work to restore Will, she'd gained an entirely different perspective. She understood in a way she never had before the implications of the ultimate cure. The line of sick waiting for a dose would stretch for endless miles: veterans with painful war wounds, cancer victims who were pale and bald after months of chemotherapy, quadriplegics who were bound to their wheelchairs, and people with every conceivable disease from around the world.

While Marian could imagine the joy brightening each face as health returned to their bodies, she couldn't keep at bay a ripple of unease—the same unease that had plagued her before. In the short term, the holy water would bring happiness to countless people. She'd experienced that happiness in saving Will, in watching him return from the precipice of death.

But in the long term, what would such a miracle drug do to their society? What would happen if people could potentially live for hundreds of years? Would they face overpopulation problems? A shortage of food? Mass starvation? More conflict and hatred and war?

In all her work testing new drugs, she'd learned that negative side effects always existed—sometimes dangerous ones. Before a pharmaceutical company could move forward with any medicine, they had to discern whether the benefits outweighed the risks.

Even so, she couldn't deny that if she had to do it over, she'd still give Will the holy water. No matter what happened to her or what her future held, she was determined to make the most of her time with Will.

Maybe after a while, she'd forget about twenty-first-century conveniences. The tastes, scents, and textures of her new life would surely begin to feel normal. And maybe she could endure the unpleasant aspects so long as she had Will by her side. After all, her other life in the present wasn't without discomforts and displeasures either. She'd had her fair share of disillusionment and regrets there too.

Even with all the rationalizing about making the best of living in 1381, the reality of what she'd done by giving Will her ampulla made her stomach twist. Would she eventually grow unhappy with her choice? And more importantly, how long would she live in a coma in the present day? She might survive years, but she also might have only days.

Obviously, as Will mentioned, they could search for more holy water. Maybe eventually they'd discover more original ampullae. If she lived long enough, maybe she'd benefit from the earthquake opening the wellspring at St. Sepulchre—if that's indeed what happened.

But even if she found more holy water, would Ellen and Harrison look in the hiding place in the crypt periodically? Or would they give up?

With the falling of darkness, she rose and allowed one of the maidservants to tend to her needs. Even though she'd dozed from time to time throughout the day, the events of the past week had caught up to her, and she wanted nothing more than to lie down and sleep.

As she climbed in next to Will, gone were the reservations she'd had about sharing his bed. The fact that he was her husband was more real than anything else. She loved him, and since she was staying in the past, she would willingly give herself to him once he was strong and well again.

She propped up on her elbow and allowed herself the pleasure of taking him in, the light of a single candle on the bedside table casting a glow over his face. His expression was almost peaceful, as if his slumber was so deep it allowed him a respite from his regrets over Thomas.

Perhaps he would never fully recover from the loss of his brother. But she loved him all the more for how much he cared about what had happened. She leaned down and brushed a kiss on his scratchy cheek. The warmth of his exhale bathed her skin, and before she could stop herself, she shifted her lips to his. She closed her eyes at the sweetness of the contact.

As she skimmed his full bottom lip, her body froze. A gust of wind swirled around her, and an instant later Will disappeared. Instead, a sturdy mattress supported her weight and elevated her head. The steady beep of monitors sounded nearby.

She'd slipped into the present somehow. Had the time continuum overlapped as it had previously? Or when she'd kissed Will, had she come in contact with a trace of the holy water on his lips?

Whatever the case, she had to use the opportunity to wake up and give a message to Harrison and Ellen that she was fine.

Wake up, Marian, she inwardly shouted at herself, attempting to lift her head from the pillow. But for as much as she tried, she couldn't move, which was no surprise since she hadn't been able to during her last vision. She could only conclude her coma was making the movement impossible, unlike during her first sightings of Will.

"They've both gone out," came a man's hushed voice across the room. A familiar voice. Was it Jasper?

"They're at St. Thomas's again," he continued.

It *was* Jasper. From the one-sided conversation, she guessed he was on the phone. She pictured him with his brown hair and athletic frame standing near a window, likely dressed in jeans and a sweatshirt.

He must have flown over when he'd gotten news about her being in a coma. The gesture was sweet of him, but after being with Will, the slight interest she'd once had in Jasper slipped through her fingers like fine dust, blown away by the merest puff of breath.

The truth was, no other man could ever compare to Will. Not even a little bit. Will was so passionate about life and those he cared about. He felt everything intensely, including his affection for her. Perhaps he hadn't fallen in love with her in the modern sense of the word, but something deep and real existed between them.

"No, they're still as close-lipped as ever." Jasper's tone was laced with frustration.

She should have told Jasper before she left Connecticut that she didn't see any hope for their future together. Of course, Jasper had always known how to deflect her concerns and insist they were just friends. But she could have been more direct. Then perhaps he wouldn't be here now, wasting his vacation and holding out hope.

"I have been trying with Ellen. But she's as cold as Marian was."

Marian's rambling thoughts converged and tumbled over one

another. Jasper considered her cold? What did he mean by that? And what had he been *trying* with Ellen?

His voice dropped. "I can only do so much before they start to suspect something—if they don't already."

Marian felt her blood begin to run cold. She was suddenly glad she couldn't move, that he didn't realize she could hear every word of his clandestine conversation.

"No, I won't threaten Ellen or resort to violence," Jasper spoke even lower. "At least not yet."

Threaten Ellen? Violence? What was going on? From the sound of things, Harrison and Ellen were safe at the moment, which was a relief after the uncertainty of the past days. But for how much longer would they be able to keep out of danger?

She waited for Jasper to say something else, to divulge his plans, but the room was suddenly silent—so much that she knew she was back in 1381. She opened her eyes to find she was lying next to Will.

He was still slumbering, the candle stub at nearly the same place it had been before she lapsed into the present time. Only a minute or so had passed, but her thoughts were vibrating like a dozen electrons.

She crawled out of bed and began to pace the length of the room, the rushes muting her footsteps. Jasper thought she was cold and he hadn't liked her as much as she'd assumed. Had he only been pretending to like her? And if so, why? What if he'd cultivated a friendship with her for other reasons, like to keep tabs on what she was doing. Or to discover her father's secrets.

She paused by the open shutters and shuddered, even though the night air was warm. While the idea of him using her was appalling, it wasn't out of the question. She'd already considered the possibility of an insider spying and funneling information to other drug companies, especially a company like Lionel. If they couldn't get details from her dad, then the next best option was to go through his scientist daughter.

She'd assumed Jasper's transfer to the Groton, Connecticut, lab at the same time she'd started working for Mercer had been coincidental, as had his placement at the desk across from hers. But in thinking back, she could see now that his attention had been too quick and too calculated.

Marian resumed her pacing and tried to recall all the things she'd told Jasper about her dad's research. She certainly hadn't used any discretion in what she'd shared, had answered all his questions, and probably divulged much more than she should have.

She wanted to deny that Jasper was capable of duplicity. But how else could she interpret the phone call she'd just overheard?

Apparently, he hadn't traveled to Kent to visit her out of concern for her well-being but to continue prying. And apparently, his numerous phone calls to her after she'd arrived in Canterbury had been for the same purpose. He'd even called her when she'd been at the bank checking Dad's safety deposit box. Had he alerted Lionel to her whereabouts? Was that why she'd been attacked after leaving the bank?

If so, then Ellen and Harrison were in very real danger. And they had no idea of the threat he posed, not only to their safety but to the safety of the ultimate cure.

Marian paused in her pacing and turned to stare at Will. Maybe if she kissed him again and ingested more holy water residue, she could travel to the present again to warn them. But even if she managed to do so at a time when either Ellen or Harrison was in the room, she'd still be helpless to communicate with them.

No, she'd have to try to send them another message in the crypt. But when?

She glanced out the window to the deepening darkness. Jasper had mentioned they were at St. Thomas's again. She wasn't familiar with all of the churches in Canterbury, but St. Thomas's was one of the closest to the cathedral. Why had Ellen and Harrison gone there? When Marian had done research on St. Sepulchre, she'd studied some of the other churches in the area. St. Thomas's hadn't been constructed until the mid-1800s. It had sustained damage during the Blitz during World War II. But otherwise, she hadn't found anything significant about it.

Were they hoping to use it as a decoy to get their pursuers to think something was located there?

With exhaustion weakening her again, she returned to the bed and climbed beside Will. Her thoughts tumbled together with confusion and distress. Maybe with some sleep, she'd gain clarity on what she needed to do next.

• • •

Will stretched, and he didn't feel even the slightest twinge, almost as though he'd never been injured. God had truly worked a miracle through the holy water. He could explain his healing no other way.

He opened his eyes to the faint light of dawn beginning to chase away the shadows. How long had he slept? One day? Two?

The quietness of the manor and the outside grounds told him everyone was still asleep.

What of Marian?

He glanced at the chair next to his bed. It was empty. Bracing himself for pain, he pushed up, only to realize once again he didn't feel anything. Anything, except the warmth and softness of a body next to his.

Marian's long hair was unplaited and spread out in waves around her. He reached for a handful, lowered his face into it, and breathed her in. She was turned away from him, but he could see that she'd shed her gown and was attired in only a shift.

He brushed his fingers across her shoulder and then down her upper arm. Swift desire jolted through him. Ere he could stop himself, he lowered himself against her. His rational side admonished him to wait, to allow her to sleep. She was likely exhausted from endless hours of tending to him.

289

But another part of him couldn't keep from reaching for her. He'd squelched his desires and had tested the limits of his patience for long enough. With all they'd been through together, surely she would accept him now, even welcome him into her arms. She'd never given any indication she didn't like his touch. Rather she seemed to burn for him as much as he did her, if the soft sounds of her pleasure and the way she melded against him were any indication.

He bent his head, parted her hair, and found the sleek column of her neck. His lips made contact with her smooth skin, and he almost groaned. He circled his hands around to her stomach, waiting for her to waken and sense his presence. He wanted her to arch into him, slip her hand over his, and give him permission to keep going.

Even though he had every right to claim her as his wife—always had—he wouldn't move forward unless she was equally ready and rested. For now he would refrain from touching her any further. After all, he would have time later. The servants wouldn't expect him to rise, not after his severe wounds. They could stay in bed all day if they wanted to.

Gently, he brushed a final kiss behind her ear and then forced himself to relax. He expected her at the very least to snuggle back into him sleepily. When she still didn't move—not even slightly—a disturbing unease pricked him, and his warrior's sixth sense told him something wasn't right.

He stiffened, sat up, and listened.

Again silence prevailed. A distant clang of a pot told him a kitchen boy or the cook was awake. But otherwise, the manor was at peace.

No, the turmoil was within. Through the growing dawn, he assessed the room, his sights returning to Marian. He grabbed her shoulder and turned her so that she was lying on her back. She didn't resist. Instead, her arm flopped to the mattress as though she were made of straw rather than flesh.

His heartbeat slammed into his ribs.

"Marian." His voice was hard and demanding.

She didn't respond.

"Marian." This time he shook her shoulders. "I command you to awaken, wife."

Her chest rose at the same slow, even pace that seemed to indicate she was slumbering. But somehow, he guessed she wasn't asleep, that something had happened to her during the night. Something terrible he couldn't explain.

He shook her again and called her name to no avail.

Panic erupted in his chest, the same kind of panic borne the moment he'd discovered Thomas had been taken for ransom by Arnaud de Cervole.

Thomas had sacrificed himself. Will had long since guessed Cervole would have released Thomas when Will demanded the exchange. But Thomas refused to go, had probably decided he was sick and dying and should be the one to suffer—not Will, who was healthy and had a family awaiting him back home.

Of course, Will had done everything he could to make the substitution. In the end, Cervole sent him away and kept Thomas. Will had been angry at Cervole, but in reality he'd been angry at Thomas too, for giving up and for leaving him. He'd tasked himself to guard Thomas and make sure he returned from the war alive. And he'd failed. Because he hadn't tried hard enough. And because Thomas had loved him too much to let him die in his stead.

Frustration ripped at Will's insides and his throat. He wanted to scream out to Marian that she shouldn't have sacrificed for him too. Even though he didn't understand how the holy water would have helped Marian, one thing was clear—she'd used her portion to save his life. And now he was alive and she was unresponsive.

He lifted her limp body into his arms and cradled her against his chest. "Marian." His throat ached with rising pressure. "Do not leave me, my love. Please. I beg of you."

More than aught, he wanted her to open her beautiful brown eyes, smile up at him with that teasing glimmer, and assure him she loved him and would stay with him forever.

But hadn't she said she was from a different time and place? He suspected wherever that might be, she'd gone home. All he knew was once again he'd failed to save the person he loved.

~ 27 ~

WARMTH STOLE THROUGH MARIAN, a warmth so encompassing she didn't want to awaken. At the voices nearby, she could feel herself rousing. Had the servants already come to help her dress? Maybe the surgeon had returned again to check on Will.

Her mind rolled as she attempted to organize her thoughts into some coherence. She hadn't meant to sleep all night. But she must have been more tired than she realized.

How were Will's wounds this morning? With how quickly they'd healed, he'd likely be out of bed and back to normal in no time.

"Nothing is happening." Even though the voice was distant, it was distinctly Ellen's.

"We might not know if it works for some time yet, love." Another voice sounded like Harrison's. "Your father's notes are dreadfully inconclusive."

Marian's heart gave a leap of hope. Somehow she'd slipped back to the present again. And this time Ellen and Harrison were in the room. She had to warn them to be wary of Jasper. Maybe if she could just lift a finger and point it at him if he was still in the room. Or try to mouth his name.

Focus, Marian. She didn't have long. She never did before the holy water wore off—maybe seconds. Mustering all the strength in her hand, she attempted to lift it. She was unprepared for the ease with which it rose into the air.

A gasp sounded nearby, and someone clutched her raised hand. "Marian?" Ellen's voice was above her, and it was laced with excitement. "Marian, can you hear me?"

Marian willed her eyes to open, put all her energy into making her lids move. Once again, she was surprised when her lashes flitted up, and she was able to see Ellen's face hovering above hers. That face she'd never expected to see again, that cover-model oval-shape with her dainty chin and prominent cheekbones. Even though Ellen's eyes were ringed with dark circles and weary lines creased her forehead, the sight was beautiful.

"Her eyes are open!" Ellen was smiling even as her voice wobbled and tears began to roll down her cheeks.

Marian wasn't sure what was happening, but she knew she couldn't waste time expressing her warning. "Jasper." Her voice was hardly a whisper and was hoarse from disuse.

"Don't worry." Ellen squeezed her hand. "He stepped out for a few minutes and will be back soon."

Marian tried to shake her head but only managed an exasperated breath. She shifted a fraction and found Harrison in his wheelchair beside her bed. His dark hair was slightly mussed, as though wind-tossed, but otherwise he was immaculately groomed as always in a crisp suit, matching vest, and bow tie. Through his thick spectacles, he regarded her anxiously.

"He'll be glad to see you're awake." Tears still ran unchecked down Ellen's cheeks.

Awake? Marian shook her head. No, she wouldn't be there much longer. She had to warn them before she was whisked back into the past. "Don't trust him."

Ellen's forehead crinkled with confusion. "Trust whom?"

"Jasper." Marian's eyelids fell and exhaustion dulled her senses.

She felt herself slipping away from them, and then sleep claimed her.

* ● ● ●

Marian woke with a start. She wasn't sure how long she'd slept again. All she knew was that she needed to check on Will. However, the drowsiness was so thick she felt as though she were climbing uphill through a dense fog.

"Will?" she managed to croak, praying he was completely restored.

A hand stroked her forehead, easing back her hair. It was too soft and feminine to be Will's and had a clean lemony-lavender scent.

"Where's Will?" she asked again, her voice gaining strength.

"Who's Will?"

Marian's eyes shot open. Ellen was sitting at the side of the bed. "Ellen? What are you doing here?"

"Waiting for you to wake up."

Harrison was there again too, a stack of old, musty books on his lap, the top one open.

Marian glanced around the room to the sight of glass windowpanes, modern furniture, the open walk-in closet that led to the spacious boudoir with the bathroom door wide open, revealing the shower.

With each detail she took in, the horror inside swelled until it was an uncaged beast on the loose. She tried to sit up against the hard mattress of a hospital bed, but her limbs were too weak—atrophied from lack of use.

Her gaze returned to Ellen, and she could only look at her sister with utter despair. "What did you do?"

Ellen's smile dimmed until it disappeared altogether. "I don't understand."

"The ampulla was for you. Not me." Marian's voice came out

stronger and clearer. She wasn't simply visiting the present time after ingesting holy water residue or having a time-slip overlap. No. She was back, had fully awakened from her coma.

Ellen's lovely features were haggard, the strain of all that had happened taking its toll on her already taxed body. "I can't believe you thought I'd drink the water while you were dying."

"I wasn't dying." At least not yet.

"I've been worried sick about you since I arrived and found you in a coma, wondering which day would be your last, thinking I'd lose you like I lost Dad." Distress punctuated each word, and Harrison gently rubbed Ellen's arm as though to soothe her. "How could you believe for one second I'd give you up if there was even the slightest chance I could have you back?"

Marian's throat clogged with the need to weep, and she let her lashes fall lest Ellen see the truth in her eyes. The truth that she hadn't fully comprehended until this moment—that she hadn't wanted to come back, that all she wanted to do was wake up in 1381 and be in Will's arms, that she ached for him and didn't know how she could live without him.

Not only had Ellen ripped her away from the man she loved, but now Ellen might have doomed herself. It was only a matter of time before the tumors came back—probably sooner rather than later with all the stress.

"It wasn't just my decision." As though sensing Marian's turmoil, Ellen's voice rang with defensiveness. "Harrison and I both agreed that if you were able to get an ampulla into the crypt, we'd give it to you. It was the least we could do for you."

Marian wasn't sure if she trusted her voice to work. But she opened her eyes and reached for Ellen's hand, squeezing it between hers. "I carved your initials into it." But even as she said the words, she knew she couldn't blame Ellen.

Marian had known she was taking a chance that this very thing might happen when she'd given Will one of the ampullae. She'd hoped Harrison would convince Ellen to drink the holy water, but she'd also known her sister might refuse. Ellen was too kind, too giving, too sacrificial to do anything that might jeopardize someone else. With only one ampulla, Marian had practically given Ellen no choice in the matter.

Tears swelled in Marian's eyes. She may have saved the man she loved, but he was lost to her all the same. Now, unless they uncovered the original spring at St. Sepulchre, Ellen would be lost too.

Whatever the case, Marian was here now. And she wanted to make the most of her time with her sister. "I love you. And I'm so glad I get to say it again." Marian held out her arms.

Ellen choked on a sob and dropped into Marian's embrace.

• • •

Harrison's private nurse and doctor came to Chesterfield Park to assess Marian's vitals and to remove all the monitors and tubes that had helped her live over the past two and a half weeks.

The medical professionals finished their examination and declared her 100 percent recovered. The astonishment on their faces as they'd exited would have been comical if Marian hadn't been so shaken by the turn of events.

Once Marian was sitting up in bed with a cup of freshly brewed coffee and piece of toast, Harrison and Ellen explained all that had transpired in her absence. Harrison hadn't known who took him captive that day in the crypt. His kidnappers blindfolded and drove him to what he believed was a secret underground laboratory where they bullied, interrogated, and bribed him for several days before dropping him back off at the cathedral.

He'd been bruised and hungry but otherwise hadn't been harmed. Perhaps they decided he didn't know enough about Arthur Creighton's miracle cure. Or they realized he wasn't planning to give away any information and would be more useful to them alive than dead.

In the meantime, during Harrison's captivity, Ellen arrived only to discover Marian was in a coma. She knew right away Marian's condition was somehow connected to their dad's. Even though she wanted to transport Marian to the best medical facility and get more help, she honored Marian's wishes to remain at Chesterfield Park and instead arranged for home health care.

With her nursing experience, Ellen spent all her time caring for Marian and finalizing the burial arrangements for Dad. After Harrison was safely home and recovered, he relayed the details of what had happened, showing Ellen all Dad's notes and summarizing his and Marian's conclusions.

"Harrison believes Dad's research has merit." Ellen was poised gracefully in a wingback beside Harrison's wheelchair. Though she wore no makeup and hadn't styled her long, straight hair, she was as stunning as always. "But I'm not sure I can buy into all the talk about crossing time barriers and miracle cures."

Cupping her hands around the mug, Marian savored another sip of dark-roast brew. "I know it sounds completely far-fetched. But Dad was right all along about the Tree of Life. The water in the ampulla contains residue that has been in contact with the life-giving qualities of the tree."

Ellen's brows narrowed above her tired eyes. "The original tree from the Garden of Eden?"

"Legends passed down for centuries indicate that seeds from the original tree were preserved and scattered throughout the Roman Empire for protection from the invading barbarians. Two of the seeds were brought to England, and one was hidden here in Canterbury. While we don't know exactly how the seed ended up in the ground—whether someone planted it or threw it out, whether it germinated or simply remained a seed—we do know that the life-giving qualities from the seed affected a water source."

"And did you find the water source your dad was seeking?" Harrison's eyes had grown intense behind his spectacles, so intense that for a second Marian hesitated. Harrison hadn't mentioned anything yet about the piece of clay she'd put with the flask. He apparently hadn't figured out the clue. Should she tell him?

But what about the worldwide, life-altering ramifications such a discovery would have? Did she want to be responsible for the good as well as the bad that could come from resurrecting the Tree of Life, something God had deemed as dangerous after Adam and Eve sinned and were ejected from the Garden of Eden?

Maybe her dad's mission to uncover the wellspring was ill-fated. Maybe it was time to let his research die with him. But could she give up helping Ellen now that she had a chance?

She focused on the steam swirling up from her coffee, her thoughts tangling and twisting just as swiftly. "I have an idea of the location. But it's just speculation."

Harrison nodded and sat back in his wheelchair. He didn't press her further, but the determined set of his mouth told her he wouldn't let the issue drop for long.

Her gaze traveled around the room as it had already a dozen times since awakening. Deep inside, she hoped for a glimpse of the past—an open shutter, the burgundy tapestries, or even the rushes on the floor—something to assure her Will was only a breath away. But as before, she saw nothing but the contemporary furnishings.

Swallowing her disappointment, she brought her attention back to Ellen and Harrison. "Tell me how you managed to get the ampulla out without getting caught this time."

After what had happened to Harrison after his first visit to the crypt, he'd been extra cautious about going a second time. He gave Marian one week as she'd instructed in her notes. Then he made arrangements with the cathedral supervisor to allow Drake to come in during the middle of the night.

Harrison planned a series of decoys to throw anyone off Drake's trail. The manservant made it into the crypt without any altercations. But on his way out, he was attacked and brutally beaten.

Since the hiding spot had been empty, Drake didn't have any ampullae for his attacker to steal. Even though Harrison was furious over Drake's injuries, he also worried Marian's lack of follow-through meant she'd gotten herself into trouble.

Of course, by that point Jasper had arrived at Chesterfield Park. When he started asking lots of questions, Harrison hadn't known for sure if Jasper was trustworthy and so tried to remain evasive.

Harrison pushed his glasses up on his nose before glancing sideways at Ellen. "When the chap began to pay Ellen too much attention, I admit, I wasn't keen on it."

Marian watched the play of emotions cross Harrison's face—first tenderness, then embarrassment. She sat up straighter. Had Harrison been jealous of Jasper? Did he care for Ellen as more than just a friend and sister-figure?

"At first I didn't realize Jasper was flirting." Ellen hugged her arms to her chest but was unable to contain a shiver. "I thought he was being nice to me because I was your sister. And I assumed we were both sad about your condition. But when he tried kissing me one night, I decided I didn't like him—not if he could cheat on you so easily."

Harrison shrugged out of his suit coat and draped it around Ellen's shoulders. She offered him a smile of gratitude, and he returned the smile, his attention lingering, as though he couldn't quite get enough of her.

Harrison *did* care about Ellen. Marian's gaze darted back and forth between the two. Why hadn't she figured that out before? Especially after seeing his home lab and realizing how hard he was working to find a cure for VHL.

Was Ellen aware of Harrison's feelings?

As though sensing Marian's scrutiny, Harrison fiddled with his bow tie. "Jasper obviously fabricated his reasons for coming. It's a shame I didn't work out his duplicity sooner."

"If anyone should have figured it out, it should have been me.

Now after overhearing his call, I have no doubt he's working for one of Mercer's competitors."

"Once you warned us not to trust him, I phoned Sergeant Huxham, my private investigator, straightaway. She searched the manor and located several bugs. I confronted Jasper, and of course, he denied knowing anything about them, but I asked him to leave nonetheless."

Marian swallowed another mouthful of dark brew. Each sip was heavenly. "So then we have no idea how much information Jasper gleaned during his visits or how much he heard through the bugs?"

Harrison cleared his throat, but before he could answer, Ellen spoke in a rush. "I didn't mean to share as much as I did. But I may have mentioned the holy water and something about the journeys into the past. Only because I thought it was all so silly, and I needed someone to commiserate with me."

Marian's pulse stumbled a beat. If the wrong people discovered that crossing time was possible through the use of the holy water, the trouble wouldn't end, it would only escalate.

"I'm sorry, Marian." Ellen's expression radiated misery. "I know you and Harrison believe Dad's research, but you have to realize how ridiculous it all sounds."

"I know."

"What if you simply had very realistic dreams?" Ellen's pretty blue eyes pleaded with Marian to agree with her.

But Marian couldn't. What she'd seen and experienced had been all too concrete. She pressed one of her hands against her chest to the pain radiating there. How could her heart ache so desperately for Will if he didn't exist?

"Ellen, love." Harrison reached for Ellen's hand, enfolding it within his. "If Marian didn't cross into the past, how else could we explain the presence of the ampulla in the crypt during that last visit?"

Ellen seemed to welcome Harrison's hold as if it was the most natural thing in the world. "I just don't know, Harrison. I can't wrap my mind around it. There has to be some other explanation."

Marian couldn't blame Ellen for her confusion. She would have been just as skeptical if their roles had been reversed and if she hadn't experienced the time crossing for herself. "You were delayed in getting the ampulla out on day fourteen. How did you finally manage to get it without being caught or attacked?"

Harrison held Ellen's hand only a moment longer before releasing it. "A genius plan, if I may say so myself." He relayed how he remembered that tunnels existed under Canterbury, a network of passageways that had been developed as early as the Roman era but then strengthened during World War II as part of the preparation for a possible German invasion. After several days of researching, he located a tunnel that connected St. Thomas Catholic Church to the cathedral.

Although he had to bargain and bribe, Harrison gained permission from the church to clear out and reinforce the tunnel, in exchange for hiring workers to do long overdue repairs of St. Thomas Church's interior as well as within the cemetery and external grounds. Lionel Inc.'s men watched and catalogued every move of the repairs but didn't discover the tunnel connection until it was too late.

"I paid one of the cathedral security to unlock the tunnel door within the crypt. When the tunnel was repaired enough to traverse, Drake made his way into the crypt while Ellen and I pretended to be fascinated with something in the cemetery."

Marian smiled. "Your plan *was* genius."

"That's because Harrison is a genius." Ellen reached over this time and grasped Harrison's hand.

Harrison ducked his head, but not before revealing his pleasure. At Ellen's praise or her touch?

Ellen grasped Harrison's hand more firmly.

Marian studied Ellen's face, searching for a flicker of some kind of romantic interest that her sister harbored toward Harrison, but she didn't see anything that hinted at more.

Even so, Ellen continued to hold Harrison's hand. "I added the droplets from the ampulla to your IV fluids, and then we waited and waited and waited. It was excruciating, wasn't it?"

Harrison nodded. "You can imagine how relieved we were that it worked. But . . . the question is: Why aren't you relieved?"

Marian wanted to be honest, but what could she say? That she wished they hadn't brought her back? She leaned her head against the raised bed and soft mound of pillows, expelling a sigh. "It's complicated."

Ellen curled her long legs up under her in the deep cushioned chair, getting comfortable. "We've got all the time in the world."

"Do we? While a comatose body in the present can live indefinitely, a comatose body in 1381 won't last long, not without modern technology to help sustain life."

Harrison's brow furrowed. "I pondered the dilemma before we gave you the holy water to revive you. But since we don't know the repercussions, I decided we had to take the risk. There's the very good chance you'll recover."

"But Dad's list of speculations indicates there's the possibility I won't. Look what happened to Dad."

"Arthur was still comatose and technically in the past. But you've returned and are fully healthy. I'm sure that will make a difference."

"Other than a few records of people having visions, have you ever considered why there aren't any historical accounts of people claiming to cross the time continuum? What if those who did, like Dad, never revived from their comas to talk about their experiences? Or if they returned, maybe they didn't live long enough to write down what happened."

"Let's hope that's not the case for you."

After only a few hours of wakefulness, she was feeling stronger and more alert. It wouldn't be long before she would be able to get out of bed and resume her life. What if she wouldn't need that extra dose of holy water to live after all? She could only pray Harrison was right and that she'd be fine.

But would she ever be *fine* again? How could she continue on as though nothing had happened to her? How could she simply pick up where she'd left off? Without Will? She wasn't sure she could.

And what should she do next regarding the miracle cure? Now that she knew the possible location of the spring, could she sit back and do nothing while Ellen wasted away from cancerous tumors?

As though sensing her inner turmoil, Ellen leaned forward and reached for her hand, finally releasing her hold of Harrison. "Please don't worry, Marian."

She tried for a smile. "It's my job to worry about you, Ellen."

It had been her job for so long that she didn't know what else to do with her life. Finding the cure had consumed her. It had been why Dad had risked everything and why she had too. After all he'd sacrificed to test his theories, she couldn't let his life's work die with him.

And yet how could she go on when she'd left her heart behind with Will?

Overwhelming longing flowed through her veins, constricting her passageways with the need for Will every bit as much as her need for oxygen. By now he would realize she was unresponsive and not waking up. She hated to think of his turmoil, how he might even be blaming himself for what had happened to her.

Harrison's expression turned somber. "What about it? Are your thoughts in order enough to tell us what happened? I, for one, am keen to hear your experiences."

Did she want to tell them? How could she explain all she'd lived through, especially the part about getting married? If she was married in the past, was she technically still married now? She guessed it didn't matter. If she lived, she couldn't imagine ever wanting to marry anyone else anyway. She'd never forget about Will. And she'd never be able to love another man the same way she'd loved him.

She placed her mug on the bedside table, took a deep breath, and then started her tale. "You'll find this hard to believe, but I'm officially married to William Durham, the grandson of the man who built Chesterfield Park."

~28~

"IT'S HERE IN THIS GENERAL AREA." Marian stood in a large closet at the end of the spacious hallway room. "I believe this was once an antechamber. And if so, the vault would exist beneath it."

"If it wasn't completely filled in." Harrison powered his wheelchair through the doorway.

Extra extension cords hung coiled on the wall. The shelves were crowded with packages of light bulbs, batteries, paper towels, paint cans, empty plant pots, and a fire extinguisher. Marian tried to picture the antechamber the day she'd taught Robert and Phillip to play hide-and-seek, the simple room with a desk, chair, and the tapestry on the wall concealing the stairway that led to the vault.

Will had lured her to the stairway landing where he'd been waiting to kiss her. And boy, had he kissed her. At the remembrance, a sweet ache lodged in her chest.

Harrison raised his flashlight and examined the walls carefully.

Marian crossed her arms over her aching heart, as if that could hold at bay thoughts of Will. After three days in the present, she hadn't stopped thinking about him. If anything, her mind turned to him more often, picturing him in the manor, guessing what he was doing, imagining him carrying on his life without her.

Thankfully, Harrison hadn't ridiculed anything she'd revealed about her stay in 1381. He'd seemed to accept her crossing through time as though it had truly happened, unlike Ellen, who'd shaken her head at Marian's stories and told her she'd hallucinated, that everything she'd experienced had been a coma-induced dream state.

"You were only dreaming, Marian."

"It was more than dreaming. And it was more than just a realistic vision." Marian held up Dad's list of time-space continuum speculations. "It had to have been a movement through the quantum energy field just as Dad indicated."

"We both know Dad was never the same after Mom died." The statement was Ellen's kind way of saying Dad was crazy.

How could Marian disagree? Not after the years of commiserating about Dad's fanatical research. In fact, Marian had been the one to complain the most. And now, after planting so many seeds of doubt, Marian wasn't surprised Ellen couldn't accept anything.

Ellen had shown her numerous online research articles with stories of recovered coma patients who also claimed to experience strange, very real dreams. At Ellen's insistence that Marian's coma stories were no different, Marian hadn't been able to stop doubt from creeping in.

Ellen couldn't be right, could she? Had her comatose dreams been so realistic that she was unable to separate out fact from fiction?

If Will hadn't been real, how could her love for him go so deep? And if he hadn't been real, why couldn't she stop from sensing him in every part of the manor? Although the house was vastly different, there were times when she could feel his presence strongly—like now, in the closet.

She'd already tried testing the ampulla for residue, hoping she could somehow go into the past and communicate with Will, to at least say good-bye.

But after Ellen had injected the holy water into the IV, she'd rinsed out the flask with antiseptic and had done the same with the other two original ampullae that Marian had left in Harrison's safe. Every trace of holy water was gone.

It didn't matter. She probably wouldn't have woken from her coma in the past to talk to Will anyway.

Swallowing the despair that kept lodging in her throat, Marian knelt and brushed a hand over the closet floor. Thick dust bunnies caught in her fingers. She had to stop focusing on the past and start living in the present, especially because she had work to do in finding more of the water for Ellen. "We could pull back the floorboards and do a little digging underneath. We might find evidence of the antechamber."

Harrison knocked on the wall, testing the thickness of it. "Are you sure such a room would be here? It seems to me if the entryway room had once been the great hall, then it would have extended beyond the parameters that are currently here."

Marian sidled past Harrison back out of the closet. The domed ceiling with its stained glass circles was tall enough to accommodate a great hall. She only had to imagine rafters across the open space to visualize the way it had once been, whitewashed walls instead of the carved oak paneling, unpolished wooden floors instead of glossy white tiles.

Had she only pictured the great hall in a coma-induced hallucination or had she really been there?

"I believe you. I absolutely do." Harrison powered his wheelchair out into the hallway next to her. "But I fear we may tear everything apart to find an old cellar that has long been cleared of anything of value. Besides, if you already searched it and only found two ampullae, then what leads you to believe more may be there?"

She was relieved Harrison wasn't trying to downplay the coma the same way Ellen was. In fact, he continued to pore over several volumes on the physics of time—volumes that had been among the books Ellen had boxed up from their dad's library. He'd only grown more convinced that with the right vibration and wavelength, subatomic particles could shift in such a way to cause a body to overlap itself in two eras.

"You're right." Her shoulders sagged. "Why would anyone place more there?" Will certainly wouldn't. Why would he have any reason to?

Harrison studied her, his eyes filled with both concern and compassion. "It's hard to get your thoughts in order, love. I can't even begin to imagine the adjustment of jumping from one era to another."

She smoothed her straightened hair, brushing away remnants of dust and static. In the snug jean shorts and silky pink tank top, she felt strangely bare and immodest after the days of being clothed from head to toe in layers of garments. She'd adjusted to the past much more quickly than she'd believed possible. Hopefully, she'd get used to being back in the present just as fast.

She continued taking her vitals every day, monitoring her condition, waiting for the first twinge that something was wrong. Her body in 1381 wouldn't last much longer—not without food and water. She wanted to remain hopeful—like Harrison—that all would be well for her present body. But they really had no way of knowing.

"Thank you for understanding," she said. "You've been a good friend through all of this. I'm glad I have someone I can trust."

Harrison rested the flashlight on his lap and tilted his head at her, his eyes wide and imploring behind his spectacles. "Marian, if you trust me, then why won't you tell me more about the engraving you made on the piece of clay that was with the ampulla. Is it the location of the original spring?"

Wasn't the piece of clay proof she hadn't just dreamed everything? What about the time she'd brought back a posy?

"If we want to help Ellen," Harrison continued, "we should

have a go at a place that will give us a more certain outcome than we'll get with excavating here at Chesterfield Park."

He was right. She was wasting time by chasing down another ampulla rather than going straight to the source. Even though Ellen wasn't showing any symptoms of VHL at the moment, that didn't mean the tumors and problems had disappeared.

Ellen had already purchased her return tickets to Haiti and was planning to leave tomorrow. After being gone from the orphanage for close to three weeks, she was anxious to get back to her children and work, especially now that she believed Marian was fully recovered. She'd given Marian permission to do with Dad's townhouse as she saw fit, assuming Marian would sell it and add to the profits of their enormous inheritance.

Marian, on the other hand, wasn't ready to let Ellen leave, not until she found a way to give her a dose of the holy water. She was also worried for Ellen's safety. They were all still in too much danger.

Marian's one phone call with Jasper two days ago had only heightened her awareness that anyone anywhere could be plotting against them. At first Jasper acted happy to hear from her and asked when he could see her again. But when she confronted him about the phone call she'd overheard during her coma, he denied everything at first before growing silent and cold. A day later, he turned in his resignation at Mercer, confirming her suspicions that he was working for someone else.

What would Lionel or other companies do if they discovered she had knowledge of the location of an old wellspring? She suspected they'd stop at nothing to wrench that information from her—including hurting those she loved as a way to gain her cooperation.

"So?" Harrison peered up at her. "This is a massive deal, I know. But the source is what Arthur went after. And it's what we need to be after too."

She rubbed at a growing ache in her temples and wished she

had as much certainty as Harrison that going to the source was the right thing to do.

"The sooner I know, the sooner I can instigate plans. Depending on the location, I may have loads of work ahead—arranging meetings with city council members, cutting through red tape, freeing assets to fund the project, and only heaven knows what else."

Before she could answer him, she had the overpowering sense someone else was in the room. She spun around in time to see a broad-shouldered, muscular man step into the antechamber. His long dark hair was tied back with a leather strip, and he wore a familiar blue cotehardie with a sword sheathed at his belt and leather boots laced against his calves.

"Will?" Her heartbeat clanged wildly.

He didn't turn but instead disappeared inside, the door falling closed behind him.

She lunged after him, fumbling with the door and swinging it open. The room was dark and contained the same shelves crowded with the same items from moments ago. There was no sign of Will, except she could hear the squeal of a distant door opening and cool musty air rising against her face. Was he descending into the vault?

"What's happened, love?" Harrison asked behind her.

Marian blinked several times, desperate to bring Will into focus. If only she could look into his face for a minute and explain what had happened to her. But the sensation of his presence disappeared just as quickly as it came.

"Did you have a time overlap?"

"Yes, I saw Will. And he was heading down into the vault." She pressed a hand against her chest, against the ache of missing him. Something squeezed hard, pinching and crushing all at once, so much that she sucked in a breath. A dull throb radiated in her left arm up to her neck and then jaw.

"Marian? You all right?" Harrison's voice sounded distant, as though coming from a different part of the house.

She spun around to face him but couldn't get her voice to work.

His brow furrowed. "You're looking very poorly."

The tightening in her chest choked the air out of her lungs. Was she having a heart attack? Although she'd never had one before, she'd studied the symptoms. Everything she was feeling pointed in that direction.

She motioned toward her heart.

Harrison watched her, confusion written on his face. He probably thought she was pining over Will, that she was grieving his loss. While that was true, she had to make Harrison understand she was experiencing very real chest pains. He had to call his physician and get help.

She swayed. Dark spots clouded her vision.

Suddenly she realized what was happening. Her body in 1381 had lasted as long as it could without the aid of modern advances. The past had caught up with her. She was on the verge of dying.

～ 29 ～

WILL STOOD AT THE CENTER of the vault, panting from his exertion. He'd torn asunder every corner, every chink in the wall, every cavern. He'd left nothing in the treasure room untouched. Nothing.

It was his third time searching the underground chamber, this time more frantically than the last. Yet he was as empty-handed now as he'd been before.

With a groan that echoed off the stone walls, he dropped to his knees and buried his face into his hands. "Saint's blood."

Marian was weakening with every passing day. When he'd sat by her this morning, the paleness of her skin was almost the same bluish white as goat's milk. Her breathing was shallow and her body more listless—the signs of death. He'd seen them oft enough in his fallen comrades on the battlefield. He'd sensed she had only hours left, if that.

Although he'd commanded his servants to work throughout the night to spoon herbal remedies into her mouth, it wasn't enough. He'd had a local physician bleed her once. But that had only seemed to weaken her more.

"God in heaven, have mercy." His whispered plea was hoarse.

He'd spent hours on his knees in the chapel begging God to spare Marian. Why would God spare him and not the ones he loved?

If only he could find another ampulla somewhere. But his searching had been in vain. He'd even returned to the crypt underneath Canterbury Cathedral for the second ampulla. Though Marian had meant it for her sister, he hadn't been able to let her sacrifice herself, had told himself they'd find another to replace it.

But it had been gone. Someone had gotten to it before him, likely someone retrieving it on behalf of her sister.

He'd pleaded with the monks to help him locate another original St. Thomas ampulla. But they could find naught beyond what they currently sold.

Of course, Will had purchased one, hoping and praying Marian had been wrong, that the blessed water would heal her just the same. But it hadn't worked any more than the bloodletting.

He groaned again.

"Sire." Thad's voice from the top of the steps penetrated his misery.

"Go away."

"A messenger is here."

"I have no wish to see anyone."

Thad hesitated the length of a dying breath. "Sister Christina sent the messenger. She received word of your wife's illness this morn and sends you hope."

"There is no hope!" Will's voice echoed off the walls and throughout the empty chambers within his soul. "It is too late." He did not want to break down and weep in front of Thad, but he had the feeling he would if Thad didn't leave erelong.

"Sire." Thad's voice drew nearer. "Sister Christina has valuable information regarding a spring of holy water at St. Sepulchre she said might help Lady Marian."

A spring of holy water? Marian had spoken of it. She'd called it a spring that had true curative properties and claimed it was once used to fill the original St. Thomas ampullae.

Will's head snapped up, and he met Thad's steady gaze. The young steward's eyes beckoned him not to forfeit Marian's life yet, to take hold of the proffer of hope even if it was a thin thread that could unravel and snap.

"The spring is likely buried deep in the ground. But Sister Christina said she will take you to the location."

Will pushed himself to his feet and stalked to the stairs. "Assemble shovels and hoes and choose another trustworthy servant to aid us. We shall be off at once."

● ● ●

"Dig deeper." Will plunged his pick into the dirt, shoulder deep in the trench. "We are surely getting close."

The branches of the ash above provided shade to their labor. The small leaves flitted in the summer breeze, capturing the air and sweeping it away before it had a chance to soothe Will's overheated face.

Through the canopy, he gauged that the sun had moved directly overhead, signaling the passing of two hours.

Two hours of digging.

Next to him, Thad's face was red and perspiring, his hair matted to his forehead, but he jabbed his hoe into the hard earth.

Will grunted and hefted another bucketful of dirt up to Johnny, the stable boy who had accompanied them. The boy's breathing was ragged and his face perspiring from the heavy lifting of the soil and rocks, but he worked tirelessly.

Will appreciated that Thad and Johnny were willing to continue to do his bidding even though by now they must believe he was addled for this mission. If they didn't discover a spring within the next passing of an hour, he would send them home.

Whilst Will hadn't supported the recent revolt, he'd learned much through it, especially the need to show more consideration to those who lived on his land and served him.

Will had heard news that John Ball, the priest who'd performed his wedding ceremony, had finally been captured. The king had hanged, drawn, and quartered Ball at St. Albans. His head was on display on London Bridge. The quarters of his body had been taken to different towns throughout the countryside to serve as a lesson to anyone contemplating further rebellion.

Without leaders, the rebels had dissipated. However, Will suspected anger, resentment, and unrest still festered like gaping wounds that needed mending. They would not easily heal, and yet the king appeared to have no intention of acting as the great physician—not now that the threat had been squelched.

Will would have to be wary for days to come and would not rush to bring his sons home. Even so, as more rebels were captured, he feared less for his life and estate.

A courier had brought a summons from the king only yesterday. Will had received the message with no great joy. His bravery in helping save the king would only garner him a more prestigious place on the next battlefield. Away from his kin. Away from his wife—if she lived. Whilst he would never dream of shirking duty to king and country, he would not relish leaving when the time came.

His wife.

Like a shooting star, Marian had shown up in the darkness of his life shining so brightly, helping him see the beauty around him he'd been missing, simple things like laughter and conversation and being together. She'd made him want to be a better man, a better husband, and even a better father. But it seemed that now, he was only glimpsing the faint streak of light she'd left behind, and even that was rapidly fading.

He kept pushing away the thought that Marian was likely dead by now. Ere riding away, he'd gone to her bedside and kissed her cheek. Her faint breath nigh his forehead had been lighter than the brush of a dried dandelion petal. He'd known then he didn't have long to find a way to save her. But he'd instructed the servants to do everything they could to keep her alive.

He paused and wiped a sleeve across his forehead and surveyed the pit with nothing but roots and dirt to show for their work.

What if Christina had been wrong about the location of the wellspring? When he'd arrived, she'd led him to the depression where she and Marian had lain that day the rebels had entered Canterbury and wreaked destruction upon the priory and many other buildings. The very same day he'd wedded Marian.

The ancient ash that stood above him was another sign that marked the spot—although he knew not how. All he could do was pray the tree was right, that it was a sacred site, the site of the water that could heal Marian and bring her back to him.

At the fresh burst of panic winding through his gut, he jabbed his hoe harder and deeper. Will doubted he'd ever be able to stop. Perhaps he'd keep digging until he reached the bowels of hell, which was surely where he belonged for having failed not only Thomas, but now Marian.

~ 30 ~

"I'M DYING." Marian managed a whisper through her tight throat.

"No!" Tears fell freely down Ellen's cheeks. "No! I won't let you."

Back on the hospital bed the rental company hadn't yet picked up, Marian was suffocating. Even with the oxygen tube as well as the medicines pumping through her IV, she was sinking and drowning, and nothing could pull her to the surface.

She struggled to keep her eyes open so she could look on Ellen's face for what she knew would be the last time. Sorrow tinged every breath. She would miss her sister. Yet at the same time, Marian understood with a clarity she hadn't before that even if she had survived, she wouldn't have been able to return to her job and apartment and carry on with life the way she'd always known it.

Her trip into the past had altered her life forever. She no longer wanted to bury herself in work and research. And she didn't want to be a self-sufficient woman who kept people at arm's length because she was afraid of getting hurt.

Instead, living in the starkness of the Middle Ages had taught her there was something special about needing others and being needed in return. She'd learned it took courage to open her heart and allow people in. And it took the stripping away of everything she depended on to realize she didn't need any of it to be happy.

She could see now the emptiness of the way she'd been living, like a paper doll flat and one-dimensional, simply flopping along and playing at life. That kind of existence hadn't been real. In fact, she hadn't really started living until she'd arrived in 1381, until she'd opened herself up to the possibility of having friendships, love, children, and a genuine faith in God again.

As it was, she was thankful she'd had the experience, even if it had been brief. She could go to the grave knowing she was at peace with life and God, as well as knowing she'd soon be reunited with her dad. The first thing she planned to do after hugging him was apologize for pushing him away and being insensitive to his heartache. Now after experiencing her own heartache, she could finally empathize with his.

Her biggest regret in the face of death was the pain she was causing to those she was leaving behind.

She held the strand of pearls that had been among her things at Chesterfield Park when she'd awoken from her coma. She'd never recovered the necklace from the prioress of St. Sepulchre. The phenomenon of the items existing in both eras puzzled her. When she'd posed her question to Harrison, he'd launched into another physics lesson about minuscule wavelets that disappear and reappear according to the laws of quantum mechanics, allowing for such anomalies.

"I want you to have these." Marian pressed their mother's pearls into Ellen's hands.

Ellen glanced down and then recoiled. "You'll wear the necklace again."

"I don't need it anymore."

Ellen hesitated for another moment before taking the strand. "Oh Marian." Her voice was laced with agony. "You and Dad never should have swallowed the water in those flasks. It was poison."

Marian wanted to argue with Ellen and convince her otherwise, but she didn't have the strength. The truth was, Marian needed another dose to survive, just as she'd suspected. As her 1381 body lay dying, she was experiencing the deterioration in the present. In order to live, she needed that second drink of holy water to heal and restore her.

Too bad she hadn't figured out exactly how it all worked earlier, how to bridge the time gap safely. Not that it would have made much of a difference, because if she'd discovered more holy water, she would have insisted Ellen drink it—even if she'd had to pry the liquid through her sister's lips.

When her heart attack had started earlier, she'd begged Harrison not to take her to the hospital. She wanted to die at home. Though Ellen had objected and claimed she'd be better off at the hospital, he'd understood and had called in the private staff again.

Now the physician and nurse stood on the opposite side of the bed studying the ECG, keeping tabs on the electrical activity of her heart, and watching the waves on the monitor.

At some point during all the examining, Harrison had disappeared, and she hadn't seen him since. She wanted the chance to give him the location of the wellspring. She had to do it for Ellen's sake, and pray that when he uncovered it, he'd never let it fall into the wrong hands.

"Where's Harrison?" Marian could hardly get out the question.

"Looking for me?" He steered his wheelchair at top speed through the door. A coating of dust covered his suit coat, and wood shavings stuck to his dark hair.

Marian couldn't find a breath to answer him. Instead, when he arrived at the side of the bed, she held out her hand. He took it in his, which was just as dusty and dirty as the rest of him.

As he studied her, his eyes turned watery behind his spectacles.

He cleared his throat before forcing a smile. "I'm excavating the closet off the entryway."

He'd arrived at the same conclusion—that she needed another dose of holy water in order to fully return to the present. And now he was scrambling to find an ampulla in the vault in order to save her. She didn't know how he'd managed to get a crew of workers there at such short notice, but it was too late. She wouldn't last long enough for him to excavate the vault. Besides, even if he managed to get it cleaned out today, there was no guarantee he'd locate another ampulla there.

His smile wobbled. "You hang on tight. Keep fighting, and we'll find a way to save you in two ticks."

"Marian is going to live." Ellen smoothed back Marian's hair, even as tears continued to trail down her cheeks.

Marian glanced at the doctor and nurse.

As though sensing Marian's need for privacy, Harrison spoke a few words to them, and they stepped into the hallway.

As soon as they were out of hearing range, Marian forced the location out. "St. George's."

"St. George's?" Harrison watched Marian's face expectantly.

Digging deep, she summoned enough strength to speak again. "Tower."

"St. George's Tower, yes?"

She blinked in answer.

"So that was your hideous carving on the piece of clay?"

She tried to nod.

"It's a good thing you're a brilliant scientist and not an artist." Although he maintained a smile, the merriment in his tone was strained.

Marian held his gaze for a long moment, hoping he could sense her charge to save Ellen.

"Many thanks, love. You know I'll do everything I possibly can." His voice was low and raw and filled with an agony that confirmed what she'd begun to suspect—Harrison was in love with her sister. Now it was up to him to save Ellen.

Blackness began to push at the corners of her mind like floodwaters waiting to overflow. She switched her attention to Ellen. Marian would never be able to look into her sister's eyes again. This was it. She held Ellen's gaze and mustered the energy of a dying soldier readying for one last charge. "I love you."

Then her lashes fell. Somewhere she heard Ellen release a cry of protest. But Marian had no more strength to hold back the murky waves that had been threatening. They flowed over her, submerging and dragging her along where they would.

~ 31 ~

"**BROTHER.**" Christina's soft-spoken voice came from above Will where he stabbed the earth in an endless battle. "I have brought you and your servants something to quench your thirst."

Will combed his hair out of his eyes to see Christina kneeling on the mound of dirt at the mouth of the trench, a leather jug in hand.

Her eyes were kind and compassionate, and her white veil and wimple always added to her serenity.

If only he could have just a scrap of her peace, he'd take it. But all he could think about was the life ebbing from his beautiful, vibrant wife.

Was he on an impossible mission? Would his time be better spent at her side during her last breaths?

"Let them drink first." He gave a curt nod toward Thad digging behind him and then at Johnny above, tugging up another bucket of soil.

Christina handed the jug to Johnny, who collapsed wearily on the ground as he quenched his thirst. Thad leaned on the handle of his hoe, awaiting his turn.

Will didn't break his digging and shoveling until Thad finished and thrust the jug at him. Only then did Will pause, drinking gratefully, letting the coolness of the well water wash away his doubts. He had to keep going, keep searching.

"Thank you." He handed the container back to Christina.

She held her arms at her sides, refusing to take the water. "You can't blame yourself again."

Her simple statement was an anvil striking the perfect blow. He wanted to sink to his knees in despair. Instead he gripped the winding root of the ash tree to hold himself upright.

"You give of your love freely without holding anything back for yourself." She leaned down and spoke softly so that only he was privy to her words. "In the end such love costs you much."

Aye, it did indeed. He felt as though he'd had his soul ripped from his chest.

"Remember, the Almighty Father says, 'There is a time for everything, a time to be born and a time to die, a time to plant and a time to uproot.' You must do all you can to plant and sow and help the seeds grow. But you cannot blame yourself when God ordains that the harvest be reaped."

Had God ordained the harvest be reaped with Marian? He prayed it was not so. His love for her pulsed through his blood, strong and deep and unstoppable. And he wanted many more years with her, to plant and sow that love in their relationship.

Christina pressed a hand to his cheek. "Do not hold yourself accountable for something only God can control."

Christina knew he'd held himself accountable for Thomas's death. Was he in danger of doing that again now with Marian?

He guzzled more water before passing the jug along to Thad. When the men finished drinking again, Will nodded his thanks to Christina. Her words had brought him a grain of comfort even if they hadn't lessened the sharp ache in his chest at the prospect of losing Marian.

Even so, it was past time to release Thad and Johnny from the task at hand. He gave the two a nod. "You may go home. I shall finish the task alone."

Neither Thad nor Johnny made a move to leave.

"I can no longer impose upon you."

Thad swiped at the sweat on his forehead but then wrapped his fingers around his hoe. "I have no wish to go, sire."

Will could admit he'd let his anger toward Thad fester, both for allowing Wat Tyler into Chesterfield Park and for permitting Marian stay behind instead of going to the Continent. But perhaps Thad had been justified on both scores. At the very least, once again, the man was proving his loyalty.

"I have no wish to leave either, milord." Johnny sat back on his heels and watched Will solemnly.

Will swallowed hard past a sudden lump in his throat and hoped his eyes conveyed his loyalty to them in return.

Christina started to walk away but then stopped. "I wanted to give you this." She fumbled through the slit in her habit for her pocket. "It may mean nothing, but as you were digging this afternoon, I pondered if perhaps it contains water from the original well Marian described."

When she lifted it, Will's knees weakened, and he nearly collapsed in the trench.

"'Tis a very old flask of holy water I found in the apothecary two days ago as I was organizing all the items that had been unearthed and overturned during the attack."

Will scrambled up the dirt wall, his legs and arms hardly able to support him. Why hadn't Christina come to him with it right away? She'd heard the news of his recovery from holy water and had asked him about it when he'd first arrived. But apparently she didn't know she was holding an original St. Thomas ampulla. He likely wouldn't have known either if not for Marian.

"From what I can surmise"—Christina shook the flask—"it has a scant amount in it, probably not enough to help even a wee babe. But mayhap you would like to take it anyway?"

When he reached the top, he dropped to his knees in front of Christina and held out his hands for the St. Thomas ampulla, identical to the ones he'd found in the vault. He didn't know how much holy water Marian had given him to cure him of his wounds. But he had to try giving her the contents of the ampulla, even if it was only a drop. It was his last option.

Christina laid the ampulla in his outstretched hands. For a second, he closed his eyes to blink back a surge of relief. Then in an instant, he was on his feet and sprinting through the woods to the stables with nary a word of explanation, praying he made it to Marian ere it was too late.

* * *

Will flung open the bedchamber door, not caring that it slammed against the wall and startled the servants. His breathing was ragged, and his chest burned from the haste he'd made in returning to Chesterfield Park.

He strode into the room with thudding steps. He only made it halfway into the chamber before the downcast eyes and somberness of the servants halted him.

With a glance at Marian's unmoving form, he froze. "Is she—?" He couldn't make himself say the word.

The woman standing next to Marian bowed her head lower in acknowledgment of what Will had left unsaid.

"No." Anger and fear rose to strangle him like a hangman's noose. He fought against the choking hold. He hadn't struggled so hard over the past three days to stop now.

He broke the icy bonds and crossed to the bed. He dropped to the edge beside her and uncorked the ampulla. With the tips of his trembling fingers, he touched her lips, feeling lingering warmth. Maybe she wasn't gone yet. Maybe there was still hope.

"Lift Lady Marian's head." He beckoned briskly to the closest maidservant. The woman immediately did his bidding whilst Will placed the ampulla against Marian's half-open mouth. He forced his hand to remain steady and then emptied the drops, making sure they went down her throat before allowing the maidservant to settle Marian in the bed.

"Come back to me, Marian. Come back." He waited, staring at Marian's pale face. He wasn't sure what to expect, what to look for, but he prayed for some sign she would recover, that the holy water would heal her, that he hadn't been too late.

Minutes passed and naught happened. Finally, defeat overpowered him, penetrating his chest and soul in one fell thrust. "Please." His voice was strained as he spoke to the servants. "I need to be alone."

Their shuffling footsteps crossed the room. At the click of the door shutting behind them, he dropped his head into his hands. Hot tears wet his palms. Mayhap he couldn't blame himself for Marian's death as Christina had admonished. But that didn't mean he couldn't give way to the sorrow ravaging his insides.

He groped for her limp hand and brought it to his lips. "I have loved you, Marian, as I have loved no other." He kissed her palm. "The time of loving you was too short. I would that I had a lifetime to show you my love of your body, soul, and mind. But I am a better man for having loved you at all."

His whisper cracked. And he could do naught more than lay his head against her hand and let his tears anoint her. She would take them with her to her grave, along with his heart.

～32～

"COME BACK TO ME." The soft words floated in Marian's consciousness. "I have loved you, Marian, as I have loved no other."

She tried to grasp them, but they fluttered beyond her reach. Instead, the whispers of angels at the brink of heaven called to her. In paradise, she would finally taste of the real Tree of Life, the one talked about in the book of Revelation, the tree that would enable her to live in heaven for eternity.

But she couldn't keep herself from chasing after that wafting declaration. *I have loved you, Marian, as I have loved no other.* It blew ahead of her, taunting her, tugging her away from the cloudy vision of heaven and pointing her back to earth.

Marian inhaled a strangely contented breath only to catch a whiff of earth and woodsmoke—the combination that belonged in the Middle Ages. Her pulse tapped with unexpected anticipation. What had happened? Maybe she wasn't dying after all.

Her eyes flew open to darkness. She couldn't see anything—no blue lights from monitors or cell phones or alarm clocks. The night was too quiet to belong to the present with only the distant call of an owl and croaking of a toad. And the air was too warm to be the temperature-controlled rooms of twenty-first-century Chesterfield Park.

Her pulse tapped again, this time with excitement. She was back in the past. How had this happened? Was it possible her dad's speculation about dying in both eras was wrong? Or did love have the power to give life, even more so than holy water or modern medicine?

"Will?" She sensed his presence nearby even before she heard the creak of the chair where he sat. His fingers tightened around hers, and she was suddenly conscious he was holding her hand.

His other hand moved to her forehead, then to her cheek.

"It is you." Joy pulsed through her as sweet as honey.

"And who else would it be, wife?" His voice drew nearer and was thick with emotion.

Her eyesight began to adjust to the darkness of the room, the starlight providing the faintest glow, so that she could see the outline of his face near hers.

"I thought I died."

"I think you did."

"Then how am I here?" She lifted her hand to his forehead and the scar above his eyebrow, then drew her fingers down his cheek along his solid jaw to his chin and up to his lips, needing to make sure he was really there.

"Christina found an old ampulla at the priory like those from the vault. I thought I was too late. But within the hour of giving it to you, you began to breathe normally again."

Marian attempted to comprehend the situation. She'd died in the present. There was no doubt about that. But Will had given her the holy water at just the right moment to prevent her from dying in 1381. Or perhaps the miracle cure had drawn her back from the dead. Was that even possible?

Now that she was here, would she need another dose of the holy water to stay alive? If she had to wager, she guessed she would need more water to secure her body's place here in 1381. But how would they find more in time?

"At least I have you for a few more days."

"You have me forever." He lifted her hand then and pressed a kiss to her knuckles.

She fought against the frustration that threatened to compete with the happiness of her reunion. Should she inform him about the uncertainty of her condition?

"What is it?" She could feel his muscles tensing.

She had to tell him. He deserved to know. "The dose of holy water you gave me woke me from my coma. But I suspect I'll need another in order to live—"

"Then you shall have it." His words came so quickly and decisively she wasn't sure how to respond. Had Christina found two ampullae? Perhaps even now Will had it in the room.

As though sensing her questions, he squeezed her fingers gently. "I have discovered the ancient wellspring."

She pushed up slightly. "At St. Sepulchre?"

"Thad and the stable boy helped me dig in the spot you showed to Christina under the ash tree. After I rode away with the ampulla, Thad and Johnny kept digging."

Marian's heartbeat did a crazy dive in her chest. So St. George's Tower *was* the location.

She had no idea what Harrison planned to do with the information she'd disclosed to him before she'd departed. All she could do was trust he'd be cautious and wise with his investigation. Likewise, she and Will would need to be careful with the holy water so its power wasn't abused.

"Thad brought a small container of the water home to me." Will started to release her and stand. "I shall retrieve it for you this instant."

"No." She clung to his hand. "I don't know if I'll need it."

"I shall give you a dose to be safe."

She shook her head. "If I start to feel sick, then we'll know." The question was, did the wellspring still retain the curative properties that it once had? She suspected it did, but she could test a dose on herself to find out.

He hesitated above the bed, towering there, majestic and fierce, every bit as darkly handsome as she'd remembered. "I can't lose you again." The hoarseness in his voice told her of the agony he'd suffered the past few days.

"God willing, we shall be together forever." Marian prayed it was so.

"God willing." His statement was not only the benediction on the past but also the commencement of forever.

She slid her fingers through his and suddenly wanted nothing more than to feel his arms around her. She longed for him to hold her, to rest her head against his chest, and hear his heartbeat all the rest of the night, telling her this was real, that this was no dream, and that she would get to be with him for the rest of her earthly life.

"I shall leave you to your slumber." He made a move to leave, but she tightened her grip.

"Right now, there is one thing I need more than rest or holy water." She was embarrassed by how sultry her voice sounded.

"What is that?"

"You."

He didn't move, but his breathing quickened.

She flipped aside the coverlet that had shielded her body. Then she scooted over, making room for him on the bed.

Still he hesitated.

She tugged his arm. "Please, Will."

"I want you to recover."

"Don't you know you have the power to help me recover?"

"How exactly?"

"Hold me," she whispered.

He released a soft moan. "Marian."

"And kiss me."

His muscles were taut and radiated need.

"The five days are over." Once the bold words were out, she felt herself flush. She wanted him to know she was ready to be his wife, that she was committed to their marriage, and that she wouldn't hold back anything from him anymore.

Her words drew him. Irresistibly, as she'd guessed they would. With a growl, he lowered himself to the mattress next to her, his weight making it sag and causing her to roll against him, right where she wanted to be.

He wrapped his arms around her, his palm on her lower back, pressing her intimately and igniting sparks in her belly. His mouth found hers, and for an infinite moment his lips plied hers, meshing their lives, their souls, and their time on earth.

When he broke away, her breath came in gasps. She wanted more.

He gathered her fully into his arms, tucked her face into the crook of his neck, and then rested his chin on her head. "Soon. Very soon. But not tonight." His hammering heartbeat told her he wanted to ignite their passion as much as she did but that he would refrain because of her health.

She melded into him, sighing her contentment at being home in his arms.

"My love for you, it fills me and consumes me." He stroked her hair. "It does not wane but grows stronger with each passing day."

The declaration filled her with the same sweet joy as earlier. She understood it wasn't easy for a man like Will to tell her his feelings. He was better at showing his devotion than speaking it.

"I love you too." She pressed a kiss into the scruff on his neck.

"A feeling, Marian? Or a choice?"

She could sense her answer was important to him, that he wanted an honest reply from her as he always did. "It's both. My love for you is deep and abiding so that when I'm not with you, I'm restless and needing you, and when we're together, I cannot get enough of you. But whether here or there, near or far, I have committed my life and love to you and you alone."

His lips lingered warm and soft against her forehead. "I, the same, Marian. I love you with my body, soul, and mind."

She rested her head against his chest, both feeling and hearing the steady thump of his heartbeat. This man. This time. This place. This was her destiny. This was exactly where she was meant to be. Forever.

~33~

December 22, 1381
Chesterfield Park, England

Marian gathered her fur cloak tighter and then blew into her cupped hands. Over the past months, she'd grown accustomed to many things about living in the past, but she wasn't sure she'd ever adjust to the lack of central heating. Even the warmth emanating from the hearth fire didn't penetrate the chill that had descended with the cold rains at the onset of the winter solstice. The chill now lurked in every corner and crept out to taunt her.

She rubbed her hands together but then paused to gaze at the wedding band Will had commissioned for her—a delicate gold with leaves spiraling throughout, a forever reminder of the Tree of Life that had given her new life here with the man she loved.

Her new life. She let her gaze sweep over the great hall from the bench where she stood in an attempt to hang a few greens on the mantel in preparation for Christmas. When the maidservants had brought her the pine boughs, they'd been surprised when she insisted on doing the decorating herself. And though she'd relinquished many duties to their capable hands, this was one she wanted—no needed—to do for herself.

As the festive day approached, Marian realized that many of the modern customs had not yet been introduced. Although she would miss putting up a Christmas tree, stringing lights, watching her favorite holiday movies, and wrapping presents, she didn't miss the commercialized stress and busyness of the season. In fact, she appreciated the simplicity, which allowed her time to focus on all the many things for which she was grateful.

If only she didn't miss her family so terribly. At times, like now with the approaching holiday, the ache went deep. Her thoughts returned to the previous Christmas when they'd all been together at Chesterfield Park. How radically life had changed in so short a time. What would Ellen do this year for Christmas without her and Dad?

"Lady." A young serving girl crossed from the front entry, the fresh rushes muting her steps and stirring the scent of the holly Marian had mixed in. The expectancy on the girl's face gave Marian pause.

She had news.

Marian tensed as the girl finished approaching. The slowness of getting and receiving information was another challenge Marian had yet to adapt to. Messages took days, if not weeks. News was difficult to ascertain. Marian was learning to be more patient and to live with a measure of uncertainty, but when it came to Will, the inability to hear from him for long stretches was sometimes unbearable.

She loathed the weeks that duty took Will away from her. Those days and nights were long and lonely. But she'd taken to spending that time in her new apothecary—a room off the kitchen where she experimented with various herbal remedies, including developing some of her own medicines.

Through it all, she was learning she could still have a purpose to her life, that she didn't have to forgo using her intellect and education just because she didn't have modern science and technology at her fingertips. Her work would look different but could still be important.

The servant girl reached out to steady Marian's precarious perch on the trestle bench. Then she offered Marian a smile. "The master is at the gates."

Marian's breath caught. She jumped from the bench, and the servant girl braced her, keeping her from falling, clearly anticipating Marian's excitement. Marian's legs tangled in the thick wool amethyst gown with delicate flowers embroidered at the hem and sleeves, with tiny seed pearls on the front of the skirt.

Will had brought the gown home for her during his last trip to London. The king's half sister had given it to him for protecting her during the attack on the Tower of London. It had been one of the many ways the king and his royal court had showered Will with gratitude for his role in subduing the peasants.

With an impatient yank of her trailing gown, she freed herself and fairly ran to the entryway, not caring such behavior wasn't appropriate for a noblewoman, the wife of Lord Durham. The king had bequeathed the title upon Will, raising his rank as well as his influence. He'd also given him more of the land surrounding Chesterfield Park.

Even better, the king had granted Will's wish to stay in Kent and serve as a tactical advisor and military trainer for home defense in the war against France. While his new position still required traveling, especially to Dover on the coast, she was thankful he didn't have to be away for years at a time.

As a servant opened the door and she stepped outside, a fine mist greeted her. Gray clouds hung low, dipping and curving with the heaviness of their burdens. The barren trees and shrubs were draped in a thin silvery coating of ice and stretched groping fingers, all too willing to catch the icy mist.

The pounding of hooves was muted by the damp ground. Nevertheless, every thud echoed with Marian's heartbeat at the sight of the man and beast stampeding down the lane. Though the figure was cloaked and hooded, there was no mistaking Will's strong form or the determination with which he rode.

As he reined in near her, the stallion hadn't halted all the way before he slid from the beast. He flipped off his hood to reveal his dark hair neatly combed, his face recently shaven, a clear attempt on his part to groom himself for her. Surely he knew she would take him dusty and gritted with travel, that nothing mattered except he was home again.

His eyes met hers, beautiful and fierce and as startling blue as the first time she'd looked into them at this very place. Without taking his sights from her, he released the reins to a waiting groom, then crossed toward her with long strides.

Her breath hitched and heat spilled through her belly like warm spicy mead. As he reached her, he wasted no time in sweeping her up into his arms, bringing his mouth down on hers in a way that lay claim to her, that said she was his and no other's. His lips crushed hers with his ravenous appetite. She was his feast. She'd learned that already. There were times of intense hunger and other times of slow, languid, and lingering tasting. Whatever his mood, she loved every moment of their intimacy.

The press of his hand and the desire in his kiss told her this was one of those times when he wanted to pick her up, carry her to their chamber, and kick the door shut behind them. But this passionate moment would have to tide them over until later.

The servants had discreetly disappeared, having grown accustomed to the passion that flared between her and Will so easily. She oft caught them smiling knowingly to one another during moments when Will reached hungrily for her. But she craved his touch too much to care what anyone else thought.

The months had been like an endless honeymoon, except for when he traveled, which had only made their reunions all the sweeter. She hoped their open affection wouldn't end now that their household was growing.

As though sensing her hesitancy, Will broke away and growled low. "Nay, I shall not stop desiring my wife just because my sons have returned."

She smiled as he bent and attempted to kiss her again. She turned her lips away so that he had to kiss her cheek. "They are faring well?"

"Verily." He chased after her lips.

She let him chase, enjoying the game. "When will they arrive?"

"Soon." He took possession of her mouth again, his hands sliding beneath her cloak. He'd gone to Dover with Thad to retrieve Robert and Phillip along with his mother, Lady Felice, and now had ridden ahead of them. Marian was looking forward to having the boys return, even if Phillip would be leaving soon for his fostering out as a page with Sir John in Rochester.

Marian reached for one of Will's hands and shifted it to her stomach before breaking the kiss breathlessly. "Your other son—or daughter—will be here soon too."

Will froze.

Marian pressed a kiss against his warm lips.

His fingers spread over the small bump where the baby was forming. She'd suspected she was pregnant before he'd left for Dover several weeks ago only because she'd gone a few months without having to use the dreaded moss-stuffed pads for her monthly flow. But since she hadn't experienced any other symptoms, she'd decided to wait to say something until she was certain. When she felt the first flutter of movement last week, she'd known.

Will caressed the swell, his eyes widening with wonder. "God be praised."

Her heart welled with sudden and deep gratitude for the fact that she was able to be with this man, to have a family with him, and spend her days by his side.

She just hoped Ellen would find the same kind of happiness in a husband. And that she'd find healing . . .

It hadn't taken long after the discovery of the St. Sepulchre wellspring to confirm the curative properties of the water. After that, Marian had placed two flasks of holy water inside Chesterfield Park's vault and tucked them away as far back in the recesses of the walls as she could. Now she just prayed Harrison would uncover them and give one to Ellen to drink.

Every so often, she went down into the underground chamber and checked on the status, only to realize the ampullae were still there. Since the ampulla had disappeared from the crypt after Harrison and Ellen retrieved it, Marian could only conclude that Harrison hadn't located the new ones, that maybe he'd abandoned his efforts at excavating the vault.

She was beginning to think she might need to do something more drastic to get his attention, to let him know she was still alive, and that she'd hidden the ampullae.

She wasn't sure what Harrison had done with the knowledge he'd learned about the original wellspring, whether he'd attempted to dig for it under St. George's Tower or not. If Harrison excavated the spot, she doubted much would be left of the curative water, especially because the amount was so tiny.

In the meantime, Will had built a protective stone wall around it, placed a cover over it, and locked it with thick chains. After discussing the potential problems, she and Will had decided the fewer people who knew about the life-giving spring, the better. They'd taken out a small amount of the water to have on hand in Marian's apothecary in addition to what they'd placed in the vault, but otherwise, they'd decided not to utilize the water except in an emergency.

And for Sarah. "Did Thad give Sarah the water?" Marian glanced down the road, hoping to glimpse the others.

Will nodded. "She drank it the first night."

Marian smiled. "Then perhaps it won't be long before we have two new babies instead of one."

He lifted a gloved hand to her face and traced the line of her cheek. Although the shadows still lingered in his eyes from time to time, Marian could see that somehow Will had been healed too, maybe not in the same way she had been, but he was no longer the deeply wounded soul she'd first met.

They would both still experience many pains and hardships in the days and years to come, but one thing was certain—they were stronger together. Their love brought a strength and healing that would withstand the constraints of time. Whether in the past, present, or into eternity, their love would endure.

Author's Note

As with many of my books, I enjoy being able to help readers sort out the fact from the fiction within the pages of my stories. You may be thinking there's no need to do so for a time-crossing book, because it's *all* very much fantasy.

However, I think you'll be surprised (as much as I was) to discover how many facts I was able to weave into this story.

First of all, many, many theories exist regarding the original Tree of Life that once grew in the Garden of Eden. As I researched, I realized almost as much searching has been done for the Garden of Eden as has been done for Atlantis. Historians have speculated about the original garden with its life-giving trees, including great theologians James Ussher and John Calvin.

Many others throughout history spoke of life-giving water sources: tales by Herodotus, the mythical exploits of Alexander the Great, the stories of Prester John from the early Crusades, and the claims of Ponce de León during his explorations of Florida. Legends have existed of certain kinds of sacred trees (including ash) that are located next to holy wells.

Over time, especially during the Middle Ages, holy water or oil was thought to contain curative properties. Interestingly, the curative holy water healings were only recorded in specific locations and only for a limited time. Two of those places happened to be in England, including Walsingham and Canterbury. *The Pynson*

Ballad recounts the miracles that happened in Walsingham. And of course, the Canterbury Cathedral windows give a beautiful pictorial depiction of the miracles that happened in Canterbury. *St. Thomas, His Death and Miracles* documents the writings of two monks, Benedict of Peterborough and William of Canterbury, who recorded over seven hundred miracles between the two of them.

Is all of this coincidence? Holy water causing the healings? Were the healings perhaps related to the original Tree of Life in some way? I suppose we'll never know until we get to heaven. What we do know is that Revelation 22:2 talks about the Tree of Life: "On either side of the river stood a tree of life, producing twelve kinds of fruit and yielding a fresh crop for each month. And the leaves of the tree are for the healing of the nations." A tree to heal and give eternal life? Possibly.

Aside from the Tree of Life and all the theories, much of what I recounted from Marian's travel to 1381 really occurred. She went back during what is now known as the Peasants' Revolt. England was at war with France (the Hundred Years' War). Because of the high taxes being levied upon the poor, they rose up and rebelled against the nobility.

The bands of peasants roamed the countryside, their numbers swelling every day. They killed, pillaged, raped, and left a trail of vengeful destruction in their wake. They really did attack Canterbury, searching for the archbishop. They coerced knights to join their cause upon the threat of death to their children and family members.

Finally, with Wat Tyler and John Ball leading the cause, the peasants converged upon London, invaded the city, and murdered many noblemen and clergy before finally meeting with King Richard at Blackheath outside of London. At the meeting, one of King Richard's knights really did wound Wat Tyler, and in doing so helped to bring an end to the disturbance.

After the leaders of the revolt had been beheaded, King Richard made little effort to make changes that would ease the oppressive way of life for the poor. I like to think that some of the nobility, like William Durham, learned from the revolt to treat their vassals more kindly.

Unfortunately, class differentiations would continue for centuries, even into the present as represented by Harrison Burlington. Please join me in the next book as the adventure and danger continue for both Harrison and Ellen.

Jody Hedlund is the bestselling author of over thirty historical novels for both adults and teens and is the winner of numerous awards, including the Christy, Carol, and Christian Book Awards. Jody lives in Michigan with her husband, busy family, and five spoiled cats. She loves to imagine that she really can visit the past, although she's yet to accomplish the feat, except via the many books she reads. Visit her at jodyhedlund.com.

Connect with
JODY

Find Jody online at
JodyHedlund.com
to sign up for her newsletter and keep up
to date on book releases and events.

Follow Jody on social media at

JodyHedlund   AuthorJodyHedlund   JodyHedlund

More Historical Romance
from Jody Hedlund

More Historical Romance
from Jody Hedlund

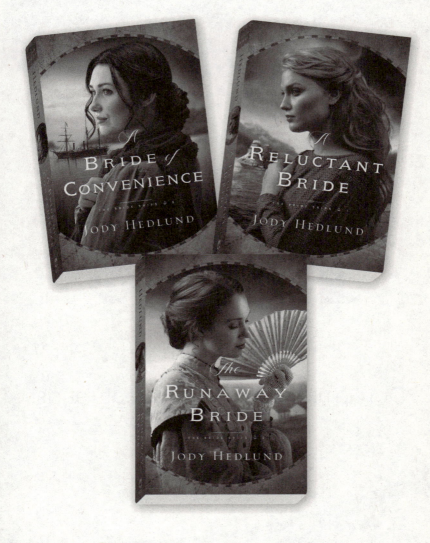